WE'RE ALL
ANIMALS

WE'RE ALL
ANIMALS

MIMA

WE'RE ALL ANIMALS

iUniverse books may be ordered through booksellers or by contacting:

iUniverse
1663 Liberty Drive
Bloomington, IN 47403
www.iuniverse.com
1-800-Authors (1-800-288-4677)

Because of the dynamic nature of the Internet, any web addresses or links contained in this book may have changed since publication and may no longer be valid. The views expressed in this work are solely those of the author and do not necessarily reflect the views of the publisher, and the publisher hereby disclaims any responsibility for them.

Any people depicted in stock imagery provided by Thinkstock are models, and such images are being used for illustrative purposes only.
Certain stock imagery © Thinkstock.

ISBN: 978-1-5320-0697-5 (sc)
ISBN: 978-1-5320-0698-2 (e)

Library of Congress Control Number: 2016914854

Print information available on the last page.

iUniverse rev. date: 09/13/2016

ACKNOWLEDGEMENTS

I would like to give special thanks to Jean Arsenault for her help with editing and also, Mitchell Whitlock and Jim Brown; my Synopsis Superheroes;-)

I would also like to dedicate this book to one of the smartest and strongest people I know, Virginia Doyle. Without a doubt, the sister I never had.

CHAPTER ONE

WE often drift a long way from where we started. Chase Jacobs couldn't exactly take credit for those words, they were merely the worthless ramblings of his father, meant to encourage in certain circumstances, warn in others. For some reasons, it was those same words that drifted through his head at that moment, but it would be much later before he had the appropriate amount of blood circulating through his brain in order to make the connection. By then, it was too late.

Lying on his back, intense waves of pleasure flowed through his groin, making it easy to ignore the ferocious pounding in his chest, as his heart raced at a frightening pace. He was on fire with beads of sweat forming on his forehead, tickling as they slid into his hairline. Feeling on the edge of the most intense orgasm of his life was overshadowing any fear Chase had of living or dying.

Nothing mattered. Not the overweight woman that straddled him, wiggling around on his dick, her unattractive face scrunched up in concentration, almost as if she was attempting to find the right spot. Audrey's large, heavy breasts were a distraction, as they bounced around, her dark nipples puckered up so tight that they were almost as unpleasant as her expression. He closed his eyes and listened to her moan and pant, almost like an animal that was after her prey, rather than someone who was in the state of pleasure.

She was a far cry from the beautiful Lucy Willis, the love of his life; until just before graduation when she decided to leave him for a man that was twice their age. Their sex life had been fair, but there was an unexpected shyness with her in intimate situations that Chase

1

could never break through. Lucy had been oddly self-conscious, always leaving on a piece of clothing when they had sex; a black push-up bra, an oversized T-shirt that hugged her perfectly shaped breasts, a skirt that covered her pantyless bum. He never really understood but found the mystery more of a turn on.

Unlike the desperate grunts Audrey made, Lucy would make soft moans, almost as if she were surprised when an orgasm flowed through her body. She would touch herself in a way that always sent Chase round the bend, grabbing her body and pushing himself deeper inside her. He didn't do that with Audrey.

It was after he came when calmness sprang through his body that he suddenly realized what a horrible decision he had made. He was horny, depressed and lonely and ended up with a girl that he found unattractive. Somewhat awkward and disappointed, he felt emotional for the girl he wanted to be with that night, rather than the one that snuggled up to him, letting out gentle moans of pleasure, as if her orgasm lasted long after his dick went flaccid.

He didn't want to be there. The sad part was that he didn't know where he *did* want to be. At home, sitting in his room, depressed because Lucy was off with another, *older* guy, probably fucking him that same night? Sitting with his parents in the living room, listening to them gossip about neighbors, watching television mixed in with meaningless chatter?

Instead, he was at a house party, with a woman he didn't care about and barely knew. He felt empty as if she had taken his soul when she fucked him. He sighed loudly and closed his eyes, the heavy bass of the music downstairs felt like it was vibrating through his body and although a part of him wanted it to stop, another side of him just went with it. He knew it was the pill; whatever shit Audrey had passed him downstairs. Chase never took drugs before that night. He never would again.

He had been sitting alone, a scurry of girls approached and talked to him, most wearing short skirts, tight jeans, and tops that allowed their breasts to almost pour out. Regardless of the heaviness in his heart, he couldn't help but feel a tightness in his groin when they leaned in to give him a compassionate hug; the fragrance of their perfumes filled him with a senses of anticipation, their silky hands were smooth and soft against his neck, while their bodies with a rousing combination of hardness and soft curves. Before Lucy, he hadn't had a real girlfriend and so his curiosity was peaked as each girl approached. What would she look like naked? How would she feel? Taste?

Not that he would find out. Although attractive with his high cheekbones and deeply tanned skin – a result of his native heritage – no one seemed to notice him. His brown eyes were bland, his long eyelashes slightly too feminine for women and even though he worked out regularly, he was still considered slightly 'too pretty' according to his sister. This was somewhat ironic to Chase, who found his lone sibling to be, what his father referred to as, a very 'hard' looking woman. Both her face and features were not complimentary and unfortunately, he didn't think she was about to turn into a swan anytime soon.

The problem was that Chase had somehow found himself in the 'friend zone' with girls. He tried to be kind and considerate. Unfortunately, teenage girls seem to have a preference for guys who acted like douchebags; obnoxious, moronic, rude and all the other things his mother had made certain Chase would never be.

Audrey liked him, though. As soon as she found him, her hands were all over him. Forget the fact that they were in a room full of people, she felt no shame in touching his leg, rubbing his thigh and telling him he was hot. He attempted to edge away, not at all attracted to the aggressive 20-year-old that he vaguely remembered from high school a couple years earlier: if anything, it depressed him. He could've been with Lucy and the sinking feeling in his stomach only grew, to the point that he felt tears burning in the back of his eyes. He fought them off.

Slowly drinking a beer, he was expressionless as Audrey continued to flirt with him, flipping her blonde hair, occasionally pushing her massive breasts up, as if the bra couldn't quite confine them. At one point, she grabbed his hand and placed it between her legs in a very obvious manner; he felt awkward and pulled it away.

"You know, I think I better go," He started to move farther away from her and noted she showed no remorse for her actions. In fact, she merely shrugged and bluntly told him the truth.

He was depressed because his 'girl' dumped him. He wasn't going to be any happier if he left the party.

Considering her words, he watched as she reached into her jean pocket and pull out a baggie. In it were two small pills. Waving them in front of his face, Chase felt frozen in the chair and wasn't sure what she was saying. Not familiar with drugs, he slowly shook his head no, attempting to explain that this wasn't an option, but she wouldn't let him talk.

"You feel rotten, but this will help," She spoke earnestly, her green eyes lit up, as she innocently batted her eyelashes. Moving close enough that he could feel her hot breath on his face, his eyes challenged hers. "It's just a little pill that will chill you out, have a bit of fun, then you go home and that's it. Tomorrow will be a new day and things won't seem so bad, I promise."

Feeling overwhelmed with misery, Chase reluctantly took the pill and swallowed it. At that point, he couldn't have cared less. He was 18, newly graduated and ready to get out of the dead-end town of Hennessey, Alberta. He would start over and in a few months, that particular night would be nothing but a distant memory.

All the anxiety he felt surrounding Lucy quickly slipped away and his body felt light, carefree and relaxed. Chase wanted to dance and move, music seemed to flow through him, his heart raced triumphantly, he felt uninhibited and light, as if he could float right out of the room. All the girls who saw him in the friend zone gathered around him on the dance floor, their fingers grazing over his chest, through his hair, and over his face and their giggles seemed to dip into every pore of his body and explode all at once. Sounding like moans of pleasure, he could picture each of them in varied degrees of orgasm and suddenly he felt like he was suffocating and rushed outside so he could breathe.

The cool evening air alerted him to the fact that he was having some kind of fucked up hallucination. Most people in the room were as high as him, in fact, some doing some very intimate acts right on the 'dance floor' area of the house.

Audrey was right behind him, her hand on his arm. She gave him a compassionate smile. He couldn't remember going upstairs with her or taking his clothes off, but he knew they had sex. His orgasm was explosive, unfortunately, it had little to do with her company. Chase suspected it wouldn't have taken much at that point.

The high from earlier quickly wore off as he rose from the bed and reached for his clothes. It was a night he wanted to forget.

"Where are you going?" Her voice was slightly demanding, as she sat up in bed. "This is my house, so no one's waiting for the room."

"Look, I gotta go," Chase replied, he ran a hand over his face, then reached for his boxers on the floor. Jumping into them, he picked up his jeans and shirt, while Audrey shuffled in bed, pouting. "I'm sorry, this shouldn't have happened."

"I don't regret it at all," Her comment was slightly attacking, but her eyes flooded with tears. "Just cause I'm not all skinny and perfect like those other girls downstairs or your ex, doesn't mean anything. You were really into it, even if you want to pretend you weren't. You wanted me."

"I'm sorry, I-" Chase miserably stopped speaking and bit his lip. "I don't know what else to tell you. I'm not interested in you in *that* kind of way. I don't want to be with anyone now."

She didn't reply. Her expression tranquil, she pulled the blanket up higher over her breasts and avoided his eyes.

Chase felt like a shit for what he did to her; did he lead her on? Feeling a sense of heaviness return, he quickly dressed and slunk out of the room, gently closing the door behind him. The music continued to pound ferociously and upon going downstairs, he could see the crowd still dancing around. He was paranoid that they'd all be waiting for him, snickering that he just fucked Audrey Neil, but as always, no one seemed to even notice he was in the room.

Just as he reached the bottom step, Lucy's best friend Maggie rushed up to him. For a moment, he felt a shiver of panic; did she know what happened?

"Chase, are you ok? You looked like you were going to be sick earlier," Her blue eyes stared compassionately into his, but he simply couldn't tell her the truth. "You're lucky, there's a lot of people who took Molly tonight and it fucked them up."

"Oh, I…I"

"Are you heading out? I can give you a drive home if you need one," She spoke gently, tilting her head to the side, an innocent gaze disarmed him. "I only had a beer earlier tonight, if you're worried that I'm okay."

"Sure," Chase replied, feeling a tinge of happiness slide into his heart, his thoughts falling back to earlier that night when she hugged him. The scent of vanilla perfume and her tiny figure in his arms suddenly had a whole, new appeal. He had always considered Maggie to be cute, but nothing had ever taken his eyes off Lucy.

A sense of revenge slid through his thoughts, but then he remembered the girl he had just had sex with and felt shame for even considering such a thought. Maggie was a nice girl and Lucy's best friend, he would be a dirtbag to even entertain the thoughts that were flowing through his mind.

But he was in for a surprise. In fact, he was in for a whole series of surprises and it started with a confession.

CHAPTER TWO

Maggie Telips was teased about her name. Throughout elementary school, she was often called 'Maggie Tulips' and then in junior high, the boys would wink at the very developed adolescent girl and ask how her 'two lips' were doing. It was crass and not surprising for teenage boys to be so cruel and although Chase always felt sorry for her, he was too much of a coward to speak out. Instead, he watched the petite young woman as she shrank in her seat, her face on fire as she stared at a book.

He hadn't really met Maggie until he started dating Lucy; and even then, he mainly became acquainted through his girlfriend's gossip and stories. Although the two were clearly best friends, Lucy insisted on keeping her relationships in very separate worlds. She didn't want Chase to spend time with her BFF because she felt that Maggie was attempting to steal all the male attention at Hennessey High School and that made her uneasy.

"I mean, don't get me wrong, I love her like a sister," Lucy spoke earnestly, tilting her head, her dark eyes wide and full of innocence, as her fingers briefly touched the space between her breasts. Pushing a strand of her long, black hair behind an ear, she sucked in both her lips, as if she wanted to hold back the words that were threatening to escape. "I just can't help but notice that Maggie is always trying to get all the boys attention. I think its cause her parents are divorced and her dad isn't around."

Chase was a little confused. He hadn't noticed that side of Maggie and on the limited occasions when he talked to her, she certainly wasn't flirtatious. If anything, Maggie Telips was quiet, maybe even a little shy and serious, especially compared to Lucy, who appeared to thrive on any attention.

"I don't understand," Chase had spoken honestly, although he quickly realized that it was a bad decision. The anger that arose in Lucy whenever he contradicted her was often sharp, harsh and not something she would soon release. It usually ended with him begging her forgiveness and being cut off from any affection for weeks, then rewarded with it again, once he said or did the 'right' thing. It was often difficult to know what that the 'right' thing was, however, so his relationship was often anxiety ridden; but he still missed it.

Now, as he sat on the passenger side of Maggie's Toyota, a car that she occasionally was allowed to borrow from her mom, his eyes traveled down her body to consider Lucy's observations. *Did* Maggie dress in such a way to capture male attention? Wearing a tight tank top that outlined her full breasts, then lay over her flat stomach, trailing down to a pair of fitted jeans, Chase could definitely see her as an object of desire as he felt a warm sensation travel to his groin, but at the same time, was she really dressed seductively? He couldn't see massive cleavage, in fact, her clothing fully covered her and was pretty appropriate for the time of year.

He usually saw her wearing jeans, t-shirts, and hoodies, just like most kids in high school. She never dressed in a revealing manner, even at school dances, where some of the girls pushed the limits when it came to clothing. Lucy was actually one of those girls, insistent that she was an adult woman and could wear whatever she pleased.

Quickly looking away, he attempted to change his thoughts, knowing that it was unlikely that Maggie would be seducing him before they arrived at his house, approximately twenty minutes away. That was until she asked him a question.

"Do you mind if we make a stop on the way home?" She inquired while playing with the buttons that shot heat through the vents. Her question seemed innocent enough, however Chase couldn't help but feel his mind drift to the land of possibilities. He suspected that unlike Lucy, Maggie would be a passionate sex partner, who wouldn't be shy with her own nudity. This image mainly came from 'secrets' that Lucy often shared with him about her best friend.

"Don't tell anyone, but…" was the prefix for many wild tales about her friends; the same ones he wasn't allowed to talk to but yet, these stories only stoked his interest. For example, she often spoke of Maggie in a salacious manner; something that Chase didn't understand since they were supposed to be best friends.

"I think her boobs got really big cause she lets a lot of guys touch them," Lucy once confessed to Chase during a party, as they watched Maggie dancing with some friends. Guys were ogling her in a such an obvious manner, that Chase almost was embarrassed for them, something that Lucy didn't miss. "I heard once that if a girl has big boobs, it's because they were touched a lot. That's why all the slutty girls have big ones."

"That doesn't make sense, does it?" Chase reluctantly commented, immediately regretting it, as Lucy shot him an angry look. He nervously shrank back. "Then again, now that you mention it…"

"I know," Lucy nodded, her hand smoothly running down his arm, her affections were his reward, much like Pavlov's dog. "It makes sense when you think about it. When you look at the girls at school with big boobs, that's *always* the case."

Chase pulled his thoughts out of the gutter and instead tried to show some respect. Maggie had been kind enough to drive him home, so he shouldn't pass judgment. "I'm in no rush."

"That's what I thought," She shot him a quick smile and continued to drive through the quiet country roads that would eventually lead them home. He wondered where she wanted to go and felt a quick jolt of desire fill him upon realizing that nothing was opened that time of night. Even the coffee shops were closed before midnight. So, if they were going somewhere-

"It's just up here." She pointed into the darkness and for a moment, Chase was a little confused. There was nothing more than a dirt road ahead and it lead back to an old dump, that was no longer in use. It seemed highly unlikely she would choose this particular area if she wanted to make out since it still smelled of rotting garbage, something the locals had been complaining about for years; a result of some people still bringing their junk, even though it was no longer allowed.

"In the old dump?" Chase asked as his eyes searched through the darkness for some fragment of understanding.

He suddenly wanted to go home. Maybe this was a little too weird for him. The entire night had been one disappointment after another and now, he just wanted to sleep and forget about everything. Driving into the middle of nowhere, even with a pretty girl, just felt hopeless, as misery filled his heart.

"I'll only be a second." She put the car in park and before he could speak, Maggie jumped out and ran to the side of the road. Using her phone as a light, she grabbed something out of a ditch, threw it in the trunk and jumped back in the car. "Okay, we can go home now."

"What? What the hell was that?" He gestured toward the back of the car, noting the gleeful expression on Maggie's face. "Did you seriously just take something out of the ditch?"

"When it's my younger sister's alcohol stash, I do." A giggle erupted from her throat and she shot Chase a humored look. "I overheard Kelsey on the phone earlier tonight. She plans to sneak out of the house once mom and dad are asleep and go grab it, get drunk with some kids."

"That's *not* happening." Maggie continued and reached to turn up the radio. A song about lost love echoed through the car and although it normally would've been like a knife in the heart, Chase was still thinking about what he had just witnessed.

"Wow, that's... great," Chase seemed unsure on how to finish that sentence. He knew that Maggie had a younger sister that was around 13 or 14, so her efforts seemed protective in nature.

"She's barely 15 and has no business being out at night getting drunk." Maggie shook her head in defiance. "A girl can get in a lot of trouble doing that around here."

"So could a guy," Chase spoke without thinking and immediately regretted it. There was some indication of a story behind his words and he didn't want to discuss his encounter with Audrey. However, as he glanced over at Maggie's perplexed expression, it was clear that she wasn't about to let him off easily.

"And what's that about, Chase?" Maggie asked curiously as she turned onto the main highway that would eventually lead to Hennessey and out of the restraints of Mento. Knowing that no police were ever in the area, she showed no reluctance to speed on the highway. "Has alcohol got you in a lot of trouble in the past? Lucy always made you sound like a saint, so I somehow don't think so."

Even hearing her name was like a dagger in his heart and Chase immediately felt ill. He turned his head and looked out the passenger side window, contemplating how to reply.

"Maybe it was a little more recently," His reply was gentle, almost like a leaf falling from a tree and softly touching the ground. He didn't know how much he should tell Lucy's best friend and continued to look out the window and in it, he saw Maggie's regretful eyes reflected in the glass. "Did you ever do something you *really* regretted?"

"Oh yes, have I ever!" Maggie let out a short laugh, a subtle hint of regret and anger filled the car. The atmosphere felt safe, warm, friendly and therefore, allowed Chase to continue.

"I mean, have you ever hooked up with someone you immediately regretted?" Chase asked shyly, slightly self-conscious, he glanced down at his legs. "Like someone you would never give the time of day if you were thinking straight?"

"It depends on what you mean by thinking straight?" Maggie showed hints of concern in her eyes, as she glanced from the road to his face. "Is that why…I mean, its none of my business, but is that why you and Lucy broke up?"

"What?" Chase snapped, then immediately came back with, "I'm sorry Maggie, I didn't mean that..I wasn't trying to be an ass, it's just that it obviously wasn't *me* that was cheating when we broke up."

Maggie was clearly startled by his response, but sympathy formed in her eyes and she reached to turn down the radio. "I'm sorry, Chase. I didn't know. I mean, she…"

"No, it's fine." He immediately cut her off. "As if she's going to tell her friends that *she* was the reason why we broke up."

"I haven't talked to her lately," Maggie confessed, her tone was even and he felt calmness fill the space between them. "I just knew you guys broke up around graduation. I didn't know why. She didn't say anything to me, one way or another."

"It's fine." He confirmed. "She went off with some older guy. I don't know his name. He's from Mento."

"Luke? Was it Luke?" Maggie's eyes doubled in size. "I mean, they call him 'Lucky Luke' for some reason, but I know she was talking about him lately."

Chase shrugged. He didn't care.

"I'm sorry, I just know she was talking about him once," Her voice drifted off and Chase didn't bother to ask what their conversation consisted of but imagined the worst. "If it makes you feel better, she kind of dumped me too."

"What?" Chase hadn't expected this piece of news. He turned and watched as Maggie slowly nodded.

"She didn't like something I had to say and well, she hasn't spoken to me since."

"Wow, I guess we are both Lucy rejects then?" Chase couldn't help but make a joke; although he quickly recognized it was in poor taste, it didn't seem to bother Maggie, who laughed. "I mean, no offense or anything."

"Nah no, that's fine," Maggie waved a hand in the air. "You're right."

Chase shook his head as Maggie signaled off the main highway and headed into Hennessey. "I can't imagine what you would say to make Maggie not want to be your friend. You guys were like sisters. Fuck, you even looked alike. I remember in Junior High when you even *dressed* alike."

"Yeah, well, times have definitely changed." Maggie coldly commented as they neared his house. He was relieved that the outside light was turned on. "I'm the last person she wants to be compared to now."

"Why?" Chase asked, confused by her statement as she eased into his driveway. "I don't get it. How did you go from being inseparable to not speaking?"

Maggie watched Chase unbuckle his seatbelt. Half expecting their ended friendship to be over something far more dramatic than it was worth, he couldn't have been more shocked when she replied. "I told her I was a lesbian."

CHAPTER THREE

"What?" His lips eased into a grin and for a brief moment, he thought Maggie was teasing him. After all, her reaction was deadpan; no emotions in either her face or voice and wouldn't such a confession provoke some kind of expression? He felt as though he should say something and rapidly searched his brain to find the words to break up the awkwardness. Then he remembered Todd Cornell: her boyfriend. "Wait, no, you have a boyfriend, right?"

"I *had* a boyfriend," She corrected him, as her fingers nervously played with a strand of her long, smooth hair as she glanced toward Chase's house. Hints of nervousness broke her original calm, cool exterior and she bit her lip and looked away. "I guess that kind of made him my... beard?"

Chase opened his mouth to reply but was lost for words. He didn't want to say the wrong thing and if his relationship with Lucy had taught him anything, it was that he had a tendency to make stupid comments. This was clearly an emotional time for Maggie, even though she was doing a great job of showing her strength, he could sense she was scared.

Hennessey was far from a progressive place. Small town mentality had a way of seeping into every area of their lives, pressuring people to live a certain way that wasn't always the best solution. He knew from his own family that homosexuals weren't accepted by many in the community. Although there were some openly gay kids at school, they mainly kept to themselves and appeared to do their best to conceal their sexuality. It was a little hard to believe that people still lived and thought in such a restrictive manner.

Lucy Willis certainly wasn't a progressive thinker. It was odd for someone their age to be so limited in their beliefs, but her family was quite conservative. He didn't have to ask what her reaction was with the realization that her best friend was gay. In many ways, Lucy was predictable.

"I'm sorry," Chase immediately apologized, then realized that maybe she misunderstand his compassion and quickly rushed to explain himself. "I mean, I'm not sorry that you're a lesbian, I just know how Lucy can be." He wasn't sure how to finish that sentence, but he noted that Maggie was already nodding.

"I understand, Chase." Her voice was barely a whisper and she cleared her throat. "I don't blame her for being kind of mad at me. I hid it from her for a long time and she's right, we're supposed to be, at least we *were* best friends, so I should've been honest all along. It was a huge secret to hide."

"She'll come around," Chase predicted, even though a part of him knew that Lucy's dramatic reaction probably was more to the facts as opposed to the secret itself. It wasn't as if Maggie told anyone else either. In fact, she had a boyfriend for the last year or more, so there was absolutely no indication that she preferred women. "I mean, it was probably a shock."

Twitching her nose as if an unpleasant scent filled the car, Maggie shrugged. "I'm not sure that will happen. She said some pretty cruel things to me when I told her. I don't think it would be in my best interest to have her in my life right now. This is hard enough for me, to come out, without having to fight with her too."

"Yeah, Lucy isn't exactly... open-minded," Chase commented, struggling to find the right words to bring Maggie comfort, but he had never dealt with a situation like this before and wasn't sure how to react.

"She's extremely judgmental," Maggie replied and nodded, her eyes scanning the steering wheel. Glancing toward his house, she suddenly seemed lost. Chase noticed his older sister peeking out her bedroom window.

"Did you want to come in for a while," Chase asked and noted the light from the family television was on, so it might be hard to find some privacy. "We can talk."

He extended the invitation, expecting that she would say no. Not that he didn't want to talk to her, but he certainly didn't want his family eavesdropping. His parents appeared to be watching television; most likely his mom, who had a lot of nightmares and decided to camp out in front of the television in hopes it would give her the comfort needed to sleep.

"Sure," Maggie quickly agreed and started to get out of the car. Chase followed her lead and watched her shove her hands in her jean pockets and follow him to the front door. Once inside, he noted that his mother was asleep on the couch, the television still on as an old Meg Ryan movie quietly played on the screen. The house was otherwise still.

"We can go to my room if you want," He pointed toward the ceiling and had another thought. "The basement is okay too, it's a bit cold, though."

"It doesn't matter," She whispered and then timidly followed him upstairs and into his room. He gently closed the door and she immediately sat on the edge of his bed. Maggie's head swung around as she took in her surroundings. Other than an unmade bed, it was pretty reasonable. "My God, you're the cleanest guy I know."

"Oh, yeah, I don't like a mess," Chase nervously responded and grabbed a crappy chair that went with his desk, a cheap discount store model that was ready to fall apart at any time. He somehow thought it was inappropriate to sit beside her on the bed. "It drives me crazy."

"You wouldn't want to see my room," She quietly confessed and hunched over slightly and took a deep breath, causing her breasts to rise and fall. Chase quickly looked away.

"So, when did you talk to Lucy?" He suddenly felt as though he was in the role of a counselor, attempting to help out a patient. "We broke up around graduation and you guys were still friends then."

"Yeah, it was around the same time, just after I broke up with Todd," Maggie replied, sitting back on the bed, appearing more at ease than when she first entered the room. "I wanted to wait till after graduation and all that stuff was over. I felt bad enough without dumping him before, you know?"

Chase nodded and considered that was less than a week. He gave her his full attention and decided it was better to listen and not ask questions.

"Anyway, Lucy and I got together and I told her the truth about why I dumped Todd. I told her I was a lesbian and she got all weird about it. She actually suggested that I was only pretending to be her friend for all this time because I wanted to get her in bed." Maggie let out a short laugh, but there was a lot of anger behind it. "As if I faked our friendship since elementary because I wanted to get her naked."

Chase felt his mind drifting to fantasy mode, but it wasn't as appealing as he would've expected. He gave a tense smile and nodded.

"She accused me of lying, being confused, everything. She didn't understand why I had Todd as a boyfriend for so long and said maybe it was his fault," Maggie let out a small, almost gleeful laugh. "As if he turned me into a lesbian."

"I don't know much about it, but I don't think it works that way." Chase made a quick observation and the two shared a smile.

"I've always known, I just… I guess, I kinda hoped I was wrong. I was confused." She attempted to explain. "I still am sometimes. I mean, I was with Todd and it was okay. It wasn't like I didn't like him, but I think it was more comfortable than anything. I don't know, maybe hormones make you kind of go with the flow sometimes."

Oh?

"I just prefer to be with women."

"Have you…" Chase wasn't sure if it was appropriate to finish his question, but it sounded as if she had something to compare it to; but as it turns out, she hadn't.

"No, not here, in Hennessey," She blushed and shook her head. "I've talked to a lot of girls online in other places. I don't think about men that way. Even Todd, I didn't. We only really hooked up when I was drunk, cause I couldn't other times. He thought I was shy, but I wasn't interested in him in that way."

"And alcohol helped?"

"Well, yes and no," Maggie replied while brushing a strand of hair aside. They made eye contact and held it for a bit longer than was necessary. "I mean, maybe pleasure is pleasure."

Chase didn't know how to respond. His heart was beating a little faster, his throat was so dry that he couldn't even speak, while his thoughts raced, pulling him into places that he knew he shouldn't consider.

That's when he heard it; the distinct sound of a creaking floorboard outside his bedroom door. Putting his finger up to indicate silence, he watched Maggie nod her head and smile. She obviously heard it too. Rising from the chair so abruptly that one of the screws fell out of it, hitting the floor with a loud ting, he rushed to the door to find no one on the other side. His sister's door, however, was being pulled shut at the end of the hallway.

Bitch.

"What was it?" Maggie asked as he quietly closed his door again and returned to the chair. "Was someone listening?"

"I'm not sure," He admitted and immediately felt bad. "I'm sorry, I think my sister might've been at the door. I know you probably don't want the entire world to know you're... I mean, that you're a lesbian."

"It's not exactly a secret anymore," Maggie replied and leaned against the bedpost with a wry smile on her face. "I don't care if people know. It's the truth. It's the real me."

Chase nodded, unsure of how to reply. He returned to his chair.

"How about you?" Maggie's voice was suddenly full of confidence and interest. "How are you doing?"

"Not great," He replied and felt all his earlier apprehensions slide away. The truth was that if Lucy was a lesbian, any sexual tension he thought was between them was quickly evaporated and therefore, he honestly could tell her anything, "One day, everything seems awesome with Lucy and the next, out of nowhere, we're done. She met someone else and that's it. Then I go to this party tonight and did something so stupid."

"What?"

"You know, I'm too embarrassed to say. It was pretty bad." He felt the heat burning his face.

"It can't be that bad."

"I hooked up with Audrey, you know that girl who threw the party?" He felt his body deflate slightly as he said the words. He was ashamed of his actions and felt the need to explain himself better, but he couldn't. There was no good explanation. "I'm not attracted to her, I mean, I don't know how it happened."

A smile quickly turned to laughter, as Maggie gleefully enjoyed the confession. At first, Chase thought she was making fun of him, until she delivered the line, "Like I said earlier, pleasure is pleasure."

Feeling some weight lifted from his shoulders, Chase couldn't help but smile when he recalled her stories about Todd earlier. Sometimes things happen and for the wrong reasons.

"Except, trade alcohol with drugs," Maggie asked, her eyebrows raised slightly as the smile faded from her lips. "That doesn't seem like you."

"How did you know?"

"Everyone knew."

"Everyone knows I hooked up with Audrey?" He asked with sheer panic in his voice, he felt the blood rush to his face again and he wanted to crawl in a hole and die. It was a small town, the last thing he wanted was for everyone to know he fucked her. It was hardly much of a claim to fame. He could almost see Lucy laughing about it now.

"No silly," Maggie replied, laughter bubbling up in her throat. "I mean, there were a lot of drugs tonight and I could tell you were high at the party, that's why I was kind of worried about you. I was looking for you after you rushed outside. I wanted to make sure you were okay."

Her words were soothing to him and he noted the compassion in her face.

"That was kind of you, Maggie." He spoke from the most honest place in his heart. "I appreciate it."

She smiled.

"It's no big deal," She finally replied, pushing a strand of dark hair aside and for a moment, a flash of Lucy crossed his mind. Their gestures were so similar that it was easy to see they had been friends for a long time. "I heard through the grapevine that she was kind of on the hunt for you. I was a little worried when I noticed you were high and I thought I should stick around in case-

"You heard she was on the hunt for me?" Chase was stunned by this piece of news. "What do you mean?"

"The party?" Maggie calmly replied. "It was a cause she wanted to hook up with you. That's what people were saying. She got back from college and learned you were single…"

"Oh God!" Chase groaned, his face sinking into the palms of his hands. "I'm so stupid."

"You're not stupid," She spoke harshly this time. "You just didn't know."

"What a nightmare."

"It's done and over." Maggie reminded him. "Leave it in the past and move on. Like me with Todd."

"Yeah, but that's different," Chase reminded her, sitting up a little straighter in his chair and making eye contact with her again, "It's not the same."

"Yeah, I mislead him into believing I was in love with him, that I was straight and we had a future," Maggie replied candidly. "You were given a pill, got high and had sex with an unattractive woman *once*. So, it's totally not the same. My situation is much worse. Do you know how angry Todd is with me right now?"

"I suppose." Chase was slightly embarrassed by his dramatic reaction and sent her an apologetic smile. "I'm sorry, Maggie."

"Its fine," She seemed completely calm. "The point is that it's all about perspective. You have to forgive yourself and move on. You never have to see Audrey again."

"That is true."

"So, forget about her," Maggie advised and sat up straight. "Focus on what you actually do want."

He was. He definitely was.

CHAPTER FOUR

Maggie's visit ended with a strong hug that set every inch of his body on fire. He managed to hide his lust behind a chaste smile as she moved away from him. Her expression suggested that she sensed his desire as her eyes sheepishly jumping toward the door, with a hesitant smirk that barely touched her lips as she reached for the doorknob.

"Good night Chase," She whispered after a quick glance in the living room, where his mother slept on the couch; the television flashing an infomercial for a weight loss product. Then Maggie was gone.

Left standing there, feeling a combination of disappointment and arousal, he locked the door before going to a nearby window to watch as the car lights turned on and she quickly backed out of the driveway. Did she somehow know what he was thinking?

A heaviness filled his chest, the same heaviness he felt since Lucy dumped him. Had it really been only days? Why did it feel like months since he last saw her, since he last touched her? Was he having these thoughts about Maggie because she reminded him so much of her former best friend? He knew that the similarities ended with the physical because their personalities couldn't be more different. Where Maggie was gentle, sweet, caring and kind, Lucy was assertive, abrupt and somewhat dominating; it was a strength that he needed. She was his guiding star and without her, he wasn't sure what to do.

Glancing toward the living room, Chase couldn't help but grimace at the promises made on the infomercial, as it guaranteed weight loss in less than seven days. After working part-time at a gym for a year, he knew that these claims were false and he felt the irritation grow as he eased into the living room and careful not to wake his mother, he grabbed the remote and turned off the television.

The light from the large screen died and his mother's tranquil face continued to be at peace. Knowing that it was the light more than the television itself that comforted her, Chase turned on a dim lamp across the room before heading upstairs. Each step pulled him back to his conversation with Maggie, a gentle scent of her perfume seemed to meet him as he entered his room. He could still see her sitting on his bed, hunched over casually, her body on full display, talking about how she had succumbed to desire with her ex-boyfriend, even though her preference was women.

He felt the blood rush to his groin and was about to succumb to his own desires when his sister suddenly flung his door opened and walked in. Her arrival was like a bucket of ice thrown on him, as he let out a large sigh.

Dressed in an oversized, light blue t-shirt and a pair of matching pajama pants, she put both hands on her hips. The dark frames of her glasses only managed to make her eyes look blacker than black, her matching hair pulled back in a messy ponytail, her lips pursed in an angry pout, she clearly wanted to give him shit. There was irony in the fact that her name was 'Angel'.

"You're a fucking dog," She snapped and Chase stepped back, suddenly feeling suffocated by her presence, as she glanced at his unmade bed. "I'm disgusted by you."

"Ang, what-

"You go to a party and fuck some girl and then you come back here and do Lucy's best friend?" Her accusations were unforgiving in nature, but that was the norm with his sister. Angel rarely listened to his side of things and filled in the blanks. She still blamed *him* for 'using' Lucy all through high school and dumping his girlfriend immediately after he was 'done'. Her feminist nature went to the extreme and for some reason, she assumed that men were always in the wrong.

"That's not at all"-

"Don't bother lying to me," Angel backed away from him, glancing around the room as if she were looking for proof of her accusation. Her eyes returned to his face, full of hatred. "It's a small town and word gets around fast, I heard you *used* some girl, who really liked you by the way, then walked out of the room and told her you never wanted to see her again. Then you come back here with Maggie. You're disgusting."

"First of all, that's not how it happened," Chase felt anxiety fill him; horrified that word got out and uncertain of how to respond to these accusations. He certainly understood how someone might misinterpret his encounter with Audrey to make him appear as the asshole, but that wasn't how it happened. "I didn't have sex with Maggie and that other girl, she was the one coming on to me. I told her I wasn't interested."

"Oh right, but you somehow still ended up naked in her bed with her," Sarcasm rang through Angel's voice and her eyes were full of hatred as they stared through him. Crossing her arms over her chest, she challenged him. He suddenly felt so drained, that it crossed his mind to just agree with her, so she would get out of his room. Instead, he shook his head no and remained silent.

"You men are all the same, just about getting your rocks off and moving on to the next girl," Angel insisted, shaking her head. Her gestures and bitterness reminded him of someone who was middle aged, rather than barely 20. Home from university, it almost seemed as if her hatred of men only grew after her second year of post-secondary education. Somehow, he doubted her accusations had anything to do with him, but for some reason, he was the target she liked practicing on the most. That had always been the case.

"Yes, Ang," Sarcasm rang through his voice, as he grew defensive, "That's all it's about. I mean, I was at a party full of hot women, but I totally wanted to fuck the most disgusting girl there, then I wanted to pick up a lesbian who wanted nothing to do with me."

He immediately regretted these words. He hadn't meant to reveal any of these details about his night, but Angel always put him on defense and he often said more than he had intended. It was a pattern they fell into as children and she still used it to her advantage; she knew the buttons to press and worst of all, he let her.

Apparently, this time, he managed to shock her because Angel's mouth fell open. "What? Seriously? But she was dating-

"It's called 'a beard', I'm sure *you* know all about them," Chase couldn't help but tossing back an insult. "Since you clearly, hate men."

"I don't hate men, I hate what they do."

"Which is *everything*," Chase injected and sat on the edge of his bed, "Admit it, you *hate* men, Ang. You'd rather have a pussy in your face any day over a dick."

He didn't even see it coming. The sharp sting to his face hadn't been the first time Angel slapped him, but yet, it always took him off guard. A part of him wanted to jump off the bed, to grab her by the shoulders and throw her across the room; but he didn't. He was taught never to hit a woman, but the animosity between them was very intense. He hated her. He hated how she looked at him, the way she dressed, her high pitch, angry voice, her cold, cruel eyes. He once told her that she should've been called the 'devil' rather than 'angel' cause she bore no resemblance to the latter.

"You're a fucking asshole," Angel shot back, her face only inches away from his own, he refused to break eye contact with her as she slowly eased away and continued to stand in front of him, her arms folded in front of her chest. "Just because I stand up against masochists like you doesn't mean I'm gay. I think *you* hate women."

"I don't hate women," Chase shook his head, suddenly feeling defeated. How was it even possible that his sister could come to such an insane conclusion? He couldn't help but feel that she was projecting something on him. "Why would you even think that? Furthermore, you alway talk about this 'boyfriend' you have, but no one's actually ever seen him."

"He's in Calgary," Angel shot back and for the first time since their conversation began, he actually saw a drop of emotion in her eyes, while her body stiffened. "And just because you fuck women, doesn't mean you *like* them, it's two very different things, Chase."

"I've slept with what? Two women in my life, how does that make me this cold, fucking womanizer you're talking about?" He shot back, anger rising in him again. "One of which, I was in love with and she dumped me for some old man. The girl at the party was a mistake and I didn't do anything with Maggie." His words seemed to knock down some of Angel's defenses as her eyes looked away and she remained quiet. "And if your boyfriend is in Calgary, why the hell did you come back here? Why aren't you there with him? Maybe if you had some dick, you wouldn't be such a miserable bitch all the time."

Unlike the first one, he expected the second slap. It was sharp and painful, much more intense than the first one and if he wasn't mistaken, Chase thought he heard a sob as Angel spun around and shot out of his room. Although regret filled his heart, it was brief and quickly forgotten.

At least she didn't slam the door, waking up both their parents. The last thing he needed was a full, family argument taking place in the middle of the night, although it certainly wouldn't be the first time. It wasn't so unusual for his parents to get involved in their children's fights, often taking sides.

He regretfully thought about his words to Angel. He shouldn't have told her that Maggie was a lesbian. It wasn't his place to reveal this secret, even though she was clearly not hiding it, he still felt that he had somehow betrayed the only person who gave two shits about him. His own family had been unconcerned with his breakup with Lucy, merely shrugging it off as if they were children who didn't have anything of substance invested in the relationship. His mother admittedly she had never liked Lucy, while his father seemed indifferent. Chase didn't bother to discuss it with his sister. Maggie was the first person who sincerely seemed to care.

Glancing at the clock, he wondered if she was sleeping. Reaching for his phone, he was a little disappointed to not find a text message from her, even though they had exchanged numbers earlier that night. He sent her a quick 'good night' message and sat the phone on his windowsill, one of the few places he had good reception in the house.

His phone vibrated repeatedly as if to indicated multiple messages and with a smile on his face, he reached for it.

His smile quickly faded.

CHAPTER FIVE

His depression continued to simmer over the long, hot summer days. Following his usual routine, he tried to not think about the emptiness in his heart. No one truly understood heartbreak until they were there, looking it in the eye and yet, few people seemed to take teenage breakups seriously, as if it was nothing more than meaningless puppy love. Chase had one thoughtless person suggest that Lucy did him a favor by breaking up with him; allowing him the freedom to get out of Hennessey and on to a bigger, better life.

When he reported his theory to Maggie, she gave him her usual, sweet smile and gently touched his arm, sending a warmth throughout his body, resulting in nothing more than a tease to his throbbing hormones. Was it possible that he was hornier than he had been in his life and yet he was spending most of his time with a lesbian, that had absolutely zero interest in hooking up with him? Even though he knew it was insensitive, Chase sometimes wanted to encourage her to give him one chance, one opportunity to change her mind.

Of course, that was ridiculous. She had been clear that her attraction for men had never been real, that her physical relationship with Todd had been something she tolerated, not wanted. It would be an asshole move to ever try something inappropriate and he was somewhat ashamed of himself for even considering it. She would be repulsed had she known the thoughts he often had about her when alone. She was just so pretty and engaging, that it was hard not to be attracted to her.

"Don't be mad at me," Maggie spoke in her soft, girlish voice, that could've been mistaken for that of a 14-year-old girl, rather than a

17-year-old woman, had he not known better. There was an innocence that rang through her words, a sweet disposition that was beautiful and angelic, with no judgment. Her fingers ran through the fragments of grass beneath them, as they sat by the quiet lake at the park, the same one most teenagers in the area had used as a private place to do everything from drink to make out. It was rare to see anyone there during the week, that was why teenagers often hid in the more sheltered side of the lake to do things that they couldn't do at their homes. He and Lucy used to go there to fool around.

"As if I could ever be mad at you," Chase replied as his face flushed in embarrassment, he looked down at the ground, as if something had suddenly captured his attention. Shyness washed over him as he slowly looked back up into her face. She seemed timid and if he hadn't known better, Chase would've sworn that their feelings were mutual; if even for that one moment.

"Well, you might be once you hear what I have to say," She teased, a gust of energy ran through her voice, evaporating any dusting of hope that he held close to his heart. Maggie turned her body more in his direction and he quickly glanced at her, pretending to not take in her long, slender legs and the tight t-shirt that left little to the imagination. It was white with a picture of a leprechaun on it, but he didn't dare take the time to read it. "I think you *are* better off without Lucy and I think deep down, you know it too."

He nodded, reluctantly agreeing with the same thought that had poked at his mind for weeks since their friendship first sprang into life. Maggie had heard it all before; he missed Lucy, he felt empty and depressed without her, so clearly that meant that they shouldn't be apart.

Maggie disagreed and insisted that it was simply too soon for him to see things logically. Logically, she added, they were a terrible match and Lucy wasn't someone he wanted to get tied down to for the rest of his life. She saw a potential in him that he wasn't able to see in himself and that was one of the many reasons why Chase was secretly falling for his new best friend.

Not that it made sense. How was it possible to still have feelings for someone who had cheated on him, while also falling for her former, best friend, who happened to also be a lesbian? What the fuck was wrong with him?

"I know you don't want to hear it," She continued and cleared her throat as if she wanted to laugh. Maggie continued to graze her fingers over the grass, almost in a caressing motion that made him envision her hands doing the same over his leg that was very close by. He looked away, immediately erasing that thought from his head and suddenly felt melancholy. "I think she would've held you back. I think you're one of the most sensitive and honest people I've ever met and I don't feel Lucy ever appreciated that about you."

His eyes lurched back to her face, just as Maggie was looking up from the ground. There was an immediate connection, a power that was pulling him toward her and rather than looking away, she silently shared that moment with him. He wanted to kiss her, to run his hands over her satiny body; but then, she sat up erectly and broke the powerful spell they shared, even if only for a moment. His tongue felt like it was frozen to the roof of his mouth as he turned toward the water and wondered what had just happened?

"Lucy wants someone who's going to jump into a bar fight or that kind of alpha dog things and that's not you," Maggie continued to speak with a smoothness in her voice, no trace of attraction could be heard. In her mind, they were just two friends hanging out at the lake, talking about life, "She doesn't appreciate you because you're nice. I don't understand, but I think there are better things for you."

Chase laughed. "So far, the only interest any woman has shown me was that Audrey chick from the party, that's it," A sardonic smile grasp his lips and he shook his head. "That was the worst mistake I ever made. I wish I never hooked up with her. Now she won't leave me alone."

"Tell her you aren't interested."

"I did," Chase pointed toward the phone in his jean pocket. "Again and again, but she keeps wanting to meet with me. I told her no."

"It's probably better you keep your distance," Maggie lovingly advised as she leaned on her left arm, inching slightly closer to Chase.

"I feel like this asshole," He turned in time to catch Maggie's sympathetic smile and her hand reached out and touched his arm, sending his body a message that his mind couldn't seem to overpower. "My sister was right, that was a dick thing to do."

"She just doesn't understand," Maggie spoke gently as she hunched over. "You made a mistake. It happens to the best of us. You didn't even know her."

"I maybe talked to her a couple of times in high school before she graduated and the night of the party, but no, not really."

"Just wait, the end of the summer will be here soon and everything will get better," Maggie was insistent. "Audrey is probably going back to school, your sister will go back to university and probably back to demasculinizing her boyfriend and you'll go away somewhere else, far away from this dead end town, where women throw themselves at you."

Chase laughed in spite of himself.

"Hey," Maggie excitedly grabbed his arm, her eyes full of light as her lips slowly parted. "You should apply for the RCMP with me! Maybe we will get recruited together."

"I don't know, Maggie, I don't think that's for me," He shrugged, a hesitant smile crept on his lips, while his eyes glanced toward the lake. "I can't see me being a cop."

"Why not?" She was unaffected by his lack of interest. "You'd be perfect. You're in awesome shape, your smart, yet compassionate. You don't really drink and you only did drugs once, just tell them it was slipped in your drink or something."

"I appreciate it," Chase spoke warmly and turned in her direction. "I really do, but I can't-

"What the fuck? Are you kidding me? This is why you aren't answering your phone?" A loud voice shrieked from behind and for a minute, Chase assumed it was directed at someone else. However, it was wishful thinking, when logic told him otherwise. "Of course!"

Immediately jumping up, it took Maggie a few extra seconds to follow. Her eyes were skeptical, as they skipped from Chase to his sister, who was rushing to meet them. Angel was alone, but with enough hostility for a small army. It was unlike her to come looking for him, she usually chose to attack him in their family home, but never in public. He suddenly feared that something had happened with their mother.

"Shit Angel is mom-

"Oh, don't worry about mom," Angel put both hands on her hips, her dark eyes full of the usual fury that rarely escaped them, harsh lines formed around her mouth. "She isn't pulling one of her fake suicide attempts if that's what you think. It's not Dad either. It's that girl you fucked and left a few week ago, she's at the house."

"She…she's at *our* house," Chase was stunned and shared confused looks with Maggie, who still appeared horrified that Angel had interrupted their conversation. "Looking for me?"

"Obviously, dumbass, she said you're avoiding her calls," Angel snapped and much to Chases' surprise, Maggie sprang forward before he even had a chance to speak.

"Hey! Don't call him dumbass," She suddenly seemed to stand taller, stronger than she ever had before, her blue eyes narrowed as she exchanged angry looks with Angel. "I don't care if he's your brother, you don't have a right to talk to him that way."

"Fuck you and you're little 'I'm a lesbian' act. Don't think I don't see right through you," Angel snapped back at Maggie, pointing toward her chest. "Wearing a skin-tight T-shirt and little short shorts around my brother, then acting like you'd rather be with a girl. Like you don't know how hot that makes guys."

"Lesbian *act*? Are you *kidding* me," Maggie snapped and moved forward as if to challenge Angel and when confronted with someone who was as strong as her, Chase noticed how she shrank back. "It's not an act. I'm not here trying to seduce your brother, I'm here to be his friend. Something you might want to try sometime."

"This is none of your business," Angel's voice rose and she pointed toward Chase. "This is between him and me."

"I don't care," Chase shouted, alarming both the girls. Although his sister's comments regarding Maggie's appearance were taunting him slightly, he forced his brain back to the actual topic of conversation. Why was Audrey at his house? "What the hell is so important that you had to look for me? I get it, Audrey wants to talk to me, but I'm not interested in her. I don't want to date her. I don't want a relationship with her. I want to forget that I ever met her."

"Well, that's going to be a little hard to do," Angel shot back, her head shaking back and forth with exaggerated attitude. "Since you fucking knocked her up."

It was as if the wind had knocked out of his sails, he felt as though his entire life was draining to the ground and disappearing into the lake. These words may as well have been a life sentence to prison, rather than an introduction to a problem that could be worked out. The hopelessness of his life suddenly seemed much bleaker, his heartbreak suddenly feeling much more manageable in comparison.

"What?" Maggie took over the conversation as if she somehow recognized that he was unable to speak. "Of course, she's going to say that, she's desperate to get Chase and even if she is pregnant, who the hell says it belongs to him."

Angel, now visibly upset, seemed to drop her defenses and nodded in agreement. "That's what I said too, but she's already talked to our parents-

"She talked to *mom and dad?*" Chase felt a cold sweat covering his body and for a moment he felt lightheaded. This had to be a mistake. There was no way he got her pregnant-

But he hadn't used a condom. He had one in his wallet. It was still there.

OH God! What must Maggie think? He sheepishly turned in her direction to see an expression of horror that probably reflected his own. She looked as if she wanted to cry. He *felt* like he wanted to cry.

"She said you weren't answering her calls or texts and wanted to see you in person," Angel replied, almost as if she were slowly putting the details together herself. "Mom asked her if she wanted to come in and wait and she did. She wasn't there five minutes and she started to cry and told us that she was pregnant with your child. Dad looked completely horrified and left the room, mom tried to comfort her, but I think she was in shock."

"I can relate." Chase shook his head and felt like he was going to be sick. "I can't believe this is happening. I don't want a kid. At least, not now and definitely not with her."

Angel opened her mouth to say something, but to his surprise, she immediately closed it. Finally, her voice quietly said, "I'm sorry, Chase, I shouldn't have come at you like that. I was just so angry, I thought, how could he do that to her?I thought you knew and were avoiding her. But now I really don't know what to think."

"I don't have a good feeling about this, Chase," Maggie spoke solemnly while shaking her head. "Did you guys not use…." Her words drifted off as he shook his head no.

"I can't do this," Chase felt like he was suffocating. "I can't have a kid. I just can't."

"Unfortunately, if what she's saying is true, you might not have a choice." His sister looked from Chase to Maggie. "She said she wants to keep the baby, no matter what."

No matter what.

CHAPTER SIX

Louise and Carl Jacobs didn't have unexpected pregnancies. They saw children as a blessing from God and this was reflected in their decision to call their first child Angel. Their mother often commented how she would stare at her little girl in amazement that she was a product of their love, that she was a reflection of each of them gathered in a small, delicate package.

The birth of their son was different. There was something extra special about a boy since they carried the family name. Louise believed that it was important that boys were given a name that indicated strength and 'Chase' reflected a great hunter, a man who would go after what he wanted and get it.

She couldn't have been farther from the truth. Chase didn't feel like he was a man who got what he wanted, especially on that humid July afternoon, as he mindlessly walked through the park with his sister and Maggie. They were silent until reaching his father's truck, which was parked alongside a camper and two small cars.

"How did you get here?" Chase asked Angel as he reached into his pocket to grab the truck keys. "I thought you had mom's car."

"I got dropped off," She replied and didn't elaborate on the details. A frown covered her pale face, while Maggie silently hung back. Chase continued to feel stunned by the news, moving mechanically, his arms feeling heavy. "Mom had to go to work and we saw the truck here so she dropped me off on the way."

Chase nodded his head and held out the keys. "Do you want to drive?"

He didn't have to communicate that he wasn't in the state to get behind the wheel; feeling shell-shocked, as if someone hit him on the head with a brick, barely managing to function on the most basic level. He was relieved when she nodded and grabbed the keys on her way by.

"I can drive you home too," Angel airily directed her comment at Maggie as she opened the truck door. "But as you know, it's only a two-seater, so you'll have to either go in the back or sit on Chase's knee."

Normally, this would've probably sent Chase in a state of arousal, but he simply felt nothing when the three got in the truck, Maggie awkwardly perching on his lap. The truck was ancient and loudly sputtered when Angel turned the key; something that had been the center of a joke a couple hours earlier, when he and Maggie first arrived at the park. Chase now longed for those innocent moments, when his biggest concern was how to hide his intense longing for Maggie. Now she was on his knee and he was unmoved by the warmth of her against his body, her naked leg touching his arm casually or the soft scent of her shampoo that filled his lungs.

It was only a short drive to Maggie's house. No cars were in her driveway, since her mom was at work during the week, whereas Maggie's schedule seemed to revolve around when the car was available, which was usually weekends and evenings. She worked in a convenience store at a local mini-mall and hated it.

She merely shot Chase a sympathetic smile as she opened the door and got out. "Call me later," Her words were gentle and smooth, almost as if she wasn't sure what else to say at that point. Probably, he assumed, because she was as repulsed by him as he was himself.

Once she was dropped off, Angel drove away and was shaking her head from the driver's side. "Unbelievable."

Chase didn't reply and assumed she was talking about the baby situation. He felt his stomach tie up in knots as they eased closer to their home and it was only at that time, that Angel decided to cram in everything that was on her mind at once.

"First of all, there's no way that girl is a lesbian cause she doesn't even *look* like one," Angel insisted, pushing a strand of her black hair behind her ear and wrinkling her nose. "I can tell it's a game to mess with you.

Girls do that all the time in university, pretending to be into other girls in order to get a guys attention. It's repulsive."

Chase didn't reply. This was the least of his problems.

"And that Audrey girl, I don't know what you were thinking," His sister lectured as they turned down their street. "Why would you have sex without protection? How stupid could you be? Some girls do that on purpose, you know? They use it as a way to snag a guy. Then again, you dated the same girl for years and didn't get her pregnant and fuck this one girl once and suddenly she's pregnant? I mean, did you do this as some sick revenge against Lucy?"

"No!" Chase snapped as they pulled into their driveway, where an unfamiliar car sat. "I can't believe she's still here."

"Yup." Angel's response was curt, showing not an ounce of compassion. "She's in there talking to dad now. Like I said, mom had to go to work and Audrey didn't seem like she was about to leave, that's why I came looking for you. I figured you were probably at the lake fucking your *lesbian*."

"She *is* a lesbian and we were just hanging out," Chase shot back as he climbed out of the truck and then he suddenly stopped, frozen on the spot. "I can't go in there, Ang."

"You *have* to go in there," Angel said, her eyebrows shot up over her glasses. "You have no choice. You got to deal with this." They both closed the truck doors and headed toward the house, although he noticed, both seemed apprehensive to go inside. "Besides, she's never going to fucking leave if you don't talk to her and as soon as I walk in the door, dad's going to fuck off cause he won't deal with this shit and if you don't come in, I'm going to be stuck listening to her."

Taking a deep breath, Chase followed his sister inside the house and immediately saw Audrey sitting across the table from their dad who looked calm, although he did raise an eyebrow when he saw his two kids enter the room. He simply muttered a 'Yup, what can you do," as he rose from the chair and passed them to go out the door, grabbing the keys on the way by.

Audrey was wearing a sleeveless, white blouse with horizontal stripes and black shorts that reached just above the knee. Her blonde hair was pulled back in a ponytail while her eyes were red from crying that she was apparently doing before his arrival. She quickly wiped a stray tear away and cleared her throat.

Chase felt a sense of dread as Angel flew up the stairs.

His legs felt like lead as he crossed the floor and a voice in his head encouraged him to turn and walk out the door. *Run!!* As if he had a choice. He eased into the chair closest to Audrey and looked her into her eyes. Rather than apologize or agonize, he simply waited for her to speak.

"Where were you?"

"Where was *I?*" Chase laughed in spite of himself, his eyes rolled to the heavens and he shook his head. "You come here and tell my family that you're pregnant and the first thing you say when I get home is, 'where were you?' Seriously?"

"They said you were with some girl." Her words were full of accusation as if he somehow had to answer to her for his behavior. "Are you dating her? Is it the girl you left the party with? The pretty, *skinny* girl?"

Deciding that perhaps this might be his way out, he decided to play along. "Yes, that's who I was with."

"Are you sleeping with her?"

Chase let out an impromptu laugh and shook his head.

"I asked you a question."

"That doesn't mean I have to answer it."

"You do." She continued to insist as if the two were in a relationship, something that completely blew his mind. "I need to know. I have a right."

"You have no right," His words were barely a whisper and he challenged her eyes. "Are you even pregnant or is this some twisted game you're playing because I didn't answer your texts."

"It's not a game, you're going to be a father and you have to start acting like one," Her words were sharp and caused Chase to laugh out loud. "Are you fucking that girl?"

Deciding that she was insane, he thought maybe this was the best way to get out of a bizarre situation. "Maybe." He lied and for a moment felt something stir inside of him at the possibility. "There's no future for us, Audrey. I tried to tell you that before and I've avoided your calls and texts because I don't think you get it. I made a mistake at the party; a *big* mistake. Nothing should've happened between us."

"Well, it did and now I'm pregnant." Her hand moved over her belly as if to indicate the product of their affair. "And your mother seems to think that you will do the right thing."

The mention of his mother was like a sharp knife in his heart, reminding him that his parents had fallen for this insane act. They believed Audrey was pregnant with his child and he knew they would insist that he take on his responsibilities, without doubting that she was telling the truth.

His mother didn't believe in 'giving yourself' to just anyone and lectured both her children on the meaning of having an intimate relationship with another person. It wasn't about lust, something that Chase struggled with when he was quite young, when his mother insisted that you only give into your desires when you are with someone you love and plan to spend your life with — she clearly didn't know he had sex with Lucy and now that she knew about Audrey, she would insist that he owed her the respect of making her an honest woman.

"Your mother and I had a long talk about relationships and how society is very casual about something as special as making love. I think she believes that we never would've had that kind of experience together if I didn't mean something to you," Audrey quipped, clearly not believing her own words. "I told her it was my first time and that it was special. I regretted that I didn't wait until we were seeing one another longer, but obviously, God meant for me to have this baby now."

Shaking his head, Chase bubbled up in laughter. There was absolutely no way she was virgin, that she shared his mother's beliefs or that she wished to have waited.

She continued to ramble, but he didn't hear a word. His mind was a million miles away, searching for an escape route, unable to handle what was taking place. Audrey must've sensed she wasn't getting anywhere because she announced it was time to leave. He was instructed to answer her calls and that she would give him further reports on her doctor appointments. Stunned, Chase didn't respond as she walked out the door, but merely let out a sigh of relief.

Reaching for his phone, he found three texts from Maggie. All indicated that she was concerned and asked him to get back to her. Glancing at the clock, he figured she was probably at work and considered going to see her; but it was across town and his dad had the truck. Instead, he texted her and quickly summed up what happened.

That's messed up, Chase. Is she crazy?

He grinned and replied.

Obviously.

There wasn't much else he could say. Horrified by Audrey's bold words, he felt a mixture of anger and misery, his body heavy as he walked upstairs and into his room. Throwing himself on the bed, a sense of panic filled him and he briefly considered running away.

Eventually, his sister would drop by his room, but she seemed uninterested in his story and merely shrugged. Any compassion she had expressed earlier that day had quickly evaporated. "You made the choice to fuck her without a condom. Live with the consequences."

His father was just as apathetic when he arrived home. He said nothing when Chase asked to borrow the truck, silently passing his son the keys before going into the living room.

Chase wasted no time getting outside and jumping in the driver's seat. He had to talk to someone who cared. He had to talk to Maggie.

The convenience store was quiet that night. In fact, the entire mini-mall embraced a silent parking lot with only a few cars close to the family restaurant in the middle. The enticing aroma reminded Chase that he hadn't eaten since earlier that day, but his stomach was tied in too many knots to even consider the possibility.

Maggie appeared surprised to see him when he entered the store. She was reading a magazine and quickly sat it aside and stood up straighter. Unlike that afternoon, she was now wearing a fitted, pale blue blouse that matched her eyes. Her jeans were loose, but conservative in nature, displaying a professional image. She looked cute.

"Chase, are you okay?"

Shaking his head, he opened his mouth but no words came out. He wasn't sure what he was anymore.

Rushing around the counter, she pulled him into a tight hug that only managed to spark his desires, which were raw and vulnerable. There was nothing he wanted more than to be with her at that moment; perhaps as a distraction or in comfort, as his heart began to race and his breath grew labored. He pulled her in closer and he could've sworn he sensed the same physical reaction in her body, but then she let him go.

"I have a customer," She whispered and rushed back behind the counter.

Feeling awkward, uncomfortable sensations, he disappeared into an aisle that held various cards, celebrating everything from weddings to birthdays and, of course, baby cards. There were tons; some for baby showers, welcoming a new baby, baby's first birthday, baptismal cards. Suddenly feeling depressed, he picked one up with an illustration of a baby in a bassinet, with two doves flying over it, pulling the child through the air.

Putting it back, he heard the bell over the door ring and he glanced over to see the customer leaving with a pack of cigarettes in hand. His eyes made eye contact with Maggie's and he suddenly realized that the lust he felt for her was probably not going to be reciprocated. Not that it would change anything if it was, but it would definitely take the edge off.

Maggie approached him, her eyes glancing at the cards in front of him. "You know, even if it's true, you don't have to be with her, you know that right?"

"I know," he sighed. "But I'm still going to be connected with her forever."

She didn't say anything but gave a sympathetic smile.

Feeling restless, he didn't stay much longer. His brain shot in 100 different directions and no amount of talking would help his anxieties. Chase decided to go home. He had to bite the bullet eventually.

His arrival home filled him with apprehension as he pulled into the driveway and saw his mother's car, wishing that his life would end at that moment, so he wouldn't have to face her.

Louise Jacobs sat at the kitchen table in the same chair as Audrey had earlier that day, drinking a cup of tea. Her dark eyes looked tired, weakened from the many dark hours of her life, but she remained silent as her son joined her at the table. He had so much to say and Chase thoroughly believed in being completely honest about everything. He felt a sense of relief when she rose from the chair and approached him, knowing that nothing would bring him more comfort at that moment than her embrace.

It happened fast. The sting of a slap had never felt sharper. It wasn't the first time she had hit him but on this occasion, he felt tears fill his eyes, simply by the shame and disgust that he saw in her eyes. Anger curled her upper lip and her eyes were red, pained and haunting. Louise Jacob's words were abrupt, to the point.

"You will marry this girl. Your careless actions and stupidity will not bring shame to my family."

CHAPTER SEVEN

Raindrops pounded against the Corolla's windshield with such intensity that it was almost impossible to see the road on that dreary night. The sky was pitch black and a heaviness seemed to surround Chase, as he sat in silence on the passenger side of the older model car. Maggie would occasionally glance in his direction but he was so distracted that she could've been naked and he wouldn't have noticed.

The weeks since Audrey announced her pregnancy had felt like a mourning period for Chase, while almost everyone else seemed to move forward. His mother, now convinced that he would marry Audrey, was elated that she would soon be a grandmother, while his father showed about as much enthusiasm as he ever did for family matters; which wasn't much. Angel, on the other hand, appeared indifferent and barely spoke to Chase since learning that she would be an aunt. If the topic was even brought up in her presence, she would roll her eyes and exit the room. Chase envied her and wish he could do the same.

It was now close to the end of the August and everything was falling apart. Rather than having an exciting summer, planning for the future, preparing to move away and start a new life, he was now saddled down to Hennessey for the rest of his life, with a family he didn't want.

One mistake. One fucking mistake and this is my life.

Of course, Maggie had heard it all before, again and again, throughout the weeks following the announcement. She tried her best to offer words of wisdom, but Chase could tell that she no longer knew what to say. There were no easy solutions. It wasn't as if his worst mistake that summer had been to put a dent in his dad's truck or get in a drunken brawl; those options looked pretty good in comparison to what he was faced with now.

Where he was miserable and dreading his future, Audrey was excitedly making wedding plans with his mother. Chase couldn't remember agreeing to marry her and yet, it had already been decided that it was the 'right' thing to do, therefore the women in his life appeared to aggressively take over his future. His mom liked Audrey. She thought she was sweet, kind and smart. How many times had she mentioned how Chase's 'new girlfriend' had completed two years of college and was currently working a casual position at a youth center in Mento, helping troubled teens.

Ironically, Chase felt like a teen in trouble; although apparently, not the right kind.

Chase briefly met Audrey's grandmother, the woman she lived with since finishing college. On top of all her other saintly attributes that impressed Louise Jacobs about Chases' new 'girlfriend' was the fact that she looked after the elderly woman in Mento, while also checking in on her great grandmother in Hennessey on a daily basis. The woman was like 300 years old and upon hearing her great granddaughter's 'wonderful' news, decided it was time to move into a senior's complex and leave Audrey the house.

His entire life had been mapped out, while Audrey's belly looked the same as it had the one night he had sex with her, showing no signs of pregnancy. He felt as though he was in the middle of a hellish nightmare, even worse than the kind where you weren't able to swiftly run away from the person chasing you; then again, it was apparent that the person chasing him already had Chase in her clutches.

The rain continued to frantically cling to the window and Chase was about to suggest that they get off the road, when he noticed Maggie doing exactly what he was thinking. The two of them were always so in tune, almost as if she were reading his mind and the only person in his life that gave him an ounce of sanity since this madness had begun. All his friends from high school - not that there were many - had all fucked off to work in high-paying jobs in the oil industry. Meanwhile, he was stuck in Hennessey, working at the local gym. At least he liked his job, the small fragment of his life that gave him confidence.

"It should let up in a few minutes," Maggie turned on her signal light and slid the Toyota into park mode. Taking a deep breath, she turned in his direction and silently stared at him. Her eyes seemed to examine every inch of his face; something that would've aroused his senses weeks earlier, now he was so preoccupied with his troubles and long had accepted that his new best friend was a lesbian. Not that he didn't still have fantasies from time to time.

Rubbing his forehead and running his hands over his buzzed haircut - an impromptu decision a few days earlier after Audrey suggested he grow it long - he took a deep breath and shrugged. "I got nowhere I have to be."

"I'm sure you would rather be somewhere other than the side of the road in a rain storm," Maggie gently suggested and let out a quick laugh. "Especially after a long day in a hot gym."

The air conditioning had broken down at the worst possible time, causing many clients to rightfully complain, while Chase was stuck in a muggy environment, the repulsive smell of sweat surrounding him all day, something he would eventually become immune to as he prayed for his day to go fast.

"It wasn't so bad, I guess," Chase considered as he stared forward and watched as another car turned off the road on the opposing side of the street. The two were on the main highway that was connected to all the small towns; the highway that could've taken Chase to a major city and away from his current hell. Other than the mini mall and Hennessey's downtown area, such as it was, there were only a few other scattered businesses including the gym Chase worked for, which was off on its own, away from everything else.

"Good thing you like your job," Maggie commented as she flickered on the wipers and the rain started to ease. She bit her lips, something he noticed she did when nervous or anxious. He knew he made her feel this way because she was looking for a way to solve his problems, but that was impossible. They weren't solvable unless he ran away.

He didn't reply. She was right, he loved working at the gym. His boss, Harold, was an awesome guy, who taught him a great deal about fitness, nutrition and the proper way to use the equipment. They recently added a heavy bag to the gym and Chase immediately announced he wanted to learn mixed martial arts. Harold had merely shook his head and corrected him. "First things first, you got to learn basic boxing techniques, there's a long road before you'll be anywhere close to being a mixed martial arts fighter."

Chase had this wonderful opportunity to learn from someone who had a vast amount of experience in professional fighting, now retired, he had returned 'home' to look after his ailing parents and decided to open a gym in the area. In the beginning, it was swarmed with local women, who had heard Harold was single. Many still came in and asked for him, but the gym owner was rarely at his workplace, having started another gym an hour out of town, he was frequently traveling between the two. Chase was often the only person working at this location, occasionally with a supervisor.

"It's an awesome job." Chase agreed and felt some relief from his usual, unhappy state. A smile perked up his lips, if only temporarily and Maggie looked pleased.

"You're really getting so buff!" Her eyes skimmed over his chest, covered by a tight, blue t-shirt he had changed into after a quick shower at the end of his shift. "I'm impressed. Maybe I should join the gym."

"I'm surprised you haven't," Chase suddenly felt in his element, sitting up a little taller in his seat. "I mean, if you want to get into the RCMP, you've got to be in really great shape, right? I know you run…"

"I do, but you're right, I have to increase my upper body strength too," Maggie said, her fingers running over the steering wheel, her eyes glancing toward the car parked opposite them, as it eased back onto the road. The rain had almost completely stopped. "I'm just waiting till I have more money saved."

"I can get you a deal," Chase offered, excited about the possibility of training his closest friend. "That's no problem. Maybe Harold will let you in for a few free sessions, to see how you like it."

"That would be awesome," Maggie said, her smile soft and genuine. "I've never been to the gym before, so you might have your work cut out for you."

"Don't worry about that," Chase shook his head. "Trust me, if you saw some of the people who come through the doors at work, you would know I've already got my work cut out for me."

"I bet," Maggie let out a short laugh and signaled to return to the street and Chase felt disappointment slide in, at the realization that he would soon be home and back to his bleak reality. "Can I go in sometimes next week? Maybe a day you aren't as busy."

"Tuesdays are quiet, in the afternoon," Chase suggested as they continued down the road. "Drop in then."

"I will," Maggie replied as they turned onto his road and then, into the driveway of his house.

"Want to come in?" Chase asked but already knew the answer. Maggie was uncomfortable in his house. The last time she popped in to hang out with Chase, casual and relaxed, she left feeling awkward under Louise Jacobs' eyes. It was clear his mother felt it was inappropriate that the two hang out now that her son was 'engaged' to Audrey. In fact, Maggie was barely out the door when his mother had made a comment to that effect.

"What difference does it make?" Chase snapped, anger crawling through his body when he considered how little of his own life felt like his choice anymore, but rather predestined by those around him. "She's just my friend."

"It doesn't look right to be engaged and spending all your time with another woman." His mother replied as she fluttered around the kitchen. Her face was weathered, old, no longer the beautiful Native Canadian woman of her youth, she now looked like someone who had graciously let herself go and never looked back. "You two look closer than you and Audrey."

"That's cause we are," He spoke honestly. "Maggie is my best friend."

"Audrey should be your best friend."

"Well, she's not." Chase heard himself snap, something he had never done toward his mother until Audrey made an appearance in his life. Now, it was commonplace. "I don't even want her in my life."

"How dare you say that?" His mother retorted as her dark eyes shot in his direction and he stepped back as if he expected her to slap him.

"Because it's true." His reply was curt and their conversation abruptly ended. Chase didn't bother telling Maggie what his mother said, but he suspected she somehow knew. She hadn't returned to the house after that day.

"You know, I think I should head home," Maggie replied and her fingers ran over the steering wheel. "There's this girl I've sort of been talking to in Vancouver, I told her I would Skype her later."

Chase nodded and felt a shot of desire spring through him, as he silently wondered what kinds of things they did when on Skype. Was it an innocent conversation or-

"Text me later," She continued and Chase merely smiled as he climbed out of the car.

"Thanks for the drive," He smiled as he stepped out, feeling a few raindrops hitting the back of his neck. "You're the best, Mags."

A flush of color ran through her cheeks as he shut the door. He watched her drive away, hesitant to enter his home. No longer a safe place to be, he once again considered running away from home, just as he had as a child. Back then, he had made a pathetic attempt to hitchhike to Calgary to live with his aunt Maureen. He didn't get far before his dad picked him up and brought him home.

His sister sat at the end of the table, drinking a cup of tea and having a lively discussion with their father, who stood nearby. Their mother was in the living room watching some crappy womanish movie about love and weddings and Chase felt like the odd one out, ignored or unnoticed as he quietly sauntered upstairs, in a way hoping to not have a conversation with anyone.

His room was Chases' sanctuary. Of course, that wouldn't be for much longer since plans were already in motion for him to move in with his 'fiance' in her great-grandmother's house.

She texted him at least a million times a day and Chase never answered. He didn't want to talk to her. He didn't want to marry her and he definitely didn't want to fuck her. She would probably have a litter of kids if his dick went near her again. In many ways, his hell was just beginning.

CHAPTER EIGHT

September can be a deceitful mistress that lures you in with the belief that the summer will never end regardless of what the calendar page tells you. Some people in Hennessey commented on how that particular month was much hotter, stickier than the entire summer had been; something that hadn't gone unnoticed by Chase. Feeling locked in his own personal hell, each day only signified one step closer to moving in with Audrey and starting a life that he hadn't asked for or wanted. However, things were about to make a drastic transformation. Like the leaves outside his window, Chase was also changing colors as fiery shades of orange and red started to shine through him.

It started on a typical afternoon as he prepared a green smoothie before heading to work. His mother sat at the kitchen table, an irritating smile glued to her face, as she flipped through some stupid bride magazine. The obnoxiously loud noise of the blender made conversation impossible; which was perfect, since he was too angry to speak. In fact, he felt a fire that was about to ignite from his stomach, exploding into a wild tantrum of rage that would leave no one unscathed.

The blender continued to work hard, pureeing the combination of kale, swiss chard, spinach, strawberries, almond milk and flaxseed that would create a late lunch. His diet was limited to skinless chicken breasts, rice, fruits, vegetables and on occasion, he would treat himself to a burger or pizza. While his parents gathered around the table with a hearty breakfast every Sunday morning, he opted for only boiled eggs, refusing the array of processed meats, greasy hash browns and most of all, bread. His sister surprisingly was the only person who seemed to understand his limited diet, but now that she was back in university, he had no one to really take his side when it came to his eating habits.

Liquifying his smoothie in order to make it easy to drink on his way to work, Chase turned off the blender and started to clean up. His few moments of welcomed silence when the blender stopped were short lived and before long, Louise Jacobs was talking about the wedding again. He didn't respond.

"I said, what do you think, Chase?"

"I dunno."

"Come on honey," She said with coaxing eyes that he now viewed as manipulative, an impression that overflowed into the entire spectrum of women in his life. Even the female clients at his work, who he once naively believed were at the gym to improve their physical shape and health, now seemed cunning and vile. Always batting their eyelashes, showing their cleavage and playing the role of scared girl when faced with the prospect of any form of exercise that would make them break a sweat. While some men probably walked into their trap, it was a mistake Chase had no intention of making again.

"Mom, I don't care," He abruptly replied while rinsing the blender.

"It's your wedding." His mother said, the smile slipping off her lips, her eyes becoming narrow and he recognized this as the look that was supposed to put him in line, but today was a new day and he had nothing more to lose.

"It's my funeral, is more like it," He muttered as he finished cleaning up and grabbed his smoothie. Glancing around the kitchen, Chase was hoping to quickly find the keys to the truck. His mother rarely allowed him to use her car, but fortunately, his dad was kind enough to leave the truck and get a drive to work with a friend.

"What? Chase, why would you say such a cruel thing?" His mother shook her head and she rose from her chair. "I don't understand you. This isn't the boy I brought up."

"Mom, I've told you a million times, I don't want to marry Audrey," Chase sharply replied, feeling irritable for every reason under the sun - the heat, his future, his lack of sex life - everything was making him feel trapped and unable to escape. Only months earlier, he was still with

Lucy and everything was completely different. Although he was slowly starting to see that their relationships was less than ideal, at least she never tried to entrap him.

"Baby, you have no choice. You got her pregnant and that was very irresponsible, so now you have to do the honorable thing and marry her," His mother spoke like a character in one of her ridiculous movies and sometimes he wondered if she was delusional. She really seemed to believe all the foolishness of romance novels; that men only fucked women they loved or would love, that babies were the result of that love and that everyone lived happily ever after. It was fucking bullshit. "You will grow to love her."

"I don't even like her," Chase replied and he immediately saw the veil of naivety fall from her face, quickly replaced by a flash of anger. It was the same anger he saw in her face on the night she slapped him and insisted he marry Audrey. Unlike that day, he was no longer that naive boy, now realizing that it was just a game and he was merely a player to be controlled. "I don't want to be in the same room as her, let alone house, with a kid and that's not about to change."

"Chase I didn't bring you up this way," She snapped, her voice a combination of shame and hurt. He was tall, well over 6' and merely looked down at her face as it tightened up into a scowl that communicated her disappointment in him. "I brought you up to respect women. You shouldn't have bedded her if you had no true feelings. Now you will have to learn to love her."

"Oh come on!" Chase couldn't help but laugh in between long drinks of his smoothie. "Are you serious? Bedded her? As if it was this grand romantic gesture? She gave me some kind of drugs, I barely remember hooking up with her and that was it. It was a huge mistake. The biggest mistake of my life. I don't have feelings for her and I never will. This isn't one of your romance novels, this is real life."

"My books are real life to some people," She retorted and crossed her arms over her chest, reminding him of an angry child. "I didn't bring you up to be amoral. Audrey loves you very much and believes this baby came to you because of your destiny to be together."

"This baby came because she drugged me, made sure she had sex with me without birth control and now my life is a mess," Chase snapped and walked away from her, something he wouldn't have done only a few months earlier, knowing that it was considered disrespectful. Grabbing the keys on the way to the door, his mother's final comments were like a slap in the face.

"You made a decision that night. You can blame her all you want, but you also decided to be with her and use no form of birth control and if you ask me, that was irresponsible on so many levels."

Without replying, he tightened his grip on the keys and walked out the door. Infuriated, he climbed behind the wheel and turned the ignition. He hated that she was right. Although it was easy to blame Audrey for everything, he had been stupid enough to have sex with her without a condom and yet, he had done it and now he was paying. He briefly considered something Maggie had said during the summer; what if the baby wasn't even his child? Audrey certainly seemed like someone who would have no modesty about getting naked and climbing on any guy, so perhaps he wasn't the only one?

Arriving at work, he finished his smoothie just as he walked in the door. The gym was quiet and his coworker Cindy was helping one, middle-aged lady with a more challenging piece of equipment. She gave him a quick wave as he walked to the employees only section and rinsed out his cup, filling it with water and looked in the mirror. The whites of his eyes were red from lack of sleep and that combined with the two day's worth of stubble on his face hardly made him highly attractive, instead, he appeared to be a dirtbag that had no pride in his appearance. He continued to sport a buzz cut, something Maggie pointed out worked with his face and his large, intense eyes and rich tan. He had merely laughed at the time, but now under closer inspection, he wondered if it was true.

A summer of frustration combined with the heavy bags in the corner of the gym had helped enhance his upper body, enlarging his muscles while creating a sleek chest met and a flat stomach. He was in the best shape of his life and yet, he knew he could do much better. His goals were lofty when it came to his physical shape and endurance and his boss assured him that he had the ability to meet them.

"You're young, strong and determined, nothing can stop you from any of your goals," His boss had insisted with complete sincerity and yet, Chase almost laughed when he considered the reality of his life. If only he knew that there were some invisible limitations that were pulling away from his goals, from his life, from his future. He was spiraling into someone else's dreams and goals, losing the biggest part of himself along the way.

Satisfied that he was ready to start another shift, he sent a quick text to Maggie and ignored the several that were from Audrey. Unfortunately, his lone friend was unable to drop by the gym that day for their regular training sessions, something he looked forward to since getting her a deal. Harold was happy to accommodate a discount for the young woman after Chase insisted they were close. He knew it came off sounding like she was his girlfriend and although he wasn't about to lie, there was a part of him proud of the fact that the beautiful young woman that gracefully slipped in the gym 3-5 days a week could be seen as such; so he didn't exactly unravel the truth yet. He needed that fantasy. Maybe, he briefly considered, he was adapting a delusional world like his mother.

His supervisor, Cindy, usually opened the gym and left after Chase's arrival. Now working full-time hours, since the student left at the end of August, Chase and Cindy were the two main employees with a couple of other trainers in on occasion. It wasn't busy during that time of year, so Harold didn't want to have much staff working at once.

"It's been kind of dead today," Cindy said as she met him on the floor, carrying her water bottle and pointing toward the one, lone customer on the other side of the room. Married with one child, Cindy rarely wore makeup and he only had ever seen her with a ponytail, an oversized T-shirt, and yoga pants. Pale and thin, she didn't appear to be very healthy for someone who worked at a gym, but she was friendly and kind to him.

"Looks that way."

"Only had a few people in," She confessed and pointed toward the window. "Too hot outside, no one wants to workout even with the air conditioning back." She let out a short laugh and he joined her. "I don't think the phone even rang."

"So a long night?" Chase asked as he glanced toward the window and the empty parking lot outside.

"Probably," Cindy smiled and started toward the door. "But at least you can get your own workout in."

He nodded and said goodbye. Glancing at the woman on the other side of the room, he noted that she was finishing and talking to Cindy, who wandered back and seemed to be waiting for her. The two left together.

Alone, Chase decided to sit behind the desk and check his phone. Deleting Audrey's messages, he replied to the ones from Maggie, who was complaining about some of her customers that day. She had one guy who came in daily, flirting with her, not realizing that he was way out of his league. They referred to him as her 'stalker' and joked about the guy that they both knew from high school.

He texted her about his conversation with Louise Jacobs before work, confessing his own frustrations with life. In fact, he told Maggie everything. Well, almost everything. He wasn't about to tell her about his hormones were in high gear lately and he was dying to get laid. He knew there were some things that girls just didn't want to know about and besides, she might think he was a perve or something.

The day dragged on and although a few people were in after work, things died off that evening. Knowing that he still had a couple more hours to go, Chase considered that he might want to work out some of his frustrations on the punching bag. Plus, he wanted to gain some muscle and it wasn't going to happen if he was sitting on his ass.

He approached the punching bags and immediately felt the wrath of the day rising inside him. As he started to wrap his hands, he considered how his entire life was run by other people. At work, he was an employee, always having to help customers, regardless of how rude or unpleasant they were; he had to plant a smile on his face, understanding in his eyes and someone else's words slipping through his lips. When at home, he felt silenced. He could argue his point, but no one was listening. His father spinelessly stood back, while Louise Jacobs took over and forced his hand into a marriage that Chase didn't want. He hated Audrey now. At one time, he felt sorry for her predicament and guilty over his part, but now, he despised her.

Anger flowed to his heart, that raced with ferocity, his breathing became heavy as he removed his T-shirt and threw it on the ground. Grabbing a set of boxing gloves, he felt arousal as he thought about his earlier conversation with Maggie, the object of his desire since they first became friends; ironically on the same night he knocked up Audrey. Although he attempted to fight it, ignore the realities of the many lust-filled thoughts that sprang up in his mind, there was no way to deny that he wanted her like he had never wanted any woman in his life. Her sensual curves, how she moved while using the various equipment in the gym, her innocent gaze as she talked about the many 'conversations' she had on Skype with women throughout the country - women she was attracted to - drove him over the edge. He wanted to touch her skin, taste her in the most intimate way and get inside her, feel her hot breath on his neck, listen to her soft moans as he hungrily thrust into her, eventually giving in to both their physical needs; the kind these women on Skype certainly couldn't give her. He didn't want to be an asshole, but it was hard to believe that another woman could bring her the pleasures he would. Lesbianism, in his mind, was like eating the icing but skipping the cake.

Maybe it was a safety factor. Maybe women felt safer with other women? He certainly did understand the desire to be with a woman, they were silky, curvaceous, with soft voices, only second to their slender tongues running over your body, teasing you, until that triumphant release that made all worth every second.

Raising his arm, he hit the heavy bag with such vigor that he thought it would break away from the chains that held it in place. He continued to pound it with all his irate anger that could've sent him half way around the world and the intense lust that could've taken in the rest of the way. He was so caught up in the passion that flowed through his body that he hadn't heard the door open.

Suddenly feeling a set of eyes on him, he turned around and saw her.

CHAPTER NINE

"Oh, I'm sorry," Chase stuttered, suddenly embarrassed by the fury he was taking out on the heavy bag. Lost in the zone, he hadn't heard the door open or the client approaching him. Abruptly removing his boxing gloves Chase grabbed his T-shirt from the ground. It wasn't until he pulled the thin material over his head and started to unwrap his hands, that he could feel the humiliation burning through his skin, briefly avoiding the eyes of a regular that came in every other evening. "I...I didn't think anyone would be in again tonight."

Knowing that this answer was highly unacceptable - he was, after all, at work - Chase was relieved when the brunette standing across from him merely giggled and shrugged to indicate that she was unconcerned with his lack of professionalism. In fact, she appeared pretty casual, her eyes full of amusement, which should've relaxed him but instead, made him face grow warmer, as he abruptly finished unwrapping his hands.

It wasn't as if she was one of the town soccer mom's, casually strutting in with a friend, only half working out, but mostly chatting about her kids. This lady usually came in later at night, always alone and rarely talked to him, but went right to work. He recognized her as being older, probably in her late 30s, but he wasn't sure. She occasionally arrived still wearing professional clothing so he suspected she worked in an office setting.

Oh...and she was hot. She was pretty enough, but her body was phenomenal. The hours she spent at the gym were definitely working in her favor. It was another reason why he felt awkward when she caught him shirtless, pummelling the punching bag like some kind of maniac.

"That's quite all right," Her voice was smooth and sent an electrical sensation through him, causing him to shuffle uncomfortably and avoid her eyes. "I didn't mean to startle you and you didn't need to stop for me."

Her grin was suggestive as her eyes connected with his briefly, before she turned and headed toward the other side of the room, walking toward a treadmill. His vision automatically zeroed in on her yoga pants and he couldn't help but notice how they clung to her. She was wearing a tank top that was loose, but not enough to hide her full breasts especially after she climbed on the treadmill and started to run. She was staring at the television across the room, currently set on a news channel, but he noted that she was wearing earbuds, so only reading the headlines across the screen.

Pulling his eyes away, Chase knew he had to get a grip and stop acting like a horny perve who couldn't get his mind out of the gutter. He decided to text his confession to Maggie. He would maybe clean it up a bit. Maybe she would reveal some sexual confessions to him too.

Hmm....

So, how's your night going Mags?

He waited a few minutes.

So boring. You?

Glancing toward the lady across the room, her breasts bouncing beneath the loose fitting tank top, he quickly looked away.

I have a client. I can't stop staring at her tits, does that make me a perve?

He waited for the longest moment, immediately regretting his comment.

Yeah, but maybe she wants you too;-)

Intrigue captured Chase at the possibility. Considering the lady was wearing a loose top, he somehow doubted it, especially since she didn't even look his way since arriving. Then again, did that mean that Maggie sometimes-

His phone buzzed and alerted his attention. It was a text from Audrey.

Can we talk? Your mom said you were at work. Can we meet after?

He deleted the message, just as another one came in from Maggie.

I think the heat is getting to you.

He wanted to ask if the heat was getting to her too, but decided against it. That might be pushing things too far. But he wasn't about to lie.

You have no idea how much it's getting to me right now.

His throat went dry as he sent the text and reaching for his water bottle, he looked up in time to catch the lady across the room looking at him. She quickly looked away. Maybe she thought it was inappropriate to be checking his phone while at work. Knowing his boss wouldn't care, Chase didn't really think anything of it, but considered maybe he should check on her, just in case?

Then again, she didn't appear to need help and maybe would be annoyed if he interrupted her. He felt his phone vibrate and he looked down.

I think it's getting to us all.

He suddenly had a fantasy about Maggie, lying in her bed, wearing a sheer nightgown, unable to sleep cause of the heat, fidgeting uncomfortably while her breasts rose and fell under the thin material. Wiggling her hips around, moaning softly as she fought off the warm caresses of the warmth that ran over her body.

He was getting hard. At least he was behind the desk and as much as he knew it was time to change his thoughts, he couldn't help himself.

It's so hard to sleep at night when it's this hot.

He bit his lip and waited. His heart was pounding a little faster, as the thin material of his boxers suddenly felt restrictive. A quick glance across the room, he saw that the lady was staring at the television, but appeared to be lost in her own world. His phone buzzed.

Tell me about it.

Slightly let down, he wondered how he could get her on the same page as his own sexual thoughts. Maybe if he revealed some more about himself, she would too? But he had to be careful, women didn't tend to appreciate such honesty when it came to sex.

I keep having dreams and when I wake up, it's too hard to get back to sleep. I think it's the heat affecting me.

Her response kind of stole away some of his desire.

Maybe you are thinking of Audrey and all this shit going on.

Glancing back up at the lady, she continued to run, staring into space as if in a meditative state.

Nah not nightmares ha..

Then, his fingers feverishly tapped a little more than he thought might be acceptable.

I'm having a lot of sex dreams.

He waited and swallowed hard.

Maybe you need to get laid.

Yes!

Taking a deep breath, his fingers tapped on the phone.

Definitely.

You should do it then.

Chase felt his desire building up and decided it was time to cool off. Pushing the phone away, he quickly changed his thoughts, although it wasn't easy. Was Maggie thinking the same thing as him? She did once say that pleasure was pleasure, would she consider maybe, just once, hooking up with him? She often commented on how hot his body was now that he was working out.

The reality seemed unlikely. They were hanging out all summer and she never did anything that suggested that she wanted to be with any man, including him. She talked about girls a lot but it was usually in a crushing on them kind of way, rather than in a lustful manner. She did have a boyfriend once and was clear on the fact that they had a sex life.

When they were drinking…

But he had drinks with Maggie on a few occasions and nothing changed.

Glancing up at the lady across the room, she was easing off the machine as if she were afraid of falling and removed her earbuds. Pushing them in the bag she had sitting beside her, she glanced toward the lady's room then up at the clock behind him.

"Is there time for a quick shower before you close?"

Following her eyes, Chase was surprised to realize that it was almost closing time. "Oh yeah, sure," He stuttered and glanced toward the parking lot. It was empty. "I actually might lock the doors now, if that doesn't…bother you?"

She let out an amused laugh and shook her head. "I know you aren't going to hold me hostage, Chase."

He grinned, wondering how she knew his name and also a little ashamed that he didn't know hers, even though he saw her around all the time. Deciding not to respond, he rose from the chair - relieved that his earlier lust wasn't quite so evident now - and walked toward the door, which he gently locked. When he turned back, she was gone. He could hear the shower starting in the lady's room and was about to start wiping down the machines and cleaning up when he heard her calling his name.

He was almost to the door when it opened and the lovely brunette, who was quiet and sweet since her arrival stood before him, completely naked. Her large breasts were definitely natural, pulled down slightly by gravity, her nipples were large and inviting. Her stomach was quite flat for a woman who was a bit older and her hips were full, round and perfect. Her pubic area was hairless, pink folds of skin were a deep shade of crimson, while he felt his dick swelling as he stood in shock, unable to talk.

Without saying a word, she pulled him close, her lips quickly finding his while she pulled him back into the bathroom. His hand immediately reached for her breast but she quickly pulled it away and instead placed it on her clit. Following her lead, as she moved his fingers in the motion that she apparently liked, he continued to work as she ran her hands first up, over his chest, then down into his shorts, grasping his dick and he let out a moan. Her fingers let go and ran over his balls, cupping them for a short moment, while her tongue tore through his mouth. She suddenly stopped, stepped back and on cue, Chase removed his T-shirt, threw it on the ground and dropped his shorts. She stared at his erection, he noted that her nipples were hard now as she took his hand, to lead him into the shower.

"Wait," He could barely find his voice. "Are you on the pill?"

She let out a short laugh. "Do you seriously think I want to get pregnant for an 18-year-old? My youngest son is two years younger than you." She reached into her bag and pulled out a used pack of birth control pills. She dropped them and they got in the shower.

The sex was fast and furious, apparently, she didn't require that much foreplay and before he knew it, she pulled him inside her and ordering him to move faster. He had no issue doing exactly what she wanted until she was panting in pleasure, one of her hands on his hips, pulling him in deeper, as her thick breasts squeezed against him as he felt himself coming fast and hard as the hot water poured down their bodies.

His legs briefly felt weak, as she turned off the water and grabbed a towel, her breath still heavy as her breasts rose and fell as she wiped herself off quickly and he found another towel and did the same. Slowly getting out of the shower, he didn't know what to say. Pleasure and relief flowed through his body and he felt like some of the tension from the past week had run down the drain.

She was now pulling on her clothes in silence and he did the same. Their eyes met and she gave him a sheepish grin.

"Do you work every night?"

CHAPTER TEN

He felt light, invigorated as they walked out of the door together. There was a hint that this affair might continue and that promise created an excitement in him that Chase hadn't felt in weeks. In a life that gave him little to look forward to, this was *it* for him. A slight diversion from his real life, which proved to be a pleasurable experience already, he could tell there was a silent understanding between them that they mutually had something to benefit from this secret arrangement.

They exchanged numbers before leaving the building. In what he hoped wasn't an obvious trick, he handed her his phone and asked her to add herself to his directory. She silently did so and it was only at that time that he would learn that her named was Claire Shelley.

Holy shit, I just had sex with Dan Shelley's mother.

Thinking back to a particular high school football incident where Dan Shelley had purposely tripped him on the field while running with the ball, Chase couldn't help but to grin.

Dan fucking Shelley; you're an asshole and I just fucked your mother.

If Claire knew what he was thinking, she certainly hid it well as he walked through the parking lot and toward her SUV. It wasn't something he did only because he was leaving, but because Chase usually walked women to their cars at night. It wasn't part of the job description, just something he thought was a smart thing to do. Regardless of all the bullshit, the female persuasion had put him through in the last few months, he really did feel protective of them. He always had. In fact, this wasn't the first time he had walked Claire to her vehicle. Of course, she never seduced him before that night.

"I will be in touch," She said as she climbed inside her red, late model Honda. It was only as the light shone down from a nearby streetlight that he noticed her eyes were a pretty shade of green; odd that he hadn't noticed before that moment. She was attractive, but her skin looked tired with a dark cast over it. Glancing at the cigarette package on her dash and empty coffee cups in the vehicle, he suspected her lifestyle probably contributed to that factor.

"Have a good night, Chase," Her voice was soft, seductive, once again create an urge inside of him that almost caused him to invite her in the gym for round two - because he was certainly ready for another round - but the headlights of a vehicle alerted both their attentions, as a small car pulled in and Chase felt his desire fall flat; it was Audrey. See you soon." She continued and started her car.

Just as she backed up and turned out of the parking lot, Audrey pulled up beside him and gave a quick wave. Sighing so loudly that Chase was sure the entire town could've heard it, he turned in her direction and approached the car. Opening the door, he immediately shook his head.

"I don't have time for this shit tonight, Audrey," His voice was full of rebellion, his eyes scanning over her pale, unattractive face and wondered how he ever allowed his dick to get him into this mess. Women really did rule the show; she got him to fuck her when he didn't really want to, now she was pregnant and held all the power in her hands. Meanwhile, along comes Claire and the minute she strips down, she had him right where she wanted him; not that this was a bad thing, but the point was that women were very powerful, underneath their innocent eyes, soft voices and intoxicating scent.

"I need to talk to you," She suddenly seemed unusually demure and he decided to get in the car. He barely glanced at her but did long enough to notice that she was wearing a maternity top; something she could've worn before the pregnancy because the shape of her body and a pair of yoga pants that didn't look flattering on her thick legs. "I wanted to talk about our living arrangements."

"I live at home, you live wherever you want," Chase was abrupt and to the point. Regardless of all the times, she attempted to encourage him to move into her great-grandmother's house, he simply wasn't interested.

"You know that can't be the case when we get married."

"I don't want to marry you!" Chase snapped and ignored the look of hurt in her eyes, followed by a quick tear that was probably meant to manipulate him, but it didn't work. Pointing at her belly, he continued, "This entire situation is a big mistake."

She didn't reply. Her face was pale, her large eyes searched his face with such a hint of innocence, that he almost felt sorry for her.

"Fine," Her reply was sharp as she pursed her lips. "If you really think this is how things are going to work, then fine. Go home, go talk to your mom."

"What?" Chase was caught off guard by her reaction. "Why would I talk to her about anything? You've already got her in your corner."

"I think you might be in for a surprise when you get home tonight, that's all I'm saying." Audrey's reply was curt, causing his stomach to twist up in a knot. Clearly, something had taken place, a conversation he assumed, while he was at work.

While I was getting off with Claire, she was talking to mom, trying to figure out how to make my life miserable again.

"What the fuck Audrey?" He snapped and sighed loudly. "You do realize that no matter what happens between us, I'll never love you. I'll never be your loyal boyfriend or husband. There are some things you can't control."

Her eyes were full of fury and for a moment, he was expecting to be slapped. There was a desperation in them that made him nervous, it reminded him of the look his mother had after waking from one of her particularly bad night terrors that sent her into fits of screaming and crying, grasping for salvation or an ounce of hope. Tears formed in her eyes and her breathing became heavy, almost hysterical as she dramatically pointed toward the door.

"Get out of my car!" She screamed, suddenly completely manic and Chase was only too happy to oblige. He was tempted to tell her that he never wanted to get in the first place, but decided against it. He merely raised an eyebrow and got out. She backed up quickly and stopped. For a brief moment, sheer terror ran through him when Audrey hesitated, the car pointed directly at him and intense fury flowed through the atmosphere and he felt a chill run through his body. Then, just as quickly she jerked the wheel in the other direction and flew down the parking lot, only stalling for a moment before squealing her tires as she pulled out onto the highway.

His heart raced and beads of sweat were running down his forehead. His body felt weightless as he walked to the truck and climbed inside. His fingers were shaking when he grabbed his iPhone and sent a text to Maggie. In fact, the message wasn't even legible.

Ace t-shirt Hogg me

A text from Maggie quickly followed. It was question marks and he managed to calm himself down enough to get the words right.

She tried to hit me.

Audrey.

With her car.

The truth was she hadn't technically tried to hit him and that realization came to him right away, but there was definitely a moment when he thought it was his fate. There was a moment, he knew that she was absolutely thinking about it.

WTF??????? Where are you?

Work parking lot.

Stay there!

It was only a few minutes before Maggie was pulling up beside him. He was so stunned, he hadn't even noticed her arrive. Glancing at his phone, he realized it was almost 10. She must've left work early.

Jumping out of the driver's side of her car and into his truck, Maggie's face was drained of all color. "What the fuck? Are you serious, Chase? What happened?"

He suddenly felt clueless, not even sure how to put his words together. His lips were moving, but his voice wasn't working. Without even realizing what was going on, he suddenly realized that Maggie was hugging him. Moving away from him, he felt calmness relax his body.

"We have to call the cops on that crazy bitch."

"I can't," Chase finally managed to talk. "She'll deny it. I don't have any witnesses and she, I mean, I don't know how to explain it."

"Okay, calm down," Maggie said, her voice suddenly soothing and controlled, she reached out and touched his arm. "Tell me what happened.

"Audrey showed up and wanted to talk. I got in her car and told her that I would never marry her, that I didn't love her and I would never be loyal to her," He blurted out everything and for a moment, feared that Maggie would think less of him, but she only nodded in agreement, her hand soft and warm on his forearm. "I just had it Mags, she insisted that I move in and all this shit and I couldn't handle it. I think maybe she talked to mom, I don't know, she made some comment about I would have to talk to my mom when I got home."

"Why is your mom on her side, I don't get it?" Maggie briefly looked away, her eyes scanning the area as if to see who could've been a witness in this situation, but she quickly looked back in his face. "So, then what?"

"She yelled at me to get out of the car and I did. She backed up really fast and pointed in my direction," Chase felt his body calming down and was surprised to find himself slightly aroused, even though there was nothing about possibly getting killed that was a turn on. "I have no proof, but I could feel it, Maggie. I know she was thinking about hitting me with the car. I'm certain."

"Always trust your instincts," She quietly replied, her fingers gently caressing his arm, her eyes searching his and he felt such a strong urge to kiss her that he actually started to move forward, she moved away and pulled her hand back. He was instantly embarrassed. Apparently, he couldn't *always* trust his instincts.

"You have to get away from her, she's crazy," Maggie said as she turned, moving away from Chase, her eyes absently stared forward, as if deep in thought.

He glanced down at her navy blue T-shirt that was very form fitting, her faded jeans and Vans sneakers. She was dressed in such a basic manner, but it didn't look basic on her. He was a little flustered and ashamed of the desire he felt for his best friend, especially in moments like this one, where it should've been the least of his concerns. What kind of animal was he, anyway? He sometimes felt as if his lust never ended.

"I can't," His words came out much more desperately than he intended, but still, wasn't that how he felt? "You're the only one on my side, Maggie. Everyone else thinks I should just cave and give my life away to someone that I made one mistake with...*one* mistake. How many people will have unprotected sex tonight and won't get pregnant? Seriously? I do it once in my life and here we are..."

That wasn't completely true. Hadn't he had unprotected sex with Lucy a few times? It was rare, but it did happen.

"I don't know what to tell you," Maggie said, her voice full of desperation. "Where is she now?"

That's when it hit him! She was probably at his parent's house.

"Fuck me!" Chase replied, his eyes now closed."Fuck me! She's at my parent's house. Pleading her case. Fuck!"

"Do you want me to go there with you?" Maggie asked and although he wanted to be a man and say no, he found himself nodding yes. "Ok, we should go now, before she causes any more damage."

"You're right." He agreed. "Are you sure you don't mind?"

"Nah, I'll just text my mom."

"Ok."

But he knew it would be a waste of time. His mother would fall for whatever Audrey said - hook, line, and sinker - he was truly, absolutely, 100% fucked.

CHAPTER ELEVEN

The sting of betrayal is always a little bit sharper when it comes from a family member. There's alway a hidden expectation that others will do it to us, that their disloyalty will shine through at the most inappropriate and unfortunate moment, however there's a part of us all that wants to believe that when things really hit the wall of misery, family will be there for us, with open arms and hearts.

Chase Jacobs didn't really want to believe that his mother would turn against him; this was the same woman who once yelled at a neighborhood kid for biting her son when he was five. She was the same woman who packed his lunches every day, always making sure there was an extra little treat hidden beneath his sandwich; which he dutifully ate, even if he didn't really like it. She was the same woman who looked after Chase when he was sick, changed the sheets when he vomited all over them and tucked him in at night.

But somewhere along the way, things changed in their relationship. Perhaps it was around puberty, when his hormones were racing and his main priorities turned to girls, sports then working out. It was almost as soon as she saw him turning into a man, she started to hate him, little by little. She never said it, but there was an indifference that he had to acknowledge, often in her disinterest in every aspect of his life. Louise Jacobs hated sport and therefore, didn't care if he made a team and her compassion was empty if he ever got injured while playing. She considered sports barbaric, training at the gym something only practiced by those who wanted to physically overpower others and she hated his first girlfriend.

Audrey was another story altogether.

For some reason, Louise Jacobs connected with Aubrey Neil in a way that she didn't even connect with her own children. She had a vague relationship with Angel, but it always had its limits. Even as children, Chase received the majority of attention whereas his sister seemed to be yelled at more than anything. Angel had a much closer relationship with their father, someone who seemed hesitant with Chase and he wasn't sure why.

By the time he arrived home from the gym that night, it was too late. His father had long retreated to bed, always avoiding any family conflicts while Louise Jacobs, appeared to be comforting Audrey. A box of tissues sat on the kitchen table on top of newspapers, flyers and mail that was up to a week old. Two coffee cups were there, along with cream and sugar, a bag of cookies and some crackers, their eyes both on Chase and Maggie as they entered the house. It was clear by their dismissive glance that they didn't believe he should've brought his best friend along. They would've preferred him to be alone and defenseless.

His mother calmly turned her attention toward Audrey and the two gave a knowing glance. She pursed her lips together tightly, her face suddenly aging before his eyes, a coldness crossed through the room and behind him, Chase could hear Maggie swallowing, nervously shuffling around, probably wishing she hadn't offered to support him.

"Chase, I've had a long conversation with Audrey and we both agree that it would be best if you move in with her," Her words curt, showing no emotion and suddenly he felt weak, powerless as if his body and life was no longer his own. "It's for the best."

"No," His voice was strong but gentle at the same time. He wasn't looking to start a confrontation, but he also wasn't willing to cave in and accept this fate. There was no way he could live in the same house as Audrey.

"Yes, you must," His mother showed no change in her expression. "After today, you no longer live here."

"What?" Chase snapped, no longer able to hold back his emotions. "You're kicking me out?

"It's for your own good."

"It's *not* for my own good."

"It is," She insisted. "You don't see it now, but you will."

"I'm going to talk to dad-

"I've already talked to Carl and he feels the same way," His mother spoke sternly, while Audrey had a look of triumph on her face.

Feeling a wave of anger rising inside him, he had to leave the room. Feeling trapped by circumstance, he rushed upstairs and could hear Maggie behind him, as he felt every ounce of wrath drop to his toes as he walked into the bedroom. Closing the door behind the two of them, he felt weak, his arms and legs like cement, pulling his entire body into the ground. He sunk onto his bed and Maggie quietly sat beside him.

"I can't believe this is happening," Chase whispered, shaking his head, a wave of grief took over and he felt broken, unable to comprehend how his life had taken such a dark turn. He hated Audrey. She was trying to force something that wasn't there. "I wish I were dead."

"Don't say that," Maggie finally spoke, her warm hand touched his shoulder, but he felt numb and unable to register anything she was saying. She continued to talk, but his brain was resisting everything. He cleared his throat and gave a brief nod, but the words were swimming through a million other thoughts that were unclear, scattered and deformed. He was 18 years old and he was dead. It was all over. There was no future. A loveless marriage, working to support a life he didn't want and he had no say. Everyone else apparently did, but he did not.

"…hope. I promise we'll think of something Chase." Maggie said quietly, her voice shaking and when he turned, she appeared to be wiping away a tear. "I'm sorry Chase, I can't believe your mother said that, I just…what kind of power does Audrey have over her? I don't understand."

"That makes two of us," Chase replied emotionlessly. "I guess I should start packing."

"I can help." Maggie quickly stood up. "Do you have any boxes?"

"There's a few in the basement, I think Angel had some extras when she went to university. I don't have much, though," He replied and stiffly stood up, glancing around at his few possessions. At that moment, he couldn't have cared less about most of them. He had his laptop, his phone, some clothes, not much else. He had hockey equipment from when he used to play, but why bother bringing that? A football sat in the corner, as well as a few fitness books and magazines that his boss gave him and other than that, few personal items. "Don't worry about that now, I mean, I have a suitcase I can use for some of my clothes. I don't even care anymore."

Maggie's face was full of worry and she bit her bottom lip. "You know, I can talk to mom, maybe you could stay at our place."

"I somehow doubt your mom wants me living at your house but thanks, Mags." His voice was sincere and he felt frozen on the spot. He knew he should be gathering his stuff, cleaning out his room, but he simply couldn't move. It was unbelievable that this was happening to him. How could he had been so stupid?

Maggie's phone beeped and she quickly glanced at it. "It's my mom, she wants me to get home."

"That's fine," Chase shrugged. "There's not much you can do here anyway."

"I'm sorry," Maggie said as she leaned over and gave him a hug. "I'm really so sorry, Chase. I can't even imagine what this must be like for you."

"Just be happy your future is wide open."

"Yours is too," Maggie insisted as she let go of him and stepped back. "We'll figure this out."

He knew she meant well, but he also knew there was nothing that either of them could do. His life had been hijacked. No thanks to his dick.

"I'll walk you to your car," Chase said and followed her out of his bedroom. Downstairs, two sets of eyes watched with interest as he gently touched Maggie's arm on the way out of the house. Once they arrived at her car, they hugged briefly, knowing that they were still being watched through the window.

She waved before driving away and Chase reluctantly returned to the house. He expected someone to say something but no one did. Returning upstairs, he felt a sudden flux of anger burning through his veins, a combination of all the emotions that had gathered up from the last few months of his life; the passion, the drive, the energy that existed deep inside him, only released when in front of the heavy bag at work. Then again, hadn't those same emotions reared his lust, the longings that were so intense that made it almost impossible to think about anything else. Hadn't his encounter with Claire earlier that night only managed to turn up the flame rather than quench a thirst? There was a few, distinct minutes when he felt powerful, in control of her pleasure as well as his own, where no one else in the world owned him. He owned them.

There were moments that he felt like an animal and this was one of them. There were times when he was hitting the punching bag that he escaped to another world, barely conscious of what was going on around him beyond hitting that bag with all the force, all the strength that drove him over the edge. He sometimes wondered what would happen if he was up against another person when this moment of disconnect happened? How badly could he hurt them? Would he merely leave them with a black eye or would he rip them apart like a caged animal desperate to escape?

Chase was different when he was with Lucy. He went to the gym and worked out, but it was passionless, simply pushing his physical limits from the times before, but now there was a hatred inside him as he hit the heavy bag. There was a fierceness that felt uncontrollable.

It was probably better that Maggie was a lesbian and only viewed him as a friend. He could never be that tender, gentle lover again. That boy was eaten by the wolves and they sat downstairs, at the kitchen table, deceptively chatting about baby showers and wedding days as if they had him by the balls. They would soon find out that no one could ever really cage an animal.

CHAPTER TWELVE

Chase Jacobs was beautiful. He reminded her of a work of art that was chiseled to perfection after hours of labor and precision; except, in this case, it was a combination of genetics and a fierce workout routines at the gym.

Maggie remembered the first time she saw her best friend with his shirt off. They had been working out together long after the gym closed, something that his boss Harold was kind enough to allow, simply because Maggie was a little bit shy when she first started to train. Her thin, pasty white arms were weak, pathetic while her ability to endure cardio was almost non-existent. The air conditioning had been broken down at the time and he removed his shirt casually, throwing it aside, while he showed her how to properly use one of the frustrating contraptions; but she hadn't heard a word.

His body, quite simply, was like something she saw on television; tanned, muscular and perfection. Although Maggie was physically attracted to other women, she certainly understood why women found her best friend so appealing. Muscles bulged underneath his shirt and without it, she could see that every inch of his torso was flawless; from his biceps to the smooth, six pack that sat just below his ribcage. It was hard not to stare. A part of her wanted to reach out and touch him, although not in a sexual way, but because she was curious how it would feel to brush her fingers down the sleek muscle. She didn't dare ask, however, because it might send the wrong message.

Maggie Telips wasn't a moron. She could tell Chase was attracted to her and there was a certain part of herself that was crushing on him, which was confusing since her main object of desire was women. Perhaps it had long been a secret, but it was definitely always there. In fact, the longer she dated Todd, the more she wanted to be with a woman. She felt nothing when he touched her; unless she was drunk and then she would close her eyes and feel no remorse for the fantasies of a woman going down on her, rather than the rough and awkward tongue of a sexually inexperienced boy. Sometimes if she really got into the moment and allowed her imagination to work, she could find herself gasping in pleasure, but most times it was an act.

Chase was different though. He was gentle and sweet. When he hugged her, she could feel the emotions pouring through him, as he attempted to control his breath. There was something about being wanted by an attractive person - even if it wasn't your sexual preference - that was empowering and seductive. She was curious what it would be like if they hooked up; was she bi and just didn't know it? Hadn't she felt safe when enclosed in his strong arms? Hadn't she felt a slight tingle when her nipples were squeezed against his hard chest? Wasn't there a part of herself that knew he would go to great lengths to bring her pleasure?

The irony was that for a man with so much physical strength, his emotional side was quite another thing. Often feeling defeated and depressed, it was kind of hard to believe that a man who had so much to offer in both personality and physical appearance, would end up with a girl like Audrey. They couldn't be more opposite and she, in Maggie's opinion, couldn't be more conniving. It was true that Chase shouldn't have considered running away from the problem when it came up, it wasn't that he was a terrible person, but because he was scared and felt backed into a corner. Audrey had always been direct with him about what she wanted; which appeared to be Chase Jacobs, regardless of whether or not he returned feelings for her or was loyal. After all, wasn't he still having sex with that stacked, older woman from the gym?

In many ways, Maggie couldn't help but feel like she was the only woman that wasn't a vulture in his life. Hadn't Lucy been controlling and manipulating? His mother, from everything he said and Maggie witnessed first hand, was completely delusional. In fairness, there were a lot of rumours about what had happened to her while growing up on the reserve, but who knew if they were even true? If they were, it would explain a great deal about why she appeared to hate Chase and possibly, men in general. However, it still didn't really explain why she would turn against her own son and favour Audrey; a woman she barely knew.

Audrey Neil was a bit of a mystery. Always quiet in high school, she disappeared to college and suddenly was back with a degree in something or another. She worked at the youth centre in Mento and apparently took some courses online during her spare time. That must've been the time when she wasn't hijacking Chases' life, Maggie decided.

The two now lived together in a chaste household. Chase refused to share a room with Audrey and opted to instead sleep on the couch in the living room. The furniture left by Audrey's great grandmother was old, stuffy and uncomfortable, but he claimed it was better to wake up with a stiff neck than beside his future bride. Her many attempts to seduce him were wasted and regardless of the fact that Maggie was openly gay, Audrey insisted that the two were more than friends and his lack of desire was because he was 'getting it' elsewhere. He was; but it wasn't with Maggie. If only the walls of the gym could talk.

Months seem to crawl by and while Maggie worked tirelessly, attempting to get recruited to the RCMP, by doing strength training, some volunteer work and even looking into university courses and learning some French, she watched her friend slowly turning into a whole other person. To her, he was still sweet, lovable Chase Jacobs, the one person who had morphed into her closest and dearest friend, but to the rest of the world he was cold and distant. He still walked female clients from the gym to their vehicles after dark, but he did so like a bodyguard that wasn't allowed to show any expression. He also no one longer talked to his family. They were dead to him.

His physical appearance made him intimidating. Tall, muscular with broad shoulders, expressionless, something she wished to emulate in order to be taken seriously during her attempts to get into the RCMP. It was necessary to seem as emotionless as possible due to the seriousness of their profession, but she never felt she could quite reach that level of sternness. She tried though and Chase was her role model.

By contrast, she often commented that her best friend would be a shoe in for the RCMP; but he wasn't interested. His goals were - or at least, had been - to be get into the world of Mixed Martial Arts and apparently beat the shit out of other men. It seemed pretty barbaric to her, but at the same time, there was something about the passion in his eyes when he spoke about these fights that he watched with his boss at the gym, that made her wonder if she showed the same zest when talking about law enforcement. It made her search deep inside herself and wonder if she was on the right track.

People assumed Chase was her boyfriend and that wasn't such a terrible thing. Other local townies kept away from her, noticing that her 'boyfriend' was huge and carried a confrontational expression that turned most cowards away. She hated that she found this endearing, but it made her feel safe. Even her own mother questioned if there was something going on, warning Maggie that he was engaged and therefore, it wasn't something she wanted to get in the middle of, in any capacity, even if they were just friends.

"Once he's married, I hate to say it Maggie, but Audrey isn't going to want you around," Her mother sternly warned, showing no compassion in her voice, but more of an 'I told you so' arrogance that she hated. "Married people are in a whole other world, especially once kids get in the picture, they tend to drift away. Trust me, I've lived it."

Her mother didn't have any friends other than relatives, so that didn't surprise Maggie. She couldn't seem to make her mom understand that her 'old' generation wasn't the same and people were more fluid now; in many ways, actually, but that's something her mother would never understand nor would she try.

But there was a part of her that had the same worry and this wasn't because of the division between married and single people, but because Audrey clearly hated her. She didn't feel welcomed in their home and her one, lone visit, was awkward, especially when she was on her way to the car and could hear Audrey scream at Chase for supposedly staring at Maggie's 'perky tits'; something he hadn't done, but clearly it indicated that she felt competitive with Chase's friend, regardless of the fact that she was gay. No one seemed to believe that she could hang around with someone of the opposite sex, especially someone as attractive a Chase and not fuck him. It was unreal.

Now that the fall months progressed into winter, the crisp Alberta air had a distinct chill that was a curt warning of the long winter that was ahead. It was a bit depressing to her, especially when she looked at her own dismal life, then felt guilty for having such a thought when she saw what Chase was up against. Audrey continued to get bigger and bigger and eventually people started to learn she was expecting Chase's child, something he was neither proud of or wanted, but was full of resentment. His life reminded her of a Greek tragedy she would read about in high school and yet, he did have free will. Could he save money, get his own place? Refuse to marry Audrey? In her mind, these were all still options. Until something abruptly changed her mind.

It was during a so-called house warming party that Audrey thrown shortly after Chase moved in. Maggie boldly arrived, knowing that Chase was the only one who didn't view her as the enemy, hoping to show him some support during such a stressful and difficult time. The party was in full swing when she arrived, several of Audrey's relatives were staring her down, but she arrogantly ignored them, sticking close to Chase, who looked like he wanted to crawl in a hole and die, as his dimwitted mother rambled on about wedding plans. It was kind of redundant, since the couple decided to hold off on any plans until after the baby was born, but it appeared to be her own, personal obsession.

The only time she left his side all night was when she went to the upstairs washroom, unaware that there was another one off the kitchen that was supposed to be for guests. Audrey must've noticed and followed Maggie upstairs because the next thing she knew, the very pregnant young woman was calling her name. Turning around slowly, Maggie would later chide herself for being too slow, too stupid to realize she was being followed, only to be shoved in the bathroom.

"What the hell are you doing up here? I don't want trash like you in *my* bathroom," Audrey's deceptive mask was finally removed, no longer the sweet, girl next door that she pretended to be in front of others, her voice was shrill. "But it's nothing new for you, is it? Going places where you don't belong?"

"What?" Maggie finally managed to say something, feeling stunned by the confrontation and unsure of how to react. "I don't know what you're talking about, I was looking for the bathroom."

"You shouldn't be *here*," Audrey challenged her, the bathroom door now closed, Maggie backed up against the shower. "Do you think I want the fucking mistress here, in *my* house, while I'm pregnant with his child?"

"I'm not his mistress!" Maggie said, but her voice sounded like little more than a whimper. Suddenly feeling claustrophobic and fearful, she reached out and gave Audrey a slight shove, but was quickly met with resistance when she grabbed Maggie's arm and twist it. Feeling pain shoot through her wrist, she attempted to fight her off but Audrey's grasp only became more forceful.

"Don't fight back," She muttered in her ear. "If I get hurt, how will it look to the RCMP? Do you think they will ever let you in if you're aggressive toward a pregnant lady? Wouldn't look very good, would it?"

Tears formed in her eyes and Maggie knew she was right. She was powerless and although she would never tell Chase about this incident, Maggie was suddenly very aware why Chase often said he felt like an animal trapped in the corner; powerless, scared….and ferocious.

CHAPTER THIRTEEN

Chase was so set on his anger toward Audrey, that he rarely thought about the baby that would soon be a part of their lives. He didn't go to appointments with her - not that it mattered because his mother was more than willing to do so - nor did he bother to ask questions, touch her belly or even consider if the child was a boy or a girl. It wasn't that he was heartless, it was more that he blocked the thought from his mind. There was some guilt underneath all the anger, feelings of remorse that would eventually surface, but the crisp winter air somehow was a comfort to him during this bleak period of his life. Perhaps because it subdued his usual fury.

This was a good thing since the holiday season brought back two women who also knew how to push all his buttons; his sister and Lucy. The first one he expected, but since he no longer communicated with his family, didn't really think their paths would cross. He certainly didn't think she would show up at his work, especially considering she appeared apathetic toward him before returning to university.

To some, a reconnection with a sister who was back for the holidays would be a warm, enriching way to celebrate the season, but Chase felt nothing when he saw her enter the gym on a Saturday afternoon. Her hair was slightly longer, making her appear more feminine, although her face was quite pale, which seemed strange when considering their shared genetics. Their mother was native, while their dad was hardly lily white. Angel had always been the freak of the family; a thought that crossed his mind as she approached him, while he wiped down the machines after a particularly busy morning. He assumed everyone was out Christmas shopping in the afternoon.

"Aren't you going to say anything to me, I've been gone since September," She curtly pointed out, as if he were supposed to roll out the red carpet before she arrived. Alone in the room, Chase was relieved that his boss was gone for the day and that the only clients around were in the changing rooms. The holiday season brought feast or famine, depending on what other activities people were caught up in, however, the true fitness geek didn't allow Christmas to interrupt their usual routine.

Shaking his head with a slight, apathetic shrug, he merely uttered a flat, emotionless 'hello' and continued to work. He avoided her eyes and hoped it encouraged her to leave.

"You know, I'm not the enemy here, Chase," She spoke calmly, smoothly, almost as if she was personally hurt by his snub, which was unlike her. His eyes flickered up and he stopped what he was doing and watched her eyelashes flutter behind the dark glasses as she pursed her lips and attempted a faint smile. "I didn't kick you out."

"No, you didn't," Chase calmly replied. "But you probably agree with it, right? Think I should just hand my life over on a silver platter to Audrey because of one fucking mistake?"

It wasn't until he saw the look of shock on her face that Chase realized how much anger and bitterness integrated each word. Her eyes reflected how much his disposition had changed over the past few months. Although the old Chase would've immediately felt guilt and apologized, his eyes were instead confrontational and he watched her look away and step back.

"I'm not saying that you shouldn't be responsible, but I don't agree with what mom did," Angel quietly replied, her fingers played with the strap of the purse that was across her chest. "She shouldn't have forced you to move in with Audrey."

"They *both* forced me to move in with Audrey," Chase sharply corrected her, but this time, she appeared unfazed, almost as if she was prepared for him to be hostile. "It wasn't just mom."

"Come on, you know dad wouldn't have a say, once mom made up her mind," Angel playfully attempted to justify their father as if it were an inside joke. Chase didn't see the humor and shot her a cold glare. "Come on, you *know* what mom's like."

"Dad has a fucking mouth Angel and if he had a spine, he could've stood up to her," Chase said, standing a little taller, he took a deep breath as a way to control his anger. He wasn't sure why every female in his life seemed to thrive on pissing him off, but he was starting to view all women the same; the clients, his family, Audrey, the women at the grocery store or at the post office. It seemed like they got some kind of pleasure getting under his skin; always complaining, nagging, never happy. Even the lady at the motor vehicles department snapped at him when he couldn't understand her broken English. Yet, he felt compelled to be respectful and try to accommodate most, with the exception of his family and Audrey, the very women who fucked him over.

"Yeah, but you know he wouldn't go against anything mom decided," Angel attempted to justify and Chase turned away from her, unable to even look her in the eye. He walked toward the desk and quietly went behind it, hoping that being closer to the main entrance would give his sister a hint to leave. He had no interest in hearing her pathetic argument. It wasn't as if his father had reached out to him in the past couple of months. "You know how they are."

"I don't care, Ang," He shook his head and leaned against the desk, purposely looking down his nose at her, a subtle gesture taught to him by Harold, who insisted that intimidation was as much about your presence and stance as it was about your physical size. Technically, Chase wasn't much larger than a few months earlier, he just knew how to display it differently now and he could see how people reacted, how they slowly inched away or pulled back as if he were an animal that could lash out at any time.

"But it's the holidays, let it go, Chase," Angel replied with a slight whine in her voice that irked him; here comes the manipulation, but wasn't that what it always came down to with people like her? "Drop in and-

"Fuck off Angel," His words were smooth, regardless of the harshness of intent. He had never told his sister to fuck off before and wasn't sure

which one of them was more surprised; her for having heard it or him for having witnessed her response. They were equally surprised, but his bewilderment quickly turned to amusement, as a grin inched his lips into a hesitant smile. "I'm not going over for Christmas, I'm not going to do whatever the fuck Audrey wants, I'm just going to sleep that day and enjoy some peace and quiet. That's my holiday plans. That's all I want."

"Come on, you can't keep punishing mom and dad," Angel attempted to reconnect, but her words only pushed them farther apart, as Chase let out a sharp laugh.

"Why? They're certainly not concerned about punishing me," He was slightly humored by his own reasoning and felt something alert him from the side. The door opened and a client entered, carrying his gym bag, giving Chase a quick nod, his eyes barely grazed over Angel. Most men showed his sister little attention. She was hardly attractive unless someone leaned toward the feminazi look. She wore no makeup, hid her curves and rarely smiled. "You gotta go, Ang, I'm training that guy."

Slightly befuddled, she didn't reply as she walked toward the door. She gave him one, last, puppy dog look; another trademark of the manipulating woman, so completely transparent. To that, he merely grinned and looked away.

"Hey Bob, how you doing today?" He called out to the client across the room, making sure to ignore his sister as she left the building.

However smooth he thought he was that afternoon, he certainly didn't fair as well a couple days later when he encountered Lucy at the mall. He ran in to grab some stuff before the holidays closed everything down and it was in the condom section of the drugstore that she appeared.

"Little late for those, isn't it?" Her words were sharp, with a slight 'Valley girl' feel behind them, almost as if she were still in high school rather than the real world. She sounded gleeful to rub it in his face and although he would've crouched in embarrassment a few months earlier, he now felt compelled to deal with her confrontation. Her long dark hair didn't hide her thin, unhealthy face, he assumed it was from the nights of partying with her new boyfriend, who was probably just excited to have a young hot piece of ass. Women were so naive when it came to men.

"It depends," Chase countered, but she seemed unaffected by his reply and merely smirked as if she were enjoying his personal hell. Another thing he had learned from Harold was that the fewer words you used, the more powerful you became. There was nothing more pathetic than a man that rambled on endlessly like a woman, a chatty Cathy that didn't have an off button; that was him, once upon a time. "What do you want Lucy?"

"Hey calm down," She showed a flicker of discomfort and shrugged off his response as if she didn't care. "I was just being nice." He noted how she pushed out her breasts as she spoke, her hand shoved in her back, jean pockets. She looked terrible and he briefly wondered if that was always the case or if Lucy were starting to show signs of her new lifestyle.

"Whatever, Luc, I gotta go," He attempted to move away and then, she reached out and touched his arm. He hated to admit it, but there was something about her soft fingers fluttering over his wrist that resurrected every intimate moment they ever shared and for a brief moment, he was a naive 16-year-old boy once again, hopelessly in love with the coolest girl he ever met, the one he never expected would give him a second of attention. He quickly shook it off.

"Seriously, though, man, how did you get yourself in that mess?" She raised an eyebrow, challenging his eyes, as she stood uncomfortably close to him. It was too intimate and he looked over her head as some slightly dirty piece of white trash walked down the same aisle, eyeballing Lucy and he briefly wondered if *this* was seriously her new boyfriend. Suddenly, the powers shifted.

"Hey Luc, we gotta get going if we're going to catch the liquor store before it closes, doll," The scrawny man, wearing a green, plaid jacket that appeared to need to be washed, along with oversized black jeans and t-shirt, while his straggly dirty blond hair fell out of an old baseball cap that wasn't even readable, it was so worn. "Luke's gonna wonder what's up."

The stranger's eyes skipped from Lucy - who was now backing off - to Chase. His eyes scanned his body briefly and his lips crept out from under a long, scruffy beard. "Well, who we got here?"

"This is Chase, my ex," Lucy suddenly seemed hesitant. Unsettled by the looks that buddy was giving him, he scowled and stared him down. Unaffected, the stranger reached out to shake his hand.

"Brad Weatherby, but everyone calls me 'Bud," He gave an unexpected and yet, infectious grin that left Chase stunned. "And I gotta tell you, if you're ever interested in working at a bar, well I got a job for you."

"What?" Chase was slightly stunned by his comment.

"He owns a bar over in Mento," Lucy explained, suddenly appearing awkward and it was clear that she was embarrassed by this guy. "He's Luke's cousin."

"And I need a guy like you at my bar," He stood back and seemed unaffected by the awkwardness of the moment, but almost delighted by his discovery. "At the doors, oh yes, those crazy motherfuckers aren't going to take on someone like you, I'm bettin' you would knock them until next Tuesday if they did try."

"What are you talking about?" Chase couldn't help but follow along in Brad's jovial nature.

"He's looking for a bouncer," Lucy attempted to decode the conversation. "He's having a lot of trouble with some of the locals and he needs someone big like you to scare them off."

"Damn straight," Brad smiled as he continued to nod his head, a self-satisfied smile on his face. "The good Lord always gives you the answer, I was just thinking this morning that I gotta find someone young and strong to watch the door at Rick's and he's good looking too, the women will flock to the bar if they see him outside."

"Wait, what?" Chase hesitated. "You want me to work at your bar? Who's Rick?"

"Oh the bar, it's called Rick's because that was the original owner, he's dead now, but it seemed right to leave the name, you know?" He was surprisingly diplomatic in his explanation and charismatic in his presentation. "Hey, you want a job, it's yours. We're open 7 days a week and I manage it, but you don't gotta work all that much. Any help would be appreciated but the weekends are obviously the busy time."

Lucy looked nervous, while Brad seemed unaffected by the intimidating nature that Chase attempted to display. He felt his defenses drop and he was surprised to actually like this sketchy looking character. His mind quickly considered the possibly; another job gave him a way to avoid his home life.

"Don't give me an answer now," Brad said before he could say another word. He slipped a card in his hand. "Call me sometime next week and let me know. You have a good night now, Chase!" He slapped him on the arm as he walked away and Lucy quietly followed.

Staring at the card, he was surprised to find it quite professional compared to the man who handed it to him. Something told him that he couldn't say no to this offer. Something told him he didn't want to either.

CHAPTER FOURTEEN

It wasn't much of a car, but it got him wherever he had to go. After he was kicked out of the family home, Chase had to invest the little money he had into a vehicle, in order to get to and from work. It was an added stress that he certainly didn't need at that time, but it was also nice to have something that was his own. However, his budget didn't get him much of a car - a really old Honda Civic, that would've been amazing in its day - but this car's day had long ended and it was hanging on by a wing and a prayer. Fortunately, most of the repairs needed were things he was able to fix himself, in the driveway of his new home. Granted, the weather was pretty crisp, but you do what you have to do.

His Christmas schedule at the gym was quite hectic and that combined with the times when Bud was available, didn't allow Chase to make his way to Mento until the first week of January. He'd made every effort to avoid Audrey and his family during the holiday season, spending most of his time at Maggie's house, who insisted he go there for Christmas dinner, since her sister would be in Calgary and it would only be the two of them. Her mother seemed suspicious of their relationship and wondered out loud why he wasn't enjoying this meal with his family, but she didn't show that much resistance to him being there.

"He's my best friend," Chase later overheard them talking in the kitchen, while he sat in the living room, checking his phone. The two were rattling around dishes and attempting to have a hushed conversation, but the walls were thin in this old house. "Didn't you ever have a best friend?"

"Not a man," Her mother's reply was curt. "Men and women can't be friends, there's always something in the background."

"What is *that* supposed to mean?" Maggie snapped.

"Feelings, attraction," Her mother's reply was sharp. "Its never just about friendship and if it is, it never stays that way. Trust me on that one, Maggie."

"I'm gay, mom," Maggie spoke quite clearly and the dishes stop rattling. "I wish you would accept it."

"You're not gay, Maggie," Her mother attempted to correct her. "You're just confused and that boy out there is attracted to you."

That's when their conversation ended. That two returned to the room and Chase pretended to not hear a word. He couldn't help feeling a spark of desire flow through him upon her mother's assumption that Maggie was confused, rather than gay and wondered if she was right.

The meal was awkward but fortunately, Chase was getting pretty used to awkward. Every aspect of his life was awkward now; his home life, his affair with an older woman and now, the conversation he was set to have with Bud about working at the bar. The idea of working for someone that was connected to his ex felt strange. Not that it mattered, she flew out of town almost as fast as she strolled in. For that, he was relieved.

Rick's Bar wasn't exactly the classiest place around, but it wasn't as bad as he imagined. Not quite 19, he was probably one of the few teenagers around that hadn't attempted to enter a licensed establishment when he was underage. Drinking had little appeal to him. Drugs had even less of an appeal. He had learned his lesson the hard way.

It was small, but for the most part, clean in appearance. A limited dance floor was in the corner beside a pretty small stage area that wouldn't allow the musicians much room, but hey, that wasn't exactly his problem. The bar was quite large, making him wonder how many kinds of poison were hidden behind it and how many people left a place like this, only to do things they would later regret, as he did after his own, last night of partying. Of course, it was closed when he dropped in to speak to Bud about a possible job.

To his surprise, Bud was a gracious interviewer. He met Chase at the door with a smile on his cleanly shaven face, shaking his hand and giving him a heartfelt thank you for taking the time to drop in. Once in the bar, he offered Chase a drink, a cup of coffee and even made reference to some donuts on the counter.

"Make yourself at home," He instructed. "Whatever you wish."

"I don't really drink or eat sugar," Chase replied, feeling unusually subdued in Bud's presence. It wasn't that he was intimidated by him but oddly relaxed. There was a comfort, almost as if he could finally exhale and feel at ease. "I will take a coffee, though."

"One coffee, coming up," Bud went behind the bar, grabbing an off-white cup from a tray and grabbed a pot of coffee. After asking Chase what he took, he worked diligently to his instructions and placed it on the bar.

"Hope it's to your likin'."

Chase was pleasantly surprised when he took a sip. "This is actually really good, Bud," He allowed himself to relax and take a long drink. "Where did you learn to make coffee like this?"

"Well, I gotta tell you, I spent a lot of years in AA and for some reason, I got nominated to make the coffee every week," His brown eyes seemed to brighten with the compliment. He still had a slight 'white trash' vibe, but overall he was wearing a reasonably nice shirt, black jeans and his hair was combed neatly, as it touched his shoulders. Pointing toward the office behind the bar, he gestured for Chase to follow him. "You get good at pretty much anything if you do it enough."

"Fair enough," Chase smirked and followed him into the office. They didn't bother to close the door. "So you aren't opened on Tuesday afternoons?"

"Nah, it's not worth it right now to open before dinner," Bud replied as he sat behind the desk. Much to Chase's surprise, his office was immaculate. Not a crumb on his desk, papers were neatly piled together, a phone book sat on the corner along with a few pens, a notepad and a coffee cup that was already full. "I try to keep it open every evening because that's when people come out, after work or whatever, but afternoons are too hit and miss to make sense. Plus afternoons tend to attract the wrong kind of people if you know what I mean? If you're drinking at 2 in the afternoon, you're probably not a social drinker."

Chase nodded, agreeing with his logic. Deciding to change gears, he addressed something that had popped in his mind minutes earlier.

"You're in AA?"

"Yeah, had a bad bout with the liquor back in the day and well," He reached into a folder on the opposite side of his desk. "Never made sense to keep it up. I made too many bad decisions and you know, got myself in some real trouble and part of the deal was for me to get off the booze and join AA. Best decision of my life."

"Does it bother you to own a bar?"

"The bar was left to me in Rick's will, actually, so it wasn't really my idea but I felt it was right to run it, since that's what he wanted," He spoke earnestly, his eyes settling on Chase. "It don't matter, liquor is everywhere in this town and at least here, I can keep an eye on people a little better. Most people don't know this, but I have a pretty good relationship with the cops and ah, let's keep that between you and me."

Chase wondered what that meant, but decided it was probably better not to ask. Nodding he took another drink of coffee. "Does it ever make you want to drink?"

"Nope," Bud shook his head and smoothed out the piece of paper before him on the desk. "It actually has no appeal to me, but I got nothing against other people having a good time. Most of them can control themselves, you know? I couldn't and well, I don't want to go back to that place. Besides, when you're sober at a bar long enough, it's kinda sad, you know?"

Thinking back to the night he met Bud, he remembered the three were supposedly on their way to the liquor store. Not that it necessarily meant that he was drinking as well, but it had been an assumption at the time.

The two went on with the interview, Bud surprisingly asking the standard interview questions before launching into what the job was about at the end.

"You'd be watching the door," He shrugged. "Not a big job, but a necessary job, especially when things get crazy in here or someone underaged wants to get in. Luckily, you're young enough to probably know who most of those people are, but hopefully, it's not awkward saying no to friends."

"I don't have many friends, so that's not a problem," Chase answered honestly, a fleeting moment of sternness quickly passed and he felt his defenses drop once again. He felt no need to put on the tough guy act with Bud; there was a sense of acceptance that filled him from the moment he arrived at the bar and it continued to grow the longer the two talked. "Whatever you need me to do."

"Like that attitude, cause you never know around this place," He smirked and Chase sensed a slight insinuation behind it. Assuming he was making reference to roughing up someone who was giving them trouble, he thought nothing of it.

"So, you probably don't have any dependents," He shuffled some papers around and found a government form. "Young kid like you."

"Well, kind of…" Chase sighed and felt a heaviness fill his chest. Bud immediately looked up and searched his face.

"Now, I do feel a story coming on here, what's this about Chase?"

Taking a deep breath, he figured it was probably best to be completely honest. Bud was clearly a guy who would be pretty open minded and why not just tell him his whole shitty story? Of course, he did the abbreviated version, feeling no need to get too much into details. He told him about his unfortunate error in judgment, the pregnancy and his disgruntle relationships with both the mother of his child and his own parents.

"Hopefully, that doesn't ruin your impression of me," Chase smirked, only half joking, he noted that Bud listened carefully to his words and shook his head.

"I never judge anyone," Bud replied and briefly glanced at the paperwork before looking back at Chase. "You know, that's a shitty deal but if you want some advice from someone who barely knows you, as I'm sure you do," A grin lit up his face. "Let it go."

"Let it go?"

"Let it go, the bitterness isn't worth holding on to," Bud replied. "you'll regret it. You know, all that matters is that baby and although you don't see it now, one day, you'll definitely feel differently about this kid. I assure you of that and as for the girl, don't force something that isn't there. You can't. Live a separate life and eventually, she'll see that you two aren't on the same page and she will back off."

He made it sound so simple and he spoke from a place of tranquility that made Chase consider his words. "Is it really that simple?"

"Everything will work out. I assure you of that," Bud said and leaned forward on the desk. "The baby is the only one you owe a thing to at this point."

"I have nothing to give."

"Exactly," Bud said with a shrug. "As for family, I'm not great at that one either. Family tends to be tied to us with a steel cable, we just can't see it."

Chase didn't reply.

"But, in the meanwhile, there's a room off this one with a couch, a microwave, a small, private bathroom, if you ever feel the urge to run away from home for a night. Rick used to stay here a lot in his day, you're welcome to as well. Consider it a benefit, since I can't afford to pay you much," He rose from the desk and walked to a door that Chase originally thought was nothing more than a closet. Rising from the desk, he followed Bud into a small, cramped room that, as he suggested, did contain a tattered couch, a wooden chair, a table that contained a microwave and a small television. A bathroom door was opened behind it and inside, Chase could see a shower and toilet.

"Wow," Chase said while glancing around. "And I can use this anytime?"

"Any damn time you want," Bud opened his arms as if to showcase the room. "It's usually free. Too many memories for me, from back in the day, you know but for you, it would be perfect. A man needs his own space sometimes and right now, it don't sound like you got much."

"The gym, once it's closed and that's about it," Chase admitted. "At home, forget it. Audrey follows me around and talks nonstop."

"Well women, they're good at that, now aren't they," Bud sighed out loud. "I can give you the keys today."

"And I can come here whenever I want?"

"Anytime, day or night, I will give you an alarm code. Long as you keep it set when you leave and turn it on after you're in for the night," Bud shrugged. "Actually, you're doing me a favor, it gives someone to keep an eye on things when we're closed. A lot of break-ins around here, as you know."

Chase felt comfort in the silence and stillness of the room. Nodding his head, he turned toward Bud. "You got yourself a new employee."

Bud's face lit up and it was strange because it was a moment he would never forget. It was the moment his life took a completely different turn.

CHAPTER FIFTEEN

There was no feeling like it. Flying down the highway, just after finishing his shift at the gym, only to go to another job; and yet, he had never felt so free in his life. Always confined to his family home while growing up, under his parent's stern rules and immediately following, trapped in a house with Audrey, he now wondered if this was what he was missing out on all along. Those few moments alone in the car, not required to follow anyone else's rules, he was a bird flying through the sky; limitless and free, restricted by nothing.

He was fortunate to work two jobs that didn't require him to be under constant supervision. When he spoke to other people, he was always amazed by how controlled most were by their workplace. Even someone much older than himself, like Claire Shelley, who often complained about her job, her boss and sometimes, even her life. He sensed her sorrow and dissatisfaction with how things had fallen into place, completely off center from her original dream and he wondered if that would someday be him too? Would he turn 40 and hate how his life had played out? The thought made him angry and anger, made him drive faster and the faster he drove, the freer he felt; even if it was for a few moments.

He spent so little time at 'home' these days, that he sometimes managed to forget about Audrey. It was never for long since she texted him constantly, angry that he was 'wasn't around'; but as he reminded her, they needed money and he couldn't earn it if he wasn't working. She didn't know where he was sleeping on the nights he didn't return home but had to accept Chases' explanation that working so much made him unfit to get back on the road at 3 a.m and therefore, he had to crash at a 'friend's' house. She was, of course, suspicious and demanded to know where that was and he merely shrugged and said, 'my boss got me this place'. He knew it pissed her off to not have him under her thumb and that gave him a small thrill. Fuck her. He wasn't going to be the only person suffering.

A couple of people knew about his hideaway. Maggie, of course, was privy to this information and Claire Shelley occasionally stopped in as their affair continued to move forward, even after she started a relationship with a 'gentleman' in town. He didn't ask nor did he care about her boyfriend. Their relationship was physical only. He liked her but he wasn't interested in complicating his life any more than it already was, but he did like to fuck her and the feeling was mutual. Their attraction was strong and the freedom of no commitment made it even more satisfying. It amazed him that they managed to keep their secret in such a small town.

His new job was pretty simple. He stood at the door, carded people to make sure they were 18, legal drinking age in the province of Alberta. It was the same thing, night after night. Skimpily dressed women stumbled up to the door and flirted with him, some attempting to get in for free by grabbing his crotch or promising him a hook up later, but he merely laughed at them and insisted they pay or go home. Their reaction was often one of shock and they would stumble around a little more and eventually, somehow, finding the money to get in. If there was one thing he hated, it was a drunk woman.

The guys tended to strut up to the door with the arrogance of someone twice their size, with the alpha dog approach that was just plain fucking irritating to Chase, someone who *was* twice their size and actually worked for it. Unlike the women, the guys seemed to sense his lack of patience and usually were pretty reasonable. They paid to get in and rarely attempted to get in when under age. There were a few with fake IDs, but Bud had taught him how to distinguish between real and fake. More often than not, he didn't care. If the ID appeared real, to the point that he could plead ignorance, he let it go. He wouldn't let underaged women in, though; ever. As Bud said, underaged girls in *any* situation they shouldn't be in was a shitstorm waiting to happen.

It didn't matter in the end. It was always the same, week after week. Girls left crying hysterically, stumbling away from the bar, often with friends holding them up. Other women hit on him at the door, something that didn't really have any appeal to him. The smell of liquor on their breath, their disheveled appearance and lack of control was another situation that Bud warned him against and the longer he worked in that environment, the more he began to see that he made a valid point. Drunk chicks were more trouble than they were worth. He always shook his head no, expressionless and unapologetic, his lack of emotion seemed to do the trick.

Fights were common. The younger the patrons, the more trouble seemed to erupt. Men were worse for fighting, but women were dirtier. With two men, you could usually sense it. There was a tension in the air that was recognizable to those who were used to such an environment. Bud could feel it immediately and would send one of the bar girls out to monitor the door while he and Chase broke things up. On his first night at the job, a bad fight broke out in the parking lot, just as the bar closed. Remaining relatively calm, he approached the two men and with the help of another patron, managed to pull the two drunken fools apart, while someone else called the RCMP, who were generally not far from the bar on a Saturday night. Usually, they were sitting in the same parking lot in wait.

He had no idea that he would be working so closely with the local detachment but Bud insisted that they be as accommodating as possible. Almost too accommodating, Chase considered, but said nothing. He learned right away what they wanted, the details that he would keep track of when they arrived in these cases, as well as how to not get in trouble himself. He would eventually discover that there was always an urge to drag these knuckle-draggers behind the bar and kick the shit out of them, but he knew Bud's policy regarding this and respected it.

Patrons quickly learned that he could take them on and were apprehensive about stepping on his toes, especially after seeing him do things like dragging a 'patron' out of the bar by the hood of his shirt, while he appeared to struggle to breathe. He obviously wouldn't kill the fucker, but he was definitely making sure that people saw that he had a bit of animal inside of him, that he was not to be fucked with, something you had to do when you worked the door at a popular watering hole.

Women were another story. The first time Chase broke up a fight between two of the female patrons, a slight grin on his face, he thought of an episode of *Jerry Springer* that he caught earlier in the week and he assumed it would be pretty simple. Women were smaller, so it wasn't like pulling two Albertan cowboy wannabe's apart; at least, that's what he assumed. As it turns out, ripping apart two women in a passionate fight proved to be much more difficult. They didn't just throw punches, they bit, they scratched and they did so in a blind rage, often with no idea who their victim was and in some cases, it was him. It was important to keep calm when stopping a fight and even more so with women because regardless of their sometimes questionable fighting methods, they *were* still smaller and therefore, he couldn't be too brutal. It was a difficult balance to find, but usually speaking to them calmly, but sternly, while pulling them apart would help. It was also a matter of holding them from behind in order to stop flailing arms and legs.

Chase quickly developed a sixth sense around patrons; who was trouble, who was in for a good time and who was there for a fight. It was something you had to learn in order to survive in such a shady environment. Apparently the winter months, he was told, were calm compared to the hot summer nights that would be coming up. College students returned to town, tourists came through and all sorts of people were around, so you had to be prepared for anything. Apparently, a student would be helping him out at that time. During the winter, it was mainly just Bud, who was much stronger than he appeared and occasionally another guy, who took the job very seriously, but was a bit of a softy and would sometimes allow people to go in without paying to 'find a friend' or some other nonsense.

Overall, he enjoyed both his jobs, but there was still something unsettled in him, which he assumed that it was his desire to leave Hennessey and explore the world. Bud insisted that was a rite of passage and it only made sense he had wanderlust at such a tender age. Chase merely shrugged and assumed it was his circumstances that drove him to want to leave, more than anything else.

He saw a lot less of Maggie, but she occasionally dropped by the bar after work. He knew that she was preparing for a written test, apparently the first step in a lengthy process of joining the Royal Canadian Mounted Police, but he was certain that she would pass with flying colors. She was researching every aspect of the process and talking to local detachment about what was expected of her, so it seemed inevitable. They couldn't get a better girl, as far as he was concerned. Although, when she went off to train, he would miss her.

It was sometime in early March that he went 'home' to do some laundry and catch up on a few things, that he was surprised to find a whole slew of cars outside. It wasn't until he walked in the door that Chase remembered the baby shower that was to take place that day.

Fuck!

Quickly rushing in through the back door and right into the basement, he was pretty sure that no one noticed him from the living room, where the event was taking place. There was so much noise from the women loudly commenting on gifts, playing games, whatever the hell they were doing, that they hadn't heard him enter the house. He threw his clothing in the machine and turned it on and then quietly walked back upstairs and finally, snuck up to the room that he was supposed to share with Audrey. There weren't many of his possessions in the house, let alone the room, but he did have to grab some more clothing, the stuff that he wore every day was in the machine, but he wanted to gather what was remaining to throw in the car.

Wanting to sneak away and hopefully not return until after the shower was over, he jumped after hearing a small knock at the door. Turning to see it was still open ajar, he was surprised to find his Aunt Maureen. His mother's sister was one of the few relatives that he communicated with and quickly shared a smiled with her as she entered the room. Her long black hair pulled into a bun, it was clear that she had been dying it for years, other wise she would've been gray while still in her early 30s. She was his mom's younger sister and other than having similar features, the two couldn't have been more different. Maureen spent many years in university and now worked in the finance department for the government. He had no idea what she did, he just knew her to be smart, ambitious and kind.

"Did you think you would sneak in here without me noticing?" She asked as she crossed the room and pulled him into a hug, softening his presence in a house that usually brought him so much tension.

"I was hoping no one would notice me, not that I even know who's here," Chase confessed, feeling apprehensive and briefly, shameful of his part in this situation.

She let go and shared a bright smile with him and he felt his defenses drop. Sitting on the edge of the bed, she gestured for him to do the same.

"So, I'm getting two stories. My sister tells me that you are excited about the baby and head over heels in love," She commented, the smile only brightening as she spoke, while Chase let out a groan of frustration. "And another that says you didn't want this baby, were possibly tricked and forced into moving in this house. I would love to think it is the first one, but something tells me it is the latter."

'I don't want this, Maureen," Chase spoke softly, fearful of what she would think of his words. "It was a horrible mistake and mom jumped in with both feet and..

"That's okay," She replied, her hand up to indicated he stop, an assortment of expensive rings sparkled when met with the sunlight that entered the room. "I know my sister. You don't have to explain. She misreads a lot of situations, unfortunately."

"Misreads? I think that's probably a nice way to put it," Chase confessed, running his hands through the short bristles of hair on his head and looked down at his feet.

"Your mom comes from a completely different world than you," Maureen replied, hesitating as if to search for the right words. "And I'm in no way trying to justify her actions, I don't believe she should've thrown you out, but I do understand why she did it. She grew up around men who weren't responsible for their actions. I assume she is worried that you will be the same."

"What do you mean?" Chase asked as their eyes met again.

"It's not my place to say, you just have to trust me on this one," Her rich brown eyes were full of love and it was hard for him to not soften in his stand on the matter. "As for the marriage and baby, I don't know what to tell you, Chase. You have to follow your heart."

"This isn't in my heart," He replied quietly, hearing the emotion in his voice, he could see Maureen automatically react. Her eyes were mirroring his sadness.

Rather than speak, she reached out and touched his hand. It was a small gesture, but it felt as though his anger seeped out of him and drained into the carpet below his feet. All that was left was despair.

CHAPTER SIXTEEN

It was his buzzing phone that woke him. Sunlight flowed through the window and touched his face but this time, it was setting, not rising in the skies. His irregular sleep patterns were the unfortunate result of working two jobs that were starting to fuck with his body, as his clumsy hand felt around for his phone. Realizing that it was asleep, he quickly rose and grabbed his cell with his left hand and glanced at the unfamiliar number and cringed. These days, there was always the fear that he would receive a call that Audrey was in labor and he wasn't prepared for that moment. In fact, the thought made his stomach swirl in nausea and dread grasped at his heart.

"Hello." It was a hesitant statement, his voice emotionless, as he attempted to shake his right hand out of its current stupor. Exhaling loudly, he felt like a hidden magnet was pulling his body toward the ground, attempting to suck the last of his life into the earth.

"Chase?" A feminine voice alarmed him on the other end, recognizing the fear that was saturated into a soprano tone that suddenly sprang his senses awake.

"Yes."

"It's Ellen Telips here," Maggie's mom suddenly spoke in a lower tone and he could hear the clicking of heels in the background, a slight echo in the phone. "I'm sorry to bother you, but I was wondering if maybe you would have time to stop by sometime tonight?"

Chase glanced at a nearby clock and took a moment to refocus. It was Tuesday and his day off from both the bar and gym, so that was no problem, however, his concern was what was wrong. Maggie's mother rarely spoke to him and never called him. Unsure of how to express his concerns, he merely made a casual reply, "yup, sure."

"Thanks, Chase, she's really upset and I feel like everything I say seems to make things worse," Her final words fell into a sob and he automatically felt helpless and weak. Frowning he listened as she regained her composure. "She didn't pass the written test for the RCMP."

Chase felt his heart sink. He knew how much that meant to Maggie. Although she had casually mentioned that the test was coming up - preparing for it months in advance - he had no idea of the date. Had she told him and he forgotten? Guilt swept over him and he frowned.

"I'm sorry to hear that," His voice was soft, quiet and he struggled to think of what else to say, but he came up empty. "I had no idea."

"She tried to keep it a secret," Her mother admitted. "She borrowed the car and went off to take it, I didn't even know." She hesitated for a moment, he could hear her take a sorrowful breath and continue. "She's devastated. I can't seem to get through to her that she can take it again, that this isn't exactly the end of the road, but she won't even talk to me. I thought that since you two are so close, maybe you would have better luck.I feel like everything I say is making it worse, not better."

"I understand," Chase replied but did he really? What if he made her feel worse? Lately, he felt like an emotionless machine, a distant reminder of his old self, he knew that wasn't normal, but wasn't sure he could ever go back to the complex person he used to be not even a year earlier. "I will go over." His reply felt robotic, but if she noticed, Ellen didn't comment.

"Thank you," She quietly replied and he heard another sniff at the other end of the phone. "I appreciate it."

"Can I bring anything?"

"She won't eat, but if you can think of anything…"

"I'll bring some food," He replied and racked his brain. What the hell did Maggie like to eat? Chocolate? She loved chocolate.

Ending the conversation, he rushed to get ready and was out the door within minutes. On the highway, he felt anxiety fill him up while frustration washed to the surface. It wasn't fair. Maggie was a good person and worked really hard and yet, she got the shit end of the stick.

Meanwhile, girls like Audrey lied and manipulated and the world fell at her feet.

What the fuck?

Arriving at the same drugstore where he ran into Lucy a few months earlier, he went into the candy section and suddenly felt like nothing was right. Chocolate? Did he really think chocolate would make her feel better? Turning around, his eyes scanned the entire store but Chase felt defeated. He finally decided to grab a box of expensive candy that he knew she loved. After paying, he headed into the parking lot and glanced at a nearby cafe. As much as he wanted to avoid bread, he was starving and the idea of a sandwich was making his stomach roar. He went in, settled on a turkey on pita bread and the largest cup of coffee he could possibly get. He got one for Maggie too.

Driving to her house, he ate the pita in about three bites, he was so hungry and sunk the remainder of his coffee in her driveway. Grabbing the candy and coffee, he rushed up the step. Suddenly feeling awkward, as if he was there for a date, Chase was relieved that her mother didn't make any comment about the gifts in his hand. She gave him a sad, pathetic smile and actually looked touched by the gesture.

"Thanks," She replied weakly and he slowly made his way upstairs, his legs like lead, he felt like a huge, clumsy monster rather than the compassionate friend. He thought he saw her younger sister peeking out her door, but wasn't sure. Finding his way to her room, a gentle knock on the door was senseless because she didn't answer.

"Maggie, it's me," His voice was hoarse, "Can I come in?

Silence. He heard movement in the room and was somewhat alarmed when the door slowly inched opened and he was met by a tearstained face and bloodshot eyes. A slight scent of vanilla perfume alerted his senses, while he felt frozen on the spot, unsure of what to say or do. Feeling stupid, he silently passed her the coffee and chocolate. Her faded, blue eyes glanced at the gifts and a smile was attempted but didn't quite make it. Her eyes filled with tears and she started to cry again. Moving in the door, his heart lurched and he silently pulled her into a hug as her body shook with sobs, he ran his hand up and down her back, attempting to be comforting, but feeling as though he was falling short.

She finally let go of him and wiped the tears away with her hand. Gesturing toward the bed, he started to follow her.

"Close the door," She instructed and he did so. "Thanks, Chase."

He turned back to see her opening the coffee, the candy sitting beside her on the bed. Walking over, he was hesitant to join her, feeling as though he should say something, but what?

"I failed, Chase."

"You can write it again," He quickly countered. "You were probably nervous, that's normal-

"I shouldn't have failed," She cut him off, shaking her head. "I planned, I prepared, I knew what was expected of me and then, I totally choked."

"We all choke, Maggie. We all make mistakes."

"But I shouldn't have," She stared at her coffee cup and took another drink. "If I can't even get through this first step, how am I supposed to do the rest? There's still a physical test, an interview, so many things, Chase. I can't do it."

"You can do it," He sternly insisted. "You can do anything, Maggie."

She looked back into his eyes and they silently communicated without saying a word. His strength was enough for the two of them and he hoped she could sense that even though he understood her fears and misgivings. "I know you can. Between the two of us, you're the one who's going to make it. You have to…"

"Chase, don't say that.." She shook her head, her face glowed a warm shade of pink, as she blinked rapidly as if to regain her composure. "That's not true. You can do anything too."

"I don't think so, Maggie." He whispered.

Neither said a word but there was a shared message that was clear and somehow caused Maggie to sit up a little straighter, her composure changing before his eyes, to someone who regained her confidence. Looking away, her lips were pursed in anger and suddenly took a long swig of her coffee and finished it off in a couple more drinks. Chase felt awkward and glanced down at his hands.

"Do you want some of the candy?" She pointed toward the chocolates.

Chase shook his head no. "I don't eat candy."

"I know, but, I thought I would ask."

"That's fine, they're all yours."

"Thank you, Chase," She sat the empty coffee cup on the floor. "This was so kind of you."

"You should've let me know." He replied, his eyes searching her face.

"You're busy."

"I don't care and you know that," His reply was stern. "You should've told me."

"I didn't tell anyone."

Chase didn't reply.

Maggie yawned and he noted that she was wearing a baggie black t-shirt and shorts, her usual nighttime attire. "I'm sorry, I never thought, you probably want to get some sleep. I mean, that might make you feel better." Glancing at the clock, he realized that it was only 7:50.

"I didn't sleep at all last night," She confessed. "I was so nervous."

"That's okay," Chase replied and rose from the bed. "I can go. Your mom's probably not crazy about me being up here, alone with you anyway." He let out a self-conscious laugh, knowing that her mother never really fully believed that the two were just friends, despite the fact that her daughter was a lesbian. "If you get some sleep, I think you'll feel better."

"No, don't leave," She stood up beside him and he immediately felt his defenses fall to the ground. Her hand reached out and touched his forearm. Tears began to flood her eyes again. "Please just stay a while with me, till I fall asleep. I know if I'm here alone, I'm going to get crazy."

He silently nodded and watched her get into bed and lay on her side, with her back to him. Removing his sneakers, he felt slimy as he crawled in beside her, even though absolutely nothing sexual was taking place between them. It was when he heard a stifled cry that his apprehension disappeared and he laid behind her, his arm wrapped around her fragile frame, he pulled her close and stared at the ceiling as the scent of her hair filled his lungs. He briefly closed his eyes and opened them again and awkwardly placed his right arm over his head and on the pillow. He would stay until she fell to sleep and would sneak out.

Closing his eyes for a moment, he felt his phone vibrate in his jeans and ignored it. Nothing else mattered at that moment. He pulled Maggie a little closer and she seemed to comfortably mold into his arms, seamlessly as if it were the most natural thing in the world. He could hear the sound of a Pink Floyd song drift through his head, the same music that had been playing on the radio during the drive to her house. Suddenly feeling relaxed, mellow, his thoughts drifted off, no longer mattering in that moment; nothing else did.

It was when he awoke in the middle of the night to a ringing cell phone that it occurred to him that maybe he had to work and had forgotten? It was Tuesday night, right? Shuffling around carefully, not wanting to wake Maggie, he pulled the phone out of his pocket as it stopped ringing. He noted that there were several text messages and they alluded to the same thing.

He was now a father of a baby boy.

...and why the fuck wasn't he at the hospital right now?

He felt his hand shake as if a bucket of ice had been thrown on him. He slowly rose from the bed, glancing back at Maggie, who continued to sleep. Sitting on the edge of the bed, he knew he would never again feel the way he had that night. The innocent beauty of lying there, unconditional love that flowed through him, it was something that was only a naive dream and real life was about to begin. And the next chapter of his life wasn't going to be something he could've ever predicted.

CHAPTER SEVENTEEN

Leland. Chase wasn't sure how he felt about his son's name, but he immediately knew how he felt about the child. Despite the anger he had toward his family, Audrey, and life in general, there was something inside that melted when he looked in his son's eyes. Although he had heard many times that there was no greater love than that between a child and parent, he had never fully believed it until the moment when he first held Leland. So small, fragile, yet strong in his presence, his son's eyes seem to beg for his indifferences with Audrey to disappear, no longer relevant, it was water under the bridge.

For the first time since moving in with his wife to be, Chase actually spent some time in their shared home. He still slept on the couch but he didn't hesitate to jump up the second he heard his son cry. It didn't matter what time or what he wanted, it was almost as if he unconsciously went to him, blindly with no concern for anything else. It wasn't until one day while soothing the crying baby that he turned to catch Audrey watching in the doorway and he realized that she had him exactly where she wanted him. This was her trap and he felt some of his original resentment return.

It was difficult to separate his relationship with Audrey and the one he had with his son. He wasn't sure where the lines in the sand were or how he could continue one while ending the other. He didn't want to marry Audrey. He didn't love her. However, he wanted his son in his life and after a great deal of thought, he confronted her with these feelings. It was time to end this situation and figure out something that would make them both happy. Having just passed his 19th birthday, he thought it was a pretty mature decision for him to make. Audrey didn't agree.

"You can't leave me now," Her words were more of a demand, rather than a suggestion and he recognized the fury that swam in her green eyes. Lines formed around her mouth as her lips pursed tightly together, she placed one hand on her hip. "We have a child together, I need you here to help out."

Chase didn't reply but instead watched her walk out of the room.

The months passed and little changed. He worked two jobs, came home and helped with Leland; who turned out to be one of the few bright spots in his life. He loved watching his transformation from a delicate infant to a capable child, slowly learning the simple things in life, always in awe of his own abilities or the world around him. It was amazing how little it took to make a baby happy and yet, how much it took to make an adult experience even half the joy.

Chase did enjoy his jobs, but things were slowly starting to change as springtime slipped into summer. His affair with Claire heated up to its most powerful intensity shortly after Leland was born, only to start to fade out shortly afterward. Meanwhile, the university girls were back in town and although he rarely mixed business with pleasure, they were starting to flood both the gym and bar and he was tempted. They were so fresh, full of ambition and they represented a positive, bright spot that he couldn't obtain in his own life but perhaps, could share with them in a few brief moments.

He was careful, choosing girls that appeared rational, leaning more toward the girl next door types who seemed harmless, only looking for some summer fun because that was all he could offer. There was one in particular that captivated him, a woman in her early twenties with curly caramel hair, with hints of red hidden in the many layers. Her brown eyes were huge, staring into his every time she approached the door to Ricky's, always insisting she was the designated driver, therefore he allowed her to enter for free. He knew she wanted him and through casual conversation, he suggested she drop by the bar later that night after it closed.

Like Claire, she wasn't shy about what she wanted, taking over their every encounter, lost in her own little world, almost like he wasn't a part of it at all; other than his dick. Not that it was a huge deal, it struck him as a bit strange. She was sexy, but not in a super thin, delicate way, but rather slightly curvy with very pale, soft skin. Her passion was insane and he was slightly relieved that the bar was empty and not close to any other homes because she was also very loud, whether it was her sexual demands or pleasure, she certainly wasn't timid.

Things got a little more interesting at the bar that summer. Just as Bud had suggested, many tourists wandered in and a lot of minors begged to get in the door. It was the night that Maggie's younger sister, Kelsey attempted to get past Chase that really surprised him. Bold in her attempts, the 15-year-old stunned him when she suggested she would 'make it worth his while' if she allowed her in the bar. When he laughed and shook his head no, she pouted and complained that he should be considerate since he was best friends with her older sister.

"If not more…"

"We're just friends," Chase continued to be humored by her immature attitude, as he glanced at the two guys behind Kelsey, clearly much older. Definitely too old to be hanging around a 15-year-old.

"Right, that's why you spent the night with her that time?" Kelsey raised one of her overly manicured eyebrows, attempting to get his goat. "No one really believes you're just friends."

"Well, we are," He calmly replied, unable to control the smile from forming on his face. "You're 15, Kelsey, get the fuck out of here."

He made sure to make the comment loud enough for the two guys behind her to hear, before shooting them a warning glance that wasn't so kind. They seemed to get the message, quickly insisting they had no idea of her age and suggesting perhaps they should part company. He wasn't so sure that this was true but he hoped it was and quickly text the information to Maggie.

She still worked at the same store that she had since high school but growing restless, she had recently started to look for a new job. Chase had suggested the bar and although she seemed hesitant about the atmosphere, she did appear comforted by the fact that they'd work together. Bud had met her a couple of times and seemed keen on the idea of teaching 'the pretty little thing' bartending, even offering to pay a course if she was interested. Chase sincerely hoped she'd considered it because he worried about her working alone at the store. Reports of robberies in nearby locations concerned him, however, he knew sharing these worries would only make her more determined to stay.

Where his life used to center on fitness, his focus was now his son. He still worked out regularly and was in phenomenal shape, but he no longer considered learning mixed martial arts to possibly compete. It was more of a casual thing now but when asked what he wanted to do with his life, he didn't dare answer. He felt his dreaming days were long over. His dreams of moving, his dreams of career success, his dreams of Maggie; they were nothing more than fantasies that were unreachable.

Life was uneventful and sometimes when he was alone in his own space at the bar, he felt a sense of misery that was more of a life partner than an occasional visitor. He was going through the motions of life and really, wasn't everybody? He looked around him and saw Maggie doing the same, unfulfilled and sad. Her aspirations for the RCMP seemed to be slow moving, her social life almost non-existent.

"Just another reason to take up Bud's offer to work at the bar," Chase coaxed her on a Sunday afternoon, as she hung around the gym before her shift at the store. "Great tips, it's busy, so your nights will go faster. Maybe you'll meet…someone?"

A small smile embraced her face. "Maybe. But most of the lesbians around here are total bull dykes. If I wanted a woman that looked like a man, I would just date a man."

"I think there's probably one, obvious difference," He teased.

"Barely," She laughed with him. "I'm attracted to women that look like women. Who aren't butch, but have a softer side. If I wanted to date a masculine woman, I'd just date you." She teased.

Chase laughed heartily, "I would rock your world!" He was only half joking. The idea of hooking up with Maggie never escaped him. He was intensely attracted to her and found himself comparing other girls to his best friend but no one was ever close either in physical features or personality. Her sister was the closest in appearance, but clearly, he wasn't about to hook up with a kid, nor was her personality anywhere close to Maggie's.

"I'm sure you would," She raised an eyebrow and quickly looked away and for a brief moment, he wondered if she was actually considering it. She left shortly after but this possibly continued to swim through his head. Was there any attraction on her end. It seemed like a ridiculous question to even ponder, considering she was honest about her preference, but did she maybe consider it? Even to just mess around a bit? Did she ever get horny and want to hook up with someone? Were girls like that?

By the time he got to the bar, he somehow managed to convince himself that it was a possibility and maybe, he could carefully ease into the topic. What if she dropped by the bar some evening and had a couple of drinks and hung out with him in his hideaway afterward, would something develop between them? He had to push the thoughts out of his head, it was starting to distract him and at the bar, he couldn't ever be distracted.

Except something was different that night. When he arrived, the two students were covering the door and told him to go inside, that Bud wanted to see him. Briefly afraid that maybe he was in trouble, he racked his brain to figure out what could be wrong but couldn't think of anything.

In his office, he noted right away that Bud was acting a little nervous, like someone who was in a vulnerable situation. He quietly entered the room and closed the door without saying a thing and sat across from his boss.

"Chase, you've been here a while now and I like to think you're more part of the inner circle than just an employee," He gestured toward the closed door behind Chase. "It takes a bit of time to develop that kind of trust, as you can image, but I feel strongly you can contribute much more to this business."

He nodded.

"I haven't been completely straight with you about a few things. This bar," He extended his arms out. "This is part of many things I do here. It's legal, on the up and up, but there are other side projects that I work on, you might say extra activities."

"Okay."

He felt an awkwardness as Bud turned the computer monitor toward him to display a frozen scene in a porn. He quickly recognized the location as that same office, but the actors were unfamiliar to him. "We sometimes shoot films here. Adult films. I got a brother in Edmonton that has a company, his customers ask for different things and we try to find the people who are interested in maybe making some extra money and having some fun at the same time."

"Okay." Chase wasn't sure what else to say. "You want me to help set up things or do camera or something."

"Something like that," Bud said and stood up and gestured for him to follow to the back room, his hideaway, and opened the door. A very attractive, naked woman about his age stood on the other side. Wearing only heels and two red ribbons in her hair, she looked almost as apprehensive as him, although glancing over his body, it was clear her comfort level was increasing. Was it his imagination or did she kind of look like Maggie? His dick started to get hard, as the thoughts of earlier in the day began to surface. He barely heard what Bud was saying.

"The big demand now,' He spoke quietly behind a dumbstruck Chase, "is something called Gonzo films, like the first person perspective, if you will. This pretty little thing will….help you out" Bud placed a camera in his hand and slipped out the door, closing it as the woman approached him. Glancing down, Chase saw the camera was already recording. He wanted to say something, but his voice seemed to get caught in his throat. Had he had time to think about it, he would've been nervous, but his thoughts were only on the woman who approached him; perfectly shaped breast, trim figure and long, lean legs. He felt his breath increase with each second.

"Keep the camera on me, try to keep it still and make sure you don't hold back and make lots of noises, people like that," She muttered and instructed him how to point and use the camera. It was pretty simple and he was slightly stunned by what was taking place, he quietly followed her instructions. Holding the camera in place, he watched through the lens as she slowly unzipped his pants and reach into his pants. When she eased onto her knees, he heard himself gasp as pleasure ran through his body from the moment her tongue touched the end of his penis, he wasn't reluctant to allow himself to gasp and moan at the appropriate moments; not that it was much in the way of acting, since this woman clearly knew what she was doing, right to the end.

He was surprised when she jumped up immediately after, turned off the camera and said. "I'll see if he wants us to do it again or if this is fine."

Stunned, Chase looked down at his groin. His pants were now zipped up again and she was in the next room discussing what had happened with Bud. They were talking about the technical side of things and he was left standing there, unsure of how he felt or what to do. No, that's not true; he did feel something. Undeniable and guiltless pleasure. He felt freedom.

CHAPTER EIGHTEEN

Although it seemed peculiar at the time, he would later reflect that it was the best possible approach. Had Bud gone into a long explanation and allowed Chase the time to consider being in a porn, he never would've done it. Although he was pretty confident in his sexuality, being recorded and then viewed by many sets of eyes was a whole other thing. Not that anyone could see his face in the movie and his real name wouldn't be used in the credits; if at all.

It didn't appear to be a turn-on to Bud, who viewed the movie like any business man; making sure that it would be appealing to the public, that the technical side wasn't too cloudy or the final results were, as he put it, 'amateur but not *too* amateur'. The girl - who he later would learn was called 'Betsy' - was a professional from Vancouver, who was an 'up and coming' in the industry. Like Bud, she was concerned about the technical side of things and how the final product appeared, as opposed to giving it a second thought that she had blown some guy that she just met. As much as it should've been intriguing, he couldn't help but be slightly horrified; which seemed ironic even to him, considering his own lack of morals.

Bud and 'Betsy' decided that they had to shoot it again. Although both assured him it was quite well done, they both thought she should strip before going down on him. 'Betsy' thought it would help the storyline - such as it was - by expressing how long she had wanted to taste him, how she had dreams, fantasies about sucking his dick. When she first told him the concept, he had to hold back his laughter because it was just so ridiculous, but then he decided it wasn't for him to say anything and remain stoic. In his mind, guys didn't give a fuck about any of that, they just wanted to see the action, but she insisted that there had to be a storyline and to that, he merely shrugged and say, 'All right."

The second time, he felt slightly more confident and except for a brief moment, when she did something freaky with her tongue and he almost dropped the camera, he felt pretty assured that the video was a success. He definitely got more into things, following her instructions to show my 'verbal proof' that he was in an extreme state of pleasure; his breathing, encouraging comments and gasping were exactly what she wanted to add to the anticipation. For that, he apparently made a passing grade.

The second attempt satisfied Bud and Betsy that they made a good film, something they could 'work with' and apparently, everyone was set to make some money. Chase would make his usual night of pay plus a handful of bills, with a promise of more to come in the future. He signed something that appeared to be on the up and up and when all was said and done, Bud assured him no one would ever know it was him.

"Unless they recognize your voice or dick," He gave a short laugh as he went through the film again, Betsy standing behind him at the desk. Fully clothed, she now smoked a cigarette and seemed relatively happy with the results, although for the most part, somewhat bored. Neither one of them appeared to see it as sexual but from a marketing perspective. "Sorry to throw this on you so last minute, Chase, but my other guy was a no show and we got people waiting on this here film, but I thought you would be perfect." He pointed toward the monitor.

"As long as no one knows it's me, I'm okay with it."

Bud started to shake his head no, but Betsy quickly cut in.

"His hand shook a little bit there."

"I think that's okay, it seems more real, less overly produced like that." She nodded in agreement. Chase said nothing.

"I'll send you this to your phone," Bud said and gestured toward the iPhone that Chase had in his hand. "It's nice to have a copy for yourself.

"Next time, I want to be on top and have him record it on his back. It's my best angle," She continued to comment, almost as if Chase wasn't in the room at all. "I can alternate between fast and slow, but you," She suddenly acknowledged him in an accusing angle, "When I say 'shoot' I mean shoot then. *Not* before, you got it. You could barely keep it together tonight, honey."

"You were sucking my dick, what did you expect?" Chase replied in defense. "This isn't exactly my profession."

"Settle down, guys," Bud replied in a calm voice, giving them both a warning glance. "In fairness, Bets, it was his first time and I didn't exactly give him time to think about it, but," He returned his gaze to Chase. "If you were to do another movie, you gotta have amazing control. Some guys take something, whatever helps you, but that's totally up to you. I'm not sure if you're gonna want to do it again."

"I don't know…"

"I think if this film does well, we could make more together," 'Betsy' replied in a matter of fact voice, as she ran her fingers through her long, dark hair. "He's not an asshole and his dick isn't too big, so it's easier to work with."

Chase sat in stunned disbelief. Ironically, he felt this whole conversation was starting to feel a lot less arousing and somewhat degrading instead. He let them continue to talk as if he wasn't there and secretly wondered what else Bud had going on behind the scenes. Something told him it was much more than a few skin flicks.

He was sort of relieved when the night was over and for once, he went home after work, rather than camp out on the couch. He felt weird about what had taken place in the back room of the bar. On the drive, he considered telling Maggie but changed his mind. This was unbelievable. What would she think? Maybe it wasn't such a good idea that she get a job at the bar.

However, it was too late. The next day, Maggie sent him a message that she had met with Bud and he had offered to pay for the appropriate training in order to work at the bar. She was over the moon.

"You might want to rethink it," He felt reluctant to explain himself further, even though he knew she would want to know why the sudden change of mind. "There's some…sketchy things going on there and it mightn't look good for an RCMP candidate."

"I'm not sure I'm a candidate just yet and what do you mean?" Maggie asked with hesitation in her voice. "You really wanted me to work at the bar last week."

"I know, but I've kind of...saw things that make me think it mightn't be a good environment for you," He replied cautiously.

"I'm not a child, Chase, I can take care of myself."

"I know, but it's just some of the backdoor stuff is sketchy."

"Hookers? Right?"

"Well, not exactly."

"Chase, tell me!"

"It's probably better I don't," He assured her. "Look, maybe the mall-

"I don't want to work at the mall," She sounded determined. "Don't worry, I'll be fine."

When it seemed unlikely that she was going to budge, he sent Bud a quick text messaging, asking that he leave Maggie out of this 'side business'. His reply was quick and professional.

You have my assurance that I only want her on the bar. We don't use locals.

He wasn't sure if that made him very reassured, especially when he was local and clearly, in one of the movies.

He continued to worry that it would get out there and someone would recognize him. Bud insisted that the industry was littered with so many gonzo films, that was highly unlikely and really, he could deny it. There were no clear indications that it was even recorded in Canada, let alone that town and office.

That made sense.

Moving forward, he reminded himself that the extra money would come in handy. Audrey was off work on maternity leave and although she wanted to return soon, his two minor jobs weren't contributing much to the growing bills that came along with having a child. Everything was so expensive; diapers, formula, baby this and that. He felt like he was forever handing money over to Audrey and while Leland kept her pretty preoccupied, she still managed to find the time to think about and plan the wedding and of course, a baptism.

"I wonder if there is a way we can do both on the same day," She wondered to him one day, while he held the baby and she made a list of people to invite to one or both the events.

He didn't reply.

"Well, what do you think?"

"I don't care about baptisms and you know how I feel about getting married." He spoke bluntly and his comments seemed to be a slap in her face, but her reaction quickly returned to hostility. He ignored her glare and looked down at the baby in his arms. It was amazing that he could love anyone at this point, but he definitely loved this tiny child, manifesting something from a place in his heart he honestly didn't know existed. "I don't love you and I never will."

"You love your baby, don't you?" Her voice became very low, her eyes were small and concentrated on his face. "You want what is best for your baby, don't you?"

"Of course, I do," Chase replied hastily. "You know that's true, but I don't think marrying you is what's best for him."

"It makes his mother happy, shouldn't that matter? To know that his mother isn't just another one of daddy's whores that accidentally got pregnant?" Her voice rose and tension filled up every corner of the room. The baby started to cry.

"Audrey, just let it go," Chase felt anger sliding through his body, taking over his arms, his legs as his heart rate increased, he felt his skin tighten, almost as if it were contracting to hold in all the rage simmering beneath the surface. He hadn't seen it at first, but she was just like his mother; the passive-aggressive that turned herself into the victim, always wanting to seem helpless and alone and yet, never taking responsibility for anything. It was a scene that replayed in his mind again and again, except that his mother insisting that he was a neglectful son who pushed a knife in her heart. She had done it again and again, always trying to prove that she was the innocent one, while he was evil and unappreciative.

"I can't let it go. I know you're fucking other women, I know it in my heart. I can smell it off you every time you walk in the door," She continued to yell over the baby's cries, her eyes filled with angry tears and Chase briefly felt a twinge of guilt. Her breathing was heavy, as her sobs took over like tremors. "I'm not good enough for you? I'm not some skinny little thing, like Maggie.

"I'm not having sex with Maggie!" He insisted. "How many times do I have to tell you that?"

"Yeah, only cause she won't let you," She snapped and rushed over, ripping the baby out of his arms so fast, that Chase felt panic fill his heart. Did she hurt Leland? His cries were becoming louder and louder, but looking into her eyes, it was clear she didn't care. He immediately jumped from his chair.

"You're fucking hurting him!" He screamed over the baby, who was hysterical, his face was red, his screams filling up the house. "What is wrong with you?"

"He's fine!" Audrey howled, but she continued to squeeze him hard and Chase felt his heart pounding furiously as fear grasped his chest, tears were in the back of his eyes. He wanted to grab the baby from her arms but was scared of her reaction. He felt a calmness take over him, his mind going into the same mode as it did at work when tension increased and fights broke out, a time when he had to remain balanced in order to have others do the same.

"Audrey, you have to relax," He instructed her with a soft voice, cautious of what she might do next and more scared than he had ever been in his life, Chase felt like he had to do anything to prevent her from hurting the baby. "It's going to be fine."

"No, it's not!" She wept and shook her head, as the baby continued to cry, his eyes on Chase. He felt as though his son was silently pleading for his help. "You don't love me, you hate me! You won't touch me, you don't even want to talk to me. You weren't even there when Leland was born, he means nothing to you!"

"That's not true," Chase assured her. "I fell asleep and didn't hear my phone, that's the only reason why I wasn't there. You know I love him."

"But you don't love me."

He couldn't respond and as if on cue, she pulled the baby close, once again squeezing him tightly in her arms, causing the child to wail.

"I do! I do!" He desperately insisted, moving forward, ready to grab the baby from her arms. He had to do something before she hurt him if she hadn't already.

"I don't believe you," She said, desperation filling her face. "You think I'm disgusting. You won't even sleep in the same bed."

"I will start."

"You will not," She challenged and for a split second, he could've sworn he saw a look of glory in her eyes.

"I will, please, will you-

A knock at the door interrupted the fight. Audrey abruptly pushed the baby in his arms and rushed to the door. Relief filled his body as he attempted to comfort Leland, feeling physically drained after an adrenaline high, he wanted to collapse on the floor in tears himself, but only had time to comfort the confused child in his arms. He quickly inspected him to see if he was okay, but still feared he might be missing something. Who could he ask? Who could he tell this to?

Wiping her face, Audrey suddenly seemed absolutely fine when she answered the door. Their neighbor and his former high school teacher, Flora Johnson stood on the other side, a concerned expression on her face. The older lady was recently divorced and about to retire, so clearly had too much time on her hands. Chase was seeing way more of her than he wished.

"Hi, I'm sorry to drop by, but I heard the baby crying from my house and was a little worried that everything was okay?" She glanced toward Chase, with a combination of worry and skepticism in her eyes. She thought he was hurting the baby. He could see it immediately.

"Yes," Audrey replied with her usual, bubbly voice, the one always reserved for company or his mother. She pointed in Chase's direction, a huge smile on her face. "Leland took a little topple and I was scared out of my mind that he got hurt, but thankfully Chase calmed me down."

"Oh, well, that's gonna happen," Flora gave a knowing smile in his direction and nodded. "Children are a lot stronger than we think. I'm sure he's fine. Do you want me to take a look?" She automatically rushed in, as if they had said yes. Chase exchanged cold glances with Audrey, something that Flora didn't seem to notice, her concentration solely on the baby as she pulled him into her arms.

Leland instantly calmed down as Flora talked to him, while simultaneously checking him out. He had to wonder if she was checking him out because of Audrey's bullshit story or because she thought *he* had done something to hurt his child. He had mixed emotions and felt his stomach lurch at the thought. He would never hurt his baby. He would kill anyone that ever hurt his baby.

After Flora seemed content that everything was fine, she made an excuse to leave, her eyes seemed to be surveying the house on her way out, while Audrey gave her a sheepish smile and told her to stop by anytime.

After the door was closed, he felt his heart grow cold. "What the fuck is wrong with you?"

She stared and him and didn't blink.

"If you ever hurt Leland, so fucking help me-

"Babies have accidents every day," She calmly replied and Chase held the baby protectively close "I can't watch him every second of the day and you're never here…"

Her words drifted off and Chase felt his body turn cold. He attempted to hide the fear that grasped his throat, causing him to not to be able to speak, but she knew. Chase could see it in her eyes. Audrey knew exactly what she was doing.

Later that night, while he lay in bed with her for the first time since the night Leland was conceived, he closed his eyes as she grunted and groaned as she straddled him and he pretended the pleasure he was feeling was from a sexy little porn star named Betsy. Then he thought of Maggie, and that's when he came.

CHAPTER NINETEEN

Summer seemed to creep up on Hennessey; the weather went from unusually cool in the beginning to humid and suffocating. It was too hot and sticky to do anything that didn't involve air conditioning and fortunately, there was none in Jacobs household because it discouraged Audrey from 'seducing' him. It was an odd way to describe it, causing him to laugh bitterly every time she said it, but then again, ever since their lackluster wedding day, her interest in fucking had generally decreased.

It was ironic and sometimes he couldn't help but laugh at the fucked up mess his life had become. He went with the flow now and didn't think about the future and on the rare occasion when Chase thought of the past, his heart filled with sadness when comparing the problems he experienced back then to the ones in his present life. Sometimes he wanted to go back in time and remind himself that it could be a hell of a lot worse and that his constant whining about missing Lucy would be the least of his problems. Suck it up and move on.

On the rare occasion that Lucy was in the area, she looked at him with a different set of eyes; they were full of compassion and caring, something he hadn't expected. The two didn't talk much and when they did, it was as if they were strangers, people who knew each other long ago. It literally, felt like years since his whole life had spun out of control and rapidly circled into another century. He didn't even know the man he used to be and sometimes when Lucy was talking to him, her large eyes looked at him as if he were a stranger, just some random guy she knew by name only.

Maggie had a cordial relationship with Lucy, but the two weren't friends. They were very adult about it when Lucy stopped by the bar but behind closed doors, Maggie would roll her eyes as a way to hide her lingering hurt. She tried to play tough but in fact, was quite sensitive. Chase saw that first hand when he finally confessed to her what was going on at home. She appeared sickened by Audrey's indirect threats and suggested he go to the cops.

"Right and she will do the damsel in distress role and they'll believe her," Chase replied with a shrug. "I have to accept that she won and I got to do what I can to make sure my son is safe. That's all I live for anymore."

Maggie didn't say anything but a flash of anger shot through her eyes and she sucked in her lips as if to hold back from saying something she might regret. The beauty of his relationship with her was that they could look into each other's eyes and silently communicated things that neither of them could say out loud. Words didn't seem to have as much meaning when expressed, so why cheapen them?

He was in love with Maggie. It wasn't something he could share with her, but it was there. Everyone else saw it; even Bud within a few days of the two working together in his bar. His keen eye picked up on it and when the two of them were later in his office discussing the porn results and the plans for the next movie, he didn't hesitate to bring it up.

"So what's going on with that little girl out there?" He gestured toward the door, leaning against one arm, curiously gazing at Chase. "And don't tell me you're just friends and all that bullshit, this is Bud here you're talking to and I know what I see."

Chase didn't respond at first, simply shrugging. "We're *just* friends. Can't be any other way."

"Why would you say that?" Bud asked and raised an eyebrow, mischief crossed his face. "I'm pretty sure a guy like you can have his pick of any girl and you guys are apparently already close. It don't make sense to me."

"First of all, she's a lesbian," He replied with a short laugh, noting Bud's intrigued reaction. "Second of all, I'm unfortunately married and third…you know what? I don't have a third."

"The lesbian one is probably the biggest barrier in this here situation," Bud replied, leaning back in the chair, his lips scrunched up in an expressive reaction. He reached for his coffee and took a long swig. "Lesbian not bi? Are you sure about that, boy?"

"That's what she tells me," Chase said with a shrug. "I could never try anything, it might ruin our friendship."

"Do you want to?"

"Fuck yeah," Chase said with a quick laugh and Bud joined him. "What am I gonna do? She likes girls."

"Ok, so what about this wife of yours?" Bud asked, rubbing both hands over his face.

"What about her?"

"So, you went and married her over the baby? Why couldn't you just share custody with her? I know you said she wouldn't let ya, but I don't get how she has a choice in the matter?"

"She's crazy, that's how she has a choice in the matter," Chase replied quietly, a sudden silence in the bar as the music changed seemed to put emphasize on his words. "Bat shit crazy. I'm afraid she might hurt the baby if I don't go along with her wishes."

"She's threatened?"

"More or less."

"I hate to tell you this, kid," Bud responded while shaking his head. "But that can happen even if you jump through every hoop she provides."

"I know, I just," He took a deep breath and looked down at his jeans and up again. "I don't want to push my luck. I know what my own mother was like and God, fuck, I mean she's exactly the same. Now I see why my dad stuck around for all those years and didn't say anything when she slapped us around."

"Did she do that a lot?" Bud asked, leaning back in his chair in fascination.

"Enough," Chase admitted and realized that he hadn't made this confession to anyone before that day. Even Maggie hadn't known about his mother's abusive side, although she had suspected it a few times, but he felt ashamed and wouldn't admit it. "She was brought up on the reserve," He referred to the reservation outside of town that was known for having a great deal of heartbreaking issues such as alcoholism and abuse. "It was pretty rough in her family, but I don't know all the details. She's pretty fucked up; suicide attempts, nightmares, extreme highs, and lows."

"Sounds bipolar to me." Bud listened intently. "My mother was like that."

"Oh yeah, same as mine?"

"She was pretty erratic, probably worse than yours. She beat the living daylights out of us kids, all the time, every day." Bud spoke emotionlessly, almost as if it were a joke, but his eyes didn't hide the wounds that were clearly deep. "My dad left us and it got worse over time, so I do understand where you're coming from and I respect your decision, but it don't mean you have to cut yourself off from other possibilities."

"I don't know if I have other possibilities."

"You always do," Bud licked his lips and finished his coffee, almost in quiet contemplation. "All I know is that you got a butterfly in a glass jar situation going on with your wife. If you keep a butterfly in a glass jar because you don't want to share them with the world, eventually they either escape or they suffocate. I don't want to see you suffocate, Chase. It ain't going to help that kid of yours and that's what you have to think of, in the long run. Maybe not this second, but eventually you're going to have to get out of that situation."

"I know," He said softly.

"In the meanwhile, life's gotta keep being interesting, maybe some side action would help to clear your mind."

Chase grinned. "There's been action."

Bud let out a hearty laugh and slapped his hand on the desk. "Now, that's what I'm talking about. Speaking of which, we're getting a lot of great comments about your movie. My cousin wants some more from you and Betsy. Says there are thousands of hits on his site even the first day. Analytics say you're most popular with middle-aged women and men from ages of 15 to death, so I think you got a little celebrity in you."

"I kind of doubt it's me that's the celebrity," Chase countered and a grin slid over his face. "I think I'm more of a prop."

"Your participation is definitely important," Bud insisted. "You're a little more than a prop, you show vulnerability and people like that kind of thing. One comment was that you showed 'passion' and sounded 'sexy'." He hesitated as Chase laughed. "Hey, it's a good thing. Most men just make comments like 'suck it' and let out a few grunts, while pulling her hair. You're not like that and that is what people like about you. Imagine if they saw the whole package."

"They're not gonna." Chase said and smirked.

"Your call but they like what you're doing," Bud replied and pointed toward his computer monitor. "Betsy wants to get together for another one in a few days, as soon as she can fit it in her schedule. We both think the element of surprise helps you, so we're not gonna tell you when, but you'll enjoy yourself. You'll be taping it like before and she wants to make it seem like you're her boyfriend, make it appealing to couples."

"Sure."

"And there will be more money this time," Bud raised an eyebrow. "And hey, it's a great distraction from real life, which ironically, is one of the reasons why the porn industry is so popular. People like to see people being impromptu and impulsive, in a way that they'd never do themselves. It's a damn shame that so many people live that way, but I guess people like keeping it safe."

"I guess."

"Maybe that's why you're such a natural at this, Chase, you just go with the flow and see where it takes you." Bud suggested as he stood up from his chair and Chase slowly did the same.

"It doesn't always work out so well."

"Yeah, but think about it for a moment," Bud suggested and stood still. "What if you'd done what you really wanted to do the night you hooked up with Audrey, what would it have been?"

"Honestly, found Lucy and beg her to come back to me," Chase made a face, unable to see his point.

"Was she at the party?"

"Nope."

"I mean at that party," Bud posed the question. "That night, if you could go back in time, what would you have done instead of hooking up with this wife of yours."

Chase hesitated, having never considered it before. What would he had done, had he not felt so limited that night, as if all the pretty girls didn't want him? What if he had taken the chance?

Maggie.

"I definitely would've tried to hook up with someone else, I just didn't think I could at the time." Chase spoke honestly as his body slouched over, almost as in shame of not giving himself enough credit. "I didn't think the pretty girls would give me the time of day."

"And now," he continued. "I see that I didn't give myself enough credit. Trying and failing with one of them would've been a hell of a lot better than what ended up happening."

The realization awakened his senses and gave him food for thought. Bud certainly had an interesting point. In a way, it kind of made him sad, but hopeful at the same time.

"I guess we can't go back," Chase shrugged, pushing the thoughts out of his head.

"No, but you can change your future." Bud started toward the door. "Before it changes you."

Chase didn't reply. It wasn't something he could even think about at that moment.

"By the way, Bud," He asked as he opened the door and started out, hesitating momentarily. "What happened with your mother and you? Do you get along better now?"

Darkness was a soft sheer over his face and with a vacant look in Bud's eyes, he waited for a brief moment before replying. "She's dead."

Something told Chase to not ask any more questions.

CHAPTER TWENTY

Chase was expressionless when told that Bud wanted to see him in his office. He merely nodded and walked into the bar making his way through the crowd. The sweet smell of alcohol filled his lungs and he ignored the women who were seductively dancing around, attempting to capture his attention but instead stayed focused. Bud had indicated his night of taping another film with Betsy was coming up and he hoped it was that night.

As much as he appeared emotionless, showing no indication of temptation when women arrived at the bar door that night, his eyes were always sending messages of temptation to his libido. The women often showed up in groups and were usually wearing revealing clothing; short skirts, skimpy tank tops, skin tight dresses and sometimes showing more skin than he thought they realized. Often intoxicated upon arrival, there seemed to be no limits to what they saw as appropriate.

It wasn't just the clothing, it was their soft, voices, their silky skin as they grazed his arm on the way by to get in the door or how they smelled; God, women usually smelled so good. It was how they wore their makeup and in some cases, how their faces often appeared to be void of any makeup at all. Women could manipulate men more with their eyes than all the cleavage in the world and he often wondered how many actually were aware of this special, alluring gift?

When he first arrived in Bud's office, he felt his expectations crash to the ground when he didn't see Betsy. Maybe it was merely wishful thinking, a cruel taunt reminded him that luck was often not on his side. Needless to say, he felt sheer relief when she walked out of the tiny bedroom behind Bud's office. Fully clothed, her face expressed the same boredom as a teenager working at a fast food restaurant. He said a quick hi and she merely shot him a fake, vague smile before starting to talk to Bud.

"So let's get going," She was abrupt and direct, with one hand on her hip as if everyone was there wasting her time. He was secretly determined to make the scene an enjoyable experience for her but he somehow didn't think she was capable of letting go to pleasure. She struck him as one of those hot girls who looked sexy but couldn't have an orgasm if her life depended on it.

"Ok, I guess that's your cue," Bud said as he turned his attention toward Chase and reached for a camera on his desk. "Remember, make some noises but don't be the creepy porn guy, if you know what I mean. I'm going out on the floor to keep an eye on things and you guys, have fun." His final comment seemed to be more directed at Betsy, who shrugged as if she couldn't have cared less.

Of course, the actress in her came out quickly, once the camera was on. Having had already warned him not to 'shoot' too quickly and giving very specific instructions on how he would know when it was okay, he merely nodded and said nothing. However, when the time came, it wasn't so easy. The combination of her moans with how she moved on top of him was almost too much, as she rocked on his dick, her breasts bouncing to the rhythm, it was hard to believe that she probably wasn't finding much pleasure from the experience, even when she touched herself and let out soft moans. He had to close his eyes more than once, distracting his mind in order to keep going; but it wasn't easy.

He also had to keep the camera from shaking too much. It had to look amateur to a degree, so a certain amount of mistakes were allowed, but clearly there had to be a sense of professionalism to guide them through to the end. Of course, the end is when things got really difficult as her 'excitement' increased and things got more frantic, Chase struggled to not 'shoot' as she so crassly put it, even as sounds escaped his throat that he hadn't even heard before while having sex. It was those final moments when he was finally allowed to let go that he grabbed her with his free hand and held her down while lifting his hips that he briefly thought she was actually getting off. There was a moment of surprise in her eyes that neither of them expected and she let out a high pitch moan and grabbed her breasts.

While pleasure ran through his body, she simply rose from the bed, grabbed the camera and checked back to what they taped. A smile finally crept on her lips and while Chase was recovering and cleaning up with a nearby towel, she seemed uninterested in doing the same. Finally, she sat the camera down and went into the bathroom with her clothes. Chase rose from the bed and got dressed, feeling physically relieved, while at the same time unaffected by her strange reaction. It was only business to her.

Luckily, it was a business that was profitable and his performance, such as it was, had been deemed acceptable. Although she certainly didn't say it to him, she would later show enthusiasm as she explained to Bud all the reasons why she felt this film would be a hit. She barely acknowledged him after their encounter was over and somehow, he thought that was probably for the best. She was a cold-hearted business woman who was out to make money in porn and that was all there was to it. As Chase had stated in the past, he was merely a prop.

After Bud and her talked business, while Chase sat nearby, scanning through his phone messages from both Audrey and Maggie, he was surprised to find one from his sister. She was heading back to university in a few days and wanted to meet up with him for a coffee. He ignored it and returned his attention to Bud and Betsy; who were now finishing up their conversation, having just sent the film off to the production house to make some final, careful edits, it appeared that his services were no longer needed, so he suggested going back on the floor. After all, it was nearing closing time and they might need his help.

"Nah, they'll be fine," Bud assured him and glanced toward Betsy, giving her a quick nod and almost as if on cue, she announced she was leaving. She didn't say good-bye or even look at Chase but merely walked out the door as if he were irrelevant.

"She's cold," He couldn't help but comment after Betsy was gone. "No goodbye, nice working with you, fuck off, nothing? What's with that chick?"

"Now, don't you worry about her," Bud replied and waved his hand and leaned back in his chair. "That's just the pro in her coming out and to be honest, that's what you want at this point. You don't want to be friendly, you do your job and move on. She's made a lot of films and you're nothing more than another dick to her, but hey, who cares right?"

"I guess when you put it that way…"

"Exactly, don't worry about her," He seemed rushed to move on to another topic. "Now, I might have some other business proposals for you soon. It's kind of dicey now, but I'll get back to you."

"You mean, this kind of stuff-

"Well, not necessarily. I have some other stuff I do," He chose his words carefully, his dark eyes had a gleam that couldn't be mistaken for anything less that salacious and Chase decided it was better not to ask. "I might need your muscle sometime in the future. I'll let you know more details later."

"Okay," Chase replied slowly, his brain curiously jumping from one sketchy situation to another, but he wasn't in the position to say anything. It was a lot easier to fall into this underground world than he ever would've imagined. Had it been asked a couple of years earlier, Chase never would've believed that this would be his future; married to someone he didn't love, with a baby, working at a bar and doing porn on the side. It was a dismal turn his life had taken, but then again, would things really be much better if he was happily married and working a 'normal' job; was that merely a myth that people wanted to believe? Not that he knew anyone who exactly had a normal life to compare himself to - but he did wonder if other people had as many secrets as him. He somehow doubted it.

When he returned to the bar after it closed, he noted the suspicious look in Maggie's eye. He ignored it. Not that it mattered. She found her way across the room.

"Where the hell were you?" She sounded oddly bitter for Maggie, something he hadn't expected.

His answer was short and to the point. "Working."

"Nah, come on, you went in the back room, I saw you," She quietly commented, glancing toward Bud on the other side of the bar, as he talked to one of the other bouncers. "You were gone a long time and some sketchy chick came out of the there before you. You're not messing around with some of the Mento trash, are you?" She curled her nose up in judgment. Perhaps working at the bar wasn't a great atmosphere for her. Maggie was exposing some sharp edges lately and he wasn't sure how he felt about this new side of her.

"It's not what you think" Chase assured her, a soft grin crossed his lips and he brushed up against her arm as he walked away and approached Bud, who seemed to realize he needed a distraction and asked him to help with some of the boxes of empty beer bottles.

She didn't ask again; at least not that night. He walked her to her car before they left and gave her a quick hug before she got in and drove away.

"Hey Chase," Bud called after him and he returned toward the entrance. It was 3 a.m and the rest of the staff was gone. "You didn't tell her anything about…"

"No," Chase shook his head. "Nah, that's the last thing I want to do."

"Okay, good. I mean, I guess it doesn't matter, I just like to keep things quiet, you know?"

"Oh, *I* know," Chase shared a smile with his boss as his phone vibrating. Reaching into his pocket, a deep furrow developed between his eyebrows and a grin twitched his lips as he read Audrey's text encouraging him to return home. "The rabbit died? What the fuck is that about?"

"Who sent you that?" Bud pulled out a pack of cigarettes and lit one up.

"Audrey and oh fuck," Chase suddenly felt his body become weak and his throat dry, as he took a deep breath. "Is that her way of saying she hurt Leland? Oh, Jesus…"

"No, no!" Bud began to laugh and started to choke on some cigarette smoke. "Haven't you ever heard that before? The rabbit died? It means someone is pregnant."

This piece of news, unfortunately, didn't make Chase feel any better.

CHAPTER TWENTY-ONE

He loved his son. His every movement was amazing; the way he twitched his nose when the smell of toast filled the house, how his eyes scanned the room curiously, as if discovering it for the first time or when he peacefully slept in his crib, his hands in tiny fists. Chase totally got why people referred to babies as 'miracles' because they really were; having said that, it was when Leland cried for what felt like hours on end, that Chase thought he would lose his mind.

Audrey was oblivious to the crying. Since telling Chase the news of her second pregnancy - followed by a screaming match that went right into the morning hours - there was a change in her. She appeared to have entered the world of fantasy, bouncing around the house like she was Snow fucking White, trying to fix everything perfectly, her face sparkling with joy as if she had somehow found the pot of gold at the end of the rainbow. While Chase, on the other hand, felt like another piece of him died each day. It was like a prison sentence that increased in severity.

As much as he loved Leland and would do anything for him, there was something about knowing that a second child was coming, that broke him. He moved back to the living room, the betrayal he had expected with the first baby rang even truer the second time around because there was simply no way that Chase could believe in two mistakes; Audrey had planned this all along. She always talked about having two children and insisted that it was 'too soon' and 'in a few years…' and Chase nodded as if he agreed when he secretly attempted to figure out an escape plan. Should he take Leland and move out? If he had a relationship with his family, maybe they could help him, but he knew they put conditions on their love. Plus their relationship had been estranged since kicking him out of the family home.

As if these feelings of hopelessness wasn't enough, Chase also felt a strong fire building inside of him and it started on the night he learned of the second pregnancy. This combined with pure exhaustion building during the cold winter months pulled him into a depression, making him even more thankful for his personal sanctuary at the bar. However making an escape from the house without having to endure a conversation with his nosey neighbor was becoming almost impossible. It felt as if she were watching, waiting for him to exit.

"Hey sorry, I'm running late," Chase attempted to be pleasant to her on one particular day when she caught him on his way out. After working two jobs the day before then returning home to a screaming match with Audrey at 3 am, followed by the baby crying the rest of the night, he just wanted to head to the bar and crash out for some sleep. A part of him wanted to shove Flora aside, jump in the car and fly out of the driveway; but he had to be the friendly neighbor, yet another role he played on an average day. It was one of many - father of the year, loving husband, caring personal trainer, frightening bouncer, a porn star with incredible endurance - the list never seemed to end. He was an actor who was always switching roles.

"Chase is everything okay, I thought I heard yelling last night," Flora asked with compassion in her eyes and accusation in her voice. It was the typical woman thing; he was always answering to a woman whether it was his mother and sister back in the day, now Audrey, nagging clients at the gym, obnoxious drunks at the bar or Betsy's stern sexual demands, women had to feel like they were always in control.

"We had an argument," His reply was curt, as he unlocked the car door and shot her a dispassionate look. Her eyes were full of concern but he suspected that it was insincere. With her blonde hair pulled back in a ponytail, she looked substantially younger than her actual age, although her voice rough from years of smoking, although she claimed to have quit, he often could smell cigarette smoke drifting from her house. "That's it."

"It sounded really bad," She pushed and Chase took a deep breathe as he challenged her eyes.

He didn't reply.

"Can I do anything?" She continued to show concern. He became more skeptical and merely shook his head no.

"I have to go," his reply was abrupt and he got in the car and zipped out of the driveway and down the road.

Relief filled him when he arrived at the bar. He had barely slept in 48 hours and his body was at the point of exhaustion as he entered the empty building, turning off the alarm, he stumbled through to the tiny room behind Bud's office.

Barely able to move in the small, cramped space, he stubbed his toe. Fury felt like an intense, electrical current that shot through his veins and sent a charge of power like nothing he even felt, as he grabbed a nearby lamp and smashed it against the wall. His heart pounded with such intensity, he feared an explosion would overpower his body, as a scream filled the room, sounding like that of a wounded animal. Rationality seemed to chime in at the ideal moment, as he found himself gripping onto a nearby chair, clasping it so tight that beads of sweat were forming beneath his shaking hand. Letting go, he sat on the edge of the bed.

What the fuck was wrong with him? This blind rage that snuck up on him was unexpected and frightening. Had the action resulted in any kind of peace, it would've been a different matter but instead, he felt sorrow floating through his body. A flow of tears came like a tropical storm, his chest shaking as if the room were frigid rather than stuffy and lifeless. He felt drained, defenseless, as his body sank to the floor, finding some stability as if it were holding the remainder of his sanity. He closed his eyes and they suddenly sprang opened.

What was that under the bed? His eyes attempted to focus, but the stale scent of the carpet suddenly repulsed him, as he sat up and then lifted the blankets to focus his eyes. It was silver. A ring? He reached out and picked it up.

The piece of jewelry looked like a kid's ring. Well, maybe a teenage girl's ring. It was a purple butterfly that was too juvenile for an adult woman, but yet, probably too old for a younger child. Did Bud have children? Chase's boss rarely talk about his personal life, other than making reference to a woman he was dating, but until that moment, it never occurred to him that he might have kids. Maybe he had stopped at the bar at some time and had a child with him. It seemed possible. If anyone knew how easy it was to suddenly be a father, it was Chase.

The concept peaked his curiosity. He didn't even know where Bud lived. Considering the money he was making off the movies alone, chances are he had a nice place. Chase ended up handing over most of his own money to Audrey to put toward the never-ending costs of running a home and her van. He managed to save some on the sly, but if he didn't have her and Leland, he would've been able to afford a more comfortable lifestyle with his jobs; the work on and off the records.

It made him see Bud differently. It made him feel more connected to his boss as if he better understood where Chase was coming from and that sense of connection calmed him.

In the weeks following news of Audrey's pregnancy, Chase found himself grow quieter. He didn't even talk to Maggie very often even though she was trying her best to encourage him, her own heart was sinking. Feeling cramped in the small, rural area, suffocated, as she described it, Maggie was anxious to leave Hennessey. Having succeeded at the first test for the RCMP, her confidence seemed to grow especially when her months of working out at the gym were also paying off, creating muscles and endurance that would allow her to take on the physical portion of the test with no issue. She was ready.

Chase encouraged her, but secretly dreaded the day she would announce moving. He knew it was coming but he was in denial, much in the same way as he was about the new baby.

Work consumed most of his days. Both of his bosses were like surrogate fathers to him, replacing the feeble man that he didn't speak to anymore; although both were vastly different, they shared many traits such as being upbeat, optimistic, always encouraging Chase no matter how grim he felt about life. In fact, they taught him how to be a man, a pool that his own father seemed to dip his toe in more than dive into altogether.

His work at the gym continued to be intriguing. Claire was gone for the summer and returned that fall, surprising him when she started their affair again. His time was pretty limited but she hardly saw this as an obstacle.

Bud continued to talk about a new actress he was currently looking into, while Betsy still showed her half-hearted attempts at making movies with Chase. Since he wasn't opened to 'showing his mug' she complained that they were limited and therefore, didn't think many options were left. Bud insisted that she was the star and that Chase not being on camera allowed her to have all the attention, a concept that she liked and soon came up with other ideas on how to make it work; including a threesome with another chick.

The truth was that he couldn't keep it together. When he watched the two women fondling each other and moaning, it seemed so incredibly dramatic and fake that he started to laugh. Betsy got pissed off and ran out of the bedroom and into Bud's office, completely naked and complained about 'that fucking moron'. Bud, always being the professional, calmed the waters and within 20 minutes, the three of them were involved in a sexual act that was somewhat acrobatic and challenging to not only keep himself from 'shooting' too fast but also holding the camera at the right angle. Anyone that thought porn was easy, really had no idea.

The year came to an end and unlike the previous one, Chase made sure to remember Maggie's birthday when it rolled around, buying her a small cake from the local bakery and presenting it to her before a bar shift in mid-December. Bud got in on things, offering them both some shots before work. Maggie declined but Chase took one, his eyes watering as the bitter taste of alcohol burned his throat, something that made Bud laugh. It did seem to take the edge off, though, which was a welcomed change.

Christmas came and went. Leland was too young to really understand what was going on but it didn't stop everyone from buying him every toy under the sun. Both families gathered together on Christmas Day to watch Audrey open the gifts for the baby.

Chase noted that his father definitely aged, looking thin and pale, while his mother focused on her grandson and barely talked to anyone else in the room. Audrey had a strange look on her face as if she had finally discovered what she married into and Angel sat quietly in the corner, uninterested in her nephew and quietly nursing a drink. When Chase announced he had to go to work at the bar and jumped out of his chair, Angel followed him outside.

"You really have to work tonight?" She snapped as she followed him outside.

"Yes, Angel, bars sometimes open on Christmas Day. I'm assuming so people can escape their families," He muttered, as he pulled his jacket closer while heading toward the car. Angel abruptly pulled on her own coat, her pale face expressionless.

"Chase, we have to talk, it's important."

He stopped but didn't reply.

"Dad's sick."

"Sick?" Chase asked, half laughing at the concept since his father hadn't even had a cold in years.

"He's very sick, Chase," Angel spoke earnestly. Her eyes started to water and to his surprise, she pulled him into a hug and started to sob.

CHAPTER TWENTY-TWO

Chase didn't have to watch the news to learn it was the coldest winter Alberta had seen in years; he felt it every morning. The drafty old living room he slept in seemed to be the coldest in the house, something Audrey gleefully commented on, her snide remarks giving her comfort, as if he deserved to suffer since he wouldn't sleep with her. For that reason, he often chose to stay at the bar and even though the back room was cold as fuck most mornings, it still brought with it the pleasure of peace and quiet; no baby crying, no Audrey yelling, and no nosey fucking neighbour at the door, trying to pry into his life.

It was a glum month and as heating bills rose, businesses slowed down. Chase naively thought it was just too cold to get out of the house, but Harold pointed out that things like gym memberships seemed secondary to costs that came with winter months; household expenses, unexpected damages brought on by the winter, not to mention attempting to catch up after overspending during the holidays. For the first time since leaving high school, Chase found his hours cut back at both the gym and the bar. Although this came as a relief at first, when things didn't pick up into February and then March, he grew concerned.

Audrey was getting huge. She could barely wobble around the house and rather than having compassion for her, he felt a sense of satisfaction that she was in discomfort. It seemed appropriate considering she had hijacked his life and turned it into a circus sideshow, rather than a fantasy come true. Not that he necessarily would've had the best life had they not hooked up, but there would've been that elusive dream to keep striving toward. Now, he felt like his life was no longer a blank slate, but a dismal nightmare that felt hopeless and limited. And it was the limits that made him the angriest at all.

He looked around and noticed other people his age settling down and thought it was unusual to see people who were barely out of high school already getting married and having kids, creating debt, whatever it was that families did together. He couldn't help but feel like they were looking for what they thought was the safest option, as opposed to what was natural. Then again, had he stayed with Lucy, would this be his life now?

His ex occasionally rolled into town, but slowly became a whole new person. She looked at him as if he were unfamiliar to her and rather than being humored by the shitstorm his life had become, she looked at him with strangely subdued eyes as if she wanted to say something but the words never quite got out. She was now in college, approximately an hour away from Hennessey and still living with 'Lucky Luke' who apparently worked in the oil fields and had lots of money coming in. He was paying for her course and it was only when she spoke of it, that she showed any signs of joy. Maybe it was maturity that he mistook for unhappiness, but something felt off with Lucy. He just wasn't sure what.

"She's depressed," Maggie said bluntly when he brought up the topic, as he watched her behind the bar, where she put glasses away before the business opened on that frigid March afternoon. She wore a fitted t-shirt and black jeans, appearing to be comfortable, even though Chase still wore his jacket. Then again, she moved so fast that perhaps the cold didn't have a chance to catch her.

"Depressed?"

"Yeah, I can tell," Maggie insisted, showing neither compassion or satisfaction in this fact. She bent over and slid a tray of glasses under the bar. A small strand of hair fell in her face and she quickly brushed it aside. "Life hasn't turned out as she thought it would."

"Ha! Tell me about it," Chase wasn't able to hold back his bitterness and it was something that only momentarily caught Maggie's attention before she silently went back to work. He felt like she was avoiding his eyes and a sting of guilt hit him. "I mean, not just me, obviously, it's-

"No," Her voice was soft as she rose a hand to halt his comments as she stood upright again. "That's fine, Chase. I don't blame you for feeling that way and yes, my life hasn't turned out as I thought at this point, but your path is definitely bumpier. I totally understand."

He squeezed his lips shut, suddenly having flashes of the latest movie he made with Betsy cross his mind. It was the one secret he kept from Maggie, but yet, how could he ever tell her the truth? He felt as if it had come between them. Could she sense it? Was she feeling the distance too?

"Chase, I think I might be leaving soon," Her words were rushed, as if she had forced them out much in the same way one would rip off a Band-Aid; fast, before you had a chance to realize what was happening and yet, the pain was still there. It was just sharper.

"What?" He suddenly felt like a child who was being told there was no Santa Claus, that the magical side of childhood had always been a lie. He knew this was coming for some time, but he chose instead to float in the beautiful waters of naivety.

"I was talking to my dad in Calgary," She started slowly, still avoiding his eyes. "He thinks that I would benefit from going there, just looking into some courses, doing some volunteer work, learning another language, I don't know," She suddenly stopped, but only to quickly glance at him and look away. "He's right, those are things that might help me get in the RCMP. I'm not going anywhere here."

"You can do some of those things here...online, right?" He made a feeble attempt to persuade her but knew it was senseless to even try. She'd already made up her mind and this day had been coming for a while. "I guess it's not the same."

"I was talking to a guy who's in the RCMP and he told me that I should gain as many experiences and knowledge that I can," She finally made eye contact with him. "He was right. My world is pretty small here. There's my sister, my mom, you, that's about it other than work. I don't have many friends anymore. Lucy ditched me and everyone else moved away after high school and every time they come back, I can see it in their eyes, that 'I knew she'd never leave' look. As if my dreams were all talk and nothing more."

"Come on Mags-

"It's true."

"Maybe it's true for both of us," He suddenly felt a stab of depression. It never occurred to him that perhaps people looked at him in the same way. "Even more so."

Maggie took a deep breath and her face faded in color. "I'm sorry, Chase, that's not what I meant. I didn't mean you, I think people see you differently."

"I'm not so sure about that," Chase replied and bit his lip. "That's how I see my own life and I want more for you."

"Chase you can have more, you have more options."

He didn't reply.

The rest of the night was an endless flow of drunks coming in, most of which Chase met with a stern glare as emotions ripped through his body; a part of him wanting to put his fist through the wall, another part wanting to hide in the corner and cry but he feared that if he were to do either, he wouldn't be able to stop once he started. He was tired of life fucking him over. Maggie was the only good thing left and without her around, there was a sinister part of him that felt as though it would be unleashed, for he had no other reason to hold it back. If there was a God, he just took and took and took, until Chase had nothing left.

His birthday came and went on one of those cold, depressing days. Maggie attempted a mini celebration with Bud before work, but he wasn't feeling it. He could see that reflected in her eyes as she passed him a German Chocolate Cake with a single candle on it. "I know you don't eat cake, but make an exception this one time. I remember you said this was your favorite."

"Come on now," Bud chimed up, waving his hand in the air as he stood beside Maggie. "Listen to the little girl, now blow out that candle and make a wish."

Chase grunted, thinking that it was a silly ritual. In fact, if he wished for something, there was almost a guarantee that the opposite would happen. Still, he followed these instructions, something that seemed to make both Bud and Maggie happy.

"Twenty years old, what I would do to go back and live those times over," Bud announced, leaning on the bar, a dreamy look in his eyes. "The things I would do."

"I'll gladly switch with you," Chase muttered and was surprised by the bitterness in his voice, it certainly wasn't his intention to dampen the moment, however, it didn't phase Bud.

"Be 20 again, looking like you, my God, bring it on!" Bud stood up straight, with a glow of excitement in his eyes that cause both Chase and Maggie to laugh. "Ain't gonna say no to that."

"Well, hopefully, you're smarter than me and wear a condom at the right times," Chase couldn't help but add, something that made the two of them to laugh even more.

"Hey now, Bud's always careful," He tapped Maggie's arm and let out a loud, yelping laugh that was causing her to laugh more, something that appeared to be contagious.

Little did he realize at the time, that it would be one of the few moments he would share with Maggie before she would move in late April. Both their lives were so busy, that it was almost impossible to get together and when they did, it was usually before work at the bar. He had hoped that they would have some private time together the night before she left, but a series of events made it impossible. Just as with the rest of his life, Chase certainly didn't have the luck of the draw and had to work at the gym, due to a sick coworker.

Maggie had intended to drop by to see him but it didn't happen. The long night at the gym, trying to help clients while keeping one eye on the door, hoping she would walk through it any minute, filled him with both anxiety and anticipation. He was distracted and couldn't wait till the night end and he could finally lock the doors and head out.

His immediate instinct was to go to her house. He had to say goodbye, tell her the thoughts that were running through his head, words that had to be said even if it didn't really matter to her. They were burning up inside of him and had been since that night he left the party, in her mother's beat up old car. He had to tell her the truth about his feelings, about what he was secretly doing on the side for Bud; he had to tell her everything. He couldn't let her go without everything coming out.

But it didn't happen. He left the gym and rushed to her house to see no lights. No one was home and the car was gone. His heart pounding in agitation, Chase took a breath and attempted to calm himself, in hopes he could rationally think of where she could be. With a shaking hand, he texted her, but she didn't reply. He sat in her driveway for longer than he meant to, staring at the dark window that had been her room, wondering why she wasn't answering him. Tears burned his eyes as he started the car and turned back on the road.

Pink Floyd poured through the car and he turned it up loud, as he sobbed uncontrollably, swerving on the road, he briefly feared that someone would see him do so and think he had been drinking and quickly forced himself to calm down. His body shook, the coldness of the outside finally meeting with his deep spirit, the part of him that died slowly each day. He thought about the night Leland was born, how he had stayed the night at Maggie's and held her in his arms. It was the only time he truly felt love flow through his heart; now nothing seemed to matter anymore, he desperately thought of his bleak life that continued to unravel until there was almost nothing left.

It was when he met a tractor trailer that his mind, for one brief moment, went into autopilot. His eyes focused on the bright lights on his face, a chill crossed over him and he felt his arm shaking, almost as if fighting off the impulse to make a sudden swerve, full speed ahead into the front of the truck. No one would care. Maggie was about to start a new life, soon to forget her old one, while the rest of the world barely seemed to see him on their radar. He was invisible. He was no one.

But something stopped him and when he would later look back on that night, it was almost as if his memory wouldn't reveal what happened. Suddenly, he was driving normal, the truck was in his rearview mirror and he felt at peace; no longer crying, no longer angry, just a calmness; the most frightening passenger of all.

Unconsciously, he drove to the bar and went inside. It was a quiet night, blues music flowed through the speakers and at the back of the room sat Bud with a clipboard on the table in front of him. Making his way to the table, his legs felt weak as if he had just run a marathon. Bud looked genuinely surprised when he saw Chase sit across from him, concern filled his eyes as he stared.

"Oh man, I thought for sure you would be with Maggie tonight," He commented and when Chase didn't reply, too stunned to talk. "She was still leaving tonight?"

"She is?" His voice was small, defeated in the same way his spirit now felt, as it dripped out of his body, slinking away into the night.

"Yeah, she ah….she dropped in earlier today and told me, they changed it up on her, I just thought," Bud hesitated and glanced down at the paper. "Saying goodbye, it's hard, you know?"

Chase nodded, slumped over in the chair, he felt as if the music flowing through him. "Yeah, it is."

"I'm sure she tried to find you, but I think it was pretty last minute," Bud assured him, pushing his paperwork aside. "You know you meant the world to that little girl."

'I'm not so sure right now," Chase took a deep breath and glanced around the dreary bar.

"Like I said, it's hard to say goodbye. Sometimes people choose to not do it because they can't."

"But why not? You know, even a text," Chase asked, glancing at the phone in his hand. "Nothing."

"I wouldn't take it personally," Bud insisted. "I really wouldn't."

Chase considered his words. "I think I'm going to stay at the bar tonight," He pointed toward the office. "You don't have something going on there?"

Bud let out a laugh. "No, course not, you're here aren't you," His answer was smooth, maybe a little too smooth, Chase considered as he rose from the chair and made his way toward the office.

Exhausted, but yet, he didn't sleep a wink that night.

CHAPTER TWENTY-THREE

The burning in his stomach started in the spring. It started with the news that Audrey was pregnant with twins and only grew stronger with each passing day. His life, now without Maggie, was bleak and dreary, his spirit, he was certain, moved to Calgary with her on that cold, winter night.

Chase thought of her all the time. He pictured her walking on the sidewalk beside busy streets, hundreds of people around and not one of them seeing her at all; just another person rushing along, her life irrelevant to them, as they stared at their phones and ignored everyone and everything around them. On the other hand, she would always be looking around, curious and anxious, taking in everything. Was she overwhelmed by the size of the city? Did the fast pace intimidate her? Was she scared? Did she make a new friend?

He hoped so. In fact, Chase truly wished that all her dreams would come true. Maggie deserved it and somehow, he could picture her life working out perfectly, now that she made the move and took a chance. He was jealous, but proud, at the same time.

The two finally connected in a brief conversation, where Maggie insisted she had made great efforts to find him the night her mother suddenly decided to move her; preferring nighttime because of the ease of traffic. Instead, she had rushed to the bar in Mento, only to realize he was back in Hennessey and by that time, her mother was sternly letting her know that they just didn't have time to go back. Never a fan of Chase, it didn't surprise him that her mom had no concern for his feelings.

"We wouldn't have had time to really talk anyway," She insisted through the phone, a slight echo suggested she was in an empty room, her voice soft and gentle. Grief filled him, nausea followed her words and he fell silent. It seemed impossible to believe that they couldn't have found the time to get together for one, last visit. Had she avoided it or had he not made himself available? Was it actually him that couldn't say goodbye?

"I will be back for visits, Chase and you know you…" her voice drifted off as if she realized that it was unlikely he would be able to visit her in Calgary. Between work and his family, it wouldn't happen. There were just too many obstructions in the way, keeping them apart that there was no need to do anything but to surrender. He didn't reply nor did she finish her sentence.

He heard the fear in her voice and although Chase knew she was happy to be away, she was definitely scared too. Who wouldn't be? It was a huge city and Maggie was so far away from everything she had grown used to in life. Fortunately, her father was there and helping her out a great deal so she wasn't alone.

Their conversation ended on a cool note. He felt secrets hanging in the air but how could he tell her the truth about anything over the phone? It was something that had to be done in person but when would that happen and was it too late? She hadn't been gone long and already, he felt the distance growing between them and it scared him.

His friendship with Bud seemed to grow when Maggie moved away. Unlike Harold, who was all business, Bud seemed interested in his personal life and enjoyed giving out unsolicited advice.

"That's just the way she goes," He commented one afternoon before the bar opened; the two sat at a table, Bud calmly rolling a joint as he listened to Chase describing his recent interactions with Maggie. "People grow apart sometimes but not always. Sometimes people can be a million miles away and still close to you in your heart more then as if they're in the same room."

Chase immediately thought of Audrey and grunted. "It seems kind of fucked up."

"Well, boy, it is," He licked the rolling paper while raising his eyebrows at the same time. "Just keep talking to Maggie. Check in frequently. It's scary moving to a big, bad city like Calgary. Trying to find your way around, trying to make friends, that there is not easy. Although, I will say it's easier than if you move in a small town like this one here. People think they know more about you and judge you harshly cause of it."

"How long have you been here, Bud?" Chase asked and turned his head when he heard a car outside.

"Four, five years now?" He replied and sat the joint aside, squinting his eyes, he peered out the window. His eyes narrowed. "Middle-aged women with bangs, they always make me nervous."

Chase opened his mouth to ask why, but Bud was already out of the chair and heading toward the door, his voice sugary sweet as it always was when talking to strangers. It wasn't that he was fake but that he poured on some fake charm, the kind most men would reserve for women that were on their radar. Turning in his chair, Chase immediately recognized Maggie's mother.

She gave him a rushed, almost nonexistent smile and turned her attention toward Bud. She talked low, Chase assumed to make sure he didn't overhear their conversation, making him feel snubbed as he turned back around in his chair. Maggie's mom didn't like him and he wasn't sure why. Even after the night she specifically asked him to drop by to comfort her daughter, her dislike only seemed to grow rather than fade away.

He could hear her walking out, not making an efforts to acknowledge him; as if he were merely a fly on the wall, rather than someone of substance or relevance. It was a sting he shouldn't have felt, but he did. Had Maggie said something to her to make her dislike him so much?

Bud returned to his seat and didn't say anything at first. Shaking his head, one eyebrow rose, he reached for his joint and lit it up. "Uppity bitch."

"She doesn't like me very much," Chase quietly confessed as he listened to the sound of a car pulling out of the driveway outside. "Never has."

"Course not, she knew you wanted to fuck her daughter," Bud let out a short laugh as he inhaled his 'medicine' as he referred to it and leaned back and with his foot, pulled over another rickety, old chair close and put his leg up on it. "They never like that.'

Chase smirks and gave him a look.

"I know, I know, you didn't," Bud put his hand up defensively. "I'm just saying you wanted to and I don't think anyone thought otherwise, including her. But her being a lesbian and all, kind of made it difficult."

Chase didn't reply and finally asked. "What did her mom want?"

"Ah, just her T4. I was gonna go and send it but I guess maybe she didn't trust me," He shrugged and took another puff, before putting out the joint on the nearby windowsill. "I tell ya, don't trust middle-aged woman with bangs."

Chase laughed. "Where did you get that?"

"Life experience, that's where" Bud replied and took a drink of his coffee. "Those severe, almost perfectly straight bangs, always spell trouble with middle-aged woman. We're not talking about the ones with a bit of wave, a bit of curl, we're talking the fucking straight as an arrow bangs, that look like they've been cut by a ruler. Those bitches are trouble."

Chase considered what he said and shrugged. He thought of former teachers, clients at the gym and even women that stopped by the bar. "You might have a point."

"Just the older ones, though," Bud said, apparently feeling the need to clarify. "The young ones with those bangs, usually sexual deviants, oddly enough."

Chase let out a laugh. "And not the middle age ones?"

"Nah, they hate men. If they're sexual deviants, it ain't with us." Bud shrugged, his eyes glazed over, he took a deep breath. "Life teaches you all kinds of things Chase and you're just getting started."

"Funny, I feel like I'm years older than I am."

"That's cause life has fucked you and it fucked you hard," Bud replied thoughtfully, his hand grazing the table as if to inspect a slight bump in the wood. "It fucks us all, but not usually at your age."

The comment defeated him. It wasn't meant to be jarring, but he was still vulnerable from Maggie's move, the news about the twins and almost feared what would be next. Life was definitely pounding the shit out of him and there didn't seem to be anything bright in the skies. The flash of bright headlights in his eyes drifted in his mind; had he made the right choice the night Maggie left town? Should he had swerved and shot head first into the large truck in the opposite lane? Would this nightmare all be over now? His pathetic life finished? Would anyone even care?

"Cheer up, kid," Bud said as he tapped his fingers on the table. "We got you a nice surprise coming up later this month. A nice, surprise to film with."

"Oh yeah?"

"Yeah, a nice little girl, you're gonna like her," Bud smirked. "I promise you that."

"And this girl," he continued. "Perfecto" He kissed his fingertips.

Chase nodded. This was a promise he had heard many times but somehow doubted that it would matter. Making the movies wasn't all it was cracked up to be and it left him feeling like someone who had broken a law but hadn't been caught yet. Not that the movies were illegal, but they still felt wrong. Then again it was an escape from his real life. It was all he had for himself, other than his vigorous workout routines at the gym; the rest of his life seemed to belong to someone else; his employers, his wife or his child. Everyone had a piece of him. If he was lucky, there was a little portion sometimes left for himself.

The days rolled along and Audrey seemed to get bigger every morning. It was now difficult for her to do the simplest thing, so she often opted to do nothing. He returned home one day to find her sitting on the couch, while Leland cried upstairs. With her eyes closed, she showed no signs of distress over the fact that her baby was screaming his lungs out; Chase ran upstairs, expecting him to be hurt but instead found him sitting on his bedroom floor with a diaper full of shit.

Quickly rushing to change the baby, Leland stared at him as if he were a savior who occasionally swooped in. Feeling grief in his heart, it shifted to anger when he finally went downstairs to find Audrey still on the couch, showing little interest in what was or wasn't wrong with Leland.

"What the fuck Audrey? You can't check on your own fucking kid?"

"He's your fucking kid too," Her eyes snapped open. "Not just when it's convenient for you to come home."

"I'm fucking working two jobs, what do you expect?" Chase shot back, but she acted as if he hadn't said a thing. Awkwardly rising from the couch, she brushed past him and started upstairs. "You might want to check on your kid when he's screaming. Leland's diaper was full of fucking shit. Full, Audrey, do you ever bother to change him?"

She continued to walk upstairs, ignoring his words. He rushed behind her.

"This might surprise you but having kids isn't just a way to trap a guy into marrying you, there's also some responsibility involved," His voice shook in anger, a fire burned through his limbs as he watched her go upstairs as if she hadn't a care in the world, as if he weren't speaking to her, as if he were invisible. "You have to look after him."

At the top of the stairs, she swung around so fast, that Chase found himself grabbing the banister, fear lurched through his heart as he momentarily thought he was going to fall down. He knew she wanted to push him. An adrenaline rush shot through his body and he flew to the top of the stairs and grabbed her arm.

"Look after your fucking kid," He screamed and in the next room, Leland quickly followed suit, his sharp cries rang through the house.

"Let go of me," Audrey's hot breath was on his face, her voice was sharp, high pitched and it was just then that he noticed she had a new haircut; her bangs were straight, severe even, as Bud's words flowed through his mind. She started to struggle, using her free hand to push him back toward the staircase. His heart began to race furiously and in that second, he wanted to hurt her and squeezed her arm harder, while struggling to get away from the stairs, his immediate instincts were to fight back and that's when he used all his force to shove her against the wall.

A huge thud shook the house as she fell to the floor and grabbed her stomach. Animal like screams came from her mouth and sent a shiver through his body, as he realized exactly what he had done. It was right then, as he felt a frigid cloud of shock blanket his body, that he turned to see Flora standing at the end of the staircase.

CHAPTER TWENTY-FOUR

The fraternal twins were premature. This wasn't a surprise to the doctor, who appeared to think that this was completely normal. He seemed content that the infants were in good health, that all was well and nothing unusual had lead up to Audrey's sudden labor. No one did, and that's what made Chase nervous.

He wasn't sure how much Flora saw before calling the ambulance - or even why she walked into the house without knocking - but with his luck, she probably arrived about the same time he shoved Audrey. It was such an instinctual reaction to his fear that she was going to push him downstairs, that he almost couldn't stop himself from pushing her away. And yet, it didn't matter; she was the woman, she was pregnant and therefore, he was the animal. No one would see it differently. Had she knocked him downstairs, Chase was sure that people would blame it on hormones or a clumsy, accidental act, allowing her to bear no responsibility. The entire community would come together to help her out and he wouldn't be fortunate enough to die, but end up in a wheelchair for the rest of his life; suffering every fucking day of it.

For some reason, life always worked out for people like Audrey. Now she had something else to hold over his head.

But he was wrong. Audrey was excited over the birth of her babies and didn't have an ill word for Chase, even when no one else was around. She conveniently forgot about almost pushing him downstairs and when he attempted to mention it, Audrey claimed that her memory was 'foggy' and he should know she would never do such a thing. Her words were sugary sweet and had he not known her better, Chase would've believed her. He assumed the doctor had given her some strong medication that altered her mood.

It was Flora that would be the problem. She hung around the hospital, her eyes full of tears when learning that Chase and Audrey had two more little boys; Chet and Devin. Chase wasn't crazy about the names but once again assumed he had no choice in the matter, but his impression was echoed in his sister's words when she later referred to them as 'redneck' names.

"Sound like names of fucking cowboys in mom's romance novels," His sister's comment was blunt when he called her shortly after the birth. "I'm sure they're cute, though."

"I'll send a picture," Chase replied and glanced toward Flora who sat nearby, watching him carefully. "I gotta go, I-

"Chase we have to talk soon," Angel interrupted him. "It's about dad-

"I can't deal with that today," Chase abruptly replied.

"Okay," She was strangely compliant. "But we do have to talk about it. He's not well."

"I know."

"Soon. You can't keep brushing me off."

"We will," he assured her. "I promise. Just not today."

The conversation ended on a surprisingly positive note that sent a jolt of hope through his body. He felt very emotional with the combination of the baby's birth and fears of what happened just before, his adrenaline at an all time high, he wasn't sure what to do with himself but he couldn't sit still. He wanted so badly to call Maggie and talk to her about what happened but the battery on his cell was getting low and he didn't even know where to start. There were so many things she didn't know, that he was scared to even say out loud.

"Chase, I know this probably isn't a good time," Flora was suddenly beside him, her hand resting gently on his arm. "But we have to talk about what happened earlier."

Noting the compassion in her eyes, he merely nodded, making sure to not show any expression as he followed her to a quiet section of the waiting room. Sitting beside her, his heart raced at an accelerated pace and he felt his face grow warm as he bit back his emotions. Chase wasn't ready to deal with this; his nerves were on edge. He was on empty.

"Those are lovely boys you have in there," Flora grinned, her eyes full of kindness as she pointed in the general direction of the nursery. He felt something inside him melt as he thought of the tiny infants that were born within a short period of arriving at the hospital. Chase had slipped away to contact his parents as well as her family and by the time he finished, Audrey had already given birth. The doctor had even commented on how she was lucky to make it to the hospital in time and although Chase knew he could've been in the delivery room for their birth, he used the excuse that he had to look after Leland to hang back. Flora went into the room with her instead.

"Thanks," Chase felt slightly emotional but hid it well. "Thanks for going in the delivery room with her, I barely had time to go make those phone calls and Leland-

"Don't even worry about it, that little guy was sure tired when your mom picked him up," She put her hand up in the air and that was when something changed in the conversation. He felt a chill enter the room and his stomach lurched, anticipating the other shoe was about to drop. "Chase, I don't know what is going on with you and Audrey but from what I've seen and heard, especially earlier today, it's not good."

Chase didn't reply, his expression stoic.

"Now, I always wondered about you two and was kind of worried, but I try to mind my business," She sounded authentic regardless of Chase's reluctance to believe her. There was something not adding up in this conversation but he was going to hold the cards close to his chest before commenting. "But I heard screaming today and I thought maybe she was in trouble. But what I saw was a shock."

Chase nodded and refused to break eye contact. Harold taught him that this was necessary when dealing with an enemy and at that moment, he wasn't sure where Flora fit into the picture. She liked to play the role of friend, but was she? His short life had taught him that women often liked to play roles that seemed appropriate at the time but they weren't always real. He had little doubt she was different.

150

"Chase, don't take offense to this but I don't think that girl is all right," Flora spoke smoothly, pointing toward her head as if to indicate that Audrey was crazy. He didn't react, still unsure of where she was going with this train of thought. "I don't know if I trust her with small children, she seems to let poor Leland cry a lot. I know you can't always be there, working two jobs and all and I don't want to seem like a busybody, but I worry."

Chase felt his body relax slightly, although not completely soften. There something she wasn't getting at and he waited, anticipating her to circle back at any moment.

"Now, I think I have a clearer understanding. There's a whole lot not right in your house," She commented and glanced away, her eyes finally returning to Chases' face. "I saw the evil in your house. I see the violence between the two of you. I fear for those children being brought up in that environment and I feel that you need help from a higher power."

What?

Reaching over, her soft hand touched his and she leaned in closer. "The Lord is always there for you, you gotta know that. You two are young, things are stressful and scary, the economy is a mess, I know how difficult this must be for you," Flora shook her head slowly and Chase felt a small smile reluctantly cross his lips. "Now, I'm not going to say anything to anyone about what I saw but under one condition. I need you to start attending church with me on Sunday and I know religion probably sounds silly or not 'cool' to your generation but it helped me out so much after my divorce and I think once you two get back on a spiritual path, everything else will fall in line."

Chase was stunned and remained silent, studying her face. She was serious.

"I know Audrey comes from a religious background and somewhere along the line, she was separated from it but this is a chance for her to get back. I think it will make all the difference in the world. As for you, I think it will open your eyes."

Chase silently nodded and glanced down. Clearly, what she meant was to start going to church or she would call social services. He knew he had no choice but to say yes.

"I think you're right," he spoke softly and she tightened the grip on his hand, a smile covered her face. "We're pretty...lost."

"It will help," She spoke in a hushed tone. "I know that your marriage isn't exactly ideal but no marriage is and you have to make the best of it for the kids."

He nodded.

"I know you're gone a lot and things are strained. I know you spend a lot of nights on the couch," Her words were barely a whisper as she picked up his hand and guided it to her thigh. Chase was too stunned to reply, when it was met by the heat of her body, with only the thin material of her pants separating the two. "It doesn't have to be that way."

That was the other thing. He didn't just have to start going to church, he would also have to start fucking Flora Johnson.

Taking a deep breath, he nodded, indicating that he understood. It was another secret to add to his gallery of shame. His life, of course, was further off track with each day and it almost scared him to consider exactly where it would go from there.

The next few weeks flew by at an exhilarated pace and the next thing he knew it was the middle of summer, rapidly leading to the fall. Another year would soon be shot and his life continued to spin out of control. When he did have a spare moment, it was almost as if Flora sensed it and called him next door, claiming to an exhausted and uninterested Audrey that she need Chase for some 'handy work.'

Much to his surprise, the sex with Flora was surprisingly good. Fast, furious, it was the relief that he often needed and for being an older lady, she was surprisingly in great shape. Her breast only slightly sagging but her legs were long, lean and it was clear that the yoga DVDs she mentioned had a positive impact that he couldn't deny.

He hadn't made any movies since the twins were born. Things were so hectic, that he generally had to leave work immediately after finishing, no longer hanging out with Bud, he missed their time together. Chase was starting to think maybe his boss no longer wanted him to perform in any of the films since he hadn't even brought it up in months.

Then one day he did.

"There's a cute little girl we're planning to make movies with, I sure would like to get you in on it," Bud commented casually after the doors were closed, as they were cleaning up the bar for the night. "She's seen your work and thinks you can do better with her than Betsy. Maybe a little rivalry there, I'm not sure."

Chase knew that there would be some extra money involved and he certainly wasn't in the position to say no, their expenses continually growing; the financial aspect of having three kids was starting to overwhelm him.

The day the taping was scheduled, Chase woke up to the sound of a crying baby - then another - interrupting a beautiful dream. In it, he was with Maggie in the most intimate way possible, finally giving into their desires for one another, on the cusp of a pleasure, he fantasized about so many times and yet, reality awoke him just as the beautiful sensation flowed through his body.

Not that it stopped him from allowing the fantasy from returning throughout the day and in a way, it almost seemed to lift him, as if it were a real possibility and not just a dream. He felt her soft hands running over his body every second of the day, a pleasure flowing through him, a temptation that was almost overpowering filling him, making it almost impossible to focus on anything.

By the time he arrived at work, he knew he was ready; in fact, he was more than ready to take on this sexual dynamo that Bud described to him. He felt powerful, strong, confident, as he made his way to Bud's office, almost not hearing his words as he passed the camera, Chase entered the room where this woman awaits him.

An electrical shock ran through him when he saw who it was; a combination of panic and excitement. The reluctance when he saw her face was almost overpowered by her naked body; so perfect, just as he would've imagined. But it was wrong. So very wrong.

Chapter Twenty-Five

"What the fuck?" Chase finally managed to find his voice, his brain and eyes in conflict on whether or not to look at her naked body; her flawless, youthful curves couldn't have been any more perfect as she walked toward him with a wide-eyed grin on her face. Chase found himself backing away, as a small, yet loud part of his brain screamed for him to get out of that room, he couldn't deny that his body was full of desire, blood rushing to his groin while his heart pounded in anticipation. "Kelsey, what the fuck?"

The fact that it was Maggie's sister was bad enough, but how *old* was she? Definitely not legal, that much he knew for sure. It was then, as he glanced at the top of her head, he noted the hair clips that reminded him of the ring he found under the bed months earlier and assumed belonged to a child. He suddenly felt nausea grab hold of his stomach, squeezing it so tight that he thought he would be sick. Comments Bud had made in the past suddenly made sense, the many remarks suggesting 'little girls' were the best, had a completely different meaning now that Chase no longer had the naive notion that he was necessarily referring to young women in their twenties, such as Maggie.

"Oh fuck!" Chase said as he closed his eye, putting up his hand for her to stop. He ignored the indication that his body was on a whole other track from his heart and mind, as she ran her hand over his chest. "Put your fucking clothes on!"

He finally opened his eyes and saw the look of hurt on her face, her blue eyes filling with tears and he quickly averted his eyes, turning off the camera in his hand. Shaking his head, he felt his heart soften. She was just a kid. How did she get in this mess? It was bad enough he was involved, but she was only - what? Sixteen?

"Kelsey, please," he spoke gently this time and pointed toward her clothing piled on a nearby chair. "You have to put your clothes on."

She wiped away a tear and slowly made her way across the room, silently starting to dress. His heart racing in panic, it suddenly occurred to him that maybe this wasn't the first underaged girl. What the fuck was wrong with him? How did he allow his life to take such a fucked up turn?

He looked away as she dressed and when she finished, standing awkwardly beside the chair, tilting her foot to the side, as if unsure of what to do or say next. Knowing that he was supposed to be the adult in the situation, Chase realized that he had no choice but to deal with this head on.

"How many have you done?" His words were soft, barely a whisper as a chill ran up his spine. "Please tell me this was the first."

He wasn't surprised when she shook her head no. Chase looked away, his heart pounded in his ears while his body still showed traces of excitement; something that greatly shamed him. In fact, he never felt more like a scumbag in his life.

Fuck!

"How many, Kelsey?"

"A couple," She cleared her throat, her voice barely a whimper, as if she were a child caught smoking.

Not making a fucking porn.

"A few?"

"I wanted to do one with you but Bud said I had to do some with this other guys first," she spoke innocently as if it were a rite of passage to get to him. Chase felt fury rise in his chest, as a picture formed in his mind. "You know, to make sure that I was ready."

"Ready?"

"That I would know how to perform."

Chase closed his eyes and ran a hand over the short bristles of hair on his face, followed by his closed eyes. He suddenly felt weak; his muscles heavy but his body light, like he had been caught in the act of doing something wrong, even though he had stopped himself.

"It's okay, I kind of liked it," Kelsey said as if this information would somehow mend the situation. "It wasn't really an act-

"Kelsey, please," Chase cut her off and slowly shook his head. "You're only 16."

"I'm almost 17!"

"You're a minor." Chase reminded her. "This is illegal."

"Teenagers have sex all the time," Kelsey insisted. "Didn't you?"

"Not on camera."

"You're only 20, so I find that hard to believe," She argued.

"I was 19, Kelsey, that's legal," Chase said and stood a little taller. "When I was your age, the only person I was having sex with was Lucy, my *girlfriend*. Not some random person on camera, for money."

He knew these words were harsh but it was too late. He could see her eyes water and he immediately felt bad.

"Kelsey, you're a kid," he spoke gently. "I know you don't want to hear that but this is something you shouldn't be involved in. You're not in trouble but if Bud gets found out, he could be in deep shit. Not that I really care about him. I'm assuming he knows you're Maggie's *younger* sister."

She wiped away a tear and nodded. "That's why he waited until she was gone."

Fuck!

Chase felt anger rise in him. This was all manipulated. It was carefully planned. Bud knew that Maggie would suspect something, so he waited till she moved away. He manipulated Kelsey to fuck some other guys for his movies in order to 'get' to Chase; whom she apparently had some kind of weird crush on. It had been planned so carefully and since Chase had feelings for Maggie, Bud probably thought he would gratefully take the opportunity to have sex with her younger sister, who resembled Maggie. Except for one thing. Maggie wouldn't do something like this; never.

"How did you know…"

"I heard some guy was making movies and I thought it would be cool to try," Kelsey shrugged. "I didn't think it would be a big deal and when I heard you did one-

"Wait, how did you hear that I did one?"

"Bud told me when I approached him about doing a movie," Kelsey replied. "He said it was a secret, though. Don't worry, I didn't tell anyone."

The fact that anyone knew made him uneasy; especially a local. The last thing he needed was word getting out. He licked his lips, his brain racing to find an answer. What should he do?

"Kelsey, this is a bigger deal than you think. This is porn and you can't take back these movies once they're out there."

"I don't care."

"You might."

"You do them."

"You can't see me in the movies."

"I can see some of you," She purred moving closer. "I can hear you. It's sexy and-

"No," Chase spoke sternly. "Nothing is happening here, Kelsey."

"Is it cause of Maggie or because I'm almost 17."

"Both," He replied and took a deep breath. "Look, Kelsey, I don't know how to fix this, maybe I can talk to Bud about taking the movies down and-

"I don't want him to take them down," Kelsey's comment was abrupt. "I'm proud of my work, I look sexy and I want to do more."

"No, Kelsey, you don't want this…" He couldn't believe that this was a conversation he was having with Maggie's sister. "And you're too young and I would never do anything to hurt Maggie and this *would* hurt Maggie."

"Fuck her! This is my life," Kelsey defiantly crossed her arms over her breasts and reminded him of a stubborn child.

"You're a minor, you can't-

"I won't stop doing them."

"What can I say to make you stop?"

"You know," She moved closer, placing her hand on his chest.

"That's not happening."

"I won't tell anyone."

"That's not why."

"I won't tell Maggie."

"No, Kelsey."

"I want you, though," She whispered. "I keep watching those movies you're in and I wish that was me and listening to you make me-

"Kelsey, no," He insisted. "This can't happen."

"Then I won't stop making the movies."

"You have to stop," He suddenly heard an adult voice coming out.

"You can't do anything about it," Kelsey insisted, her blue eyes boldly stared into his, while her hand continued to travel over his body. "I won't stop. If you tell my mom, I will tell everyone about you."

Fuck!

"Kelsey," he attempted to ignore her hands running over his chest. "This isn't about me, this is about you. You're like a little sister to me and-

"I don't think your sister would be doing this to you," She muttered, her breath labored, as her hand traced past his belly button and Chase fought back his impulse to give in, convincing himself that she was only a couple years younger than him. Reaching down, he removed her hand, their eyes met and he shook his head. "This is not a road you want to go down and I wouldn't be much of a man if I let you. You're too good for this Kelsey."

"I just want to be with you."

"That can't happen."

"Why not?" She asked defiantly. "You cheat on your wife, so it's not like you have a real marriage. You can't have Maggie, even though it's clear you want her. I'm almost 17, you're barely 20, we're practically the same age."

"Practically isn't enough," his voice was soft.

"What if I were 18, would you say no to me then?" She was wide-eyed and it was a question he couldn't answer. "If Maggie gave it her blessing, if I was of age, if it wasn't on camera anymore. Would you?"

Considering the fact that it was well over a year away and not something she'd probably even care about by the time she turned 18, he also realized that this might be the only way to stop her from making more movies. "Yes."

"Really?" She asked, her face full of hope and he felt deceitful but at the same time, he had to get her out of this business. There was no other option.

"Yes, when you're 18, *if* you still feel this way, then I will."

He couldn't believe he was actually making this deal or that he had to; it was ludicrous to even consider.

"I have to find a way to get those movies offline," Chase heard his thoughts entering the quiet room and she stood back, suddenly shy in his presence.

"I didn't really make them."

"I thought you said you did."

"I did," She nodded earnestly. "I mean, I was being filmed but Bud said I wasn't quite ready to go live yet. It was kinda practice."

Chase had a bad idea what the practice run was really for; he wondered if Bud used it as one of his personal jerk off materials and he felt sick even thinking about it. Had he sold the opportunity to be with her? He looked away and didn't say anything for a long moment, while Kelsey appeared nervous. "Kels, did you do anything with Bud?"

She shrugged nervously and he knew the answer. He felt as though his world was crashing down, the person he didn't want to see in Bud now had a glaring light and he couldn't ignore it any longer. "It was like an audition. I didn't have to really do much, I-

The anger started deep inside him, burning through his stomach until it lurched forward, finding it's way to his throat, as it filled every inch of his body. It was a power that was unlike any other, he felt as if he could tear the side of out the building his bare hands, a murderous explosion filled him as he flew out the door. The worst possible situation would be to find Bud in the other room, calmly using two fingers to type an email, as if nothing unusual or illegal was happening in his bar, but that's exactly where he was when Chase charged at him.

Stunned, fear filled his face when Chase grabbed him by his shirt and ripped him up from his chair. "She's a fucking minor, you piece of shit.!"

"I...yeah, but she's just a-

"Listen to me, you're getting rid of every movie she's in right now or I swear to God, I will fucking kill you, right here, right now and no one's going to give a shit when they find out what a fucking slime you are," his voice was calm, almost tranquil as he uttered the threats, despite the fact that he was squeezing both of Bud's shoulders so tight, that he was expecting to feel a bone break beneath his own fingers, his grasp so strong that he thought he would never let go.

"I..yes, yes. I will," Bud replied, terror running through his eyes as Chase loosened his grip. "I will, I will, I swear.."

His hands shook as he deleted files, opening them first to show that they were Kelsey. There were two; one with him and another with some old guy that made Chases' skin crawl, he felt his stomach turn and momentarily feared he would vomit. However, he was able to pull back his emotions and focus.

"Is that it, are those movies on the site?" Chase demanded. "On an external hard drive? Anywhere?"

"No, no, I swear, no!" Bud's voice shook as he rose both his hands up as if to surrender. "You can look."

Chase decided against it.

Glancing toward Kelsey, she looked more frightened than Bud; if that were possible.

"If I find out otherwise or that you have anything else going on with underaged girls here, I swear, I will come back and I will fucking kill you and then, I'll burn this fucking place to the ground, you got it?" Chase asked, not recognizing the person speaking as if a stranger had taken over his body.

Bud nodded yes and there was no doubt that in his mind, he meant it.

Turning toward Kelsey, he gestured toward the door. "I will meet you outside. Wait by my car."

She moved quickly, silently and slipped out the door, closing it behind her.

Turning back to Bud, he held nothing back. "You're one sick fuck, you know that?"

"I did it for you," Bud attempted to justify. "She came around and I thought that you-

"Wanted to have sex with Maggie's younger, jailbait sister?" Chase attempted to finish his sentence. "Seriously?"

"She's a lot older than she looks," Bud attempted to reason.

"So you thought you'd take her out for a test drive?" Chase felt his anger rising again and he forced himself to stand still.

"That wasn't my idea," Bud spoke defensively. "She insisted on it and I..I was weak. She's a nymph, that girl she's-

"Just stop," Chase cut him off. "Stop right there. I don't want to hear it."

A silence followed as Bud stared at him, not even blinking, as if in fear of what Chase would do if he even moved an inch.

Chase felt heavy when he left the bar that one, last time. Disappointment and shame filled him and only increased when he went outside to find Kelsey standing by his car. His anger toward Bud felt slightly unjustified when maybe he was no better.

Chapter Twenty-Six

Chase started to calm down on the drive home. At first, he didn't talk to Kelsey, nor did she speak to him. Like a shame-filled child slumped over in the passenger seat, he felt compassion for her as she chipped at her pink fingernail polish, her expression encompassed various degrees of pain and misery, almost as if there were a dam about to break. He felt pity for her and although she attempted to display her femme fatale side at the bar, she now resembled the dreary teenager she actually was; this softened his anger.

He remembered sitting on the passenger side of Maggie's car only a couple years earlier, feeling very much as he suspected Kelsey felt at that moment. Of course, the situations were completely different but when you experience that combination of remorse, defeatism as if you are the lowest form of a human, you recognize it in someone else. He wanted to say something but they were back in Hennessey when he spoke again.

"Are you okay?"

"No," She sniffed. "What do you think?"

Chase took a deep breath and ran his hand over his head. He didn't understand teenage girls when he *was* a teenager, let alone now, that he felt more like a 40-year-old man, rather than a mere 20. He didn't want to say the wrong thing, but he couldn't *not* say anything.

"Kelsey, it's going to be okay," he calmly assured her. "Trust me, Bud got rid of everything and we can forget this happened. You're lucky because nothing was put online. I'll even double check when I get home but I'm sure everything is fine."

"Don't you get it! Everything is not fine," Kelsey sobbed, a shot of anger mixed in with her cries alarmed Chase and he felt unable to speak. "I don't feel like anything is fine. I don't care if the stuff we did is out there or not. I want to be with you, Chase and you think I'm some stupid kid. You only did what you did tonight because I'm Maggie's sister, otherwise you couldn't have cared less."

"That's not true."

"It is, if you didn't know me, you would've had sex with me and never even thought twice about it," she insisted as he glanced over to see her wiping away a tear with her hand, while makeup started to run in the corners of her eyes. "You would've fucked me, we would've made a movie together and you would've never asked my age."

Was that true? Chase felt a heaviness fill his chest and he glanced at her. She *did* look slightly older than her age but would he even considered that Bud would hire a minor? Did he have blind faith in someone he shouldn't have trusted at all? These questions weighed down on him as they got closer to Kelsey's house and she stared out the window beside her.

When he pulled into her driveway, she flew out of the car and ran up the steps of her house. He noted that Ellen Telips wasn't home and was kind of relieved since he didn't want Kelsey's mother to start asking too many questions. Then again, should she know? Should he call Maggie? There didn't seem to be any right answer. Was he just covering his own ass?

Back at home, he found Audrey on the couch, head in hand, while three children cried upstairs. He didn't say a word but made his way up to the bedroom of the twins, realizing that both needed a diaper change, while Leland appeared to want attention more than anything. He calmly went through the motions, while his mind was back on Kelsey.

Fuck! Why didn't I get her number?

Knowing that he couldn't exactly ask Maggie for her younger sister's number, he reluctantly texted Bud. He replied quickly, with an apology, an explanation, and Kelsey's cell number. Chase ignored the first two comments but reluctantly realized that maybe that in his own twisted way, Bud thought he was doing him a favor. It was sick and fucked up but he had a nagging feeling that this was what was going on.

Kelsey, it's Chase. Are you ok?

She replied right away.

No. Can you come see me?

He immediately recognized that maybe he made a mistake.

No, I have three screaming kids that I have to look after.

After a brief pause…

Can I help?

Chase grinned at the idea, although he certainly would've appreciated any help he could get at that point.

No, thanks though.

Feeling overwhelmed, but satisfied that the kids were all calmed down, he went back downstairs. Audrey was lying on the couch.

"You're back early," She commented without opening her eyes.

"I quit the bar."

"What?" her eyes flew open. "Chase, we need the money."

"I still work at the gym full time, Audrey."

"We need more money, this is way too expensive."

"Maybe you should've thought of that when you decided to not use birth control."

"The woman isn't the only one responsible," she snapped.

"Yeah, I asked you if you were on the pill both times and both times you said yes," he reminded her. "I offered to use a condom other times and you said no and here we are, you're living your dream life." his comment was purposely sarcastic, with every intention of hurting her.

"You hate me, don't you?" she asked.

He didn't reply as he left the room. Going outside, he briefly considered sitting on the step and breathing in the cool, evening air, just being alone for a few minutes. However, deep down, he knew that the second he sat down either Audrey or Flora would be there talking to him. Not that he had a chance, his phone rang. Assuming it was Kelsey, he grabbed it and started to walk toward the car.

It was Angel.

She was crying.

"It's stage four," she sobbed loudly, her words barely coming out as her voice shook.

"What?" Chase asked even though, on some level, he knew exactly what was going on.

"Dad, he has stage four Cancer," she sniffed. "Mom just told me."

"What?" Chase thought back to a brief visit their mother made to the house the day before, often stopping in to help out with the babies. "Mom saw me yesterday, she didn't say anything."

Although their relationship was still pretty strained, it struck him odd that she wouldn't tell him something that was so serious. "Are you sure, Ang?"

"Yes," she sniffed, her voice slightly calmer. "She called me and asked I tell you too. They're both in shock, Chase, he's scared and mom's running around like a lunatic, as usual."

"She doesn't want to believe it," Chase commented, leaning against his car, his legs felt weak beneath him. He reached out to touch the door to steady himself, but it was as if nothing felt safe. His world continued to fall apart around him like a nightmare that never ended.

"Neither do I,' Angel had a softness in her voice that made her barely recognizable. A layer of anger had dissolved, her vulnerability suddenly was apparent in a way that made Chase question if it had really been there all along; he just hadn't noticed.

The rest of the fall flew by as his father's health declined. Chase felt as though his life was a non-stop merry-go-round that was flying out of control. He worked. He came home, changed diapers, fed children, did laundry, then went back to work. In between, he got in his regular workouts - the only time he had to himself - while occasionally doing 'handy' work at Flora's, which oddly came as a diversion from his regular life, a minor distraction that often satisfied him more than he expected. She also was around all the time, in attempts to help a grateful Audrey out with the children.

His life was insanity and on days when he thought things couldn't get worse, he would get a call from Kelsey, who wanted to talk. Occasionally she sent him a totally inappropriate image that she thought would change his mind, especially after she turned 17 and suddenly felt that her prison sentence of being a minor was almost over; therefore making Chase a more intimate part of her life.

"I'm counting the days!" She once commented to him and he was surprised when he felt a jolt of desire rising in him, but he didn't tell her. He could never tell her.

Maggie was almost a distant memory, rarely calling or texting since her move. He did his best to stay in contact but wasn't getting the impression she wanted to do the same. She was slowly moving through the various tests involved in becoming an RCMP officer, although her desire to do so seemed depleted, at least that's what Chase sensed from her.

Maggie was a very different person now but he couldn't put his finger on what that change was or when it happened. He got the impression that she was seeing someone and sometimes wondered if she was 'allowed' to talk to him anymore; something he couldn't help but resent, considering he was married with children and always found time for her. He wondered also if she knew about his relationship with Kelsey, although it was pretty innocent in nature. At least, his side was innocent.

It kind of hurt him when Maggie seemed to show little interest in his father's illness. Not that she knew his dad well, but she was *his* friend and it was a pretty heavy situation. His dad was dying. There was no denying it. No one talked about it in their family but it was clear that Carl Jacobs was quickly going downhill. He had waited too long to go to their family doctor, insisting that he was fine but in reality, cancer was eating away at him. It started in his prostate and quickly moved to his stomach. The doctors talked chemo and surgery but in the end, it was desperate attempts to keep a dying man alive and uncomfortable for his remaining days.

There were days that Chase felt like it couldn't really be happening but it was. Angel came home for her Christmas break and demonstrated her sorrow over their father's deteriorating health. It was her final year of university and vital that she do well, now that she settled on a Bachelor of English with feminist something or another; Chase didn't understand what this meant in the real world but decided he would appear stupid if he asked, so he didn't.

Angel and their dad were always close; whereas, Chase felt distanced from his father. It didn't make it any easier to see him fade away, suddenly realizing that life was only temporary and there were no promises, it seemed to renew something inside himself. There were days, he felt a glimmer of hope, the lost 18-year-old from two years earlier had returned, reminding him that his life was more than babies and bitter, demanding women. He was still in there, somewhere, waiting to be dug back out again.

It was shortly after Angel's return from school that Carl Jacobs died peacefully in his sleep. It was as if he waited for his favorite child to return home, sitting on his bedside, she said he opened his eyes and stared at her for a moment and seemed to nod, before closing his eyes forever. It sounded so beautiful when she repeated it and although Chase hugged her as she sobbed, he felt nothing. His own relationship with their father had never been strong, flimsy at best, especially since Chase was kicked out. It was almost as if a stranger died. He didn't shed a tear during or before the funeral. How could he mourn a man that barely lived, but went through the motions? Would Chase be the same?

In truth, it was that thought that really haunted him, brought sorrow to his heart. Was his faith the same? Was he already dead, just not yet in the ground; too busy being everyone's puppet on a string, going through the motions of this excuse for a life?

And that's when he cried.

CHAPTER TWENTY-SEVEN

His mother believed that it was a bad omen to light a candle unless it was during a power outage. Louise Jacobs insisted that doing so for any other reason was a way of 'inviting darkness into your life' and therefore, the children were never allowed candles on their birthday cake nor could Angel ever light a candle in her room; it was unacceptable in their mother's eyes. She insisted that a terrible tragedy would follow.

Several days before Carl Jacobs' death, apparently, she arrived at her son's home to discover Audrey had lit a candle. It was an innocent act that was meant to freshen the air in a home that smelled like baby shit; she had forgotten about her mother-in-law's peculiar beliefs regarding candles and was stunned when the older woman blasted her for such an 'inconsiderate act'. Audrey attempted to calm the older woman with the assumption that her irrational beliefs stemmed from grief and anguish due to Carl's deteriorating state.

"Chase, I don't want to alarm you, but I think your mother might suffer from some form of mental illness," Audrey said to him one morning over breakfast, as he wolfed down a huge bowl of steel cut oats and attempted to scan his phone for news. He almost choked on a strawberry that was combined in the mixture and immediately began to laugh.

"Really, Audrey? All these great psychology classes you took in college and the ones you take online now, and you *just* started to see that my mother has a mental illness?" Chase asked and felt laughter rise from his belly and light his whole body on fire, as he considered her attempt to make a serious diagnose of something that was crystal clear to the most uneducated person. "Really? What was the first clue? When she practically threw herself on dad's casket at the funeral and made a huge scene or when she insisted that the name 'Leland' was actually evil and he was cursed? I mean, how many clues did you need?"

"It helps me understand your issues more clearly," she continued, ignoring his attempts to belittle her suggestion, purposely showing her as little respect as possible. Audrey always bragged up her education as if he were a moron in comparison and took herself a little too seriously, so it was nice to remind her that *even* he was able to make an uneducated guess.

"Sure, Audrey," Chase said in the most patronizing voice he could find, unconcerned with hurting her feelings; in fact, since his father's death, he somehow felt more free, as if nothing owned him anymore, like no one had a grasp on him. He had even seriously considered leaving Audrey. Perhaps, the best way was to do everything in his power to make her hate him. It was better that she hate him than he hated himself.

"Your mother's odd behavior made you into this weak man, who feels the need to 'look after' women, in some discipline or another, to have their approval," She continued to ramble as Chase finished his oatmeal and gulped the remainder of his coffee. "She controlled your life, I see that now. She made you scared of everything."

"What the fuck are you talking about, Audrey?" Chase took his bowl and cup to the sink, carefully rinsing out both of them.

"Look, you even rinse out all your dishes, just like your mommy use to tell you to do," Audrey attempted to poke at him but Chase didn't care. He could see what she was doing. In fact, she did it all the time. If Audrey could somehow needle at him to start a fight, she did. A few times she was successful but most of the time it didn't work. Chase didn't give a fuck what she thought or said. It was irrelevant. As long as she looked after the kids, he didn't give a crap what she did.

"It's called common courtesy," Chase calmly replied, as he returned to the table and reached for the phone, sliding it in his pocket. "You might want to look into that while studying all your psychology books."

Ignoring his last remark, she continued. "Did your mother molest you?"

"What?" his reply was sharper than he meant it to be but the ridiculous comment was too shocking to take in a rational, calm manner. "Where the fuck did that come from?"

"Just the way she talks about you," Audrey replied, her lips barely disguising the smile behind them. "She talks about you as if you're an Adonis, perfect in every way, lovingly, while she barely talked about your dad even when he was dying."

"Cause she was in denial of his death," Chase snapped, suddenly feeling a crushing anger take over where calmness prevailed only seconds later. She knew the buttons to push. "All mothers put their kids on a pedestal. Well, *real* mothers."

He threw in the final comment as he grabbed his jacket and headed for the door, suddenly uninterested in continuing this conversation, smart enough to realize on what path it was headed. She was trying to egg him.

"I'm a real mother!" she shot back, her voice rushing behind him as she grabbed his arm and pulled him back, almost causing Chase to lose his balance. Instinctively, he attempted to pull his arm from her grasp, as the two started to struggle; him to get away from her, while her to hold on. Upstairs, Leland started to cry, followed by the twins and in that moment, Chase wanted nothing more than to run away and never come back. Frustrated he turned around to tell her to check the kids, that he had to go to work, when he felt his head swing back as a heavy hand tore across his face with such great force, almost knocking him against the nearby wall.

Fury tore through his body like a lightning bolt and he grabbed her by the shoulders, attempting to push her back, but she continued to claw and pummel his chest, her face full of rage, both eyes squinted to almost slits, as if she were suddenly a different form of herself; the ugliest form he had ever seen. Unable to hold her back, unable to stop her from hitting him, he shoved her. Watching her fall to the ground, attempting to grab the kitchen table behind her, Audrey's eyes were full of terror as she hit the ground and let out a cry.

"Get out!" She screamed and Chase wasted no time in doing so. His heart raced, while anxiety began to replace his original anger, fear of what he had become. If anyone had told him he would ever attack a woman, ever push a woman, Chase never would've believed it. He had such respect and admiration for the so-called fairer sex, that the idea of ever hurting a woman seemed unfathomable; until now.

He wanted to hurt Audrey. He wanted to say the words that sent the sharpest cuts through her soul. He wanted to grab and shake her. He wanted to see her in misery, in pain. He hated her. He hated everything about her; how she looked, the way her voice lazily spoke, slowly, as if to be condescending to those around her, the way she attempted to manipulate and play a different role for everyone. She was one to talk about others having a mental illness! What kind of mother allowed her children to cry non-stop without looking after them? What kind of mother attacked her kid's father? What the fuck was wrong with *her*?

Chase was grateful that nosey, old Flora wasn't out tending to her garden that morning because the last thing he wanted to deal with was her too, on top of everything else. He started the car and tore out of the driveway. It wasn't the first time, but he was starting to feel like it would soon be the last. He couldn't handle it anymore. He couldn't handle living in that house. He couldn't handle Audrey. If it wasn't for the kids, he would've been long fucking gone.

But then he looked into his three little boys eyes and his feet were nailed to the ground. He couldn't leave them with that lunatic. He couldn't walk away.

Could he?

When he got to work, Chase felt himself cool off; even if just slightly. The parking lot was deserted, which meant that he would be able to work on his boxing; something that always made him feel better. It calmed him. It helped him regain control.

But it didn't that day.

He was met instead by Harold and the news that felt like a rug was ripped out beneath him. The gym was closing.

"I can't make it work anymore," Harold explained, as the two sat in his office. "I had to choose between this and the other gym and this one isn't doing well, especially with the new exercise classes that are going on in town, a lot of people want something new and different."

"Can we do something like that here?" Chase felt as though he were grasping at straws, his brain searching for an answer.

"I've already thought of it," Harold confessed and gave him a sympathetic smile. "I'm sorry, it's not going to work out. Believe me, I hate delivering this news as much as I'm sure you hate getting it, but I can offer you a great recommendation and of course, if anything comes available at the other gym, I will let you know. I know it's a bit of a drive but it's the best I can do right now."

He had a job until the end of the month. All dreams of leaving Audrey were gone; he was stuck.

Feeling desperate after Harold left, he text Maggie with the entire story. She didn't reply.

The night was long and no one came in. It was one of the evenings when the specific class that Harold spoke of was taking place. It was always dead on that night.

It angered him that his boss hadn't made more of an effort to change the situation. Why didn't he grow, try to introduce new things to the gym? Things that made it fun? It seemed like the logical thing to do, yet, people weren't always prone to logic.

He was so preoccupied with his thoughts and worries, Chase almost didn't hear the door open. Feeling drained and depressed, he felt a glimmer of hope when he saw Kelsey walk in. Her eyes somehow seemed enormous and innocent, her coat opened over a fitted sweater and normal jeans, but somehow she filled them out a little too well for him in such a vulnerable moment.

He looked away, not wanting to give her any signs of hope, feeling more depressed by the temptation he knew she was about to offer. She had been friendly, yet relentless since that night at Bud's. The worse part was that he really did like her, but it was almost as if she was Maggie's polar opposite in every way. It was ironic when he considered how much he lusted after Kelsey's sister to no avail, only to have the opposite situation with the youngest of two Telips' girls.

"What's wrong?" she immediately zeroed in on his face, her question simple and yet powerful at the same time, as she tilted her head, her right foot tilting inward in a nervous gesture.

"I lost my job," Chase replied and avoided her eyes. "Harold's closing the gym."

"Oh," Her comment was soft, sensual, causing him to look up as she hunched forward. "I'm sorry, Chase."

He didn't reply just gave a quick smile.

"I feel responsible for you losing your last job."

"You're not responsible," Chase answered gently, suddenly appreciative of some compassion. Where else would he find it, especially when considering he had no support now that Maggie was gone. Clearly, she had forgotten him along the way. "It's no one's fault, it just is…I guess."

"What are you going to do?"

"I don't know," Chase let out a short laugh. "Throw myself over a cliff somewhere."

She fell silent.

"You wouldn't really do that, would you?"

"What?" Chase asked, a glint of humor in his voice, he quickly felt guilty when he saw her eyes water. "No, it's a joke Kelsey, I was joking."

Awkwardly, she rushed over and hugged him. It was a quick hug, but just long enough, He could smell a flowery scent fill his lungs, as her long hair brushed across his face and her delicate fingers briefly touched his back. A chaste hug, all things considered, but it helped to soften his disposition.

"I'm sorry, Chase." she stood up and pushed back a strand of hair. She placed a hand on his shoulder and ran her fingers back and forth, slowly gliding past his neckline to touch his naked flesh. The temptation build up in his quickly, almost uncontrollably and he couldn't deny that he instinctually wanted to give in to them; lock the door, take her in the shower as he once had with Claire Shelley and unleash all his cravings until she moaned in pleasure; but he couldn't. He immediately felt shame. She was only 17. What the fuck was wrong with him? Was it because she reminded him so much of Maggie? Was he some kind of fucking deviant, pedophile? Was he nothing more than a dirtbag?

Then again, as she always reminded him, there was only a couple years age difference between them. He would turn 21, where she was on her way to 18; how could it be any more fucked up to be attracted to her than have sex with the much older women like Flora, who was early retired, but she was still *retired*. His desires were strong. Was that normal? It wasn't like he had any other guys to talk to this kind of thing about. His high school friends were replaced by Maggie and they were all gone, moved on to bigger and better things in the city.

Just then, the door swung open and one of the regular clients, a middle-aged woman, walked in. Her eyes evaluated the situation between Kelsey and Chase, clearly not pleased by what she saw. Kelsey seemed unconcerned and merely shot her a dirty look. She gave Chase a quick kiss on his cheek and said bye, before rushing out the door.

CHAPTER TWENTY-EIGHT

For the most part, Chase didn't mind staying home with the children when Audrey returned to work. It actually surprised him how quickly he fell into a routine with Leland, Chet, and Devin; it was just a matter of having everything on schedule, from feeding times to cleaning the house while the children all slept. Once he got the hang of it, things actually went quite well. Not to suggest everything was perfect; there were days when he was ready to pull his hair out but for the most part, the months leading into springtime flowed along nicely.

Audrey insisted it was only because *she* had gotten the children on a schedule that he was having any luck at all. For some reason, it was impossible for his wife to accept that perhaps the children felt more at ease with him than her, therefore things flowed much more smoothly while she was gone. He sensed the resentment in her voice and saw the jealousy pouring out of her eyes when she arrived home to a silent, clean house rather than the disaster Chase often found himself returning to when he still had a job.

Not to suggest that he felt great about himself since becoming unemployed. In fact, he hadn't realized how much people's work defined them until he didn't have a job. Removing that one factor from life created a huge empty space in his identity; making him feel pathetic when he went to the grocery store, surrounded by all the local moms, as they eyed him over a shopping carts. At first, he felt a sense of shame, even though he had done nothing wrong. He felt like he owed everyone an explanation; little did they know that just a few months earlier, he had been working close to 60 hours a week and now, he changed diapers, cleaned up messes and tried to keep the household together.

Flora and his mom were a huge help. It was difficult to take all three kids anywhere, so he often would bring Leland along while he ran errands, leaving the twins with one of the two women. He wasn't so secure with his mother being alone with two babies but he noticed that she was protective of the children, almost as if they were her own. Her voice was tender when she spoke to them, a tone that greatly differed from the one she used with the rest of the world. Chase wondered if she had once spoken to him and Angel in that manner but somehow doubted it.

Although their relationship had improved since the arrival of the children, Louise and Chase would never have a close bond again. She was off in her own little world, almost as if his father hadn't died only a few months earlier. Angel was still a basket case since Carl Jacobs passed away, often calling Chase in tears, the stress of her final year of university combined with her deep sorrow was almost too much and he was left trying to boost her up when she was at her lowest point. He certainly understood how that felt and although they hadn't always had the best relationship, Chase did recognize when it was time to step up.

Since she was also in Calgary, Chase sometimes wondered if her and Maggie's paths ever crossed; but then realized how ridiculous that was and never asked. Calgary was one of the largest cities in Canada, so it was unlikely for it to happen but it worried him that Maggie seemed to have but fallen off the face of the earth. When he attempted to ask Kelsey if her older sister was okay, she often got defensive, as if he were only using her to keep a connection with his former best friend.

"You know that's not true," Chase would attempt to reassure her, but it was clear that some resentment lay beneath the surface, perhaps not so much with him than from within the Telips family. He sensed there was a lot of comparison going on; Maggie was a good student, quiet, a hard worker and had a sweet disposition. Kelsey didn't want a part-time job, despised school and was more bold, more vocal than her sister ever was; she wore revealing clothing, showing off her cleavage, displaying her smooth midriff or tight jeans or yoga pants that left little to the imagination. She spoke her mind, often abrupt, bordering on rude, but she didn't care and sometimes, that was the problem.

Chase didn't want to go anywhere with her in public for fear people would think they were a couple. Some rumors were already swirling around town that they were having a secret affair, something that didn't exactly help his position in the community. He suspected that this might've been a contributing factor for the dirty looks from local women, as if he were a sexual deviant, chasing after jailbait while married to a woman with three small children.

Not that he was doing anything with Kelsey but he did enjoy her company when she stopped by the house. He appreciated that she often jumped in to help with the kids or household tasks such as unloading the dishwasher and folding laundry.

"Your old lady wears pretty sexy underwear for being a mom," Kelsey held up a pair of frilly panties one day as she folded a huge basket of clothes that were overflowing onto the floor. Neither Flora or his mom were there on that day, so he didn't have to deal with their dirty looks when the brazen teenager arrived at the door on the cool, June afternoon. Not that their attitudes affected Kelsey; her original shyness long gone, she would coo over the babies, carrying them around as if it was second nature for her and although he originally was nervous of the idea, Chase had to admit that the boys loved her.

"She's not my 'old lady'," Chase corrected her from the other side of the room, where he was cleaning a smashed cookie from the curtain. Now that Leland was starting to walk, Chase always had an eye on his eldest son to make sure he didn't rip the entire house apart or hurt himself in some way.

"You *are* married to her right?" Kelsey asked, as she sat the panties down and pulled both twins into each of her arms as if they were merely a couple of grocery bags, momentarily causing Chases' heart to catch in his throat, fearing she would drop one but they were fine. Chet was grasping a strand of her hair while Devin seemed fascinated with her left breast. "That makes her your old lady."

"I barely consider her my wife."

"Well, you got these three," Her eyes glanced over all the children. "Obviously, you hooked up at least…twice, right?"

Chase raised an eyebrow, his face tightened up. She seemed unaware that Devin was pulling on her bra strap and that Chet was sucking on her hair. A large blob of drool suddenly dropped on her chest and rolled down her cleavage. Kelsey glanced down.

"Hey Chase, can you get that for me," She glanced at her breasts. "I don't want to put them down."

Past circumstances proved that the babies hated it when Kelsey put them down. Of course, past history also showed that Kelsey did almost anything to get close to him, tempting his desires, especially now that his sex life consisted of fast hookups with an older woman or at his own hand during his very short, morning showers.

Grabbing the closest roll of paper towels - something he had in every room now - Chase cautiously wiped the drool off her chest. Reluctantly, he reached between her breasts to get the drop that was rapidly running into the hollow between her breasts. Feeling a twinge of arousal, it was quickly depleted when the door opened and Audrey walked in. Glaring at the two of them, Chase feared she would attack Kelsey but she didn't say a word.

Having already met the youngest of the Telips' girls, Audrey perhaps caught on right away that unlike Maggie, Kelsey wasn't intimidated by much and wasn't sensitive to what made other people uncomfortable. Catching the reaction at the door, she merely shrugged and said, "Your kids sure drool a lot, Aud."

Rushing to the other side of the room to stop Leland from ripping the long curtains down from the windows, Chase barely caught Audrey rush over and rip both children from Kelsey's arms. The babies were alarmed and immediately started to scream. Chet reached out for Kelsey as if he couldn't bear to be removed from her arms.

"You shouldn't have them, what do you know about babies?" Audrey sneered and turned away.

"I know how to keep them from crying," Kelsey muttered and eased past Audrey, showing no signs of intimidation under her dark glares. "See ya Chase." She breezily commented as she bent over to pick up her backpack, her breasts almost pouring out of her bra when she did so and it took everything in Chase to look away. Then she was gone.

"Why was she here?" Audrey snapped and exhausted by the day, Chase ignored her question and grabbed Leland. With cookie smeared on his face, it was an excuse to get a washcloth in the bathroom to wash it off. His mind continued to go back to when he cleaned the drool off Kelsey, the soft noise she made when his hand gingerly wiped the clear substance, as her breasts seemed to rise a little higher as he did so, his desires rising at the possibilities.

Pushing it out of his mind, he didn't allow it to return until after dinner, while in the basement pummelling the punching bag that Harold had graciously given him after the gym closed; in fact, he helped Chase to install it, making sure it was secure before leaving, shooting back an apologetic look as he glanced at the three small children in the living room. It was clear he felt guilty over laying Chase off, but both of them knew it was unavoidable.

It was his time in the basement when he could escape. Pounding on the heavy bag in the corner, all his desires and frustrations unleashed, flowing through his body, escaping through his pores of sweat, grinding through his muscles as he found relief with each attack on the punching bag. His breath released the intense desires that never were far away, his need to have a normal, physical relationship with a woman, rather than forced encounters with his wife or Flora, but a connection that was mutual and not just physical. He somehow missed out on that stage and wasn't sure why. Either he really wanted someone who didn't want him or vice versa. It was never on the same level but mismatched and minimal nutrition for a body that craved so much more than he was finding.

Removing the gloves, he threw them on the ground and went to take a shower. The kids already in bed, Audrey was on the computer in the living room and they ignored each other as he went upstairs and closed the bathroom door. It was only in there that he allowed himself to think about Kelsey's cleavage and give in to his longings, under the hot spray of the shower, as his hand worked rapidly to bring himself some pleasure.

Drying off, he pulled on old sweatpants and a hoodie before returning downstairs, relieved that Audrey was now in the bedroom, he collapsed on the couch and glanced at the clock. His chest rose and fell beneath the blanket and his eyes started to drift shut when his phone vibrated. Assuming it was Kelsey, he was surprised to pick it up and see Maggie's name show up.

We need to talk.

A sudden jolt of happiness flowed through him, his eyes suddenly wide open, he didn't hesitate to hit 'call'. Feeling the warmth of her voice on the other end, it took a minute to realize that she was pissed off.

"Why are hanging around with my *sister*?" She finished the sentence as if talking about a rampant disease, rather than a family member and Chase felt defensive at not only his actions but also on Kelsey's behalf.

"What?"

"I know you guys are spending time together and I don't like it," She was breathless, apparently walking, he could hear the anger in her voice. "She fucking 17 Chase, what are you doing?

"Nothing," his voice immediately sounded defensive. "Was this Audrey, cause-

"It wasn't Audrey, you know I don't talk to Audrey," Maggie snapped and a loud honking in the background, along with voices and music flowing together only made him relieved to be somewhere quiet that night. "Everyone in Hennessey is telling my mom how Kelsey is always hanging around 'that married Jacobs' boy. One woman called mom tonight and said not to be surprised if Kelsey came home pregnant."

"Well if she does, it wouldn't be because of me," Chase insisted, having a flash of his earlier fantasies in the shower and quickly pushed them from his mind. "Come on, Maggie. You know me better than that, I'm not doing anything with your sister."

"Then why is she suddenly hanging around you?"

He didn't know how to reply truthfully. He hesitated, which seemed to increase Maggie's suspicions.

"*Seventeen*, Chase and barely that," Maggie snapped.

"I didn't touch her," Chase insisted. "Look, she started to come around the gym, I think she's just a lonely kid, it's nothing." He hurriedly explained.

"A horny kid is more like it," Maggie snapped. "Keep away from her, Chase. She's trouble."

The call ended. Chase felt a chill cover his body and as he sat the phone down.

CHAPTER TWENTY-NINE

Chase could only remember going to the reserve once when he was 7 or 8. His father insisted that it was 'nowhere for a child'; the very provocation Louise Jacobs needed to break out into a fury. This was frequent when he was a kid, hardly the demure and comforting woman she was with her grandchildren, her anger was like a volcano that would quickly explode at the drop of a hat.

"You are ashamed of me and where I come from!" She shouted, while Carl Jacobs automatically pulled back and fell silent but Chase's mother was only getting warmed up. Her eyes grew small as her face tightened into a chilling frown, causing her youngest child to hide under the table while Angel stood in the doorway with tears in her eyes. "You think we're all trash, a bunch of dirty Indians with no morals, just animals!"

Their father would never fight back no matter how insane their mother became. He would instead sit in silence, causing her anger to peak until she either threw things against the wall or fell into a heap on the floor, tears flooding her eyes.

Chase wasn't sure which scared him the most.

The next day as they drove into the secluded area, Chase began to understand his father's reluctance. Discovering generic versions of their own house, he immediately noticed one with a portion of the roof caved in and yet, didn't he see young faces looking out the window? Did people live in that house? He remembered feeling sad and frightened at the same time. Why didn't they live in nice homes like him? Why did a few of the houses have broken windows with discolored plastic replacing a portion of the missing glass? Weren't they cold? How did it happen? Why didn't they replace the windows? He wanted to ask his mother but remembered how angry she got when his dad brought up the topic the previous night and so remained silent.

Stopping in front of a small house, faint yellow in color, Chase noted that the grass was much too long in the yard, a few wildflowers growing in the midst, almost as if attempting to rise above the blade of dry sprigs of grass that smothered them. He wondered why they didn't cut their lawn and try to make it nice like people in his own neighborhood. Maybe their lawnmower was broken, he decided.

In silence, he followed his mother out of the car and up the short step that looked to be roughly painted an unflattering shade of brown and chipping off, he ran his fingers over the paint and dry pieces broke up beneath them, falling to the ground. Just then, the door flew open and an overweight woman with glasses and long, straight hair appeared, her face had a gleeful smile; she didn't hesitate to reach out and pull Louise Jacobs into a hug, giving her a quick kiss on the cheek.

Her eyes quickly caught sight of Chase, who nervously fidgeted, unsure of how to react but feeling some comfort by the stranger. "Is this your boy?" The woman asked, her tone gleeful, excited as her eyes ran over him. His mother turned, wiping away a tear, she nodded and smiled. The stranger gave a warm smile and leaned forward. "Such a handsome little boy!"

She ushered them both into the house, Chase immediately recognized the smell of toast, his eyes glancing to the right. An older boy sat in small room off of the kitchen - what appeared to be a combination of a bedroom and living room together - he glanced at Chase, appearing indifferent to their arrival, he stuffed some toast in his mouth and returned his attention to a small television set in the corner, a morning talk show was barely audible.

Sitting with his mom at the kitchen table, Chase remained silent as the two woman started to talk about how long it was since they saw one another, apparently they had been childhood friends and lost touch through the years. Glancing around the small kitchen, that barely allowed enough room for a table and three chairs, he noted that it was cluttered, the cupboards full of containers and clean dishes piled to one side, as if there weren't enough room to put them away. Then again, upon glancing at the limited doors on both the top and bottom, perhaps there wasn't room.

The floor was badly broken up, missing tiles were obvious next to the shiny, gleaming white vinyl squares that were left behind. The entire room was remarkably clean despite the compact area that hardly allowed his mom's friend - he thought her name was Mary - room to move in the kitchen, searching the cupboard for a 'treat for the boy', despite his mother's insistence that Chase was 'fine.' In silence, he watched her pull open doors that displayed generic foods, mostly mac and cheese and various noodles that his own mother often referred to as 'garbage' when Chase asked for them at the grocery store. He wondered why her friend thought this food was okay? Was his mother wrong?

He noted her face was solemn as she again insisted, 'Chase is fine, right honey?'

Chase nodded but reluctantly asked for a glass of water. His mother frowned and he wasn't sure why but Mary seemed unaffected by his request, almost joyful as she pulled out a bottle from the fridge and poured a glass. She passed it to him and Chase noted how kind her eyes were, a huge smile covered her face and he felt at ease. "I got some yesterday at the store." She seemed to be assuring Louise Jacobs. "If nothing else, I always make sure we have lots of clean water."

Suddenly feeling comfortable with the nice lady, his shyness momentarily disappeared, 'How come you don't use the tap like we do?" he gestured toward the nearby sink. Immediately, he sensed that he asked something bad, as his mother's eyes swooped down on him like a fierce storm while Mary appeared unaffected.

"Our water isn't good here, Chase," She calmly answered his question. "We have to buy it in the store."

"Oh," he replied and although he wanted to ask why he could tell by his mother's stone face reaction that he somehow stepped out of bounds. "Okay."

His mother's mood seemed to lighten when Mary offered kind words to describe Chase and for a few brief moments, he secretly wished that *she* was his mother. He didn't care if her home was kind of small and needed stuff fixed, he liked her and she was kind. Glancing toward the living room again, he noted that the older kid was watching him, his disposition was one of despair as he slumped over a pillow.

It wasn't until they got back in the car later and started to leave, that his mother yelled at him. "Mary is poor, Chase, couldn't you see that?" Her words were ice cold, like a shard of glass that ran through is veins, he didn't reply. "How could you be so stupid? They can't afford water for themselves, let alone us. I told you before we left that I had some in the car if you needed it, why didn't you listen?"

He couldn't remember her telling him that there was water in the car. Mary didn't seem angry, so he wasn't sure why it was such a big deal; but like his father, he decided to not say anything.

Chase grew up feeling dumb. He didn't do well in school and tended to daydream a lot, maybe that was because he wasn't smart enough to listen. Other kids did well; Angel excelled in school but Chase didn't understand a lot of things and sometimes, he didn't really care either. He hated history. Math was stupid. Other than gym class, it was pretty boring.

His parents had never seemed concerned with his grades, almost as if they expected him to not do well, his father praised him for excelling in sports, always a big kid, he was aggressive and intimidating. He often considered that was why he was so drawn to anything physical; his body always long, lean and strong. It was something that the world encouraged and so his marks, unfortunately, hadn't seemed quite so important.

Audrey always made him feel stupid. She laughed when he messed up something that he was apparently supposed to know; basic things in the news or in everyday life, things that often didn't really interest him.

"Good thing you're pretty," Audrey said gleefully as if he had nothing else to offer. "Cause you're not the brightest bulb on the tree."

Chase acted indifferently but deep down, it bothered him that he wasn't smart. For that reason, he started to make an effort to learn things. He would turn on the news, occasionally researching topics he didn't understand on the Internet or turned on documentaries while around the house. Still, he was self-conscious and sometimes felt that perhaps it was better to keep his mouth shut and make people wonder if he was stupid, rather than speaking and proving it to be true.

He often wondered if that was why Maggie stopped talking to him. Perhaps she hadn't realized how dumb he was until moving away, to a city full of intellects that could talk about more than a limited range of topics. In a way, he hoped that was the reason and not simply because she no longer cared for or had forgotten him. Although, now that there were so many rumors swirling around about him and Kelsey, chances were good that she would be happy to never speak to him again.

After their conversation, Chase sent Kelsey a brief text, explaining that he thought they should stop spending time together. He went on to tell her about the rumors and how it wasn't a good idea that they were seen together, that people were getting the wrong idea and that Maggie was upset. He chose his words carefully, concerned with hurting her feelings and his text was followed by silence. It was probably for the better anyway, he decided, she needed to find some people her own age to spend time with and she was constantly provoking his desires, something he wasn't exactly proud of and it was about time he stopped sexualizing her, even if it were just in fantasies.

But it wasn't that easy. His dreams that night were full Kelsey and they were anything but innocent, almost as if his subconscious was working against him every step of the way; taunting and seducing him into a place that was wrong, regardless of the escalated ecstasy he felt in his dream life.

He woke up hard and to the sound of a screaming baby.

Pushing her out of his mind, the day had gone pretty smoothly until she showed up at the door later that afternoon, as if nothing had happened. For a moment, he wondered if the text went through but she quickly assured him that it, in fact, had.

"Why are you letting people like Maggie and my mother scare you from being my friend?" She asked pointedly, throwing her bag on the floor. She wore a somewhat conservative blouse and jeans, much to his relief. "If you stop talking to me, then you're doing exactly what they want. Why don't you do what *you* want?"

"You really want me to answer that question?" Chase grunted as he picked up toys that Leland left everywhere earlier that day. The child was a little daredevil and seemed to go in circles all day, while the babies cried for attention, food, changing, love; it never seemed to end. As much as he hated to admit it, he enjoyed having Kelsey around, she always seemed to lift his day and perhaps she was right; was he just worrying about what others thought?

"See, I knew you wanted me," Kelsey said with self-satisfaction in her voice as she collapsed on the couch, leaning over and watching Chase cleaning up the room. All the children were taking a nap. "You want me naked, on top of you, just like that Betsy chick in that movie you did."

The visual wasn't something he welcomed but it took over his imagination and he felt his face turning red.

"I knew it!' She spoke jovially and sat upright. "That's why you're so upset by what Maggie said, cause you have a guilty conscience. You want to fuck me raw and you know it!"

"Kelsey, I-

The door opened and Chase immediately felt his heart race as he glanced out the window. At least Audrey's car wasn't home but instead it was his mother, who walked in without knocking and immediately frowned when she saw Kelsey on the couch.

"Who is that?" She nodded toward the teenage girl who watched her with big eyes. "Chase, what are you doing with this child?"

"I'm not a child!" Kelsey spoke defiantly and Chase gave her a look.

"She helps me out after school," Chase replied and shot Kelsey a warning look, something she surprisedly upheld to with a nod. "She just got here."

"Well, she's not much help to you if she's sitting on your couch, is she?" His mother shot Kelsey another cold glare as she headed for the stairs. The rebellious side of him glanced at Kelsey and felt temptation build in him, suddenly fighting an urge to pull her into another room and succumb to his desires, as his mother went to tend to the children. Almost as if she were reading his mind, she flashed him a smile and raised an eyebrow. He stood in the middle of the living room, if even for the briefest moment, considering the possibility. In his mind, counting how many days she was from turning 18.

She stood up and started to approach him when the door opened again and Flora walked in. Ignoring Kelsey all together, she focused on Chase and seemed unaware of any sexual tension in the room, she excitedly told him about her niece from Vancouver coming to visit the next day. Kelsey appeared deflated, hunched over, she wandered over to pick up her bag and silently walk out while Flora continued to brag up her niece, apparently, a doctor who she hadn't seen in years. She seemed unaware or unconcerned that Kelsey left while Chase felt his heart drop.

She was also the 'dumb kid' that no one took seriously.

Chapter Thirty

Chase was different. He never looked at her like she was a piece of trash like the kids at school did, but like she was an actual human being.

It was interesting to Kelsey how a girl was all sugar and spice; you know, until they're a teenager and suddenly on the cusp of womanhood and therefore no longer pure and cute in anyone's eyes. You were no one's doll when you turned 12, just another awkward teenager that they didn't want to deal with. No one wanted to hear or see you.

Unless your name was Maggie.

Kelsey's older sister was a princess. A big, perfect, lesbian princess. Her marks were ideal. She wasn't chasing after boys, so she couldn't get pregnant; and really, wasn't that all mothers cared about, that their daughter didn't embarrass them by getting knocked up in high school? How many times had their mother yelled at her that she 'better not come home pregnant'; a speech that wasn't ever used on Maggie, even though she use to screw that Todd guy, back when she was 'straight.' Even then, their mother assumed that Maggie was being a 'good girl' and keeping her legs together while Kelsey was the wild one, out getting laid every weekend.

Well, she kind of was, but not before her mother started to suggest it. At that point, what did it matter anyway? Hey, if you're being accused of it, you may as well do it, right? Exactly.

So she started to experiment with boys and it was okay. Honestly, she didn't regret it. At first, maybe a little bit, but that was more cause she was scared of rumors starting at school, but not really, you know? It was that she couldn't quite understand what the big deal was about cause if she wasn't meant to do it, then why did she *want* to do it? That didn't make sense.

So that was that. She went out and had her fun and Maggie, being a stick in the mud, did everything to eliminate her fun. She was like the chastity police; always on duty, not getting it from some chick, so she had to stick her nose in Kelsey's life. But what else was new? You can't be mom's favorite if you aren't being a narc.

It was the time that she found Maggie snooping through her room that really pissed her off. Supposedly for her own good, she claimed to think that Kelsey was 'on' drugs. Who the fuck is 'on' drugs in Hennessey? People experimented with drugs; smoked some weed or popped a pill or two to relax but it was nothing. No one that she knew was a crazed drug user, shooting up in the lame ass, downtown Hennessey, offering to suck off someone for their next hit. Kelsey pointed this out to her sister that she wasn't a cop *yet* and real cops didn't search your room on a 'hunch'. Then she threw her math book at her, hitting Maggie on the shoulder. Of course, she went crying to their mom and Kelsey was the one who got in trouble.

Please! People shoot people for going on their property, I just hit her with a book.

It pissed her off that Maggie was such an uptight bitch. Of course, that's what men wanted, right? The ones that pretended to be so perfect and virginal, even though it was almost *never* true. Those bitches were the worse; her sister was the queen of them all. *Cow.*

Anyway, she turned out to be the cock block when Kelsey was trying to get to Chase. Even back in the day, when she would try to get his attention when he dropped in for a visit or whatever but he never saw past Maggie. Like everyone else, she had him fooled into believing she was all that, wrapping him around her finger; being the cock tease, wearing her tight little shirts to go see him; like seriously, what lesbian does that? Not for boys, they don't.

It was the day Kelsey tried to get in the bar and Chase laughed that broke her heart. She acted cool and stuff but when she got back home, she cried. Like, she cried a *lot* because he thought she was a dumb kid. It was humiliating and actually, at that point, she kind of hated him.

Her anger grew when she realized that he was like everyone else but for some reason, it bothered Kelsey more that he felt that way. She became a little obsessed with it actually and went to see Bud and asked if she could get a job at the bar.

Bud took her seriously and gently informed her that she was too young. Not that he was the moral police, he quickly explained, but there was laws blah blah and of course, the fact that her stupid sister worked there didn't help. She explained to him that she wasn't exactly some moronic kid even if Maggie and Chase thought so.

"Oh, you know Chase too?" Bud asked in a kind, almost soothing voice.

"Yes, he's all in love with my sister," Kelsey spoke cooly, rolling her eyes and glancing around the room. "I mean, she's obviously not into him cause the lesbian thing, but he's in love with her. She snaps her fingers and he runs."

Bud nodded, slowly agreeing with her, which was kind of surprising. Most people told her that she was stupid or didn't understand but he sincerely agreed with her words and recognizing her audience, she continued.

"And like, he's so hot, he could have any girl but he's married to some cow and horny for my uptight, lesbian sister," she rolled her eyes again and noticed Bud giving her a sympathetic smile, as she sat further back in the chair, suddenly quite comfortable and enjoying their talk. "Guys are so weird sometimes."

"They can be, little lady, you got that right," he rocked in his chair and seemed to take her in. "You know, I suspect that maybe you got yourself a little crush on Chase."

Kelsey blushed and shrugged.

"You know, I think you have to find a way to get his attention and separate yourself from Maggie. I think once he sees you as your own person, he will see what a honey you are," he gestured toward the door as if to indicate Chase were on the other side. He wasn't though, it was his night off. Probably home banging that crabby thing he married.

Still, she was intrigued by Bud's words. He was smarter than expected and tilted her head, inspecting his eyes. "How?"

That's where the porn conversation started. He showed Kelsey the video and although she was slightly embarrassed to watch the smidgen of it in front of Bud, she was a little intrigued when he told her who the star was behind the camera. She knew it was him too. She knew it was his voice.

She tried to act cool, like it wasn't a bit arousing, asking how long this was going on.

"Not long," Bud turned the monitor off. "Just done a couple but it's a secret, so you can't tell."

"I won't," Kelsey assured him.

"I'm trusting you," Bud reminded her.

"I promise."

"I'm gonna send you this video to watch at home and if you think that doing something like this would be of interest to you," He started to type on his computer. "Let me know and we will hook you up."

She was uncertain. Porn was pretty sketchy but if she got to do it with Chase, he would have to see her as an adult. He would have to take her seriously. Still, it seemed kind of extreme and sure, she liked Bud but the suggestion of 'auditioning' for him felt kind of weird.

Still, she was relieved when she got home and discovered the house was empty. She rushed up to her room and quickly turned on her laptop. Turning on the video, she felt that familiar heat between her legs that only increased as she watched the chick grinding Chase until he grabbed her by the ass and seemed to push her even further down on his dick, as things ended on a triumphant note.

She wanted him so bad. She was going to show him she was no child and could do things with him that Maggie wouldn't.

She called Bud the next day.

Unfortunately, before she could get to Chase, there were a couple of auditions that she wasn't crazy about but wasn't that part of the deal? It only made sense that she had to prove she wasn't some inexperienced amateur who wouldn't be able to perform on camera. Both the videos were her 'interview' and then, it was a matter of waiting to get to Chase. At first, it seemed to take forever and so, she feared they had only fed her a line. But the day finally did arrive and she was nervous and excited at the same time.

Of course, it didn't play out like she had thought. Defeated, naked in front of Chase, she had never been so humiliated in her life. She quickly realized - or thought she realized - that he was like everyone else. He thought she was a loser too. She hadn't meant to cry but wasn't able to stop herself when he demanded she get dressed and that he had no interest in hooking up with her.

It wasn't until he took her out of there, after threatening Bud, that she realized that he cared and cared a lot. She was stunned when he grabbed Bud by the throat and for a split second, she feared he was going to literally kill the man. Frozen on the opposite side of the room, she felt guilt that it was her that instigated this situation. Every muscle in his upper body seemed to bulge out, just the Hulk, she was expecting for his shirt to start ripping open and for him to tear Bud in half; no one had ever stood up for her before and definitely not with so much passion. Never.

Still, there was that fear that he was, once again, doing something to help Maggie and not her. However, their relationship grew since that day. He actually listened to her when she talked and didn't treat her like a fuck up. He didn't put her down, despite what he knew about her; the dirtiest thing she had ever done with both Bud and that other guy, he didn't judge. He was protective of her in a way that no one else was; not her family or friends. The others only scolded her but they didn't really seem to be doing it *for* her, but rather, because they thought she was too fucking stupid to figure things out on her own.

He respected her. He talked to her. They were friends.

And she knew he wanted her. He didn't say it but he didn't have to; he looked at her how he used to sometimes look at Maggie. His eyes would scan her body, even though he pretended to not notice what she was wearing, he always did. He had this ridiculous fear of being with a minor, something Chase was obsessed with as if age was anything more than a number. She wasn't 12, she was 17. Why was eighteen such a magical number anyway? Technically, she was only a couple years younger than Chase.

She totally loved him. He was so handsome, so cool and caring. He looked after his kids, something that her own father hadn't even done;

still wasn't doing, unless you count the fact that Maggie stays with him and truthfully, Kelsey didn't count that at all. Chase was a good guy, her hero who swooped in and threatened someone's life over her. Over *her*!! No one ever gave a fuck about her ever before and now he did.

But some stupid nosey cows were talking about them hanging out and her mom was all in her face about it.

Don't come home pregnant. Keep away from Chase Jacobs, he's a married man. He shouldn't be hanging around teenage girls. What's wrong with him? He has a lovely wife and three kids, that's not enough for him?

She heard it all before. It didn't matter if she attempted to explain that they were *just* friends, everyone seemed to think it was impossible that either of them could keep their hands off one another; her cause they thought she was a slut, him because he had a nice body and well, there were rumours about him and other women. If they were true, he obviously wasn't happy with this Audrey cow. It seemed unreal to her that he ever hooked up with someone so gross in the first place, but then again, her own track record wasn't so great either. Everyone did stupid things sometimes. She assumed he got married cause of the kids. At least he was a good guy that way.

Chase was her only real friend. He was the only person that made her feel like she mattered. Everyone else overlooked or insulted her; something that was apparently acceptable to do if you were 'just a kid'. How did that make it okay?

It wasn't because she was horny for him; although that definitely factored in and it wasn't because he was so hot, with his buzzed hair and just enough facial hair to be sexy and his dark eyes that were almost black. She loved how he smelled when he was near, how he would smile and tease her sometimes, but most of all, she loved how he listened to her. He listened when she complained about her mom or school, life, whatever was on her mind. And it wasn't just that he listened, but that he gave her his full attention. Like, the eye contact and everything. He alway replied to her text message and sent her little smiley faces. She sent him hearts.

But sometimes it hurt. Like days when she tried to talk to him and everyone interrupted and treated her like she was trash that wandered in. Women were the worst too. Men never made her feel as trashy as other women. She could fuck every guy in the community and it would be the other women that would make her feel like a whore bag, not the men. Men just got *it*. Women got off on belittling one another; either to their face or behind their backs, it was always the same. Her mom did it all the time to her face and behind her friend's backs. They thought it was okay but it wasn't.

You know, all these stupid talk shows act as if women should support and respect one another, idealizing their bodies 'no matter what their shape' (which was a nice way of saying 'if your fat' cause no one encouraged women with perfect Barbie doll figures to love their body; then they're 'too skinny') and yet, it was bullshit. Women hated one another. They didn't want to see the chick next door get the hot boy, have nice tits or have it all. Everyone nodded and smiled in the right places but that's cause that's where they are told to nod and smile; not cause they really believe it. Fucking bitches.

It wasn't that she hated other women, it was the fact that they hated her. Kelsey used to hate herself too until she realized that's what they wanted, then she stopped and started taking what she wanted.

And now, she wanted Chase. She loved him and knew that he deep down, he cared. And well, that was more than anyone else had to offer in this lonely life. One day he would love her too. She knew it.

CHAPTER THIRTY-ONE

It was difficult to be angry at the world when he looked in his children's eyes. They were so small, so vulnerable and yet, when they cried, their presence became undeniable and strong; a force that erupted like a volcano at the slightest touch. They needed him in a way that no one ever had and possibly, ever would and he was intensely aware of that fact. Always fearing that he would do something wrong, he often wondered if other parents felt the same way.

Yet at the same time, he was isolated from the world. He certainly had no one else to talk to about his concerns. Mothers in the neighborhood weren't interested in stopping by; they had when Audrey was home alone with the kids. For some reason, a father was different. It was almost as if the world thought that he was destined to do a horrible job, yet no one wanted to help out but rather stand back and watch, almost waiting for him to fail. It was a bit stressful and made him nervous whenever he went out in public with the kids.

Audrey took the children all out at once, he assumed because she loved the attention from other mothers as if she were a saint that should be honored for monitoring them all at the same time. He thought it was kind of ironic and idiotic at the same time. Ironic, since she barely watched them at home, when no one's interested eyes were on her and idiotic because it was too much to have three young children out by yourself. Why not take turns and allow his mother or Flora to babysit the other two? It also gave focus to one child, making them feel special rather than a part of a herd; and didn't everyone want to feel special?

He learned that not from a podcast or one of his online gurus that he regularly listened to but from a daytime talk show. Audrey would laugh but he enjoyed his one program in the early afternoon; it was upbeat and fun, the pretty and confident host discussing rather ordinary topics but making them interesting. He could've listened to her talking about toothpicks all afternoon and enjoy her. It caused him to wonder what made some people so charismatic and others so bland in comparison. Was he charismatic? Judging by how few people were in his life or even seemed interested in talking to him, he kind of doubted it. But how did you become charismatic?

His favorite television host talked about enjoying life and being bold, living in the moment and appreciating the small things. Although his enthusiasm was strong, it was easier said than done, often more complex when trying to put it into practice. How did you tame all the voices of negativity that lurked in the background; the ones that told him he was stupid, that he fucked up his life, that no one cared?

He tried to create a more positive life in small ways. Helping the Filipino lady at the grocery store when she attempted to balance a baby and groceries while getting in her car. Carefully approaching her, he knew that a lot of people in town referred to her as the lady who 'married her way into Canada' and like him, had few friends. Having Leland with him probably made him seem less threatening, although her eyes were full of skepticism at first as he opened the trunk and placed her groceries inside, they were soon replaced with kindness and a compassion that he needed to fill his soul. He merely smiled as he walked away, knowing how it felt to be on the outside looking in, hoping that someone would give him the same compassion in return.

She was the only brown woman in town; unless you counted his mother. He didn't count his mother. She was part of the indigenous community from a couple hours away, therefore people weren't surprised by her presence. She wasn't a 'foreigner'; something the locals didn't appreciate in the least. They avoided the Filipino lady as if she had somehow squirmed her way into 'their' country as if she were a thief in the night.

It was for that reason that Chase was surprised to meet a young, Cambodian woman a few weeks later. He had woken in the middle of the night when car lights flashed in the living room window, momentarily making him believe that someone was in his own yard. Groggy, he slowly rose from the couch and made his way to the window to see a Jeep parked in Flora's driveway. After a slight commotion earlier that night, he was concerned that an unwanted visitor was returning again, perhaps in a different vehicle this time? It didn't make sense, but little does at 4 AM and so, he was hesitant to approach, but at the same time, felt it was necessary.

Shirtless, he stiffly headed out the door wearing only boxers, pulling on a pair of running shoes on the way. He wasn't sure what moron would be waiting for him but was too tired to care at that point. Having just settled Devin down after a long, explosive crying spell, he wasn't in the mood for any kind of trouble.

Rather than finding that pathetic little man returning, once again harassing Flora's niece, he was shocked to discover a young, Cambodian lady in the driver's seat. With tired eyes, she almost looked as alarmed to see him as he was to see her. Opening her window, she seemed unmoved by his puffed out chest and stern inquiries of who she was and why she was sitting in Flora's driveway. He was skeptical when she admitted to being 'the other niece, Vanessa' and almost as if used to it, she went on to explain that she was adopted and that the young lady he may have met earlier that night was her younger sister.

A 'city girl' for sure, she sat up very straight, her makeup and hair not out of place, her long sinewy arm casually stretching from the Jeep, reaching for her rearview mirror, she exchanged smiles with him while hers seemed to be an invitation waiting to be opened, he was hesitant to move. Unsure of what to say, he finally nodded and said, "Okay."

She was harmless enough, their flirtation seemed to wake him instantly, suddenly self-conscious of being half naked in the yard, Vanessa suggested he get in the Jeep.

"It's kind of cold out there." She commented as her window eased up and he climbed into the passenger side. He only meant to talk for a moment before going back inside but one thing quickly led to another and it was difficult to hide his attraction to someone when only wearing boxing shorts.

Her breath was quickly labored as she climbed on his lap, pulling up her skirt, she wasted no time straddling him. She smoothly pulled him inside her and he gasped as she tightened around him, almost making him lose it right away as she leaned back, her hand on the dash. Her eyes closed, Vanessa seemed to be lost while she let out small moans that quickly increased and became more powerful as she moved faster and Chase fought to not come too fast, desire building up so quickly that when she finally showed signs of orgasm, he wasted no time as she suddenly became an uncaged animal of lust, as she bounced roughly as if his dick were some unbreakable dildo unattached to a real person and in fact, when she finally opened her eyes, it was almost as if she had forgotten he was there.

It was weird.

Of course, like everything else in his life, it got weirder the next morning when he had to have coffee with Flora, who was insistent he 'come over and meet' her other niece. Of course, he and Vanessa played the role of strangers quite well; not that it was such a stretch considering they were pretty much unfamiliar to one another outside of their sexual encounter. He played along and it was awkward but Flora and her younger niece Natasha didn't seem to notice. For which, he was relieved.

Not that he had to contend with them long since the girls were gone almost as quickly as they had arrived. Fortunately, before that happened, he did have an opportunity to get to know Natasha a little better, something that he hadn't expected. Chase wasn't even sure where his courage came from that day when he saw Vanessa and Flora leave, knowing that the other niece was still in the house. Assuming that she wouldn't want to talk to him, he almost didn't go; even after he spotted her sitting outside alone, staring into space.

Something inside him coaxed Chase to go however, his legs felt heavy as they crossed the lawn, her eyes non-judgemental as he approached, he shyly asked to join her and assumed that she was just saying yes to be kind, until she offered him a beer which gave him a license to stay a little longer. The two of them ended up talking about everything; he found her surprisedly down to earth and compassionate.

Their talk lasted long into the afternoon until about the time that both Flora and Vanessa arrived home, followed by Audrey, as she flew in his driveway, her anger evident by her hostile driving alone. Seeing him with the beautiful young woman, actually enjoying his afternoon would push her over the edge. He decided to go home and face the music.

The screaming started immediately. They were barely in the door when Audrey pulled on her martyr costume and in front of the curious and frightened children, started to yell at him. Accusations of his infidelity came flowing out.

"I saw you last night."

She didn't have to say one more word. Nearby, Leland was watching them both curiously, a thumb stuck in his mouth, something he did when nervous. Chase wanted to rush over and comfort him. Audrey wasn't having it.

Grabbing his arm, she dug her nails into Chase as she pushed him back, her green eyes glaring as she hissed, "I saw you fucking that brown bitch last night. You fucking pig. Practically in our yard, for the entire neighborhood to see."

Chase struggled to be released from her grasp, his attention focused on Leland and the twins, who were now crying. Tension crawled through the back of his neck and he struggled to get away, accidentally pushing her at the same time. Falling back, she grabbed onto the couch for support, merely getting her bearings, she sprung ahead and attacked Chase. This time much more viscous than ever before, pure hatred filled her eyes as she pummelled his chest furious, like a caged animal that was released, as the children all screeched around them, he pushed her back and in the process, she almost fell on top of Chet.

"Get a hold of yourself, Audrey," He yelled, pulling Leland into his arms, the child quickly dug his face into Chase's neck, his eyes closed as he sobbed uncontrollably. "You're scaring the kids."

"Like you give a fuck about the kids!" She screamed, ripping Chet from his seat, fury continued to burn in her eyes and for a moment, he felt locked in fear; would she hurt the children? What was she going to do? His brain raced and something told him he had to stop this insanity. He couldn't ignore it any longer.

"Audrey, please," He spoke calmly, as Leland clasped onto him as tightly as possible, his body tense and Chase suddenly felt powerless, unable to fight anymore. A peacefulness filled the room, a light switch seemed to go off in Audrey's head, as if suddenly aware of what she was doing, tears filled her eyes and she collapsed on the floor with the baby in her arms.

"Audrey, I-

"I want you to leave Chase," She shook hard as she cried, the first tears he had seen from her in years, if ever. She completely fell apart at the seams and crumbled before his eyes; they all did. The babies were crying, she was crying as he stood helplessly, racking his brain but was unsure of what to say. Finally considering her request, he nodded his head.

"OK," Chase felt the tension lower in the room. "If that's what you want-

"It's what I want," Audrey spoke calmly, now comforting her children. "This was a mistake. It was a mistake. You and me, I was wrong. I was *so* wrong. I can't make you love me and this isn't...we can't do this..."

It was the most rational thing she had ever said.

"But the kids," Chase heard himself saying as the entire room seemed to slowly calm, return to normal.

"I can deal with the kids," Audrey replied calmly. "I have family. Your mom is always around. I have more people than most mothers do to help me and of course, you too. I just don't think you should be living here."

"I'm not saying you should leave right now," she continued. "But soon as you can figure things out."

And that was it. Their routine was the same that night and Audrey insisted she had to get out of the house. Preparing a bath, she put on some makeup and after a short visit to Flora's house announced the two were going out for a late dinner.

The atmosphere changed that night. No longer tense, anger disappeared, a huge weight removed from his chest. Even the children were calmer, sleeping through the night, with not even a cry till the next morning. Everything felt different and although he didn't know what was next, Chase knew that things were about to change drastically. He was about to get his life back and in fairness, so was Audrey. They were poison together and the agreement to end their marriage seemed to be the antidote. It was as if a light suddenly took over the house, their relationship different, expectations now lost and an unexpected friendship formed. It was chaste and would never lead to another relationship, but it was mutual, respectful, if not unexpected.

It was a few weeks later when he learned about Flora's niece Natasha. His heart broke with the news. He would always remember her, though; she was the woman that inspired change in his life and yet, she probably had no idea of the impact she had on him. With courage in his heart, his life was about to switch gears and he didn't even see it coming.

CHAPTER THIRTY-TWO

Change can be exciting but it also can be as scary. The unknown is a world that we're scared to enter, yet it's not as frightening as monotony. It's difficult to find the right balance and at that point, Chase would've welcomed any stability in his life. Upon the end of his relationship with Audrey, the two of them looking into the easiest and cheapest way to obtain a divorce even though they still resided under the same roof. Jobless, Chase felt as though his options were limited and his anxieties set in, keeping him awake at night while the rest of the house slept soundly.

Jobs were becoming few and far between. The only positive was that the bar scene was picking up as the summer drummed on and Chase found some casual, part-time doorman positions, but for the most part, employment was drying up in the years since he left high school. At the time, overwhelmed with work, especially when most people his age left town in droves, they were now returning with the big city job market tightening up. The economy was the shits and people were grabbing the first jobs they could find, despite their education and goals.

Lucy and 'Lucky Luke' were two of those people. The pair returned to town and moved in with Lucy's parents.

Not that Chase wished her to be unhappy, but it was a nice change of pace to see things come full circle and perhaps it healed an old wound in him. He could finally put his 18-year-old insecurities aside, now recognizing that he probably lucked out when she left him; for Lucy was now doing little more than partying every night and sleeping every day. Hardly a rock star, she attempted to maintain the lifestyle, much of which occurred at Bud's bar from what the rumor mill (that being Kelsey) told him. It wasn't an appealing picture, but if she was like most people he used to see at the bar on a daily basis, Lucy was apparently fighting demons that were deeply hidden inside of her. Chase often wondered about her relationship with Bud and in light of the kind of projects he worked on the side, wondered if he managed to recruit her as well? It was a scary thought.

Kelsey was a constant. Having finished high school, she was now babysitting for a few families in town. She seemed like an unexpected choice to look after children but apparently her experience was vast since she was thirteen. Kelsey had a reputation for remaining calm when dealing with kids, always making them laugh and having fun, therefore providing a valuable service to local parents. Even Audrey had been talking about hiring her a few days a week to help out once Chase found a day job.

Chase really hoped to be gone by then. Where he could afford to go was a looming question. Raising three children was hardly cheap and even though Audrey was looking to get her foot in the door with a government job, she still wasn't quite qualified and found it difficult to study around her work schedule and time with the children. There weren't enough hours in the day for her and yet, for Chase, there were sometimes too many.

As the hot summer raged on, Kelsey dropped by the house wearing as few clothes as possible, leaving little to the imagination, she was hardly shy in letting him know that the countdown to her 18th birthday was on. In a few short months, she insisted he would have no more excuses to turn down her advances; something that was getting tempting as the rest of his life started to fall apart. He was much too busy thinking about where he would go and what he would do at that point, to even consider the possibility of fulfilling his promise. However, it was the day that he commented on this out loud that he surprised himself as much as Kelsey.

"I may not even be here by then," he confessed to her as the children calmly took part in their own separate activities in the living room. The twins played with some blocks while Leland experimented with a toy that made barnyard noises with each touch. Chase was relieved to sit down.

"What do you mean? Where the hell are you going?" Kelsey asked defiantly, unconcerned that children were nearby; not that they hadn't heard foul language from Audrey many times over. "Can I come?"

"I don't even know what I'm doing yet, I can't look after you too," Chase commented, his eyes scanning the carpet for broken cookies or crackers; they had just dealt with a mouse issue the previous month and he had since become very alert to anything that might invite rodents in.

"You don't have to *look after* me," Kelsey sternly commented, sitting up a little taller. Today she was wearing a tank top, rolled up to show her stomach and a pair of denim shorts that could've been a little longer. "I'm an adult woman, despite what you or everyone else thinks. When Saint Maggie was my age, no one ever felt like they had to look after her."

"Cool your heels," Chase calmly replied, his hand shooting up to indicate she stop. "I'm not suggesting that you need a babysitter but I would be a bit worried about you, just as I would've been with Maggie at the time, believe it or not." Hesitating for a moment, he continued. "Kelsey, you are very bold sometimes and I'm worried that might get you in trouble in the wrong situation."

"I can handle myself," She blushed and he quickly realized that Kelsey probably assumed he was referencing her attempt to make a film with him a year earlier. "Sometimes being bold pays off, it's not necessarily a bad thing, is it?"

"You got me there," Chase replied and relaxed in his chair, an old Lazy Boy inherited from one of Audrey's relatives. "Maybe I need some of that boldness to get a job."

"What about the bar downtown?"

"It's only casual, a few shifts here and there," Chase replied. "Not great and I keep looking, but I don't know what I'm going to do."

"Is that why you are thinking about moving?"

"I may not have a choice. I can't stay here," He waved his hand around the room. "Audrey said it was okay for a while but do you really think I want to be here much longer?"

"Take me with you."

"Kelsey, I-

"Take me with you!" her words were stronger, this time, sounding much more like a demand than a suggestion. "I want to go somewhere. I want to live. I can't live while I'm here. I'm suffocating in that house with my mother. I'm suffocating in this town."

"Kelsey, I-

"Will you stop that!" She leaned in, her hands on each side of the chair, caging him in. The scent of perfume filled his lungs, desire flowing through him in a way he couldn't easily deny as he stared into her eyes; a deep blue that was completely unlike her sister's, who were always guarded, while Kelsey's eyes were full of warmth and curiosity, a warmth and peacefulness flowed through her face. "I want to go. I'm an adult now, whether or not you want to see me that way. I want to leave Hennessey."

"Ok, but that doesn't mean it should be with me," Chase attempted to explain, although he wasn't really sure where his objections came from, other than his own strong temptations. Perhaps it was the warning from Maggie months earlier to stay away from her that still lurked in the back of his mind. It was odd that he would even consider it, though, considering that his former best friend barely talked to him now. Their conversations were limited to idle gossip, a mere glimpse into her life, he really had no idea who she was anymore. Other than a day job at an office a receptionist and some other project on the side, she continued to take courses and strive to join the RCMP; her attempts slightly futile but she never really explained why that was, merely suggesting that she hadn't made it yet. He often wondered if she would even tell him the news when she was accepted.

"But why not?" Kelsey replied, once again standing over him, her arms crossed in front of her chest. "Cause Maggie won't let you?"

"I didn't say that."

"Cause you don't like me?"

"I didn't say that either."

"Cause maybe you like me a little too much?"

He didn't reply.

"That's what I thought," Kelsey returned to her original seat across the room. Patting Leland's blond head on the way by. "Chase I'm not that kid from Bud's office. I feel like you'll always see me that way and sometimes see yourself as a pedophile if you give into what you want but I'm here to tell you that I've been good. I've waited for you, I've been patient and now I'm almost 18, so what's the problem? Are you worried about what people will think? Audrey? My mom? *Your* mom? Maggie?"

In truth, she was right. He wondered how it would look if he were suddenly to move with Kelsey Telips. He knew Audrey would be indifferent; already assuming the two were hooking up in secret, while her mother hated Kelsey almost as much as Ellen Telips hated him. Maggie assumed he was looking for her in another woman and although that had crossed his mind in the early days, he now saw them as two, very distinct people. They couldn't have been more different. So what *was* his problem? Did he simply fear what others thought? But would anyone ever approve of any decision he made? It sometimes seemed unlikely. Lately, everyone was the expert on what he should do with his life; going back to school to take trades or study professions that 'paid well' or doing manual labor that would pay well short term. Nothing really seemed like the right fit.

"To a degree," Chase admitted and wasn't sure how to explain it. Even though she was almost legal age, something still felt wrong about having any kind of relationship with her, let alone moving with her. Maybe he sought his freedom more than anything. Maybe he didn't want anyone around. "I don't know, Kelsey. I don't know how to answer your question."

"You can't because there's no answer," She replied glumly and left shortly after, leaving him only with his thoughts.

The truth was that he was scared and didn't know what to do next. Anything that complicated his situation further was too overwhelming for him; he had to think of his kids, was it best to leave them in order to earn a pay cheque or should he be closer at hand, instead finding work in Hennessey? Should he go back to school? If so, what was he supposed to take?

The truth was that he was left with nothing. What inspired him? What could he see himself doing in the future? Had he ever really loved his past jobs or the idea of them more, than the actual work itself? There were just too many questions and not enough answers. Maybe he didn't fit in anywhere.

It wasn't until he confessed this feeling to Maggie later on, in a series of texts that he felt some sense of inspiration and comfort. Although he was quick to point out that she was lucky because she knew what she wanted to do, Maggie was quick to point out that wanting something and finding a way to get it was two very different things. Lately, she had been asking herself why being an RCMP officer appealed to her so much? Was it the money? The status? Did she really want to help people or was it more out of the idea of what she thought an RCMP was or what they did? When she heard news stories about officers being in some dicey situations - some of which not surviving - she often had to ask herself a lot of serious questions and like Chase, she didn't have the answer.

We're all in the same boat.

Her text was short but powerful in meaning.

It wasn't until a few days later after he put his true fears and concerns out to sit in silence, that a possible glimmer of hope arose and gave him something to consider. It was a late night text, one he wouldn't see until the next morning that grasps Chases' attention and peaked his curiosity.

Would you consider moving? I might have something for you.

Yes.

CHAPTER THIRTY-THREE

The 'yes' was probably a tad too abrupt; logically it made no sense to move away to more insecurities and fears, unsure if he would do any better in another place. Even though the city had more possibilities, it also had more people competing for the same jobs. Plus he had kids to think about; would it really be a good idea to move away with three small children left behind? Leland, Chet, and Devin were so young; would they even remember him if he was gone for too long.

It somehow felt like the wrong thing to do but then again, he had no income. Other locals did it; both men and women went away to work and returned on occasion. In fact, from what Chase understood, this was becoming normal in different parts of the Canada. People were uprooting for work because they had no other options. Neither did he.

Maggie was vague about the job she had in mind for him but he got the impression it would be as a doorman. That didn't sound like it would provide much of an income but Maggie insisted that there was more to it than what he did for Bud. However, she wouldn't provide many details through her text messages. He wasn't sure if there was a reason or simply because she was too busy. He understood that she worked two jobs; one as a receptionist and another, more mysterious position that she never had fully explained.

When she finally did call, their conversation was brief and straight to the point.

"I talked to my boss and she wants to meet you."

Overwhelmed by the mere fact that she was actually talking to him again - something she hadn't done since learning about his friendship with Kelsey - Chase opened his lips to respond but couldn't talk. He felt like there was so much to say and yet, where did he start? He still felt as if their old business was sitting like an elephant in the room and before they could return to their former friendship, he had to address it. There were so many things he had to tell her, wanted to tell her and yet, she was very businesslike and appeared uninterested in talking about anything other than the opportunity that she was presenting him.

"Maggie, I think we should talk about-

"She wants to meet you in person but said if that's not possible that you can through Skype, but I would think it would make more sense to come here," her words were full of confidence, yet there was a chill they sent through him, as though he were merely a stranger and she was the secretary setting up the appointment. Maybe, he decided, it was simply because of her daytime job that she had automatically taken this particular tone, one that was crisp, cold and direct. "You wouldn't have to stay long, just do the interview and go back home or you could crash at my place for the night if you want."

Her offer fell flat; emotionless and raw, hardly an old friend excited to see her former best friend but more like a relative, you felt obligated to put up for the night. It was a sharp dagger through the heart but the final in a series until he accepted the reality of this situation. Their friendship was a mere formality, a connection from the past and nothing more; then again, would that change when they finally were faced to face?

"Nah, that's good, I can go for the day," he replied, feeling that it was probably a relief to her to not have to deal with him beyond the short period it would take to introduce him to her boss.

"So, what is this for again?" he decided it was best to stay away from the topic of them being reunited since it clearly was beating a dead horse and instead challenged the idea of this job being feasible. "I don't really understand. Can I look up this club online so I have a better idea?"

"It's not really online," She replied, the sounds of traffic flowing behind her. "It's kind of more of an exclusive club, not where skanks go to on a Saturday night."

"Oh."

"You'll have to come on a Saturday since I won't be available to make the introductions during the week," Maggie muttered, appearing to jump past the first question, not really giving him much of an answer and for a second, he wondered if she was still on the phone. "Jolene already knows about you and said she trusts my judgment, so she'll meet you. Is this Saturday good for you?"

"Yes, but I-

"Great, try to get here early and maybe we can have lunch first," Maggie continued to speak to him like a stranger. "If not, that's fine too. I will see if we can have a meeting with her for 1."

And that was it. The conversation was over.

A text quickly followed.

Don't bring my sister with you.

Although he certainly hadn't planned on it, an indignant part of him had a flash of Kelsey on the passenger side of the car but he quickly brushed it aside. That could be more trouble than it was worth and he would be nervous enough without having to contend with her too. He decided not to mention it to anyone but Audrey.

Wrinkling her nose, something she did when unsure of what was being presented to her, she finally shrugged and didn't reply.

"You think it's a bad idea?"

"No, it just sounds like maybe the pay may not be proportional to the cost of living," Audrey sighed and spoke calmly, a new person since they decided to separate, their friendship was unexpected and pleasant. He felt like she was in his corner, something he never would've expected in the past. "But, it can't hurt to check it out."

"I'm not sure it's a great idea to move away with the kids."

"Lots of people do it, Chase." Her response surprised him and he nodded, realizing that maybe she was right. "I think it would make sense and as long as you help financially and come back to visit the kids."

Reluctantly, he agreed and stared at his hand.

"It's pretty nice that Maggie is trying to help."

"I guess."

Audrey didn't reply. Studying him carefully, she calmly took a drink of her coffee.

"She's not the same as she used to be."

"People change," Audrey replied.

"I guess the city changes people," Chase repeated the same words he had heard from his father many times. Hadn't he said that to Angel before she made the move for university? Now finished, she still lived and worked there. He thought it was interesting that in the whole time he considered this move, it never once occurred to him to reach out to her. In fact, after their father was buried, their phone conversations eased off until they became nonexistent. It was almost as if their father was her final tie to Hennessey and in a way, it was almost a relief to not pretend that there was a connection within the family.

"Life changes people," Audrey gently corrected him and he had no words.

Saturday morning came quickly and his actions that morning were automatic. He got up early, helped change and feed the kids and jumped in the shower. Late morning, Chase was on the highway, passing farmland that surrounded his town and although it was the main industry in the area, it was work that he swore he would never do. A brief stint working at a farm at 15 was enough to turn him off ever trying again. Maybe that was the snob in him coming out, at least that's what his father had suggested at the time, that Chase was too 'uppidity' to work manual labor but it his disdain for the work was immediate. It was grueling, unfulfilling and the people he worked with belittled him, taking advantage of his youthful naivety and physical abilities.

Then again, wasn't it the same when he worked for Bud? Perhaps he had only hired the eager, unsophisticated version of Chase, knowing that he would make the ideal candidate for his side business in porn? Hadn't he known that if put in a room with a naked woman, most horny young men would probably cave to the sexual promises, not really thinking long-term regrets? It seemed so clear now, causing Chase to feel obtuse upon reflection.

These thoughts took him all the way to Calgary almost as if he were in a daze. It was amazing how much time flew by, how many things had changed since those days. A brief moment of melancholy passed through him, as flashes of the past jumped uncontrollably through his head, almost as if on their way to leave permanently, never to return again; it was his private goodbye to the past that no longer seemed relevant.

Calgary offered a new life, a new existence, one that he deeply desired. He was stagnant now, unable to grow and much like Kelsey had suggested, unable to breathe in the small town. Maybe some people succumbed to this feeling and allowed it to take over and perhaps, he was one of the few that didn't want to live in such a limited world, where he had never really fit in.

He wasn't very old when the local men started referring to him as a 'faggot', something that he took more personally back then, an innocent teen who simply didn't want to work on farms, didn't want to be a country boy who went out 'muddin' on the weekend with the other teens nor did he really drink, so that took that entire possibility out of the spectrum. He didn't do drugs and in fact, the only thing that most considered 'manly' about him was the fact that Chase played sports; and he did that exceptionally well. Strong, tall, he wasn't the kind of kid that slinked back when confronted by an aggressive player or a devious attempt to get him kicked out of a game. He had a few fights and that's probably what enticed him to take up boxing and eventually start attracting girl's attention.

Calgary would be different. There was a place for everyone in a city. That's why misfits such as himself flocked to the urban areas, the place that attracted every kind of person, from every background and belief system. It was a mixing pot of every idea, thought, and opinion, attempting to live in harmony. Not that it always happened but people liked to believe the city made it easier to mix if not mingle.

Maggie was supposed to meet him for lunch but it seemed she didn't have the time and encouraged him to go to a location that was easy for him to find and she would meet him later. He did. Chase ate alone in a pub that was easy to locate once entering the city, he guessed that this probably was one of the main attractions to the chain restaurant that was filled with beautiful women; slender, tall, curvy, his eyes jumped around in amazement.

He was going to like this city.

But when Maggie walked in the restaurant, he quickly forgot everyone else. Only her eyes watched him. A stranger in more ways than one, she was more sophisticated, dressed carefully in a mid-length skirt and a white blouse. It was clear that she was no longer the teenage girl in cutoff jeans and a t-shirt, in fact, even her makeup was heavier, applied to perfection it seemed, her hair slightly shorter and without a single piece out of place; he felt like a hick beside her. Although a glance around told Chase that he probably fit in that room better than she did, dressed casually like the others.

He was surprised when she hugged him and yet, it felt cold. It was fast, abrupt and then she quickly moved to the other side of the table to sit down. He did the same.

She stared at him in silence, as if taking him in and yet, he couldn't read her expression well enough to know what she was thinking. Her face was blank, fine lines around her eyes suggested that she was a facade about to crack. He didn't know what to say, so he said nothing.

As it turns out, he didn't have to because she said it all.

CHAPTER THIRTY-FOUR

Everyone speaks dreamily of the moment they fall in love. It is as if rainbows, sunshine and shooting stars enter the horizon and the world is suddenly a wonderful place to live. It was an illusion that Chase assumed many naively believed and yet, why didn't anyone talk about the moment you fell *out* of love? That terrible, cold thud as your ass hit the floor and the truth about the person standing in front of you suddenly brought you back to a dark, humbling reality? It was as if your soul turned to a rock and your youthful innocence, your wide-eyed hopefulness, leaked onto the floor and dried into the ground, leaving a stain in the same way blood would on concrete. It didn't matter if you found a way to remove it, in many respects, it was never really gone.

Looking into Maggie's eyes as she spoke, Chase wasn't sure if he really heard much of what she said. Their conversation was impersonal as if they were strangers. It was a brutal truth that was a bitter pill to swallow and a part of him wanted to rise from the chair and leave. The fantasy that had sat in the back of his mind was gone and that was the hardest thing in the world to accept, especially when it was the one thing that kept him going all along. Nourishment for one's soul is harder to find than that of the body.

He simply nodded in silence, his eyes suddenly unable to focus on her, almost in the same way as if he were to stare at the sun. His focus drifted around the room, which suddenly appeared sad and pathetic, expressionless people talking, eating, depleting his hopes even further than they already were, he wondered if he had made a mistake. Maybe there was no place in the world for him.

Chase did manage to catch a few words here and there; enough that he could've passed the test had Maggie quizzed him on their conversation but yet, he wouldn't commit to it fully. If she noticed, he sensed she would've cared even less than he did. He wondered why she was doing this at all? Did she feel some sense of obligation to him or was this merely for her boss, Jolene?

We used to be best friends.

Chase wondered if close friends even existed outside of high school. Perhaps that's why so many married couples referred to their other half as their 'best friend' in Facebook photos, maybe they had no one else at that point and if you're committed to someone, it wasn't as if they could argue the point. Then again, maybe they were merely empty words. It was starting to seem as though most words were when you really got down to it. People liked to talk and say meaningless shit. Perhaps that is why he preferred to stay in silence with only his thoughts.

The conversation continued on the way to his car and Maggie gave directions on how to get to the location where he'd meet her boss, Jolene Silva. With the incredible buildup that suggested Jolene was a queen among women, he was rather surprised when they met her in a small office, one that was almost isolated from everything else. It was a dark, dreary building that appeared somewhat abandoned by most of its tenants and although he was curious why he decided not to ask.

They arrived at a simple, unmarked door that looked as if it had been awkwardly painted with a brush and Maggie gave a gentle knock. A voice that carried an enticing accent called out from the other side and he stepped back as Maggie pushed her way forward, sticking her head in, while simultaneously blocking his view of the person inside.

"I have him here."

"Send him in!" Her accent somehow seemed thicker and when he was finally approved to enter the room, he was met by a curvy, Columbian woman that he could only guess was in her early 40s. She was quite beautiful in a refined way, wearing a professional skirt and blouse, her perfume flowed across the room with her, as she reached out to shake his hand. Her rich, brown eyes studied him carefully, but seemed reserved in their friendliness, as if unsure of what to think of him, yet she still managed to give a stronger sense of warmth. He noticed that Maggie had slipped out and closed the door behind her.

"Come, sit down," She was curt yet her tone did hold a certain amount of friendliness that didn't make him feel bullied, so much as encouraged to follow her instructions. The office was simple, as was her desk and the chairs on each side. A single lamp sat aside as if it wasn't being used, a Mac opened, she quickly closed and edged it over, almost as if to clear the space between her and Chase. She now appeared friendlier, her eyes warmed into a deep brown, a mixture of intrigue and curiosity swept over her face.

"You, you are very tough one aren't you?" Her words had a sense of jovial behind them that he hadn't expected and Chases' lips fell into a smile.

"I don't know about that."

"No no, I mean, you can handle yourself in a fight. You are strong, powerful." Her words started off as a question seemed to end as a statement. She gripped her hand in a fist in order to demonstrate what she meant, her face tightening up as did her chest. "Know what I mean?"

"Oh, yes, I mean, I think-

"No, I know, I know," Her voice softened assuringly, as she leaned forward on the desk, her large breasts resting on it, her eyes grew in size. "There is no need to be bashful with me. I can *see* you. You are a strong man. That is what I want for this job. I need a strong man to look after my girls."

Her girls?

"I need someone who can protect. I want them to feel protected, you know? Yes?"

Chase quickly nodded. "Yes, I mean, I think I understand."

"Did ah, that one," Her fingers pointed toward the closed door behind him. Maggie must've been waiting outside, he assumed. "Maggie," she said the name slowly, almost in the same context as if she were talking about a disease. "Did she tell you what I do?"

"No."

"It is a business for women. It is very popular in other places, big places, New York and California." She spoke loudly, with confidence and yet, it a tone that was nurturing and kind. "You know?"

He nodded.

"Some people, they like to call it a 'sex club', but I do not know. That sounds...*gross*," She repeated the words as if not sure if her pronunciation was correct. "I do not like that term. It sounds disgusting and creepy, I do not see it that way."

"It is a club for women and only women. It's a place where women of a certain class can come if they want to experiment," she hesitated, leaning even further ahead on the desk, reading his expression. "with other women."

Oh.

"It's not for men," She shook her head. "It is not just any woman off of the street. It is a very...selective group of people who might want to learn about their bodies or try stuff with other women. It doesn't mean they are gay, just curious and it allows them to come to our events and do so, but not with others knowing, right?"

Chase opened his mouth but didn't respond.

"That one, Maggie, she said you would be open to this and would not be in judgment," she gestured toward the closed door again. "She said you were trustworthy to keep the secret, which is very important. I need someone who does not talk, as I see already, you do not do much of."

"I can keep a secret," Chase assured her.

"Now, don't you get all dancing in your pants," she blatantly pointed at his crotch. "This is not for you. It's not for your entertainment. You will be outside, minding the door. Although from time to time," her lips pursed together, she tilted her head. "You may be required to throw people out, that kind of thing, for the most part, you will not be allowed to see. That's something we cannot allow for women protection and privacy. They don't want to be viewed, you know?"

Chase nodded, but he didn't really understand. A sex club for women that weren't gay? Is that what Maggie did?

Almost as if she were reading his mind, Jolene answered his question. "Maggie," she continued to say her name as if mud were climbing in the back of her throat. "She, she doesn't do something funny. She is like a..what you call, hostess? She shows girls in, explain the rules, that kind of thing, you know?"

"You would be seeing the door, making sure that only people with the special cards come in. Most do not know where we are or what we do, so if someone approach, they are good. I will show you the card," She opened a drawer and pulled out an average looking business card. "They do change, from event to event. They will not necessarily indicate what we are, like this one, if you look at it."

At a closer look, he realized that it appeared to be the business card of a podiatrist. "It is confusing on purpose so that we do not get others try to get in or media people. We don't want media people."

"How do you get your...customers?" Chase asked his first question.

"Clients? We find," Her answer was short but direct and he merely nodded. "We do not want just anyone. We want attractive and women who are clever, not dirty women. We do not want prostitutes or strippers unless we hire to entertain. We have a clean environment and a good reputation."

"I'm sorry," Chase hesitated and her eyes studied his face. "I'm not sure if I really understand what you do here."

"We invited certain women, women who may be curious sexually for other women and for a fee, which is quite high, we provide them with an atmosphere that allows them to experiment if they want." She answered slowly as if choosing her words carefully. "There is privacy form to fill out. No one can tell anyone about what they see or do here. It's confident...confidential. It is a fantasy land for women that are not lesbian but are curious. No one can bring their phones in or take pictures. If they do, we may remove them. *You* may remove them and they will not be allowed to come back."

"Does that happen much?"

"No, not here in Canada but in other places, yes."

"So it's just like, someone's house or a bar where you do this?"

"We do it different places," She answered carefully. "We rent hotel suites sometimes, but others, we create like a fantasyland in a bar we borrow...rent and we make it plush, comfortable, relaxed. We serve drinks. We have toys for those who want them and we have private areas. It depends on how many we have, where we go."

"So, what kind of women come to something like this?"

"Many," she smiled for the first time in the meeting. "Women from different countries and ethnicities, women who are married, women who never been with woman before and others who have, women in business, women who stay at home with kids, women who are shy, women who are a bit show-offish, I don't know, I guess famous women sometimes but that," she pointed toward Chase. "Top secret. Celebrities sometimes. You cannot tell. Some wear masks to hide their identity too. It's a personal thing. Whatever makes them comfortable."

"The parties sometimes go on all night, but not everyone stays all night. Some just watch and talk, others participate with one or more people. Some, they never want to leave," Jolene let out a laugh, her head falling back slightly. "That is when I know I do well. Those come back and they pay, well, they pay well."

"Wow. I didn't know this existed."

"You show no judgment."

"I'm the last person that can show judgment," Chase spoke honestly. "I've done some crazy things." He decided not to go on.

"I can tell this about you," she spoke pointedly. "Maggie suggested you would be open minded and that's hard to find in men. I mean, in this type of environment. I need someone who isn't trying to get a peek." She demonstrated peeking through her fingers as if they were a peek hole. "You cannot look."

"I won't."

"I know this about you. I can see it." She suddenly was jubilant. "I like you Chase."

"By the way, what is that name? Chase?" She shook her head in confusion. "Does Chase not mean to run behind someone?"

"Yeah, it's a weird name." He smirked. "My mother is a strange lady."

"It is the hormone when they have baby. They go a little crazy." Jolene said while pointing to her head. "My mother pick 'Jolene' from that song, by Dolly," She said 'Dolly' extra loud and pushed her own, large breasts forward. "I think she somehow knew, ah?" She glanced down at that and began to laugh heartily.

Chase felt his face grow warm and for the first time since arriving, looked away from Jolene as he smirked. "Maybe." Was all he could say.

She laughed harder. "You blush, it is so cute! I like you Chase. I like the shy boy. My country, they never shy like that."

"Where is your country?" he finally looked back in her eyes.

"Canada."

"I mean, where *was*...where are you originally from?"

"I am from Columbia." She confirmed what he suspected. "Have you been?"

"Nah, I haven't been anywhere, actually."

"You must go!" She stood up from her desk. "The women, they would love you there. You and your blushing face."

CHAPTER THIRTY-FIVE

Maggie was waiting by the main entrance. Busy checking her phone, a grin on her face, for a moment she didn't even seem to realize that Chase was approaching her. Startled when she suddenly looked up, her expression returned to her usual, blank exterior. It was as if they were strangers, a reality that was digging into him like a splinter that seemed to get sharper with each moment, almost to the point that he felt as though it was time to make an excuse and leave. Jolene had his information, so Maggie had performed her part of the mission. She was off the hook.

Her expression turned to one of worry as they silently left the building and headed for his car. It wasn't until she was on the passenger side that she spoke again.

"So, what do you think?" She sounded skeptical, as if unsure of his reaction. She nervously picked at her nails; although now, unlike when she lived in Hennessey, they were manicured perfectly. "What did you think of Jolene?"

"I like her." His answer was simple and purposely changed the topic. "How do we get to your place from here?"

Taking in her instructions, they made sense with what he knew of Calgary, although it was a little difficult to adjust to big city driving after living in the country for so long, he did manage. It wasn't until they were sitting in front of her apartment building, that either spoke again. It was awkward and he would've been content to end with a simple 'goodbye' and head back home. On the road, he would be able to think; to allow his emotions to flow through him again, rather than crouching in the corner.

"You know Chase," she started slowly as if carefully picking her words, once again leaving him with a sinking feeling of talking to a stranger rather than an old friend. "I know Jolene is kind of hard to understand, so I'm not sure if you fully know what she was telling you about the job."

"Sex club for women," His reply was gentle, yet abrupt and he nodded. "I think I got it. She wants me to mind the door and keep it quiet."

Maggie appeared content with the response. "Okay, I guess you do understand then, but Chase," she hesitated again and he felt himself growing slightly frustrated. "Are you okay with it? I mean, it's kind of…different."

"Maggie, I don't care," his response was sharper than he intended, but he hated when women over-analyzed something that was relatively simple. "I don't care if there's a huge orgy or if they're sacrificing a virgin; as long as I get a paycheque, I'll do the job and follow her rules. It's pretty simple."

"I thought-

"Maggie, I'm hardly the moral king, why would I have an issue with it?" he reminded her, considering that she really only knew the half of it. Although Maggie knew he wasn't exactly loyal to Audrey, she didn't know the full extent and certainly, not about the movies or her own sister's attempt to seduce him. "It's fine, don't worry about it."

"You know I work for her too, right?"

He shrugged.

"Okay, umm, okay then," she replied, her face slightly flushed. "I guess you're just waiting for her call or did she hire you on the spot?"

"She said she'll call."

"Okay, good," Maggie said, staring at the dash as if more words were on the tip of her tongue but rather than say more, she reached for the door, saying a quick 'goodbye' and got out. No hugs or emotional ending, he felt his anger rising to the top and he would've done anything at that moment to attack a heavy bag; a combination of dejection and fury ran through him. His personal disappointment over, what felt like an ended friendship with Maggie, along with a slow, burning anger that had been gaining strength since meeting her at the restaurant. It was as if he had been tossed aside, no longer qualifying as 'friend' material and why? He could've easily accepted the excuse that Maggie disapproved of his friendship with Kelsey, but something told him it was something more and that was merely an excuse.

Kelsey. He thought about her a lot on the drive home. She'd be heartbroken if he left Hennessey and yet, he wondered if perhaps that would be the best thing for her. Maybe what they both needed was to be away from one another. It didn't matter that she was edging toward her 18th birthday, he knew that there was a deeper reason for rejecting her and yet when he attempted to justify it even to himself, he really couldn't.

The truth was that he was intensely attracted to her. It wasn't just her physical attributes that enticed him - although they certainly were powerful - it was her spirit that gained her the most attention. Her wide-eyed innocence combined with her excitement toward life, a positive disposition that rarely faded and when it did, never for very long. Where Maggie was always kind of guarded; seductive, yet standoffish, Kelsey was the polar opposite; open and warm. There was a reason why his children loved her, they could see something in her that was comforting and safe and perhaps, he did too.

Did he worry about what others thoughts? Was it a matter of having to deal with the disapproval of Maggie and did it even matter what she thought anymore? Why did she care? It wasn't as if Kelsey had taken a position in his life that she, herself, wanted to fulfill. Hell - she didn't even want to be his friend anymore, let alone an intimate relationship with him. It didn't make sense. The two sisters had a terrible relationship, causing Chase to wonder if Maggie even knew what her objections were toward the two of them.

Kelsey was anything but shy about what she wanted. Her late night text messages were often suggestive, as were the photos she would send to him. He feared that his children or Audrey would see some of these images and insisted that Kelsey practice better judgement in the future, as if he were an authority figure attempting to set her straight; while at the same time, he felt blood rushing to his groin when his thoughts secretly slipped to Kelsey's sexual openness.

And then he felt like a dirty perve; what the hell was wrong with him? She was Maggie's *younger* sister; the same one that used to sneak out with boys and drink by the lake when she was 14. The one who was always getting in trouble? The one who had screaming matches with both Maggie and Ellen Telips; occasionally at the same time.

His heart sank. No wonder she felt like such a misfit. She was one in her own home.

With the windows down, sunshine flowing through and bronzing his already dark skin, Chase flew down the highway and eventually lost the traffic that stemmed off in various directions, little of it going in either the Hennessey or Mento area, he had the road to himself. It was probably about a half hour from home when his phone rang. Slowing down, he felt his heart race in anticipation as he put on his turn signal and parked on the side of the road. A semi flew past him, sending a gust of wind through his opened window and along with it, a shitload of dust that filled his eyes.

Blinking rapidly, he grabbed his phone, tears forming where the dust landed, he sniffed and answered the call.

"Chase?" Jolene asked, her voice dragging out the word in an almost musical way and he noted it was very different from how she said Maggie's name, which was almost in disgust. "Is this you?"

"Yes," he replied while wiping away a dust filled tear, sniffing at the same time as his nose started to run. "Hi, Jolene."

"Hello," She replied with a deeper accent, that seemed to come out more with some words than others, something he was really liking about her. She was sexy, but not in the least pretentious, like a lot of attractive women. "Are you crying, Chase? You do have the job, so no need to cry."

He laughed at her remark. "Nah, I just got a bunch of dust in my eye when you called and.." There was an awkward silence at the other end. "Did you say I got the job?"

"Yes!" she let out a throaty laugh at the other end. "You're *silly*. I even said to one of your old bosses today, on the phone, 'I'm going to have fun with that one' and he said 'yes, Chase was one of my best employees'"

"Oh," Chase let out a self-conscious laugh. "Oh, you must've talked to Harold?"

"Nah nah, it was the other one, Brad?"

Oh. He had hoped she wouldn't call him.

"He really liked you a lot, told me stories about fights you broke up, dealing with some minors, that kind of thing," She said the word 'minors' in such a way that alerted Chase. Had Bud told Jolene about Kelsey?

Now, you're being paranoid.

"Oh, yeah?" He replied.

"Yes, he said you were good with people but you were tough when you needed to be and he admired that about you," she replied while rattling around a piece of paper, making him think she possibly wrote everything down. 'He said you left due to scheduling conflicts with this other job but that he didn't have much work for you anymore, so we will fix that here, Chase. I will give you work."

"Thanks." He heard the relief in his voice and he felt his early frustrations drain away.

"Now, I will be in touch with Harold too. I am waiting for him to call me back." She spoke slowly, drawing out each of her words. "But I still feel strongly you are perfect for this position and for once, Maggie got something right."

What?

"I will get you to start soon and I have training for you," she continued, speaking slowly as if to choose her words carefully. "It's not…difficult? Yes, difficult, that is the word. I will have different things for you to help with, helping set things up for me too, like my assistant, I guess."

Oh

"I need someone strong to carry and also, I need someone who does not talk. Women talk too much, you know? I do not need that," she continued. "I need someone who works more, talk less, you know?"

"I know."

"I already told Maggie you would be staying with her when you start until you can find a place."

Told?

"And she said that is okay," Jolene continued to talk. "But there may be somewhere in her building, I told her to check."

Hmmm...

"You do not have to live there, if you wish to go somewhere else but I think your first priority is to get here and work."

"Yes."

"So, I'm thinking next week?" Her voice seemed to mellow out, her tone almost passive. "Would that be okay for you?"

"I'll make it work." Chase confidently replied.

"Perfecto!!"

Chase let out a small laugh.

"Hermoso dia!!" she let out a victorious laugh. "Beautiful day!"

"Thank you," Chase replied, his comment warm and he felt a rare jolt of happiness. "I appreciate it."

"You will be paid well," Jolene continued. "We will talk more about that when you get here but it will be good. It's going to be good."

He certainly had nothing to lose. They ended their conversation with intentions of talking more the following day, ironing out the details. Before returning to the road, he checked his text and found a new one from Maggie, confirming everything Jolene just said.

Chase felt as though he was floating on the way home. Suddenly his life was in a whole new hemisphere that he couldn't have imagined only a few days earlier. He had felt so hopeless, the possibilities were limited and yet now, everything had changed again. He liked Jolene and suspected that he'd enjoy working for her. Although, it surprised him that Maggie had even helped him out, judging by her coldness when the two of them met but he wouldn't question it.

As he drove through the small town he had always considered home, he suddenly felt like more of a stranger than he ever had before; the reality was that he had never really fit in there and for the first time, he was starting to think that maybe that was a good thing.

Chapter Thirty-Six

Delivering the news was another story. He had, for some reason, expected a stronger reaction from everyone than what he received. Audrey was indifferent, as she fed one of the twins and appeared preoccupied, uninterested; while the children were simply too young to understand. He felt a sting when Audrey mentioned a new boyfriend that was now in her life and how he loved children; almost as if she had been looking for his replacement long before their official breakup. He remained silent and expressionless.

Taking a deep breath, he nodded and turned around and headed toward the door. Once outside, Chase realized that he didn't really have anywhere to go. He didn't care to tell Flora and in a way, was hoping to avoid her all together before moving. Standing by his car, he texted his sister the news then called his mother for a brief conversation. Rather than ask his plans, show any excitement or regret that he was leaving, her thoughts immediately skipped past and directly to her grandchildren. It was as if he hadn't told her the news at all, as her questions were about Leland's recent fever and to remind him, yet again, of something funny the twins did a few weeks prior. It was like talking to someone locked in a time warp, a world that consisted of only the things she wanted to know about, as opposed to the facts. Chase wasn't sure about having her around the children but Audrey insisted his mother was delusional at worst and never alone with the kids.

Who else could he tell? Feeling some reluctance, he sent a quick text to Bud, thanking him for the pleasant reference and he then sent another to Harold, warning that he might get a call. His reply was immediate.

Great news, Chase. I will be sure to give a terrific review and I might be able to hook you up in Calgary. I have a friend that owns a gym.

Chase wasn't sure if that was for another job or simply getting a deal at a gym but he was open to anything at this point and knew that Harold was probably the only person excited for his new opportunity. He knew that one person wouldn't be and that was Kelsey.

He hated going to her house in case her mom was home; never a pleasant meeting, since she seemed to hold a long-standing grudge toward him and Chase wasn't sure why. Luckily, she wasn't home that evening but Kelsey was. With somber eyes, as she met him at the door, Chase didn't even have to tell her. She already knew.

"You got the job." She bluntly commented, her voice was soft as she slowly moved toward him with reluctance in her step. "Didn't you?"

"You talked to Maggie?" he stood awkwardly outside her door while she leaned against the doorframe as if to block him from seeing inside. A short gust of wind flowed through him, deeper than anything ever had before, as he stared into her expressionless eyes. It wasn't the reaction he had anticipated.

"I didn't have to," her comment was abrupt and her eyes roamed to the ground and back up to this face. "I just know."

"Kelsey, I know you're upset with me-

"You don't know anything, Chase," Kelsey replied bluntly, although her face was expressionless, he could see tears forming in her eyes as she closed the door. There was no anger, no emotional goodbye, just a simple, unsettling ending. Then again, as he drove to Calgary a couple days later, he realized that they had all been unsettling. It was almost as if his departure was met with dispassion. No one was excited about his new opportunity. No one appeared to care that he was moving. Someone displaying a new haircut on Facebook would receive more of a reaction than he did from the very people he thought would be happy for him.

Moving his few possessions into Maggie's apartment felt awkward, even though she was friendly and helpful, grabbing a few bags and lugging them upstairs. Most were clothing, the essentials since he was never the kind of guy who collected much of anything; outside of personal items, a laptop, his iPhone and pictures of the kids, along with some messy drawings, he really had nothing to bring.

He was surprised to discover that Maggie had a spare room. He had assumed her apartment would be small and compact but it was a reasonable size and although she admitted to not being home much, she didn't volunteer information on where she was all the time. He assumed it was because she had two jobs; both in an office setting and part-time for Jolene, mostly on weekends and holidays.

"I talked to the landlord and there may be another place in the building," She assured him and glancing at the calendar on her phone, quickly continued. "It's almost the end of the month and he expects someone will be moving out. Meanwhile, you're welcome to stay here."

Her comment was emotionless; neither making him feel as though he were an imposition or welcomed. It was easier to nod yes, say thank you and head for his new room. He had briefly considered inviting her out for dinner but almost as soon as he was settled, Maggie left and wouldn't return for a couple of days. Had she taken an overnight bag with her? He hadn't noticed.

Once alone, he roamed through the apartment, noting that it barely looked lived in. Few groceries were in the refrigerator, just some vegetables, a carton of almond milk, a jar of natural peanut butter and a package of moldy multigrain bread. Although her bedroom door was closed indicating it was off limits, he couldn't help himself and gently turned the knob and walked in. Also appearing as if not lived in; the bed was made with a pretty pink blanket, the pillows were numerous and fluffy, very feminine. He didn't want to pry beyond glancing around but curiosity pulled him toward the nightstand but nothing was in the drawer other than some sinus medication and something for period cramps.

It wasn't very exciting. What had he hoped to find? Sex toys and lingerie on the bed? Even Audrey's room had more personality, which this one lacked, seeming almost like a hotel that only carried the bare essentials. He left the room, making sure to close the door behind him.

His first night in Calgary was awkward. The sounds of the night were quite different from those in the country but he quickly fell asleep, awaken early the next morning to a garbage truck near his window. The empty apartment made him feel homesick, the stillness was something he wasn't used to at all.

Checking his phone, he was disappointed to have no texts. His heart sank a bit when realizing Kelsey was clearly still upset with him; but what else was he supposed to do? He needed to find work and move forward with his life, something that wouldn't happen in Hennessey.

He wasn't required to go to work until after lunch. He met Jolene at the same office where she conducted his interview. She wore a black and blue dress that fit over her curves perfectly, along with high heels and dark, maroon lipstick. Unlike everyone else in his life, she appeared quite excited about his new job and move.

"So did Maggie and you have some fun last night?" Her question appeared to be loaded and perplexed him briefly. "You two are friends, right?"

Chase shrugged, wrinkling his nose, he slowly shook his head. "We use to be," he replied. Jolene's smile dropped.

"I thought you two, you are close?" she appeared confused. "Like best friends, maybe?"

"Use to be," Chase quietly replied. "We aren't now and I can't really tell you why."

"You do not know?"

"No."

She nodded, her face solemn as she glanced at some sheets on her desk. "Well, I guess people, they do change. I do not see Maggie,' Jolene said her name with the same disdain as the first day they spoke "I do not see her as friendly but she works well, so I say 'okay' and that's all."

Chase nodded.

"So no evening out? Drinks? Party? No?" She asked and shook her head no, along with Chase.

"oufff!" She made a face and sat back in her chair. "She not talk to you, or what?"

"She left," Chase replied. "I don't know where she went."

Jolene raised her eyebrow, almost as if she was aware but didn't reply. "Hmmm…well, Chase, I do see something on here, this form, you fill out?" She lifted both government forms off her desk. "This sheet says here, you have three dependents. Three?"

"My kids."

"Three?" She repeated, her eyes appearing slightly glazed as she stared at him. "You, you young boy, have *three* babies?"

"Yes."

"You do not know birth control?" She made a face. "*You* are still a baby."

Chase cracked a smile for the first time since moving to Calgary and nodded. "I know birth control. My wi-, I mean, my ex-wife didn't always use it."

"Oh you boys, you have to protect yourself," She warned and continued to flip through the mountain of paperwork he had to fill out.

"I know, the first was definitely unexpected and the other two are twins," he said, scratching his cleanly shaven face self-consciously, avoiding eye contact. "It's complicated."

"It sounds to be." She pushed the sheets aside. "Okay, so as I explain before, this is a very secretive job. You cannot talk about it. Its like that movie says, the first rule of the sex club industry is that you do no talk about the sex club industry. And the second rule of the sex club industry is that you do no talk about the sex club industry. Understand?"

Chase grinned at the *Fight Club* reference and nodded. "Yes, I do understand."

"Not that you appear to talk much," she continued, slowly, as if picking her words carefully. "I guess actually, the first rule is not to call it a 'sex club'. People do not like the term. We like to call it more of a lady's, I don't know, I guess a lady's garden of Eden, where women are free to explore their sexuality and not feel repressed or restricted. Women pay top money to explore and are surrounded by same kind of women. Women who like to try things, not be labeled. It's almost like, a social gathering, where ladies can meet others, see what happens."

The idea did entice Chase and he felt the blood rush a little faster through his veins every time he thought about the kind of activities that probably happened at these events but he appeared stone-faced and merely nodded.

"Now, you will be expected to handle the door, as I s'plained before and you must dress to impress. I like you to wear a suit, do you have?"

"Yes, I have a suit."

"I will have to see it. I want you to look sexy but yet, professional. If I do not feel it works, we may have to go shopping, ok?"

"Ok."

"For now, you can wear whatever but over time, I want a more professional image. This isn't just a bouncer job but you will be my assistant. If I need to set up a party, if I need errand run, if I need you to do anything you are required to help where needed."

Chase nodded.

"We will sometimes travel in Canada. Not the US but you should have a passport in case, do you have?"

He nodded yes.

"Perfect. I will mostly be traveling in this country - Toronto, Vancouver, maybe other cities later, but for now, just the big ones, right? And we will tell people we are party planners, nothing more. I work for my brother, Diego. He's in the US and started this business there and wanted me to oversee it here in Canada."

"We've had success already and a lot of demands," she continued after taking a drink of her coffee. "Women love our parties and want more but I needed help and that's why I hire you. It's a lot of work."

"Great."

"A lot of work."

"No problem."

"Very good then," she pushed the sheets aside and opened her MacBook. "Let's get to work."

CHAPTER THIRTY-SEVEN

He was a nervous wreck. Jolene was the first female boss that Chase ever had, so he was always scared about how he should act around her. Women in general always made him kind of nervous. If life had taught him anything, it was that the fairer sex often grew angry or frustrated with him, often without him really doing much to provoke such a reaction. He wasn't really sure if he said or did the wrong thing but eventually, they all grew annoyed with him; his mother, Lucy, Maggie, Kelsey, even the women he had affairs with in the past. It sometimes felt like it wasn't what he did say but more, what he *didn't* say that pissed them off.

Jolene was probably the exception to that rule but it took him some time to realize it. She was patient, strong and didn't appear annoyed if he fucked up. Not that he fucked up on anything major but on the small things he misunderstood because of a slight language barrier. "So what? We just fix it." She would say with a mere shrug, her voice neither lifting or changing, her body language continuing to be relaxed. In fact, it was probably a week in, while the two were shopping for suits, that she burst into laughter, her head swinging back and she clapped her hands together.

Dumbfound, Chase glanced down to make sure the zipper wasn't opened in his pants or that his shirt buttons weren't crooked but everything was perfectly fine. The sales associate appeared to be perplexed, almost nervous, as he rushed away to another customer. Jolene didn't seem to notice and shook her head.

"Chase, you like a lost little boy scared of his mommy," She spoke gleefully, wiping a stray tear from her eye, while a smile glistened on her pouty lips. Gesturing toward the suit he was wearing, she shook her head. "You look nervous when I say that I do not like. It is not, it is not you? You know? It...I do not like, I think it is not a good color for you.I want to see white shirts, they look fresh, you know? That shirt, that yellow, banana color shirt, it is not good."

"I guess," He glanced in the mirror and shrugged. "I'm not great with fashion. The sales guy said-"

"Sales guy stupid, your skin, it looks yellow too," She rushed through the store and grabbed a white shirt. "You need white, it looks so nice on you with your dark skin, it brings out the white in your eyes and teeth. You look good!" She glanced down at the dark gray suit. "The suit, I don't know. I do not like. We will find better."

With an extra bill added to his credit card, Chase was a little nervous. He was about to move into a new apartment downstairs from Maggie and his expenses were building while Audrey was back home, demanding money. Even his mother started to ask for some money, now that her finances since Carl Jacobs' death and insurance were dwindling. Chase could barely afford to support himself. Although his job paid well, Calgary wasn't a cheap city and he wasn't scheduled to receive his first pay cheque until the day of his move.

Jolene somehow managed to haggle him a deal; probably because her abrupt nature had a tendency to sometimes scare those around her but she was really quite harmless. Her comment in the dressing room was a bit of an awakening to him and something he thought about in the days to come. Why did women intimidate him? When he thought of his mother lashing out when he was a child, her anger seemed to erupt out of nowhere, often with Chase unsure of what he did wrong. Audrey had been the same. Whereas other women, those he was attracted to, intimidated him for completely different reasons.

The only woman who didn't intimidate him was Kelsey; but now that he had moved, she ignored him. He had made a few attempts to text her but she never replied. At a certain point, he realized that it was probably for the best anyway. Perhaps it was time for her to move on, not be obsessed with him, with dreams of seduction floating through her head. She was better than that and really, she was better than him. He had fucked up his life but Kelsey still had a chance.

After moving into his new apartment and growing more comfortable with his job and the city as a whole, Chase reached out to both his aunt Maureen and sister, in hopes of meeting the two for dinner some evening. It would be a way of killing two birds with one stone but his attempts were futile. His sister was tied up with her boyfriend and work, promising that she would get together with him when things slowed down but he almost felt like that was just an excuse. Wasn't he busy too? Working long hours for Jolene and recently locating Harold's friend Billy's gym, the potential of a second job came into the picture. Meeting the owner, a guy he immediately recognized as native, the two instantly connected.

"Harold has a lot of great things to say about you," He eased into a smile as he showed Chase around the facility; which was three times the size of the gym that Chase used to work at for Harold. When he made this comment, Billy gave a short laugh. "I bet, out in Hennessey, I'm guessing the demand for a gym probably isn't anything close to what we got."

Chase felt a little embarrassed by his wide-eyed comment, fearing he sounded like an ignorant hick, he didn't reply.

"It sucks that it didn't work out for him but it's a tough industry," Billy commented as he continued to give him the tour. "Harold said you're into boxing, we've got a ring, heavy bags and everything on the second level." He gestured toward the nearby stairs leading to the basement portion of the building. Walking into the room, Chase felt as though he was in heaven. It wasn't a huge, bright room like the rest of the gym, but it was exactly what he needed. A young man appeared to be training a young, black woman in the ring, both barely glanced in his direction. "We got it all here."

Chase nodded and a smile lit up his face as he looked around at the array of heavy bags and smaller, speed bags. By the time he left, he got a reasonable membership and was also asked if he would be interested in occasionally taking a shift in the future.

"We don't have a lot of work right now but sometimes we need a casual and you never know what will happen, right?"

Chase agreed that he would be interested, time permitting and left the gym feeling pretty reassured, confident about what the future held. Although he had a lot of doubts when first moving to the city, he was slowly starting to see things work out in his favor. It still stung a bit that family and friends seemed indifferent about his decision, he managed to push that aside and decided not to dwell on it.

He often would Skype the children back home but they seemed uninterested in him, often appearing frustrated that they were being pulled away from other activities. Audrey could be heard in the background reminding them that 'Daddy is really busy, we have to talk to him when he's available' but he sensed their rush to get away, only saying a quick hi; the twins were too young to comprehend what was going on, Leland going between crying for him to come home, while other times appearing bored by their conversation. It pulled his heart strings more than Chase would've expected. It appeared that Audrey's new man, a quiet guy he went to high school with, was turning out to be a better father than he had ever been. Maybe he deserved what he got, Chase decided.

The loneliness that he never expected with such a busy schedule, would creep in at night and on his day's off. Sitting alone at the computer in the evening, while others could be heard walking by outside his door, going out to restaurants and bars, left him feeling lonely. It was the darkest hours in the night and early mornings, when he felt his desires churning, wishing to reach out and feel a warm body beside him when Chase felt at his lowest point. He briefly considered going on a dating website for some companionship; he even thought about going out to a bar to find a quick hookup but felt awkward doing so in a strange city and instead stayed home, inadvertently learning some porn stars by their first name.

Women gave him some attention but everyone he met appeared to be part of a happy couple. Jolene was gorgeous but totally off limits. He certainly wasn't about to cross that line, even though in his private fantasies, she rocked his world. Her body was perfect; curvy and lean, her lips full and enticing, he had to purposely ignore these factors while working together - something he fully acknowledged would've been impossible even a few years ago - her sexy voice, full of confidence and strength, empowering and with never ending optimism. He imaged having sex with her many times, always with her aggressive, passionate and vocal in her pleasures. She would wreck him; he was sure of it.

Meanwhile, he made many attempts to smile, flirt, but city women were harder to get to know. Many were pleasant but like Maggie, somewhat cold and maybe even judgemental. It depended on how he was dressed; when wearing a suit, they were chatty and eyeballing him but in jeans and a t-shirt, even one that showed off his muscular body, they were less friendly. It was strange. What the hell did they want?

By Christmas time, the dry spell was starting to get to him. Was it possible that he was hornier during the holidays? While everyone else was singing Christmas carols and shopping for snowmen ornaments and candy cane scented everything, he was starting to curiously check out escort ads in the back of the free papers he found at the local bus stop. It was the day that Jolene caught him, that he felt completely humiliated.

"Don't go there, you'll get funny things growing on your *deek*," she ripped the paper away from him in the middle of McDonald's, where he had been waiting to meet her for an early breakfast. Her booming voice brought unwanted attention, while his face grew hot from embarrassment.

"I was just looking-

"Stop looking!" She sat across from him with a large coffee in her hand and glanced down at the ad. "You, you do not need this, you're handsome. Go talk to women."

"I wasn't seriously looking at-

"You get funny diseases from these women," she promptly closed the paper and pushed it aside. "You will grow lumps on your *deek*."

He opened his mouth but couldn't talk. It was bad enough it was his boss, but also an attractive woman, who saw the desperation ringing through his life.

"I set you up."

"No, Jolene, it's not-

"I will set you up," she shook her head. "Don't worry, we take care of you."

Then it was business as usual. Many parties were coming in upcoming weeks, something they had taken great pains to plan and the two of them would be required, along with Maggie and a few casual staff members he briefly met, to travel to Vancouver, Montreal and spend two nights in Toronto. They had already hosted parties in Calgary but with them, he merely stood at the door while beautiful women flocked into a venue they rented for the evening. What happened behind closed doors, he could only imagine and something told him, his imagination had nothing on reality.

Originally, Chase intended to go home to be with his kids during the holidays but when a huge storm hit Calgary two days before with more warnings to follow, Audrey suggested that he stay put in the city and come after the holidays. Although he felt loneliness strike his heart at the possibility of spending Christmas away from the kids, another part of him felt almost like it was a rite of passage. It was clear that Audrey and her new boyfriend were forming a new family and he was now being pushed out. It felt as though a jagged piece of glass were ripping through his heart but he reluctantly agreed, knowing that he had to do what was right for the kids.

His aunt Maureen insisted that he drop by during the holidays to spend time with the family but he made an excuse for Christmas Day, choosing instead to sleep in, watch some television and eat take out pizza. He'd never been a Christmas fanatic, things had often been a fucked up mess during the holidays while growing up, his mother often getting crazier during the season, something he now recognized was due to her feeling justified drinking despite her medication. Holidays with Audrey were as uncomfortable as their entire relationship and well, what else did he know about Christmas? It certainly wasn't the kind that holiday movies represented.

All was calm that evening, so he decided to go for a walk. Wandering down the street, he was surprised to find a cafe opened with a lone employee behind the counter. He noted her bored expression as he wandered in, glancing from side to side, Chase wondered out loud if she was about to close since no one was there.

"People have lives, I guess," She shrugged, looking up from a textbook, she scratched around her eyebrow piercing and pushed a strand of bleached blond hair behind her ear. She was cute. Appearing to be his age, she had sort of a rocker chick look, with heavy eye makeup and dark, perfectly manicured eyebrows. She stood upright and he immediately noticed the tattoos peeking out from underneath her uniform and he briefly considered that Jolene would give him shit if he showed up to work with a tattoo peeking out from underneath his suit.

"Not me," Chase let out a short laugh.

She looked him up and down curiously as if he were under evaluation. "Can I get you something?"

He wasn't sure how it happened. A simple coffee and conversation in an empty dimly lit cafe somehow ended with him having very rough sex with her in the staff room at closing time. He hadn't intended on things getting so crazy, but she was incredibly aggressive for such a petite woman; biting his shoulder until she drew blood, screaming at him to fuck her harder as he pushed her against the wall and she dug her long nails into him. He was so aroused that the pain didn't matter, having her hard nipples press into him while he moved inside her was pure heaven as she gasped in pleasure as she grabbed his ass with one, powerful hand, forcing him in farther, she gasped and panted and finally seemed to relax as she made sounds that resembled an animal in pain.

It was awkward after as they dressed and made their way toward the door. She walked as if in discomfort but didn't ask for his name or number. Waving bye, she warned him that he better leave soon before her boyfriend got there.

Message received.

CHAPTER THIRTY-EIGHT

"Pretty empty apartment, isn't it?" His aunt Maureen immediately commented after arriving at his door on Boxing Day, a container of food in hand, along with a small, neatly wrapped gift. Guilt filled him when he realized he hadn't bought her anything. In fact, he hadn't bought any gifts but sent some money to Audrey to make sure the children had a nice Christmas. He hadn't even bought his boss a card, despite the fact that one from Jolene sat on his countertop.

"Yeah, I'm not here a lot." He confessed and glanced around at the empty living room and gestured for her to sit down on one of the bar stools that were left in the apartment when he moved in. There was an island separating the kitchen and living room and the two sat at it after Maureen placed the food and gift on the counter and gave him a brief smile.

"Typical bachelor," Her brown eyes gleamed underneath her glasses, her sparkling rings caught the light as she gestured around the room. "I can hear an echo when I talk."

"Yeah, I'll get some stuff later. I'm trying to catch up a bit on things right now," He confessed and gave a self-conscious smile, glancing at his sweatpants. His attention back on Maureen, he noted that she was dressed as if it were another day at the office under her leather coat, he quickly decided that she probably just stopping in on her way to somewhere else. She was a bit overdressed for a casual visit with her nephew. "Can I get you something? Coffee? A bottle of water? I guess I don't really have much."

"No no," she waved her hand and shook her head. "I can't stay long. I'm on my way to meet Jack and some friends for a dinner party."

He knew Jack was her long time boyfriend but had never met him. He noticed his aunt kept their family at arm's length from her Calgary life and really, could he blame her? He was starting to see why, now that he felt disregarded since leaving home. It felt as if no one contacted him unless they wanted something; and that something was usually money. No one checked in to see how he was doing, how he was navigating the city but almost as if he no longer was a part of the family.

"You didn't have to bring anything," his voice was soft as he glanced toward the gift and food on the counter. "I feel like shit, I didn't get you anything, it's just that-

"No no," She reached out and touched his arm. "It's okay, Chase. I didn't want you to buy me anything, I just picked up a little something. The food was leftovers from yesterday. You should've joined us!"

"I don't know." He avoided her eyes.

"It's hard, isn't it?" She asked, her eyes full of kindness and her lips formed a sympathetic smile. "Being away from the kids for the holidays and the weather was hardly ideal for traveling. It's hard."

"A little harder than I expected." He confessed. "It feels weird. Everything does."

"I know," her eyes squinted with a broad smile and she pointed toward her head. "I remember those days too. You feel as if the city is going to swallow you up and everything seems unfamiliar and a bit scary, even for a big, strong guy like yourself," she teased and he laughed in spite of himself.

"I don't think it matters how big or strong you are in this city."

"We're all scared when we do something new, move somewhere new, make major life changes," She reminded him as she leaned against the counter. "But it's a good kind of scared. It usually means we are heading in the right direction."

"Here's hoping."

"There was nothing for you in Hennessey Chase," Maureen continued, reaching up to touch the heart pendant on her necklace. "I know you have a family there, that's not what I mean, I just feel it was a dead end for someone like you. You outgrew it long ago and once you outgrow something, it's time to move on."

He glumly nodded.

"It will get easier, I'm sure of it," She reassured him and jumped up from the stool and he followed her lead. Reaching into her pocket for a set of car keys, she rushed forward and gave him a brief, yet warm hug, before rushing toward the door. "We will get together again soon, okay?"

"Of course."

Although their visit was brief, it gave him a jolt of optimism that he hadn't felt in weeks. There were days he felt like an imposture, playing a role that didn't really belong to him but he continued because he didn't know what else to do. He tried to not think about it because regardless of how much time went by or how much Jolene seemed to like him, Chase always feared the day would come when she would suddenly realize that she had hired a clueless moron. Maybe she was desperate when she hired him, suddenly with more business than she could handle and he seemed good enough for now.

Dressing up for work felt strange. After working in bars and at the gym since high school, he felt awkward putting on a suit going to work. Not that he wore a suit every day but for now, Jolene let him know the days he would need one. That ended up being most days. At least he didn't feel underdressed beside her, who was always in a dress or blouse and skirt; not that he could picture her in jeans and t-shirt.

The weeks flew by and another birthday passed with little fanfare. He didn't care. Unlike most people his age, he felt like a 40-year-old man with responsibilities, rather than most his age, who would probably spend the night getting drunk and fucked by some random girl after the bar. He was a bit envious of that freedom, those who hadn't been tied down young, who were able to mindlessly live, feeling no responsibilities pulling them in any direction. Most guys his age only had to worry about either school or a job; no kids or ex-wives to constantly ask for money, bringing with it a list of problems and complaints that never seemed to end. There were no complications.

Even the men his age who were fathers usually only had one kid. One kid was easy. One kid was a joke.

He was a little disappointed when his former best friend forgot his birthday. In truth, Maggie would occasionally pop by to check in on him but that was rare and the visits usually linked to something regarding work. She never asked personal questions or offered information on her own life. He suspected she was seeing someone but he wasn't sure.

Kelsey wasn't very different. After a brief, cryptic message over the holidays, there was nothing. He responded to wish her a Merry Christmas, a few days later, a Happy New Year, as he headed to a work event that involved many beautiful women entering a private party and probably satisfying each other all night, while he minded the door with emptiness filled his heart.

Maggie was there that night, as usual, doing her hostess duty and he was tempted to ask about Kelsey but decided it was better to not bring up the topic. Chances were she had moved on from her crush and had a boyfriend taking up all her time now. He hoped it was true. She deserved to be with someone who could love her, unlike him, who had nothing more to give. That part of his life was over.

It wasn't that he was a cold-hearted asshole. It was more there was a vacant place where his feeling had once lived. He no longer had the emotional moments that filled him in his teens. He never cried. It wasn't something Chase would admit to many but he shed many tears as a teen. His relationship with Lucy had been emotional torture, something he hadn't recognized until he was able to stop and reflect, during those long nights alone in silence. The four walls of his apartment brought so much to the surface, things he hadn't had time to consider until he was suddenly alone every night; no children crying, no loud music throbbing like when he worked at Bud's, no distraction of a woman.

When he thought about it, it was actually quite surprising that he didn't hate women. Sometimes he felt like they hated him. They hated that he was silent when he should've been talking. They hated that he was strong when he should've been weak. They hated that he was passionate when he was supposed to be compliant. They hated that he was compliant when he was supposed to be passionate. He always seemed to have it backward and the rules changed far too frequently.

Jolene was the obvious exception. It was one evening over a glass of wine after a long day of finishing some details on an upcoming party planned for Edmonton, that he broke his normally quiet disposition and started to reveal things he wouldn't normally say. He felt it was professional and smart to not talk about your personal life or thoughts at work, so couldn't believe when he suddenly blurted out his feelings.

"You're like, the only woman I've ever respected."

He immediately clasped his mouth shut.

Fuck

Jolene appeared almost as shocked by the reveal as he felt for having said it. Her eyes widened and she tilted her head to the side. "Ahh, I do appreciate you, Chase. I do."

"I probably shouldn't have said that sorry-

"Nah no, you feel that way, you should say it," She confirmed, her eyes filled with emotion and she slowly nodded. "I can see why you would not always respect women. Your ex-wife, I get the feeling that was complicated, no? And Maggie," She said her name as if it were a dirty word. "That one, I do not know. She works well, but do I like? I don't like her."

"Maggie isn't the same as the girl I knew," Chase took a deep breath and quietly confessed. "I was so head over heels for her when we were younger. I mean, obviously, I was tied down with a wife and a kid really young, but man, I thought she was amazing. And I don't know, she's not that girl anymore."

"Well," Jolene pursed her lips. "It's good to know she used to be more...likeable? Is that what you say? Nice?"

"She was," Chase laughed. "I wanted her but it didn't happen."

"She's a lesbian, no?"

"Yes." Chase let out a self-conscious laugh. "I know."

"So what happened? You not friends? I don't understand." Jolene asked with some hesitation. "She really wanted you to have this job. I do not understand. I thought you were close from the way she talked at the time."

"I don't know," Chase hesitated. "Actually, yeah, I do know. Her younger sister is what happened."

"You do sexo with her?" Jolene's eyes bugged out and a mischievous grin lit up her face. "You bad boy."

"No, no, not like that," Chase laughed. "Not that her sister didn't try but Maggie was mad that we were friends. Her sister was younger than us. Just a kid."

"Ah, so, one sister didn't want you and the other did. How weird."

"Welcome to my life."

"You did not like, I mean, the sister, you like her?"

"Yeah, she was awesome but she was young. I mean, she wanted to hook up when she was 16."

"So?"

"I was like 19 or 20 at the time."

"So?"

"What do you mean so?" Chase teased her. "She was a kid. I didn't want to get arrested."

"You wouldn't get arrested for that."

"Yeah, well, actually, yeah you can," Chase laughed at the humored expression on Jolene's face. "It's called having sex with a minor. It's illegal."

"Oh this country, sometimes, I don't understand." Jolene waved her hand in the air. "When I was 16, I was dating men who were probably 25, are you kidding me? Who cares?"

"Well, to me, it's not right."

"She was 16, not 11."

"Now you sound like her."

Jolene shrugged.

"Did you respect her?"

Chase thought for a moment. "Yes, very much so. That's why I didn't try anything with her, not cause she wasn't attractive."

"I don't understand you," Jolene shook her head. "Maybe it's language barrier, but I do not understand."

Neither did he. But he soon would.

CHAPTER THIRTY-NINE

All is never lost. Everyday introduces new hope even after exploring the darkest places in our soul. Sometimes life is just about getting through the heavy, difficult periods, much in the same way that you would drive through terrible weather on a winter's day; you cannot deny or ignore it but take it on and face the pummeling snow, knowing that it won't always be this way.

Chase knew all about dark storm clouds. He had faced many in his life and sometimes, it made him distrust the days when everything seemed to be running smoothly. It was that distrust that made him nervous about losing his job and ending up on the street, empty and alone. He saw the homeless as he drove to and from work and recognized himself in many of their faces; young and aboriginal. Despite the fact that he was half white, since moving to Calgary, Chase felt like you were either white or 'something else'. His dark eyes, high cheekbones, and dark skin indicated that he was in the latter category. Oddly, in Hennessey, it hadn't been a big deal.

When he first moved to Calgary, he assumed that people were nervous of his presence at a nearby corner store because he was a large man; both tall and muscular but as time wore on, he began to question if it was because he was native. Did people think he was somehow a threat or dangerous? The idea shocked him because it was not something he experienced until moving to Calgary. Ironically, he had assumed that a large city would be more tolerable, not the other way around.

When he brought up his observation to Jolene one day over lunch, she merely shrugged as she continued to browse the menu.

"I'm Columbian," she casually threw into the conversation. "I'm a drug lord here to sell drugs to children."

"Ha?"

"It's a stereotipping, Chase." She replied as she closed her menu. "People have racist eyes about everyone else."

"Oh, *stereotyping*?" Chase asked as he took a drink of his water.

"Yes, stereotyping, yes, I know, I say wrong," she shook her long, dark hair from side to side and made a face. "People watch too much TV and think what they see there is what we are like. We are not TV people, we're…real people, you know?"

Chase nodded.

"There are good and bad everywhere, no matter what color you are, you know?" She gestured toward Chase and pushed her menu aside, her eyes staring at the waiter who was chatting with another customer nearby. "Now my brother, he thinks all white people are racist."

"Really?"

"Yes, he thinks white people think they are like, how you say, kings in the community," she put an invisible crown on her head. "But I do not, I do not think so."

The waiter made his way over to the table and their conversation ended.

Chase was very aware of these words each time he went into the convenience store near his home and felt as though he had to be extra nice to the staff, in order to prove he was not dangerous. Of course, that would've been easier if the staff hadn't changed on a regular basis.

He grew more comfortable in his new home and with the silence of his apartment. It was quiet most nights, other than chatter outside his door when people passed by, he barely heard a peep. He slowly started to enjoy the tranquility and although he missed his kids, he didn't miss hearing them cry non-stop. Perhaps it was shameful for him to appreciate this small pleasure, so he would never tell anyone. It wouldn't be considered acceptable to feel such a way.

The silence wouldn't last. It was a spring day when a knock at the door interrupted his nap on the couch; the one piece of furniture, other than a bed and television, that he invested in. Slightly disheveled, he slowly rose up to a seated position, wondering if he actually was having a dream but a second knock let him know that someone was waiting for him in the hallway. Assuming it was most likely Maggie, who occasionally showed up at his door for a brief moment, he slowly wandered toward the door, his legs slightly stiff from a recent workout that pushed his level of fitness to a new level. He expected a short, mechanical conversation that would end quickly, allowing him to return to his nap.

He barely had the door opened when caught up in a dramatic embrace that was easily soap opera worthy, the familiar scent filled his lungs and for a moment, he was back in Hennessey. Kelsey was in his arms.

Neither said a word until she let go and stepped back. Wearing slightly more makeup than she had at home, there was a maturity that hadn't existed when he last saw her. No longer wearing ripped jeans and skin tight tank tops - regardless of the weather - she was dressed more like a young lady who was about to go to a job interview, rather than the 'kid' he remembered. Her hair was pulled back in a neat ponytail and she carried a purse. Had he ever seen Kelsey with a purse; A backpack, definitely, but not a purse.

"Can I come in?" She was direct, as always and still having not said a word, he moved aside as she slid by him. He slowly closed the door, unsure of what to say, he said nothing. "I can't believe I'm here; in Calgary, in this apartment, with you."

"I didn't know you were coming," Chase was cautious to not give her the wrong impression. He *was* happy to see her but didn't want to overemphasize that fact, nor did he want to hurt her feelings by giving the impression he wasn't happy with her surprise visit. "I mean, Maggie didn't mention it."

"She didn't know either," Kelsey raised her eyebrow and let out a little laugh as she sat on his couch. "I came to see dad but he shipped me out to her house. I think his 'lady friend' probably didn't appreciate me being around. Then again, Maggie was always his favorite - well, *everyone's* favorite."

It was the typical Kelsey comment, letting him know that some things never changed. There had always been a rivalry between the two.

He had no idea where it stemmed from or how it started but it always came back to favoritism. Kelsey felt as though she were the black sheep of the family and no one ever corrected her.

"I don't know if that's necessarily true," Chase commented and stood awkwardly beside the couch. To sit down on either side, would require him to be very close to Kelsey and he wasn't sure if that was a good idea. "I think-

"Trust me, it's true," Kelsey insisted as she removed her coat to reveal a slightly loose top that didn't exactly hide her figure. Of course, he didn't have to look either. "Dad barely spent a day with me and after he did the formalities of taking me out to dinner, buying me some 'clothes that actually fit'," she gestured toward her top and shrugged. "he introduced me to his girlfriend, who looked like she was offended that I was even in the same room, then he 'suggested' that I go stay with Maggie for 'a while'. I guess that was his nice way of saying that he didn't want me to stick around for long."

"So, you got here yesterday?" He asked as he made his way to the kitchen, attempting to process their conversation. "You're staying with Maggie?

"As of today, I am," She confirmed and sat back on the couch. "She's gone but she was gracious enough to meet me for like, five minutes and let me into her apartment."

Chase grinned but didn't say anything. That scenario sounded vaguely familiar.

"And here I am," she commented and glanced around his place. "You really need to decorate, Chase."

He turned back and shrugged. "Do you want some water? Coffee?"

"I'd kind of like a 7UP with a shot of vodka."

"I don't drink pop or alcohol, really…"

"Always a saint," she teased.

"Hardly."

"If you weren't, you would've fucked me," she bluntly reminded him, her blue eyes danced around and she waited for his reaction. When she didn't get one, Kelsey continued. "I'm only here for a minute, Chase. I'm fine."

He didn't know what to say.

"So what do you think of all this?" She pointed around the room. "The apartment, Calgary, being away from Audrey? You know she's totally nailing that little nerd she's dating? The one that looks scared of her? I think she gets off on that, you know, like literally gets off on that. Know what I mean?"

Chase nodded. "You're probably right."

Kelsey glanced at her phone and suddenly jumped up, grabbing her jacket and purse. "I was on my way out but I'll see you a bit later." She headed toward the door. "I just wanted to pop in on my way through to say hi."

"OK, well, we'll talk later?" Chase asked as he followed her and watched Kelsey reach for the doorknob.

"Of course," she replied, turning quickly, he noticed her right eye turned in a bit as it often did when she was nervous, something she tried to hide but he could see it and gave her a warm smile. "Bye."

Then she was gone. Locking the door, he slowly made his way back to the couch. The scent that reminded him of fresh cookies seem to linger where she sat and he found himself feeling slightly aroused by that remaining presence.

He wasn't sure how he felt about her being in Calgary, only a couple floors above him, staying with Maggie. Was it permanent or a short visit? He wasn't really clear what brought this on or what he should do? Was Jolene correct and he being too much of a prude? After all, she was probably 18 by now? Perhaps that hadn't really been the issue so much as the one that was safe to say out loud.

Rather than to deal with his thoughts, Chase decided to go to the gym. There was something about hitting a heavy bag that brought him to a completely different place. With his focus on boxing, rather than his life, he could separate himself from the problems that lurked around. Financial concerns, fears, dreams, hopes; everything took a backseat when he was working out, almost as if those minutes put him in the zone, a place that extracted him from real life; a place that hadn't always been very kind to him.

After an invigorating workout followed by a shower, he found the relief he sought and his body was light as he walked out of the gym, heading toward his car. It was once inside, he noticed a message on his phone. It was from Kelsey, asking him to stop by Maggie's place when he had a chance. He replied, saying he was on his way home and would drop in when he reached the apartment building.

Excitement built in him, happiness for having a friend nearby, yet nervousness over what he would discover. There was some bitterness in their last conversation and he wondered if she was ready to reveal why she hadn't spoken to him in months. She indicated in her message that there was something of urgency to deal with, therefore he thought back over the months to once again attempt to understand why their friendship seemed to end after he left Hennessey. Had he said something that perhaps she took the wrong way? Maybe it was good if they finally cleared the air.

It didn't happen.

Arriving at Maggie apartment, he was stunned when the door flew open and he was pulled inside. Completely naked except for a pair of blue panties, Kelsey showed no modesty, as she pulled him close and started to kiss him. Stunned, he could hear his brain screaming no, while his body was quickly aroused as she pressed against him. He immediately felt his breath become labored as her hands briskly moved under his coat and t-shirt, running up his naked skin, one running over his back, while the other reached into his pants, his breath becoming heavier.

Jumping back and self-consciously covering her breasts, she grabbed her top from earlier and started to pull it on and it took a second for Chase to realize that her reaction had nothing to do with him but that Maggie had just walked in the room. Her face was full of fury, while holding her hand was a masculine looking woman, wearing glasses and a man's leather jacket.

Oh, fuck.

CHAPTER FORTY

The warmth of desire was quickly replaced by the heat of embarrassment as anxiousness ran through his body, his heart racing erratically in exchange for the anticipation of pleasure that had filled him only moments earlier. That split second erased every promise he'd ever made to Maggie to keep away from her younger sister and in fact, it probably indicated that his attempts to comply with her wishes were never true. That fact alone crushed his desire even more than being caught.

However, any beliefs that Maggie's fury would be directed at him were soon forgotten. In fact, it was almost as if he weren't in the room at all and in no way involved in the physical act she had witnessed, as Maggie flew across the room to attack her sister. It happened so fast that it took a few seconds to process what was going on as the two young woman wrestled with one another, Maggie's tone at an almost unfamiliar high pitch, shrill and almost deafening as Chase quickly jumped in to pull the two women apart. Not that it was easy as Maggie aggressively pushed ahead to take another grab at her half naked sister, who almost appeared to be more stunned than angry.

"You're a fucking whore," Her accusations were sharp, like daggers bludgeoning her sister, as hatred poured out of her eyes, furious tears ran down her cheek. "Why couldn't you ever be fucking normal?"

"Says the *lesbian*," Kelsey shot back without missing a beat, her eyes snapping in anger but yet it took little to no energy to hold her back from attacking her older sister. Instead, she firmly stood her ground and appeared ready to fight off this attacker, as opposed to provoking another round.

"Oh, so being a lesbian isn't normal?" Maggie shot back and pounced forward, only to be pulled back by Chase who was having a moment of deja vu from his days working at the bars. The original tears were now dried up, her reaction turned sour, Maggie's face seem to pale as she argued. "Of course, you're like everyone else who can't accept who I am."

"I never said I didn't accept who you are," Kelsey firmly corrected her, showing an assertiveness that Chase wouldn't have expected. "What I meant is that I never believed you were a lesbian, in fact, no one does. It's an act. It's an act and you know *why*."

Her sharp comment had a chilling effect on Maggie who finally pulled back, her eyes full of disbelief, she appeared almost frozen, glaring at her sister.

"There's a difference between wanting women and hating men," Kelsey continued and almost as if she saw herself with the upper hand in the conversation, she appeared tranquil, focused, her voice smooth. "Chase was the only man you didn't hate until you thought he was like the *rest* of them."

As if suddenly remembering Chase was there, Maggie's attention switched to him, if only briefly, before she looked back at her sister who shrank in front of their eyes. She looked remorseful and Chase racked his brain as to why but wasn't able to make sense of the situation. It was as if a piece of the puzzle had suddenly appeared but he hadn't figured out where it belonged.

"I don't hate men," Maggie finally volunteered, her voice small like that of a child, she shook her head and looked at Chase. "It's not like that."

"It *is* like that," Kelsey insisted, continuing to hold her ground. "You can try to talk your way around it or believe whatever you want but you know it's true and you know why."

Suddenly overwhelmed, Maggie broke down in front of them and made a quick dash for her room. Slamming the door behind her, an awkwardness followed as Chase turned to see the young woman that had arrived at the apartment with Maggie, still standing at the door in disbelief. Appearing nervous, it wasn't clear if she was about to dash out the door or if her feet were nailed to the floor but Chase offered her a quick shrug, unsure of what else to do. He finally turned toward Kelsey.

"You should go talk to her."

"I don't want to go talk to her."

"You're her sister, you should talk to her."

"Look, Chase, she doesn't want to talk to me," Kelsey insisted as she picked up her pants and casually pulled them on as if nothing out of the norm had occurred. "You've been watching too many girly movies or something because in the real world a scene like this doesn't end with sisters hugging and expressing their love for one another. It's messy, it's dirty and it's way too heavy."

Glancing toward the stranger who still stood at the door, as if waiting for permission to move, Chase decided to address her instead. "Do you...I mean, do you want to try to talk to her?"

"Oh yeah, you should totally do that," Kelsey finally addressed the stranger, who appeared to be shrinking back. "You should go in there now when she's weak and vulnerable, you'll totally get her naked."

"I...I..I just met her and I.." She nervously replied to Kelsey's suggestion, shaking her head, causing Chase to feel sorry for her. Clearly, she happened along at the wrong time and place and was caught up in a mess.

"Look it's fine, you don't have to go see her or you can, if you want, it's really up to you." He spoke evenly, hoping that she would go comfort Maggie but sensing that it wasn't likely to happen. In a way, it was for selfish reasons since he didn't want to approach Maggie himself and yet, someone had to since she was clearly very upset. "No one's judging here." He shot a warning glance at Kelsey who pursed her lips and said nothing.

"I think I should go."

The stranger barely squeaked out her response and slipped out of the apartment. Kelsey stared into Chases' eyes. "Come on, let's just go. Don't play into her games."

"I don't think she's playing a game, Kelsey." He quietly insisted. "What the hell was all that about?"

"She never told you?"

"Told me what?" Chase responded with a shrug and glanced toward the closed bedroom door. "She hates men?"

"Why she hates men?"

"I didn't even know she hated men."

"She does, except you," Kelsey insisted and grabbed her bra from the couch, slipping it on underneath her shirt, her pink nipples briefly peeking out from underneath her shirt. "She has for years since *that* guy."

"What guy? Her ex from school? Todd?"

"No no!" Kelsey shook her head, as she finishing adjusting her top and fixing the pockets of her pants. "Not that loser, I mean the guy from when we were kids."

"I don't understand."

"Mom dated some guy when we were kids and he molested us." She spoke casually as if they were merely were talking about the weather, rather than a serious and traumatic issue from her childhood. "I was really small but Maggie remembers more, I guess."

"You were molested?" Chase was stunned by the news, his heart raced in anger and he wracked his brain attempting to think of who Ellen Telips used to date but of course, this was many years ago and he had no idea. There had always been a lot of stories about child molestation in Hennessey but only a few compared to Audrey's hometown of Mento, where it was said to have happened within more families than it hadn't. "Oh my God, Kelsey, I can't. I mean, I didn't know. I'm so sorry."

"It's fine," She shrugged casually. "We had counsellng and I'm obviously fine now but Maggie isn't. I think that's why she is a lesbian. I don't think she actually wants women, I think she's scared and distrustful of men because of what happened. Bi-curious maybe but who isn't, you know?"

Chase attempted to process everything Kelsey was saying and suddenly, so many things started to make sense. He wasn't so sure that that terrible experience wasn't still affecting Kelsey but didn't share his thoughts. As for Maggie, he wasn't sure if it was true that she hated men or that her choice to be with women was simply her nature inclination but for some reason, it shed some necessary light on things.

"I have to go talk to her," he suddenly felt it was necessary and brushed past Kelsey, who appeared unimpressed with his decision but didn't reply.

Knocking on the door, he was met by silence. "Maggie, it's me. Can I come in?"

A weak 'yes', came from the other side of the door and he slowly turned the knock to go inside. Glancing back at Kelsey, he saw her face fall as she sat on the couch, appearing disheartened at best.

Entering the room, he noted that not a thing was out of place. The only indication that the room was lived in at all was a messy blanket that Maggie lay on top of, her arms hugging a pillow, she didn't look up at him as he closed the door. He wasn't sure what to do but his mind flashed back to the time she was rejected by the RCMP; the night he slept with her in his arms, knowing how deeply he was in love with her but not understanding why it wasn't mutual. He was just a kid then and although some things never changed, their relationship had since that night.

"Maggie," he hesitated for a moment, unsure of what to say. "Kelsey told me."

She sniffed, pushing her face even further into the pillow, waves of misery ran through her body, as she sobbed. The last time he witnessed a woman crying this hard, it was the night Aubrey asked him for a divorce, beaten to the edge of her soul, digging deeper than she ever had in her life, his ex-wife admitted that there was a darkness inside her that had to be removed and he suspected the same of Maggie but he wasn't sure how or if that was possible. Although his own childhood of abuse consisted of being slapped and yelled at regularly, he couldn't even begin to understand how someone got over something as deeply disturbing as molestation. Then again, how could the parents stand by and do nothing? If it was his kid, he would kill the person who inflicted such longstanding pain on his child. He wouldn't even think twice.

Moving closer, he was hesitant to sit on the edge of her large, queen sized bed. It made his own look pathetic and childlike in comparison and he found himself glancing around the room. It was like something out of an Ikea catalog, even the blanket beneath the hand he leaned on felt smooth and crisp as if it were new. Realizing that this shouldn't have been his focus, he wasn't quite sure of what to do or say, so he remained silent.

She sat up on the bed, continuing to hold onto the pillow, her makeup running down her face in globs of black, her hair disheveled and out of place. She looked in his eyes and nodded. "About what happened when we were kids?"

Chase nodded and offered a fleeting smile, unsure of how to appropriately respond.

"I always wanted to tell you but I couldn't," Maggie admitted as she glanced toward the nearby window, the blinds covered it with only glimpses of sunlight shining in. She held the pillow back and stared at it as if her words were directed at the object rather than him. He didn't take offense to this, knowing it wasn't an easy subject to discuss. "I wanted to the night that I was so upset about the RCMP. It really wasn't about the RCMP. It was because I wanted to help kids like me, to protect them, to make a difference and when I couldn't get in as fast as I wanted, I felt like it somehow brought all that back up again. I know it doesn't make sense but when I was pursuing that goal, it felt like I was fighting back. Like I was getting a part of myself back. That I was going to get out there and make a difference."

Chase nodded.

"I was devastated because it felt like another slap in the face. Almost like the guy who did it was winning," she pulled the pillow closer and hugged it. "And I was losing."

"You weren't losing, Maggie." Chase insisted. "You were surviving."

"Surviving isn't enough, though, Chase." She replied and bit her lower lip. "I want to heal. I want it behind me but where do I start? How do I start? No one really understands it. Not the shrink who writes notes about me, watching my every move, trying to get me to take stupid pills. I can't make them understand how it feels. How it feels to be powerless and confused because this was a man that my mom let in the house and who bought us things and took us places. He wasn't some dirty old man on the playground, you know?"

Chase silently nodded.

"I don't know how I get past that and I've tried. I've tried to push it behind me but it keeps popping back up and I can't stop it."

Silence followed until Chase finally spoke.

"I don't know if I ever told you this but when I used to babysit the kids when Audrey was at work, I watched a lot of afternoon television," he smiled and noticed Maggie do the same. "And I don't claim to be an expert on anything but I remember someone talking about this once and I paid attention, because I'm a father and my worst nightmare would be if anyone were to ever do anything to the boys. I wanted to understand what to look for, you know, maybe signs that someone is like that…"

"There aren't really signs," Maggie commented, her face slightly brighter.

"I know but I remember the lady talking about this topic saying that it never went away," he chose his words carefully. "I remember thinking, how can someone live with this every day? I know I couldn't. And then she said that it wasn't about dealing with it and moving on, it was about learning to accept that it happened and that it didn't make you less of a person, that you weren't at fault but you weren't a victim either. She said you can't let it define you."

"I don't think I"m letting it define me," Maggie whispered. "Do you?"

"No, but I think if you're not telling people close to you then maybe it makes you a bit of a victim. Cause, you know, it's kind of like you're a kid again and you feel like you have to hide that guy's secret," Chase reasoned. "Does that makes sense? I mean, if you had told me this years ago, at least I would know, right? Maybe, like that night of the RCMP thing, you could've told me that part of it and I could've helped you more because I just took it you were overly disappointed. Maybe you would've felt better if you said it and got it out, rather than holding it in."

"Yeah, I don't tell anyone," Maggie nodded. "I don't want people to think I'm damaged or fucked up. Although, maybe I am."

"You're not fucked up," Chase corrected her and reached out, carefully touching the hand that sat flat on the bed. "But you gotta trust people enough to tell them the truth, so they can help you. So, they can understand."

"Does it make a difference?"

"It does, to me," Chase replied. "It would help me make sense of a lot of things."

"It's not why I'm a lesbian, by the way," She replied. "Although, I used to have a crush on you but it wasn't in that kind of way."

"I know." Chase squeezed her hand.

"That's why I wanted you to stay away from Kelsey. She thinks she's okay but she's not."

He nodded.

"I thought she would've told you already. I thought you knew for years and just didn't say anything."

"I didn't."

"I was angry that you never brought up something so important."

"I didn't know."

"I'm sorry," Maggie squeezed his hand back. "She tells everyone, so I assumed that she had told you too."

"No."

Everything was still. Truth flowed through the room and everything suddenly felt light. They were 18 again and would never grow old.

CHAPTER FORTY-ONE

It was a few more days before they realized that Kelsey was gone. Chase assumed she was pissed off when he talked to Maggie after their fight and took off for the afternoon but would return. Maggie assumed that her younger sister took all her stuff and went back to their father's place or possibly, even to stay with Chase. She had no job, wasn't in school and therefore, no one else really missed her. After a couple of days, however, alarm bells started to go off.

Chase was helping Jolene finish setting up at a venue for their event that night when Maggie rushed in, breathlessly, her eyes flooded with worry. Jolene had been mid-sentence when abruptly interrupted, her irritation quickly dissolved upon hearing Maggie's muffled words, as tears began to flow down her face. If anything, Jolene looked stunned by this reaction.

"Chase, please tell me you have Kelsey at your place?"

Frozen on the spot, his heart raced as he quickly assessed the situation and with regret, shook his head no. "I...I assumed that she was at your place."

"No, she took her stuff," Maggie rushed through her words. "Has she text you?"

Chase shook his head no but grabbed his phone in case something new had developed. "No, she hasn't. I texted her and she didn't reply, but she's ignored my texts for months, so that's not anything new for her."

"Fuck!" Maggie shouted while simultaneously started to cry harder. "I don't know where she is! She's not at my dad's and she didn't go home.

And if she's not with you, where is she? Oh my God, she's so crazy, what if she went to some stranger's house. She doesn't know the city, Chase-

"Why don't you call the police?" Jolene interrupted and walked over to join them, having just dropped a massive stuffed animal, the entire room looked like a combination of a child's birthday party and a luxurious, naughty night in. Sex toys that he hadn't even known existed were placed throughout the venue, not to mention candy dishes of condoms to keep things 'sanity', a creepy kind of reality that he tried not to think about as he helped Jolene create this ultimate fantasy environment that women paid big money to experience. It felt like the most unlikely atmosphere to have this particular conversation.

"Maybe you *should* go to the police," Chase added as he glanced around the room. "I don't think we want them coming here, though."

"Good point, we take you to the police. Maybe talk to them and see, yes?" Jolene's words were strong, showing the assertiveness needed in this kind of situation. "I'm sure she is fine but, I don't know. Maybe if everyone text her, she will reply to someone."

"I texted her a thousand times and she hasn't replied," Maggie was insistent, she stopped crying and was now panicky. "I shouldn't have said those awful things to her, I was horrible to her the other day."

"Maggie," Jolene spoke calmly, although Chase was sure he heard a condescending tone underneath her expressions of concern. "We all get upset sometimes. It does not mean the world eats us, it means we are upset. She's not a little child."

Chase had to admit that Jolene had a point. Kelsey could be erratic and emotional but she wasn't a moron either. Perhaps they weren't giving her enough credit. As much as he wanted to find her to make sure she was okay, he also didn't think it was necessary to assume the worst. It seemed a tad dramatic, then again, maybe he was being too casual?

"She's my sister, you don't understand," Maggie responded like a child herself, causing Chase to be apprehensive and decided to say nothing. "What if she's hurt?"

"You will learn if she is, but for now why make assumes that she's in danger?"

Neither of them corrected Jolene's grammar. Although she insisted that they did in order to improve her English, she always got defensive and angry when they tried.

"Chase, can you text her?" Jolene calmly asked. "Give me her number, I text her too."

"She doesn't know you," Maggie reminded her.

"I do not care, Maggie," Jolene spoke her name in the usual disdainful tone. "I will tell her who I am and to let us know she's okay."

"She won't reply." Maggie insisted but gave her Kelsey's number, while Chase sent out a pleading text for her to let them know she was fine.

"Ok, I will text too." Jolene concentrated on her phone, something she did when texting. She spoke and wrote slowly at times, self-conscious of making errors, although no one seemed to mind when she did. "There. She will respond."

"She's not going to-

"Ah, there she is," Jolene cut off Maggie. "She says, 'I am fine. Tell them to leave me alone'."

Chase and Maggie exchanged looks. Jolene turned the phone toward them to prove her point, Kelsey's number showed up clearly, as did her reply.

"Now," Jolene continued, "Can we please get back to work. We have a lot to do. Unless, *Maggie,* you have another emergency?"

Looking crestfallen, Maggie shook her head no. She was in charge of picking up supplies and Jolene added more to her list before she exited the venue.

"That Maggie," Jolene shook her head as she pulled a second love seat into the centre of the room, creating a 'space for intimate conversation', "A good worker but too dramatic. Young girls, always are too dramatic." She stopped and rolled her eyes. "I was too but one day I saw that nothing is worth it."

Chase nodded. He couldn't disagree with that statement. He didn't understand why women made such uncomplicated situations difficult when most things in life were simply a matter of problem and solution. You had a problem, you solved it. You didn't like something, you changed it. You weren't happy, you find happiness. He got that women were wired differently and overthought things, but it seemed like a waste of time to him. Then again, maybe he should've given more thought to things. Perhaps that was the balance between men and women he decided.

"What happened, Chase?" Jolene asked, after moving the chair slightly to the right, she sat down. "I need a break. So, what happened? Mr. Jacobs, tell me a story. Make it a good, I've had a long week."

Grinning he joined her in the 'intimate conversation' area, sitting beside her in another plush chair that was a pricey rental from a business that was usually quite happy to see them arrive. The Latino man would actually clap his hands and bow when they walked in his door. "Well, hello Ms. Silva! What a pleasure to see you again!" They would give a rushed kiss on each cheek, then get right to business. Chase remained quiet.

"There was a bit of a ruckus the other night," He said and immediately noticed a curious look on her face. Realizing that it 'ruckus' probably wasn't a word she was familiar with, he corrected himself "I mean, there was a bit of…drama, as you put it."

"I gather, so tell me more…"

Chase hesitated for a moment, glanced toward the door as if Maggie might still be there and launched into the detailed story. Jolene looked intrigued, reacting to every tidbit; giggling when he told of Kelsey meeting him naked, about Maggie showing up with her 'friend' and then the blowout, followed by what he learned about the Telip girls' childhood. She pouted with the story's conclusion.

"Well, I do understand now. Kelsey left because she was embarrassed," Jolene spoke evenly. "She puts on a good act but she felt stupid and maybe, a little awkward for not telling you the truth sooner. Maybe even a bit jealous of your friendship with her sister, even though it is *just* friendship, you know?"

Chase nodded and considered her words.

"I think it will blow over," Jolene nodded and Chase joined her. "It's sister stuff. But the molesting thing, it does explain a lot. There's a lot, how do you say, weird things with Maggie. She's not okay but at least you know why. I do too, I guess, so that's good."

"How did you get Kelsey to respond to your text so fast, by the way?"

"I told her I might be hiring again," Jolene gave a mischievous grin. "And that you recommend her."

"I did?"

"Of course not but she will meet us later today, so you can talk to her." Jolene insisted. "I get the job done, as they say."

"I guess so."

"Every problem has a solution and sometimes, those solutions aren't necessarily as complicated as we like to think," She raised an eyebrow as an older man walked in the door. "There's the owner of this place," she gestured in his direction. "I must talk to him about something, you can finish arranging things here, you know what I want, yes?"

"Sure," Chase rose from his seat and got back to work. Trying to arrange furniture and setting up for an event while wearing a suit was hardly his idea of comfort but considering she was doing the same in heels and a dress, he wasn't about to complain. Jolene was all about having a professional image and she insisted that this was something that could be lost in a second. He learned a lot from her and actually, she was probably the best boss he ever had. Even this situation with Kelsey, she calmly and rationally knew how to resolve it.

Kelsey dropped in later that morning, looking fresh and together as she pulled her suitcase behind her as if she was a gypsy with no place to go. Wearing a similar outfit as previously, he was relieved that she wasn't dressed like a teenager hanging out at the mall all weekend but rather an adult woman. Not that he thought Jolene was even remotely interested in hiring her but he still wanted her to look respectable in front of his boss, who judged people harshly at times. Also, he knew she already didn't like Maggie and hoped her impression of Kelsey would be better.

"Hey Chase," She spoke casually, as Jolene watched her from the corner of her eye across the room, where she and the venue owner were making sure a special swing was firmly supportive for 'the girls'. He didn't ask and in a way, preferred not to know; the early intrigue of working for female sex parties wore off quickly for him.

Not aware that they were being watched, Kelsey shrugged out of her lady-like coat, that reminded Chase of the one Jolene owned and displayed a figure fitting leopard print blouse and tight black pants, leading to a long pair of sleek boots with heels. She plunked down on the chair that Jolene was using earlier that morning, only briefly glancing around the room but appearing unmoved by the setup. "What's up?"

"I could ask you the same."

"I was out, discovering the city," She replied as if there was nothing out of the ordinary about disappearing for a few days. "So did you fuck Maggie?"

This question came up as Jolene started to make her way back to the centre of the room, where Kelsey sat. She made a funny face when she heard Kelsey's bold question.

"No, she's still a lesbian, Kelsey," Chase spoke firmly, a little insulted by the question.

Jolene interrupted their moment of hostility, clapping her hands together. "Well, you must be the missing Kelsey that I'm hearing about all morning?" Her voice had some softness in it as she leaned up against the chair arm that was opposite of Kelsey, who suddenly sat up slightly straighter. "I hear you were on an adventure, maybe?"

"I was exploring."

"You look fine," Jolene commented and glanced toward Chase. "Didn't I tell you? She's fine."

"I think Maggie thought she might not be," he calmly remarked.

"As if she cares," Kelsey said and rolled her eyes. "Maggie is all about Maggie drama and only Maggie drama."

Jolene let out a short laugh. "I like this one, Chase." She pointed toward Kelsey.

Kelsey seemed to light up with this comment and turned toward Jolene.

Chase suddenly realized that it was up to him to make an official introduction. "Oh sorry, Jolene, this is Kelsey and Kelsey, this is my boss, Jolene."

"Pleasure," Jolene rose from her seat and reached out to shake Kelsey's hand. "Nice to meet you.

"You too," Kelsey looked slightly enamored by the attention and Chase realized that there may be a reason for that; she didn't get a lot of it, at least, not that easily.

"You and I, we must talk," She gestured toward the door. "Chase we are going to go for a coffee across the street. We will be back soon."

Kelsey looked stunned but quickly jumped up from her seat and grabbed her coat and suitcase.

"You can leave that here, Chase will be here and will look after it." Jolene pointed at the luggage and Kelsey mindlessly let go. "Ok?" She turned her attention to Chase.

Nodding, he replied. "Yeah, sure. Jolene, can you grab me a coffee on your way back?"

"I grab you lunch on the way back," She winked at him and led Kelsey toward the door.

He wasn't sure what was going on, but something told him that Jolene had something up her sleeve. Regardless, he suspected that Maggie wouldn't like it.

CHAPTER FORTY-TWO

Where Kelsey had been for those unaccounted for days, Chase would never know. He suspected Jolene had the answer but decided to leave it alone. The less he asked, the less he knew. Eventually, Maggie would bombard him with questions and it was better if he had nothing to tell her. He had his own family drama.

It was that same afternoon, after rushing around with Jolene and eventually going home for a quick nap before the party began, that he received a call from Audrey. She hardly ever picked up the phone to reach out to him, usually preferring to communicate through text, Skype for the kids, he immediately sensed something was wrong. He was right.

"Albert is moving in," She referred to her boyfriend who had suddenly appeared in the picture shortly after the couple officially broke up. Chase had his suspicions that Albert had actually been around before but didn't care. It was water under the bridge. Even this piece of news didn't really concern him, other than how it would affect his children.

"What about the boys?"

"He loves them."

"Are you sure he's...okay?"

"What do you mean by 'okay'?" Audrey spoke with a tinge of offensive in her voice. "What are you implying, Chase?"

"I mean, he's not....fucked up or anything?"

"More than you, you mean?" Audrey asked as bitterness crept in. "Does he fuck other women on the side, take off all hours of the day or night? No, Chase, he's not 'fucked up'."

Ignoring her suggestion, he continued, "I mean he's not, you know, too friendly with the kids?"

"What are you trying to say?"

"I was thinking of someone who recently told me about being molested as a kid-

"Oh, you were talking to Kelsey and Maggie?" She asked nonchalantly, her frustration seemed to dissolve. "Chase, I'm a professional counselor, I think I would know the signs. Albert isn't a pedophile if that's what you're suggesting."

He cleared his throat and said nothing. Closing his eyes, he felt a surge of mixed emotions; relief that the kids would have a father figure around, yet disappointment that he was about to be replaced by another man.

"Chase, this really is for the best," Audrey spoke up as if sensing his concern. "Trust me, this will work out. Just be available to the kids if they need you."

That was the concern. He didn't think they did.

"Did you just find out about Maggie and Kelsey? I thought one of them would've told you long ago, where you're so...close." She changed the topic and in a way, Chase was kind of glad. He felt a heaviness in his chest when they talked about the kids and welcomed moving away from the topic. It was too much to deal with right at that moment, with a lack of sleep and too much caffeine in his system. He knew Audrey saw him as nothing more than a sperm donor; an absentee father who was a child support payment away from being irrelevant.

"Ah yeah, I had no idea."

"Kelsey told me about that a while ago around the time she was babysitting for me, so I assumed you knew," Audrey explained. "I kind of saw the signs, though, to be honest."

"You did?"

"Yeah."

Another twinge of hurt stabbed him, causing him to wonder why neither of them felt comfortable talking to him about it, yet Kelsey had been forthcoming with Audrey, who was hardly a friend. He didn't verbalize his concerns but instead ended their conversation with the excuse of having to return to work. It was kind of true.

Lying on the couch, he felt nausea creeping in, left with an unsettling feeling that filled ever corner of his body, he realized that his busy lifestyle was merely masking these unsettled emotions that he hadn't wanted to deal with for so long. Losing his father, his lack of a relationship with the man who had brought him up and here he was, being the exact same parental figure to his kids. The difference being that his father was physically in the same house while he grew up but was he ever really *there* at all? He never stood up for Chase nor did he really show any involvement as a parent. Like father, like son. Chase hadn't really been 'there' for his kids either, except for those months he was jobless while Audrey went out to work.

Then again, he couldn't go back to Hennessey. Even if he did, the kids had adopted their new father and he was more stable than Chase had ever been. Was it better to leave things as they were or did that make him a terrible father? He considered contacting his sister to talk about it, but clearly, she wasn't available to him. Since moving to Calgary, they met only once and it was strained and awkward. She brought her boyfriend, who stared at Chase as if he were a freak show and neither had ever suggested meeting up again.

His former life was crumbling and even though he had hoped to have a clear path between his past and future, sometimes that wasn't possible.

The day floated on into the evening and after a shower, shave and change clothes, Chase was back to work at the same venue he had helped Jolene set up early that same morning. He was tired but it didn't really matter. This was the easy part of his job. He simply had to let women into the event, comparing their special cards to a list of names, in case someone tried to sneak in with a fake one. Things were pretty underground, so the majority of people weren't even aware that this kind of event even existed. They moved cities so quickly, most not willing to talk about their experience, therefore keeping it a small, selective club. He noted that many were from out of town, often from neighboring cities and provinces, probably to keep animosity. The women were beautiful, though; it was rare that someone unattractive slipped through the doors and although this was an enticing concept to him early on, it seemed to fade as the weeks and months went on.

The only unfortunate thing was that their parties ran really late. Sometimes until 6 in the morning, depending on how late guests decided to stay. He wanted to get home and sleep but was stuck guarding the door for the night, in case there was any trouble or some random person attempting to get in. Occasionally, Jolene would watch over things and allow him a break but their staff was quite limited. Bartenders tended to belong to the establishment they used for the parties, however, the staff was asked to sign a confidentiality agreement, promising to keep quiet about what took place; although most were used to that anyway. The staff was also monitored carefully to make sure they wouldn't do or say anything to make Jolene's clients feel uncomfortable.

It was around 1 AM that night when Jolene rushed out and grabbed Chase by the arm, abruptly pulling him inside. Knowing the door locked automatically so that no one could wander in once he left the entrance, his concern was why she was silently dragging him through the event. She had been clear that he was to never see what happened inside these parties, so obviously something was very wrong. He could see it in her eyes.

Although rushed, he did see a lot as she pulled him through. For a moment, he was stunned; while many women were simply talking, touching an arm or hand of another lady, things didn't look as raunchy as he originally imagined. However, the deeper they got inside the bar, the more that changed. A stripper was dancing around a pole to *Pour Some Sugar on Me*, completely naked except for a pair of thongs, while women watched, one suddenly jumped on stage with her and although he knew Jolene wouldn't like that, she clearly was concerned with something else, as she continued to pull him through the crowd.

That's when it got weird. The things he thought would be a turn on and make him weak in the knees, actually kind of made him feel awkward. Women were making out, some were openly using sex toys, unaware that he was even passing through, locked in their own desire while others watched, finding pleasure in what they viewed. Women were going down on one another in dark corners of the bar, many areas set up in advance for 'some privacy' but clearly, not that much. The entire thing was like a sexual zoo that seemed to get more and more bizarre as they moved through. Stuffed animals were a little weird for him, as were some of the toys in use, but he averted his eyes only to have something overhead grab his attention. It was Kelsey. Naked and on the swing that Jolene had put so much care into having installed earlier that day.

Oh, fuck!

Deciding that it was better to pretend he hadn't seen that, he felt mixed emotions about her role in the night, deciding silence was the answer more and more in his life.

The lights were brighter as they wandered down a hallway that led to the ladies' washroom; although that particular night, women were free to use either washroom, since other than occasional male staff, only women attended these parties.

Maggie met them, dressed professionally in a form-fitting red skirt and blazer, a look of horror on her face that told him that something was *very* wrong.

Oh, fuck.

She moved aside with a pleading look in her eyes as he passed and Jolene's hand seemed to grow tighter around his wrist. They entered the ladies room, to find a young woman passed out on the floor, with what appeared to be vomit running down her face and chin. She was as white as a ghost and his first assumption was that she was dead.

"Chase, the cocaine, it took her," Jolene commented as he glanced from the lifeless woman on the floor to those who stood around; one he recognized as the owner of the establishment but there was also an unfamiliar woman crying, he assumed she was a friend or someone who had discovered the unconscious woman. The owner had been asking her some questions and ushered her out.

"Chase, you must take her out of here," Jolene was clearly distressed. "Take her to the hospital."

He apprehensively touched the woman's skin, it wasn't cold but it wasn't exactly warm either. "Is she alive?" Chase searched for her pulse and thought he found one, but then again, was that wishful thinking on his behalf? Was that his own heart pounding through his chest, forcing blood to rapidly move through his body that he was feeling, as his shaking fingers pressed into her neck. She was a thin brunette, dark curly hair disheveled, drool was running into her ear, while the stench of vomit was strong. He noted some was on her thin, purple top.

"But shouldn't we call-

"No no no! We cannot," Jolene abruptly shook her head and the establishment owner joined in, leaning down to look Chase in the eye.

"No man, we can't have that kind of attention," he was insistent. You got to get her out of here. Take her out the back."

"Is your car there, Chase?" Jolene appeared more upset. "I come with you."

"No no, you gotta stay here," The owner insisted, while Chase decided to ignore both of them and carefully slid his arms under the woman and pulled her off the ground. Her head fell back with such abrupt force, he was frightened she was dead. Her body was so light, yet there was a heaviness that could be felt surrounding her as if she were an angel with cast iron wings.

"I'll take her, but what do I say."

"You found her outside." Jolene insisted. "I've done this before, trust me."

"You saw her outside when you were driving down the road, heading to the bar down the street," The venue owner gestured toward the door. "She was on the sidewalk. You saw her and stopped the car, grabbed her and brought her to the hospital."

"You didn't call 911 cause you feared it would take too long," Jolene added. "But she wasn't here, you weren't working, I don't care, do not tell them she was here. We don't want an investigation."

Chase nodded and without saying a word, rushed toward the back emergency exit, rushing into the silence of the night. He quickly located his car and at first, hadn't realized Jolene was right behind him.

"I help." She grabbed his keys, opening the door and helping him get the woman inside. Although she continued to show calmness, it was clear a great deal of anxiety was lingering in the wings; she was scared.

"Chase, I trust you," Her eyes were glossy as if tears were being fought off. "Okay?"

He nodded and jumped in the car, wasting no time getting on the road and speeding to the hospital. Fortunately, it was close, so the story that he felt it would be faster to bring her there than to wait for an ambulance seemed likely.

Arriving at the emergency, he flew into a parking spot and threw the car into park, jumped out, pulled the strange woman out the passenger side and ran into the emergency room. After repeating his rehearsed story of finding her on the sidewalk nearby, he was asked to go to the waiting room until the police arrived to talk to him. In the combination of rushed staff and lack of people around to notice during that late hour, he managed to slip out the door and back to his car. There, he felt his emotions pulling him down. No longer on the high of adrenaline, he felt overcome by anxieties, weak as he glanced at the now empty passenger seat and worried that the stranger was possibly dead. There had been much concern when he brought her in but something told him that being dressed in a suit and tie probably gave his story more credit than had he walked in wearing jeans and a t-shirt. Now he understood Jolene's logic.

He managed to calm himself enough to drive back to the event, although he felt like a zombie, as he made his way through the streets and finally, the same parking spot he had before his rushed trip to emergency.

Chase sat in his car for a long time. Frozen, he was unable to move and felt a sense of calmness flow through him, while pain shot through his arms, an undeniable ache that resembled that after hours at the gym, begging for a hot shower and to sleep. But would he ever be able to sleep again?

Chapter Forty-Three

"It is something I should've told you before," Jolene spoke as the two sat at the bar, long after the patrons had left, as the sun began to peek through the morning skies. They were all tired. The venue owner, Bob, was behind the bar and had poured them each a shot after an eventful night. Maggie, Kelsey, and the others were now long gone, Jolene insisting that they discuss this incident later. Chase wished more than anything that he was home in his own bed but at the same time, didn't know if he would be able to sleep even though exhaustion was overwhelming his body. He felt as though he was slowly shutting down, each limb was heavy, his back was starting to ache and there was a sharp pain traveling from behind his eyes to his ear, that were impossible to ignore.

"It does not happen often but sometimes," She pointed in the general direction of the washrooms and although it felt like Jolene was about to say more, her words suddenly halted and Chase felt as though he could lay his head on the bar and sleep. He wanted to talk about this but more than anything, he wanted to leave.

"Many bar owners will tell you the same thing," The older man with a touch of gray in his hair spoke matter-of-factly to Chase as if he were a part of their inside clique that was allowed to know this secret information. He was also wearing a shirt and tie, something Jolene would've insisted on, although Chase noted the tie was now loose as if he welcomed the moment when he could take it off completely. Women didn't understand how constrictive and uncomfortable they could be;

like a symbolic noose around your neck, much like a collar you would put around an animal, just before you took him for a walk.

When Chase didn't reply, Bob appeared slightly awkward and continued to talk. "It can fuck your business if you have this kind of attention on it, especially if the person dies. People want to blame the bar even though it's not the bar's fault. Customers sneak it in."

Chase nodded in silence and stared at his empty shot glass. He got that but having worked for Bud, he knew that a lot of seedy things took place at a bar; in fact, Chase knew that more than anyone else. Chances were good that this guy was hardly the innocent victim of any accusations but at that moment, he didn't care either. He wondered what happened to the girl. He worried that someone spotted him leave and maybe he was caught on camera. There was no way he could justify leaving when he was specifically asked to stay and talk to the police.

Maybe that was the key word; *asked.* No one told him he couldn't leave but then again, that wasn't exactly their job either.

"What about the girl?" Chase spoke up. "Will she tell the cops?"

"That she was at a girl on girl bar? Probably not." The man behind the bar snickered while his eyes were self-consciously glancing toward Jolene as if looking for assurance.

"No, she will not tell," Jolene insisted. "When the payment is made, there is a form that they must click 'yes' to before they can move forward. It states that no drugs are to be brought on the premise."

"Does anyone actually read those things before they sign?" The bar owner asked with a smirk on his face, as he leaned forward, almost seductively glancing over Jolene's body.

"It does not matter. It is all our words over hers anyway. We say no, we did not find her." Jolene insisted. "Worst case, if they find out about the party, Chase can say he had to leave the party to get something and that's when he saw her outside. She was taking drugs, no one will believe her and no one saw anything at the bar."

"What about the woman that was in the bathroom?" Chase suddenly remembered her frightened face.

"She will not talk." Jolene sat up a little straighter. "I talk to her. It's taken care of."

A chill ran through him that he chose to ignore. He wasn't sure if he knew all the details but he also knew that it was better to not ask. The worst possible situation was that he would be caught in a lie but chances were good that the police didn't have time for every OD case they ran into on the weekends, unless....

"What if she dies?" Chase couldn't help but ask the question that had been lingering all evening.

"She will not die, Chase," Jolene assured him. "She got to the hospital. She will be fine."

He didn't speak and neither did the venue owner.

It was well after 7 AM when he finally arrived back to his building. Turning the corner to his apartment, he was surprised to find Kelsey sitting outside his door, tapping vigorously on her phone. She suddenly looked up and quickly jumped off the floor. Her eyes widened as she began to talk but he immediately put up a hand to indicate that she stop.

"Kelsey, I'm exhausted and it's been a really long night, can we talk tomorrow?"

"Chase, were you there when that girl died?" Kelsey shot back as he froze, his key halfway into the lock. "She died, right? You got rid of the body, right?"

"Kelsey," He laughed in part because of his exhaustion and in part because of the absurdity of the question, followed by the relief of knowing that the stranger's death was an assumption, rather than a fact. "She's not dead, she Oded and I rushed her to the hospital. Where do you get this stuff?"

"Maggie said she didn't look good when you took her away."

"She didn't look good but most people don't when they've Oded, Kels," he pushed his apartment door open and noted that she made herself at home, walking into the apartment despite the fact that he was exhausted and just wanted to sleep. "But I assure you, she was alive when I got to the hospital."

"Did you stick around?" She asked as he closed the door behind them.

"No."

"Can I stay?" She pointed toward the couch.

Shrugging, he threw his keys on the island separating the kitchen and living room and walked toward the bathroom. After throwing some water on his face and looking into his own red eyes in the mirror, he felt the miseries of the night creep up on him as he slowly recalled the events that would forever be etched in his memory. What if that woman died? It was completely possible, wasn't it? He chose not to think of it and sensed that this would be a dark chapter in his life that he'd never truly be able to put in the past.

Slowly opening the door, he was relieved to see Kelsey settled on the couch as he made his way to bed. Undressing, leaving on only a pair of boxers, he climbed into bed and closed his eyes. Expecting that he would immediately fall into a peaceful sleep, instead, his mind ran continually as he drifted off. Nighttime visions of the woman's corpse in his car, decomposing before his eyes inhibited his entire being, as he suddenly awoke, feeling a pleasurable sensation traveling through his groin. His hand reached down and he felt a face. It was Kelsey sucking his dick. As much as his usual inclination was to tell her to stop, in that moment he had no desire to discourage her, seeking the physical pleasure accompanying as a distraction to the last 24 hours.

His desire built quickly as he sent out a sharp gasp just as she stopped. Moving away, but only briefly while he put on a condom, he could see she was naked as she silently climbed on top of him, she pulled him inside of her and he gasped as a warmth filled his entire body as she moved on top of him, quickly picking up her speed as she moaned loudly, her legs straddling him with such strength that he was unable to move, as waves of pleasure were overwhelming and were welcomed, as his hands reached out to touch her body, squeezing her breasts as she moaned softly, her eyes closed as if she was only focused on finding the pleasure she sought. It happened fast. Really fast. Had she not displayed such clear signs of satisfaction, he would've feared that he was the only one who benefited from the encounter. His heart rate still not subsiding as she pulled away from him, a relaxation flowed through him and he craved another encounter with her immediately, even though he knew his limitations; he needed time to recoup.

Without saying a thing, she rose from the bed and went into the bathroom. He closed his eyes for a moment feeling peaceful for the first time in weeks; satisfaction was something he cherished now that he had fewer opportunities to obtain it and he was surprised to not feel guilt or discomfort about having such an intimate encounter with the same girl who used to chase him around Hennessey, practically begging him to sleep with her. It always felt so wrong but at that moment, it felt right.

He wanted to tell her this but when he opened his eyes again, she was gone. Not in his bed. Naked, he jumped up and looked through the apartment to find no trace she had ever been there. Had it been a fantasy? Maybe a dream? Had the anxiety of the night before caused him to create an illusion as an escape?

Sitting on the edge of his bed, he glanced at the clock and saw it was well after noon. He grabbed his phone but as usual, there were no texts. He sent her a message that didn't mention what happened, just a simple, 'where are you?' that would not be answered. She never answered. Maybe it was her version of silence that gave her a sense of power.

He sent Maggie a message and asked if he could drop by to talk about the previous night. He got a simple 'OK' and after a quick shower, he grabbed a banana on the way out the door.

Arriving at Maggie's apartment, he secretly hoped to find Kelsey but she was nowhere to be seen. Casually, after the two talked about the OD victim from the night before he brought up Kelsey's name.

"So, Kels is working at parties now?" He carefully entered that forbidden territory and noted Maggie was rolling her eyes.

"Oh, don't even get me started. That swing thing was her idea. I think Jolene had planned to hire someone to swing naked and I guess Kelsey, being insane Kelsey, decided to volunteer her services."

"I'm surprised you didn't say anything."

"I can't. Jolene's the boss and if you hadn't noticed, she doesn't like me very much," Maggie reminded him and shrugged, brushing aside a strand of her hair. She wore no makeup and was dressed in a casual t-shirt and yoga pants. It felt weird to sit across from her and not feel an attraction. At least, one that wasn't as primal as it used to be when his entire life seemed to be lead by his desires.

"Did you say something to Kelsey?"

"Does it matter, Chase? She doesn't listen to me." She shook her head. "I don't even know where the fuck she is. She was here last night and I woke up today and she was gone."

Chase shook his head. "She likes to disappear."

"But where? Where's she going?" Maggie put the question out that he had wondered too. "I mean, where's she going in a strange city? Who's she with? That's what worries me."

He nodded and didn't reply. She hadn't said a word to him during or after their encounter. Still, he thought he felt something surge between them, something stronger than he would've expected but her absence implied it wasn't mutual.

"I don't know. I'm wondering that too."

"I guess we will never know." Maggie insisted and let out a little laugh. "I think she has been hanging out with you too much, she doesn't talk."

Chase let out a self-conscious laugh but didn't reply.

It was on the following Monday morning, a rare one when Maggie was actually available to join him and Jolene at the office, that the police walked into the room and his heart stopped.

CHAPTER FORTY-FOUR

Although sheer terror briefly crossed her eyes, Jolene was quick to regain her composure and standing tall with her usual unshakable confidence, she nodded toward the two RCMP officer's as they approached. "Good morning, can I help you with something?"

The younger of the two glanced in Maggie's direction and that's when Chase got a sick feeling in his stomach. Jolene was expressionless while Maggie's face completely drained of color, as her eyes glanced from one officers face to another. It was as if the two Constables were suddenly aware of the strange combination of reactions in the room, judging by how their eyes were analyzing the situation, Chase made every effort to remain stone-faced. The last thing he wanted to do was to bring suspicion onto himself. He remained calm as he listened to them talk.

"We're looking for Kelsey Telips regarding an investigation," The older of the two officers spoke while the other one continued to watch Maggie's reaction; tears were forming in her eyes, while some color returned to her face, but in this case it was dark hues of red that were anything but subtle. Chase could tell by Jolene's expression that she wasn't happy with Maggie's emotional reaction, as she pursed her lips tightly together. "Her parents said she was staying with Margaret, or Maggie Telips, sister. We were told she might be here."

"Kelsey is my sister," Maggie replied in a whisper and quickly cleared her throat and turned in her chair. "What did she do?"

The Constable glanced at Chase and Jolene, returning his gaze to Maggie. "Do you know where she is? We need to ask her a few questions regarding an ongoing investigation. Is she staying with you?"

"She was but I haven't seen her since Saturday night," Maggie spoke earnestly. "She tends to take off and not respond when we message her. I don't know where she is right now. I can try to text her if you want?"

"We have her number," his reply was direct, his expression unreadable. "I would also like to speak to you as well for a moment."

"You can have my office," Jolene spoke evenly, her eyes glanced toward Chase as she reached for her purse. "We can leave for a while so that you can talk to Maggie." She was moving away from the desk and following her lead, Chase rose from his seat and noted that Maggie was giving him a begging glance. The last thing he wanted to do was stick around for this conversation. He had no idea what Kelsey was up to but he was finding her antics to be draining and confusing. Where she once was a whimsical young woman who was full of energy and light, she was now mysterious and there was a darkness, a secretive side of her that he didn't understand.

"We would appreciate that," The constable nodded and Jolene gave him a brief, small smile and glanced toward Chase, who quickly followed her toward the door.

"Maggie," Jolene called over her shoulder as they reached the exit and Chase reached for the doorknob. "Text us when you have finished."

It wasn't until they were outside that Jolene had a flash of anger cross through her dark eyes as she shook her head and gestured toward the building's main exit.

"Idiota!" Jolene snapped and reached in her purse. Pulling on a pair of oversized Gucci glasses, she snapped her heels against the pavement, as they headed toward the closest coffee shop. "How can she act like such a whiny girl the minute the police walk in the room? It makes us all look guilty."

"I think she was worried that something happened to Kelsey since she always goes missing," Chase attempted to explain as he rushed to keep up with Jolene's quickened pace, the smell of diesel filled the air as a large truck passed them. The chatter of young girls behind them was hard to miss, as he turned and saw a group of young woman ogling him as they followed him and Jolene on the sidewalk. His boss didn't notice; she was still stewing over Maggie's reaction.

"You never act weak with the police, you do not do that!" She complained as they entered the coffee shop and walked up to the counter. The young woman working at the cash was Latino, a smile lit up her face and she immediately addressed Jolene in Spanish.

"Hola!"

The two talked rapidly with words that were unfamiliar, yet intriguing to Chase, as he stood back and after the two women laughed, the lady behind the counter glanced at Chase and made a comment to Jolene.

"No," she replied and said something else as the young woman grabbed two large cups and wrote something on them as she nodded at the same time, a giggle rose from her throat and she shrugged. He looked away, having no idea what they were talking about but suddenly wished he knew Spanish.

It was only after they were at a table that Jolene's original demeanor dropped as she explained to Chase that the woman thought he was her 'boy toy'.

"She asked if you were my younger boyfriend," Jolene giggled and placed her purse on the empty chair beside her. "She said you are so handsome. But I say no, you work for me."

"Oh," he wasn't sure how to respond to this, his mind still back with Maggie and the RCMP officers, it was difficult for this conversation to distract him in the least. He watched as Jolene tapped on her phone as a strand of her long, dark hair fell forward into her face. Taking a drink of his coffee, he remained silent with his thoughts.

"I tell Kelsey about this," she pointed in the general direction of the office. "She's replying, I can see."

"She's replying?" Chase almost choked on his coffee. Kelsey never replied to him or Maggie but always to Jolene? Why was that?

"Yes, she say that she knows what this is about," her eyes met with Chase's and she stared for a long moment. "She said you would too?"

"I just assumed when they walked in, it was over what happened on the weekend," Chase admitted. "I don't know why they're looking for

Kelsey. She hardly ever talks to me anymore, so if she's in some kind of trouble, I don't know what it's about."

"She's coming here," Jolene replied as she looked at her phone, perhaps not even listening to his words. "She said she will explain."

Chase had a quick, inappropriate flash from the weekend and felt a tinge of desire that caused him to look away and unfortunately, glance in the direction of the barista behind the counter. She gave him a quick smile and he felt color fill his cheeks.

"Chase, what is going on with you?" Jolene's voice was soft, almost vulnerable. "What is with you and Kelsey? Did something happen?"

"What do you mean?"

"You *know* what I mean," she gently replied. "Why are things so weird between the two of you?"

"I don't know."

"She doesn't answer your texts? I understand her not replying to Maggie, but why you?"

"I don't know."

"But that doesn't make sense."

"Ever since I moved, that's how it has been." He replied as she took another sip of his coffee as the sun touched his face through a nearby window and he glanced toward the sidewalk, where people were constantly rushing by, many with their heads down looking at a phone. "I don't know."

Jolene didn't reply and changed the subject.

"I hope Maggie doesn't get nervous and talk about anything with the police," she anxiously tapped her long nails on the table. "I do not want her talking about what's going on with the business or anything stupid."

"I don't think she will," Chase offered. "It sounds like this has something to do with Kelsey."

"I do not trust Maggie."

"Why not?"

"She wanted to be a police like the ones that were at our door today." She pursed her lips. "I do not trust that."

"You don't trust the RCMP?"

"No, I do not trust any police." Jolene shook her head defiantly. "No matter where I do not trust."

He merely nodded. It was better not to ask.

Their conversation went back to work, the topic of Saturday night faded away and for the most part, Chase was somewhat relieved by this shift. Eventually, Jolene received a text from Maggie stating that the RCMP were gone but she didn't offer any other details. Jolene merely rolled her eyes and pushed her phone aside. Kelsey arrived shortly after, breezily entering the shop, dragging her suitcase behind, as if it were just another day; as if it were normal to have the RCMP looking to speak with her, as if she hadn't crawled into Chases' bed on Saturday morning and snuck out after he fell asleep, as if nothing was out of the ordinary.

"Morning," she sat down between Chase and Jolene, a smile on her face. "So what's going on?"

"That is what we want to ask you," Jolene asked, her eyes searching Kelsey's face, her expression anything but pleased. "Why are there cops showing up at *my* door looking for *you?*"

"Yeah, that, I'm sorry," Kelsey replied and glanced down at her fingers. "I didn't think they would go there. I guess cause I'm staying at Maggie's and she's never home, they had to find her somewhere and you're probably listed as her employer and-

"What is going on? Do I need to know?" Jolene appeared impatient. "We have a lot of work to do today to plan six parties in and out of Alberta, we do not have time for this...*shit*. What is going on?"

Kelsey didn't reply at first, her eyes slowly glancing toward Chase. "It's got something to do with stuff that happened in Hennessey, where Chase and I are from."

Wracking his brain, he suddenly knew exactly what she was referring to, at the exact same moment as she said his name. "It's got to do with Bud"

"Bud?" Jolene asked and made a face. "What is a 'bud'?"

"It's a guy," Kelsey replied and shifted her gaze toward Jolene. "From back in Mento."

"What?" Jolene appeared even more confused. "What is a bud? And Mentos? You mean like, candy, Mento?"

"No no," Chase replied, a little frustrated by Kelsey's inability to see that Jolene struggled with English and was confused by their strange terms and names. "She's talking about a man who's nickname is 'Bud'. His real name is Brad but everyone calls him Bud. He's the guy you got a reference from before I started to work for you? Mento is a town next to Hennessey, where I'm from, that's where the bar was located."

He noted the understanding in Jolene's face as she nodded slowly and scrunched up her forehead. "Bud? Why do you have such weird names here? Bud? Chase? Do you not have normal names in little towns?"

"Nothing is normal in small towns," Kelsey spoke lightly, letting out a sharp laugh.

"So, what does this have to do with you?"

Kelsey opened her mouth to say something, immediately shutting it and looking in Chases' eyes. "It has to do with the…films.."

Shit! Fuck!

"From the back room?" Chase asked and Kelsey nodded. "The cops found them?"

Kelsey nodded again.

"And saw you?" He asked and she continued to nod. "And they want to ask questions about it? Do they know about me?"

She shook her head no, hesitated and shrugged.

"I don't think anyone knows about you and I'm pretty sure Bud isn't going to tell after you threatened to you know, kill him."

"What?" Jolene's eyes grew in size. "What is going on, Chase?"

He took a deep breath and hesitated, his eyes glancing toward the window. He couldn't avoid the truth and when he considered what happened on the weekend, something told him that Jolene wouldn't be someone who would be shaken by the truth; no matter how dark.

"When I lived in Hennessey" Chase exchanged looks with Kelsey, who quickly looked away as her cheeks flooded in color. "When I worked at this bar, I didn't know but the owner had a side business in pornography."

"Porn?" Jolene's lips parted and fell open as she moved forward in her seat. "Tell me, were you two…." She glanced at Kelsey. "Did you?" Jolene looked into Chases' eyes.

"Yeah, me but not with Kelsey, I mean, it was just a couple and ah….I was filming it in like a first person perspective, so no one can see my face." Chase stumbled and hesitated to continue, feeling flustered and awkward. "But they could see everything else."

"Oh." Her eyes doubled in size, but yet she didn't appear shocked or offended. "So you did these movies for this Bud person?"

"Yeah, I needed the money and it was stupid but I just did a couple." Chase could see that Kelsey looked on the verge of tears but felt he couldn't lie to Jolene. She would know. "And I was a kid, like 19 so I didn't see how stupid it was at the time."

"And this one," She pointed toward Kelsey.

"Bud got her involved. She was only 16 at the time." Chase spoke clearly, attempting to ignore the discomfort at the table.

Glancing at Kelsey, he noted that her crimson cheeks seemed to be fading. He wasn't about to embarrass her in any way but simply stick to the facts. She gave him a quick smile.

"And you threaten this Bud person?"

"I threatened him because she was only 16, a kid," Chase replied and noted that Kelsey was continuing to avoid Jolene's eyes. "I was furious and threatened him because I wanted him to destroy the tapes, which I guess he didn't."

"He did." Kelsey's sudden remark surprised him. "I know he did."

She had both Chase and Jolene's attention.

"There are other tapes." She replied and cleared her throat. "I made after you left town. The police raided him and found them. That's why they wanted to talk to me."

Chase felt anger rise inside of him. He had tried to help her. He had tried to save her from herself.

Misinterpreting the anger in his face, she continued, "Don't worry, your tapes you were in are gone, they don't know about them. They only want to talk to me because I wasn't quite 18 yet."

He didn't say a word as he felt the fury fill every inch of his body, as his heart raced like a freight train through his veins. Grabbing his coffee, he stood up and exchanged looks with Jolene, who said nothing; but he knew she knew. He knew she knew everything as he walked out the door.

CHAPTER FORTY-FIVE

Lucy once accused him of trying to be a 'superhero'. Confused by why she would make such a comment, a naive 17-year-old Chase laughed self-consciously and shrugged, not knowing how to respond. It was after he rushed to help a lady outside of a grocery store when one of her bags broke and cans of food rolled in various directions in the parking lot. Chase wasted no time rushing over to help her pick everything up, as she grumbled about the cashier overloading the contents.

"Damn teenagers are clueless," The older lady sharply remarked while glancing at Lucy, who apparently represented the cashier in the store. "It's common sense that these bags are cheap and will break."

Lucy rolled her eyes while Chase attempted to help the lady even further by carrying them to her car. When he returned, his then-girlfriend shook her head and criticized him for always trying to 'save' women. Giving a tentative smile, he quietly shrugged.

Chase had spent his entire life trying to be a 'good guy'. He was a compliant boyfriend to Lucy. He tolerated Audrey's bullshit, even when she made his life intolerable. He was a good kid growing up, never doing anything to cause shame to his family; never coming home drunk or stoned, always had passing grades and never got into trouble. And when he had that opportunity to have sex with an underaged Kelsey at Bud's a couple years earlier, he ignored his mounting desires and told her no. Not only did he tell her no, he threatened Bud within an inch of his life to keep away from the minor, to destroy anything he previously recorded so that the naive teenage girl could avoid making a huge mistake.

Not that it mattered. As much as he didn't want to see what Maggie had been attempting to tell him for years, Kelsey was a train wreck. That's why Maggie had given up on her, showing little interest in helping her kid sister. He hadn't seen it before but clearly, she had been exactly where he was at least once; frustrated and confused, gobsmacked that someone so smart could be so incredibly stupid. It made him wonder how many other things he didn't know about her. For example, where did Kelsey go when she disappeared from Maggie's apartment?

He didn't understand. What was his role with women? He thought about romantic comedies he used to watch with his mom while growing up. Women in these movies always seem to be damsels in distress, looking for the strong, handsome man to swoop in and save the day. Yet, the real world wasn't like that at all. Women didn't want or appreciate any help he gave them. Even the lady from the grocery store, whom he helped when her cans of dog food went flying across the parking lot, hadn't as much as thanked him for his consideration. Women thought they wanted something until they had it, then they took it for granted.

Jolene was the rare exception. She appreciated his work and perhaps, that's why he continued to be loyal to her. Always clear about what she wanted from him, Chase knew his role.

Jolene. Shit.

Chase left the coffee shop so abruptly, infuriated with Kelsey, he hadn't considered that maybe she was wondering where he was or when he'd return. Walking aimlessly, he attempted to cool off, when noticing that his gym was just around the corner. He remembered thinking that it was fortunate that it wasn't a long drive from Jolene's office, although both were a distance from his home, it was nice to have some portions of his life in a decent proximity.

Heading inside the building, he stopped briefly at the door to send Jolene an apologetic text then walked inside to the familiar stench of sweat and stale air, his membership pass quickly located in his wallet, he glanced around the almost empty room. Smiling toward the girl who worked there as a personal trainer, he wandered downstairs to what was referred as 'the boxing corner'; even though it was actually a pretty large section of the gym, although underground, which seemed kind of appropriate to him.

Noting that no one was in the room except for a skinny kid who was putting something in a gym bag, Chase headed toward the heavy bag in the corner. Removing his suit jacket and abruptly throwing it on a nearby chair, he roughly loosened his tie, slowly rolled up his sleeves in a trance-like state as anger slithered up from deep, inside him. He grabbed the first pair of boxing gloves he could find and felt the fury spreading through every inch of his body to his fingertips. Rather than to wrap his hands, he just slid them into the red gloves, noting the famous name brand in large print across the wrist, he continued to feel a rage quickening the beat of his heart. Without a second thought, he started to pummel the bag with all the ferocity that ran through his body.

The anger roared through him like a lit match gingerly falling into a drop of gasoline; explosive and furious, he felt his body temperature rise and stopped briefly to remove the gloves, throwing them to the ground. Glancing around, he saw no one else in the room; not that it would've mattered. Pulling his tie apart, he threw it on top of his blazer, followed by his shirt. Underneath he wore what Kelsey referred to as a 'wife beater'; a term he had never appreciated and picked up the gloves again.

Closing his eyes, he had a moment of complete peace that seemed to lift him from the ground, almost allowing him to float across the room. But this moment of calmness didn't last and was quickly followed by an intense wave of anger that sprung from places he hadn't thought about in years; the times his mother slapped him across the face in a drunken rage, with tears running down his face, while his father sat quietly nearby, neither condoning her or defending his son, something that was more confusing than if he had taken a side. How many times had that happened and why had it seemed to be easier and easier for his mother to do each time, eventually showing no signs of remorse over her actions?

He feared her being around his sons, but when he explained why to Audrey, she had acted as though he exaggerated and that his mother would never hit her grandchildren. Claiming to be an expert in psychology, she had diminished his concerns as if he were a hysterical man, exaggerating the facts. As usual, he was treated as if he were valueless and irrelevant. Once again, he was belittled, this time in front of his three children, as she laughed and told him to stop being a pussy.

He hadn't even realized he was hitting the heavy bag again until a gasp from behind pulled him from his blind rage, as he turned to see a young woman wearing glasses and an unflattening workout ensemble entered the room. He laughed in spite of himself while she appeared almost frightened, as the trainer from upstairs followed her down the stairs, only appearing slightly alarmed by the sweating man, wearing a business wear from the waist down, and a sweat filled muscle shirt on his upper body. He was tempted to rip it off but thought that might come across more dramatic than intended but after noticing the glasses lady's look of disapproval, he shot her an angry look and just did that; grabbing the thin material with the claw-like gloves, he ripped it off, tossing it in the corner and made his way back to the heavy bag.

The next round was hardly subtle and rather than tiring out, he instead seemed to be increasing his vigor and fury, as thoughts of his ex-wife disappeared and were replaced by Maggie; how hard had he tried to be her friend, even after she left? He had even avoided her sister when she asked, distancing himself from her both physically and mentally, only to be discarded, rather than allowed to know her vulnerable, most personal secrets? Hadn't he told her all of his? Wasn't that what women claim to want? Men to be vulnerable and honest and yet, when they were, it seemed to almost repel women, as if it were unnatural unless you were on a movie screen.

Then there was Kelsey. This thought made him halt his movement as sadness filled him. He had tried to help her. He had tried to stop her from making a huge mistake, writing it off with no judgment as being an impulsive and inexperienced move, attempting to help her move on with her life and get a fair shake. Yet, she only went back to Bud and made a movie - or movies, he wasn't even sure how many were out there? Who had she done them with? It made him as sad as it made him angry. He felt a flood of despair overrun the anger and for a minute, he thought tears would take over where the fury had so abruptly ended, but they didn't. Instead, he felt a calmness return, as he looked across the now, empty room.

Removing the gloves, his hands stiff, he gingerly returning them to where they gathered in a collection, he calmly walked back to his ripped muscle shirt and picked it up, followed by the rest of his clothes and headed toward the locker room, where he, fortunately, had some soap, deodorant, and a towel. It wasn't until he was in the shower and the hot water was pounding against his skin that he felt weak as if his emotional morning had drained every fiber of his strength, as it ran off his body and down the drain. He felt nothing; no anger, no sadness, just nothing.

Once out of the shower, he dried off and put his clothes back on, throwing the ripped muscle shirt in the garbage. He felt lighter, relaxed, as he walked back upstairs, passing the lady trainer on his way out. She gave him a sincere smile and wished him a good day. He halted for a minute, looked in her eyes and said, 'thank you' before walking out the door.

Although the spring air was warming up, a dry chill wasn't completely gone and he was thankful for putting his blazer back on, even though he originally didn't think he would need it. People rushed by him, cars moved slowly on the street and the smell of urine seemed to suddenly be everywhere but he didn't care. He walked back to work, only glancing at his phone briefly, knowing that Jolene wasn't upset and Maggie sent a few frantic texts that he wasn't ready to deal with yet.

Back in the office, Jolene was sitting behind the desk. Her expression was solemn when he entered the room. For a minute, he feared she would fire him after learning the damaging information that morning or after walking out of the coffee shop. Instead, there was some concern in her eyes.

"Are you Ok?" she showed no expression but he sensed her questions was sincere rather than just a pleasantry to gap between an awkwardness and what she really wanted to say. Her dark eyes watched his intently and her face was relaxed. She wasn't anxiously tapping her nails on the desk or fighting off anger, so that was a good sign.

"I am now."

"What did you do?" She asked. "Or should I ask such a question?"

Chase couldn't help but let out a short laugh. "I went to the gym. Hit a punching bag. Scared some chick then took a shower and here I am."

"How did you scare this, how do you say, this *chick?*" She wrinkled her eyebrows.

"Oh," He let out a laugh. "Sorry, there was a woman who saw me hitting the punching bag and I scared her."

"It is a gym, no? Wouldn't that be ok? I mean, would that be what you do at a gym?"

Chase took a deep breath and broke out in a rare smile. "I was hitting it pretty hard."

"Were you wearing that?" She pointed at his tie.

"I took off my shirt and tie," He admitted.

"Ohhh…maybe she like?" Jolene teased and winked at him.

"No," Chase continued to smile, his whole body relaxing as he sat down in the chair across from Jolene. "Nah, I don't think so. I think she thought I was an animal."

"You know, Chase," Jolene spoke thoughtfully. "We're all animals. Some of us are cute, cuddly and some of us are wild and crazy. But most of the time, we are all of these things, you know?"

He smiled and nodded.

"We are complicated. *Life* is complicated. No?"

He nodded again.

"This situation from this morning, I do not blame you for walking out," Jolene commented airily. "I slap her for you."

Chase felt his eyes double in size. "What? You slapped, who?"

"Kelsey, I slap her for you," Jolene spoke confidently. "She was being an *idiota.* I slap her hard."

Chase was stunned. "You slapped Kelsey? In the middle of the coffee shop?"

"No, in the ladies room." She spoke nonchalantly. "After you leave, I say we should come back to the office. I told her to talk to Maggie. She did not want to and that was a final straw for me, so I told her we should visit the lady's room and when we got there, I slap her across the face."

Chase was silent, still shocked by her words. Was he misunderstanding her?

"I tell her to get skinny, white *puta* ass back to this office," Jolene spoke sternly, loudly tapping her fingernail on the desk. Her face was tight, her eyes black and she pursed her lips. "I say, you go talk to your sister and you do not tell her about Chase and the movies. But you do tell her that he tried to help you and you were too *stupid* to listen. I tell her either she walk in on her own or I would drag her back every step of the way by her hair." She grasped her hands together and then regained her composure. "She did as I tell."

Chase heard himself laugh. He hadn't even realized it was coming until it did and then, he almost couldn't stop. He wanted to hug Jolene for her passion and intensity, but instead just thanked her.

"No, no thanks, it was necessary. This is too much drama, Chase. These girls bring me too much drama," She shook her head. "I tell Maggie that she needs to deal with her sister at her own time. We do not have time for this here and Kelsey, after she talk to Maggie, I do not want to see her again. Goodbye," she waved toward the invisible person at the door. "Go away, I do not want to see again. Maggie is working two jobs and isn't usually available to me, so she need to think what she want."

Chase nodded and saw exactly what Jolene was talking about. Everything she said made sense but he still couldn't believe how she treated Kelsey and when he commented on that, she merely shrugged.

"She lucky that the police wanted to talk to her today so I could not leave a bruise."

To that, he fell into hysterics and she began to giggle with him. Neither said a thing for a few minutes until Jolene finally spoke.

"Chase your heart, it is big, but you cannot help people like that. I know you want, but," she stopped mid-sentence and shook her head. "It is not good, you know?"

"I know," he nodded and glanced down at his tie. "I was thinking the same thing."

"Good. We learn lessons today."

"We learned some lessons today."

"We *learn* lessons today." She attempted to correct his grammar incorrectly and to that, he smiled. How could you argue with a woman who just slapped someone for you?

Chapter Forty-Six

It wasn't that Jolene had an issue with the movies, as Chase would later discover. After a long, hectic day of catching up at work, the two sat in a quiet restaurant for a late dinner and a glass of wine. Not normally a drinker, it was definitely a welcomed treat after a day that was both emotionally and mentally draining; first from his commotion with Kelsey in the morning and later from the vast amount of arrangements both he and Jolene had to rush to organize.

The company's parties were becoming more and more popular; who knew so many women were interested in 'exploring their sexuality' as Jolene tactfully put it. He often wondered if she was one of these women but somehow doubted it. Then again, she was a woman of mystery and he really didn't know much about her life outside of work. If she was married, she wore no ring. If she had kids, she had no pictures on her desk and made no reference to them. Then again, he didn't talk about his kids much at work either and in a way, he preferred that level of professionalism. That's why he hated that Jolene knew about the movies he did for Bud. It wasn't like he did a lot but it didn't reflect favorably on him. It was after his second glass of wine that he attempted to approach the topic with his boss.

"It is not important," she shook her head and downed the last of her red wine, signalling to the approaching waitress for another glass. "Chase, you do good work for me, why would I care about your past? I think…I think it is you who cares about this more, no?"

He considered her words briefly before nodding. "It's not one of my proudest moments, no." Chase hesitated when their waitress approached them and when she asked if he would like another glass of wine, he hesitantly said yes. It was after she left that he finally continued. "I can use the excuse of being young but I knew it was stupid back then."

"So, how do you go from working as a doorman to making such a film? I do not understand."

"I didn't even know my boss was making films. I had no idea," Chase shook his head, his wide-eyed innocence sang through even though he hadn't realized it and he briefly smiled at the waitress as she approached with his second glass of wine. "He just talked to me about this side project and the next thing I knew, I was in a room with a naked girl, holding a camera." He let out a short laugh. "As ridiculous and unbelievable as that sounds."

"Chase, I believe anything," she seemed to relax as she drank her third glass of wine, showing no real signs of intoxication, he was a little reluctant to start drinking his own glass. "There's a lot of crazy in the world, we just don't always know about it. Sometimes it is what goes on behind doors that we do not know. There is a lot of business people who say their business is about one thing and stuff is going on, you know?"

"Yes, yes I know," Chase laughed. "I always wondered how Brad ran the bar on such little business but I was a kid and didn't really think about it a lot. Now I realize that he probably had a lot of things going on I didn't know about."

"It does happen." Her voice was small this time and his eyes averted to her face; her lips were pursed as if she was attempting to not say something, as her eyes narrowed and she nodded slowly. He was starting to wonder if their business had some things going on behind the scenes that she wasn't telling him and if it did, would he be in trouble if she were ever caught? Then again, was he being judgmental? Perhaps racist, assuming that since she was Columbian that there was an illegal aspect that he wasn't aware of; since the night the woman Oded in the bathroom, he occasionally wondered if the drugs were brought in? What if there was something else going on that he wasn't privy to, always being away from the parties?

As if she were reading his mind, Jolene brought up the very thing that concerned him since the weekend.

"She is OK, that lady from the party? She is OK."

"She is?" Chase wasn't sure how else to respond. "You know?"

"I check." Her answer was simple, vague as if she didn't want to get into details. "She OK. You save her, Chase."

"I didn't save her, I took her to the hospital."

"Nah, you save her." Jolene insisted as she hunched slightly in her chair, her eyes falling to the glass of wine. "He did not want me to send her to the hospital. The owner? He wanted to throw her out and hope for the best."

"What?" Chase was a little surprised by this comment. "The venue owner? He wanted to throw her out?"

"Yes, he say, 'I don't want trouble' and I try to tell him it did not have to be like that," Jolene spoke solemnly, still avoiding his eyes. "That is why you save her life. You are a hero."

"I'm not a hero," Chase let out a short laugh, thinking back to Lucy's comments from when they were teenagers. "I don't even know if I *want* to be. No one appreciates it."

"I appreciate it," Jolene returned her gaze to him and gave him a small smile. "You do not do it to be appreciated. You do it because it makes you feel right. You do it because it *is* right. Not so that someone can pat you on the back."

She was right. He felt a wave of shame when he considered her words. It was never for them, it was for him. Maybe it was simply a life test that was made specifically for him.

He nodded and didn't reply. Taking a sip of his wine, he fell silent. Sadness filled him and he wasn't sure why.

"These bars do not want, I think you say, 'blood on their hands'," Jolene said, rubbing her hands together. "They want secretly. Just like your old boss, they want to hide things and they do no care who gets damaged. Bob wanted to put her out with the *putas* and junkies. He say, no one will know the difference. I say no."

"Your boss, Brad, in a way, he do the same. He did not care about Kelsey being a minor. He did not care about you. He cared about money. That is it. He got sloppy and he got caught. If he did not have young girls, he would not have had that problem. That is what I think," Jolene paused as she lifted the glass of wine to her mouth. "My brother,

Diego, he can be the same. That is why it is better for me to run things here. He does not care. He would agree about that lady. She would be on the street in a second if he were here."

"Your brother is cold?" Chase asked, only hearing about the company owner briefly, having not met him, he pictured him as an older, unfriendly Columbian man who probably was the opposite of Jolene in every way.

"Yes, sometimes but when it comes to love, he's a stupid man," she gestured toward her heart. "He can be very, what you say, lead by his dick? But that is okay. He will learn."

Chase assumed this was her way of saying that he was a womanizer. If he was a successful businessman and had an ounce of Jolene's attractiveness, he probably had lots of women rolling into his bed. Chase's own desires creeping in, he was jealous of a man with so many options, when his own conquests had diminished since moving to a city.

"Chase, I do not want you to get a bad idea of my brother, I do not mean he's a bad man necessarily but he thinks fast, he's impulsive," she spoke slowly as if to pick out her words carefully. "He's a bit wild. He's a daredevil."

Chase nodded, unsure of what to say.

The evening went slowly from that point on and while the wine relaxing him, he couldn't deny his attraction to Jolene, someone who originally intimidated him too much to even consider but the wine seemed to ease these fears. It was while in the bathroom and looking into the mirror a little later, that he reminded himself that she was, after all, his boss and unlike his younger days when he was, as Jolene would say, 'lead by his dick', he had to be smart. He couldn't do anything to screw up this job or his relationship with Jolene.

But the fantasy was there. It followed him home that night as he entered his apartment, hoping to enjoy it alone, he discovered a note stuck to his door.

Sorry Chase. I love you. Kelsey

Pulling it from his door, he stretched a long piece of bubble gum that she apparently used to attach it and after spending five minutes removing the remainder of the sticky substance, he felt his original desires quenched as he walked in the apartment. Half expecting to find her inside even though she didn't have a key, he was relieved that the day was over.

Checking his phone, he quickly realized that this assumption was probably a bit abrupt, after noting messages from Maggie. She wanted to talk to him.

He sent a brief messaged of one word.

OK.

Five minutes later, she was at his door. Wearing yoga pants and a fitted T-shirt, she bashfully entered the room and walked toward his couch. Neither of them said a word for a minute.

"Chase, I'm sorry about this whole, entire mess," she finally commented in a quiet voice as she sat on the edge of the couch, as if not to get too comfortable. "I'm sorry that Kelsey is such a fuck up. I'm sorry that I didn't know about the film thing and I appreciate that you tried to get her out of it. I mean, I was originally kind of pissed that you didn't tell me but I thought about it and I understand. I think I see where you are coming from. You wanted to protect me and Kelsey but I don't need protection and Kelsey, you can't help her. Fuck, she won't even help herself!"

Her last words were full of fire, anger that swept in suddenly, followed by a single tear. "I can't help her, Chase. I've tried, so many times. When we were living in Hennessey, I didn't tell you a lot of things that I did try to help her. I wanted to keep it within the family. The boys she snuck in the house, the drugs, the alcohol, it just seemed like she was always doing something stupid and I couldn't make her see why she had to change. I couldn't help her."

Chase nodded.

"Remember the time I was driving you home? The night of the party?" Maggie let out a short laugh. "We stopped and I grabbed the backpack she had hidden in the ditch? So she could go out partying later? That wasn't the first time. I always had to be two steps ahead of her. That's why she hated me so much. When she first started to hang around with you, I thought it was because she was trying to get you in her web, that's why I said to avoid her. I was a little pissed at you for not seeing what she was like but then again, I didn't exactly let you know, so I didn't have the right to be angry. I just…get so frustrated with Kelsey."

Chase shot her an understanding smile and she returned it.

"I told her today that I give up on her," She suddenly added, tears filled her eyes again and she blinked rapidly. "I can't handle her anymore. I told her she wasn't welcome back here, that she had to go to dad's house or back home with mom but she can't stay here. I can't have that in my life. She won't listen and she didn't even see what she did wrong or why she was being so stupid. She thinks she's going to be this big porn star and all these men will want her or something."

Chase looked away and thought about the night she seduced him, suddenly very relieved that he wore a condom, he was also ashamed of their encounter. He could never tell Maggie.

"It's fucked up. She needs help. Like, seriously help. She's delusional and impulsive and crazy!" Maggie commented as her hands both jutted into the air, frustrating rang through her voice and Chase related to her statement.

"I hadn't realized it was that bad," Chase admitted. "I definitely didn't know she went back to Bud's"

"I always knew there was something off about that guy," Maggie commented as she ran a hand through her hair. "He was kind of slimy but I had no idea it was something like that. I actually thought you were in on it with him, whatever it was."

"No," he replied, perhaps a little too quickly but she didn't seem to notice. Maggie shook her head and sniffed.

"I kind of get that vibe about Jolene too, actually," She placed her hands in her lap and leaned forward. "Especially after the other night."

"Well, she didn't want to alarm people, so she asked me to take her to the hospital." Chase attempted to cover things up. "The lady, she's OK. Jolene looked into it."

"You really trust Jolene?" She raised her eyebrows.

Chase shrugged.

"That's what she tells you, doesn't mean it's true or what happened was OK," Maggie insisted. "She should've called 911 and had them enter the premise. It didn't matter what was going on unless we were doing something illegal."

Those words stuck with Chase and he felt the need to defend Jolene. "Nah, it's just that she was worried about the woman's privacy."

"Yeah, maybe," Maggie considered and shrugged. "I'm not sure if I'm going to stay on. She told me today to figure out what I want and after talking to the RCMP today, I actually felt like I want to try to get in again. I got quite far than just stopped. I was busy and not so sure that it was right for me. Now I kind of think it might be worth looking into." She hesitated. "After the Constable questioned me and seemed satisfied that I had no idea about Bud, I asked him some questions and he encouraged me to try again. I think I will."

"You should."

"I might. I think I will have to quit with Jolene though," she grinned. "I don't think Jolene likes police."

Chase smiled and didn't say a word.

CHAPTER FORTY-SEVEN

Bud was arrested. Chase later heard that Lucy's boyfriend, 'Lucky Luke' was also being charged. Although dicey, it didn't appear to be the fact that they were taping porn that was a problem but that there were minors involved. Apparently, a 17-year-old Kelsey wasn't the youngest woman they had making movies; something that made Chase physically ill to learn. It became a huge controversy in the Hennessey/Mento area, bringing local, then national news teams to the area, asking local residents about the matter. Most were shocked that this kind of thing was going on, including some staff who claimed to be in the dark. Chase wondered if that was true.

He knew the day would come when the RCMP would want to interview him. Unlike Maggie, he was relieved when they arrived at his door. It was the same officers that spoke to Maggie and he could tell they immediately recognized him. He wondered if he thought it was strange that both he and Maggie left town after working for Bud, once again working for the same employer, one that dealt with some underground parties that weren't illegal but did have a shady side to them. If this was a concern, however, it wasn't clear.

Having never experienced a police interview before, he hadn't known what to expect and felt his heart race the entire time, even though the questions were simple and he remained expressionless, showing no signs of nervousness. He told the Constable that he worked the door and that was it. He had two jobs, so it was only a couple days a week, he hadn't noticed anything shady and was as shocked as everyone else. When asked if minors were allowed in the bar, Chase shook his head no.

"Not on my watch," his voice was calm as was his appearance, as he made eye contact with the officer, something that Jolene insisted was important if they were to interview him. He wasn't sure why or how she knew such a thing but felt it was solid advice. She was right. It seemed to work. The questioning felt almost unofficial, didn't last long and when the officer left, he appeared satisfied with the answers.

The early recordings of Kelsey had been destroyed, so they had no idea about the first attempts to profit off her youthful ignorance. Technically, if they did ever find any of Chases' movies, he was of age and his face wasn't even in the scenes. The girls didn't know or seem to care about his name and chances were, they were long gone anyway. Worry had filled his nights and an occasional disturbing dream haunted him but for the most part, things got back to normal a couple weeks later.

Maggie quit. She focused on her office job while working toward joining the RCMP. She seemed lighter, stronger than he had ever seen her before and almost like the old Maggie; but not quite. There was still a distance between them and even though a part of him missed their old friendship, another part of him recognized that as time moved forward, he would build new friendships. It just wasn't easy in the city, where everyone seemed to be in their own little world.

Jolene hired a new lady to be the hostess and fired her a few days later. Three girls followed, until she finally found one she liked, ironically another Columbian. The two chatted in Spanish in front of him, making him curious to know the language but at the same time, not paranoid that they were ever saying anything about him until he caught his name one day. Later, Jolene would explain that the new girl, Daniela had a crush on him.

"But no, not a good idea, Chase," She shook her head and frowned. "It is, what they say? Don't eat where you shit?"

"Shit where you eat," he corrected her and grinned. He had no interest in Daniela, so it didn't matter.

"Yes, well it is the same, no?" She breezily shook her head and took a deep breath. "I cannot afford to lose another girl when you break her heart."

To that, Chase laughed. "Don't worry, Jolene, nothing will happen between Daniela and me."

Jolene looked skeptical but didn't say anything.

It didn't make her shy about getting his attention. Accidentally rubbing against him, making that small moaning sound that was almost unnoticeable but rose the hairs on the back of his neck. It was almost like she sensed that he wasn't exactly getting any lately and was going out of her way to grab his attention. She made innuendos, touched his leg when they were talking, bent over in front of him with a short skirt, everything that seemed to distract him and he secretly wondered how women were allowed to get away with this at work. As a working man, if he touched a female coworker's leg, rubbed up against or spoke inappropriately to her, he would be in trouble. Not with Jolene but with most workplaces, he would probably be fired for sexual harassment. Yet when women did it, clearly it went under the radar. Jolene saw it many times and glared but said nothing.

Eventually, Daniela got a new boyfriend and rather than attempt to seduce Chase, she instead told him detailed stories about her sex life. He wasn't sure which was worse.

The summer months were the busiest. Work was insane. Often out of the city and province, they were on the road a lot. Spending time at airports, waiting for flights, while Jolene tapped impatiently on her phone or laptop, attempting to do work on the run. Everyone grew impatient, tired and the heat was insane, especially during one particular weekend while working in Toronto. The air conditioning wasn't functioning properly in the venue they were holding an event and Jolene yelled at the owner to get it fixed before the night started. When this didn't happen, she ordered in a huge shipment of ice and although curious, Chase wasn't going to ask how it played into the night. It ended up being their most successful party.

The summer rolled forward. He worked. Rarely did he date. He went to the gym a lot but was ignored by most women, which he didn't understand. The women in Calgary didn't seem to like his type, many were ironically more into the same kind of rugged rednecks he grew up with, something he didn't understand. They also liked men with money.

He dressed well but when women learned he was only an assistant and not making a 6 digit income, they seemed less interested and drifted away. One woman even asked if he was in the NHL because of his size and physical status. When he said no and told her the truth, she shrugged and walked away.

By the end of the summer, he was starting to feel a little desperate and the rejection was starting to get to him. He never had this issue when he lived in a small town. He never had this issue when he was younger. It was strange and the complete opposite of what he would've expected. He even attempted online dating, which ended up being a complete joke. He had one hook up with a crazy woman and never saw her again. For that, he felt somewhat fortunate. She had somehow managed to steal food out of his fridge before leaving the next morning, the oddest way to end a one night stand.

By the fall and his one year anniversary of being away from Hennessey, he thought about going back for a visit but the idea was met with a lackluster response. Audrey suggested he didn't.

"The boys are just getting used to you not being around," she spoke impatiently into the phone. "So maybe it's better that you didn't."

"But I haven't seen them in a year," Chase calmly replied.

"Chase, you forgot Leland's birthday this year and you hardly ever talk to the kids online," she was rushed as the sound of the boys yelling in the background erupted emotions that tore through his heart. "I don't think it's a good idea if you come back, at least not right now. Maybe you can talk to them on Skype later this week."

He didn't reply. He couldn't reply. It was as if his tongue was heavy, frozen to the bottom of his mouth, emotions roaring through his chest, fighting to get out. He was his father. He was *that* kind of father. He was the father Maggie and Kelsey had; never around, only with occasional phone calls and gifts but no real connection in their lives. To them, it had been normal but created a series of issues. Was Kelsey the way she was because her dad wasn't in their lives? Would his kids be fucked up too? Then again, they had a replacement father that they seemed to love.

It wasn't that he didn't want them to care about Audrey's new boyfriend. He certainly wanted them to be happy, for her to be happy, but he couldn't help but feel as though he had been replaced. Almost like having a pet that died, burying it and joyfully moving on with a replacement, eventually forgetting about the rotting corpse beside the oak tree.

He remained silent and she must've sensed his remorse.

"Look, Chase, it's okay. The boys are okay. At least they don't see us fighting, that would've been a hell of a lot worse." She reminded him and he nodded, even though she clearly couldn't see him through the phone. "I know this is hard for you. It's not like the kids don't see you as their father anymore, but Albert is here with them and even when you lived home, you weren't as present. You were always working."

"I don't hold that against you," She continued. "I don't say anything bad to them about you. It's not like that at all. I just think right now, it's better to not confuse them. It's what is best for them."

He reluctantly agreed and spent the next few days depressed. He was even quieter at work, as Daniela chirped on about her new man and all the things he bought her on their latest shopping trip. She rattled on while Jolene was attempting to do some work and she finally told her to 'shut up and go run some errands.'

Fortunately, Daniela was an obedient employee and scared of her boss, so quickly jump up and left with a list of things to pick up and people to phone and confirm various details of their upcoming events. Shaking her head after the door closed, Jolene rolled her eyes.

"She works well but oh, does she ever stop talking, that one?" she complained, shaking her head, "Ah ah ah! Dos Mio!!"

Expressionless, Chase nodded.

"And you, what is wrong with you?" her voice went down in tone, indicating that she hadn't the same frustration for her more mature employee. "You quiet. What is wrong?"

"Just stuff with my kids back home."

"Ah, do you miss?"

"Yes, but unfortunately, my ex-wife doesn't seem to think I should go see them."

"What?? No no no, you are the father, you have a right."

"I know but she had a good point," Chase said as he sat upright in the chair, where he was slouched over a laptop, doing some research for

Jolene. "The kids are getting used to the new boyfriend, to not having me around and she thinks that they will be confused if I go back now."

Jolene frowned then shrugged. "Maybe she is right, I do not know. What do you think?"

"That she's right," Chase avoided her eyes and glanced back at the screen. "I don't know. I feel like I'm one of 'those' fathers that are never around. It's a lot harder than I thought it would be when I left. It's so hard to know what's the right thing to do when you're a parent."

"You were a young father, no?"

"Too young, that's part of the problem," he replied. "I can't help but wonder what my life would've been if I hadn't had kids so young, got married, all of that. Where would I be now?"

"Not necessarily anywhere better," Jolene commented and although he thought she was about to say something more, she hesitated and he could see emotions on her face. She quickly recovered and shrugged. "I do not know."

He didn't reply nor did he work. Staring at the screen, he bit his lip and opened his mouth to reply, when the door suddenly flew open. Assuming it was it was Daniela bringing them a surprise coffee, as she often did before heading out to take care of other things, especially if she thought Jolene was pissed at her. He started to turn around and without thinking commented, "Thank God, I so need a coffee, I-

He was met instead by intense, dark eyes staring down at him. The man wasn't very tall, he was guessing probably around 5'7" but what he didn't have in his physical statue, was definitely made up for in presence, as his brutal glare and deep, brooding expression sent a chill through the room, specifically through Chase. Although his eyes challenged the stranger's, there was an uneasy feeling that rose the hairs on the back of his neck and made his heart race. Expecting some kind of trouble, he immediately jumped up from his chair, abruptly closing the laptop and sitting it on Jolene's desk.

"Can I help you?"

The stranger showed no emotion but continued to study him, his eyes roaming over Chase as if to assess his strengths and weaknesses.

"Diego, come on!" Jolene stood up from her desk, one hand on her hip. "Is that any way to be? You don't come here ever, and now here you are, barging in like some kind of crazy man."

Ignoring Jolene, he continued to stare at Chase. "If you want coffee, go get it yourself while I talk to my sister." His comment was sharp but yet his voice much weaker than expected, almost jovially, as if he were enjoying the moment. "And get me an Americano while you're there."

"Diego!" Jolene snapped as she leaned over her desk. "No no, you do not come in here and order my assistant around, you do not do that!"

"I pay him, so technically, he's my assistant," Diego's eyes fluttered toward Jolene and back to Chase as he raised one eyebrow.

Chase was stunned. This was Jolene's brother? Other than being Columbian, there was no resemblance. Although he still had a slight accent, his English was almost flawless, as he stood a good inch or two below her with her heels. His skin was lighter than his sisters, while his eyes and hair much darker. He was cleaned shaved, wearing a suit that even Chase could tell was quite expensive. If he had anything in common with his sister, it was that Diego was quite stylish and approximately the same age. Had he been asked to picture Jolene's brother, he couldn't have had it any more wrong.

Hesitating for a moment, Jolene shook her head. "Chase, would you mind getting us all a coffee?" she returned her attention to Diego. "Even though he's not a personal slave that I order to run my errands."

Diego sucked in his cheeks and with shining eyes, his lips pursed into an odd smile, as he glanced at Chase, giving a quick eyebrow flash.

"You like to push my buttons," Jolene stabbed her nails on the desk.

It was clear by Diego's face, that was definitely the case.

Chase nodded to Jolene and headed toward the door. On his way out, he heard Diego say, "I expected more of a *guero* but I'm almost whiter than him."

"Diego!" She snapped at him as Chase closed the door and headed out of the building toward the coffee shop.

CHAPTER FORTY-EIGHT

If things seemed tense when Chase left, they were anything but when he returned. The laughter could be heard from the hallway, as he juggled the tray of coffees while opening the door. Inside, he found Diego sitting in his own chair, leaning back comfortably, unaware that Jolene's assistant had returned. A completely different version of himself, he was laughing joyfully at something his sister was saying in Spanish, slapped his own leg and tilted his head back.

"Ah Chase, thank you!" Jolene said as he made his way toward the desk. For some reason, he found his eyes suspiciously glancing toward Diego, as if expecting him to trip him or something juvenile in nature, however he was instead met by the same black eyes and a quick brow flash. Turning his attention back to Jolene, he shrugged and gave her a small, awkward smile, as he sat the coffee on her desk. Taking his own, he reached for his laptop and commented that he would do some research on the other side of the room while the two of them had a chance to catch up.

"No no, not just yet," Jolene gestured toward a spare chair on the other side of the room and without saying a word, Chase replaced the laptop on her desk and went to grab the chair. After moving beside Diego's, he sat down and started to drink his coffee. "Since my brother, he does not understand how to be polite, I will properly introduce you. Chase, this is Diego."

Switching the coffee to his other hand, he awkwardly leaned forward and shook Diego's hand and nodded. "Nice to meet you."

Diego's face twisted into a smirk and he nodded back, his eyes continuing to analyze Chase's face as he strongly grasped his hand.

There was something unsettling about Diego's gaze he chose to ignore, instead turning his attention back to Jolene and drinking his coffee a little faster than normal, unsure of what was about to take place.

"Diego is in town a couple of days. A surprise visit, as you say," she twisted her own burgundy painted lips into the same expression as her brother, almost as if mimicking him, while her eyes studied his face. "Which is quite unusual since he never comes here *ever*."

"Not ever! Come on," Diego defended himself as he stood up and reached for his coffee and Jolene did the same. "You exaggerate!"

"It's been a long time. Since I don't know," She took a quick drink of coffee and made a face. "Bitter."

"I think you have mine," Diego replied after taking a drink of his own. "This has too much sugar for me."

He stood up and traded. Chase got a whiff of his subtle cologne as he leaned forward.

"How could you not know?" she accused, pointing at the cup. "There it is, a giant 'J'. Does Diego start with J? No, it does not."

He grinned as he returned to his chair and didn't respond.

"It starts with whatever I tell you it starts with."

"See what I mean," Jolene commented toward Chase as if she had already had a conversation with him about her brother. "He is like a child, no? Ah Ah Ah!" She shook her head and took a deep breath. "So what brings you here to us today?"

"What brings you *here* today?" He corrected her English, causing Jolene's face to scrunch into a glare but she remained quiet. "I'm here to say hello to my sister, of course, and to see how things are going in my Canadian office."

"Things are going well," She seemed to choose her words carefully. "I do not need any help if that is what you are suggesting."

"Not suggesting a thing," he spoke calmly, focusing his attention on Jolene, almost as if Chase weren't in the room; not that he minded. Drinking his coffee, he felt awkward and was doing a mental checklist of all the things he had to do that morning rather than witnessing this strange conversation. "Maybe I just wanted to say hello to my sister. Did you ever consider that?"

She didn't reply but watched him carefully.

"So tell me, Chase," his attention shifted and tension filled the room. "Do you like your job here?"

Showing no emotion, Chase slowly turned and met eyes with Jolene's brother. Nodding, he was hoping that this would be the only question asked but it quickly became clear that Diego was waiting for him to go on. "Yes, I enjoy it. Jolene," he gestured toward his boss. "She's great. I think we work well together."

"I see, I see," Diego nodded and glanced back to Jolene. "So Chase, I hear you recently helped us with an awkward situation. A girl who Oded and you took her to the emergency."

"Which was the *right* thing to do," Jolene immediately spoke up, her tone was assertive as she sat up straighter in her chair.

"Hey," Diego shrugged, innocence crept in his eyes. "Did I say it wasn't? Obviously, we don't want someone dying. Am I right, Chase?"

Feeling as if he were being tested, Chase simply nodded and ignored Diego's probing eyes.

"Jolene, you worry too much," Diego intercepted and turned back toward Chase. "She always did. This one, she's a worrier. Whereas me, I live in the moment and what happens, happens."

Chase grinned. He could only imagine how many stories were behind that statement. He pictured orgies, drugs, and guns; chances were good there were many sketchy things in Diego's past. He sensed it. He sensed a strange, unspoken vibe between the brother and sister. He knew Jolene knew a lot that she would never reveal. Fortunately, Chase didn't want to know either.

"It's my motto if you will," he titled his head down, his eyes looking up at Chase, continuing to study his face. There was an element of mystery to him and he suspected that this combined with Diego's good looks, he wouldn't have a problem going anywhere and picking up pretty much any woman he wanted. It was amazing how some men just had *it*; that thing that women wanted, that most men didn't truly understand.

"That motto has not always served you well," Jolene spoke up, her eyes glancing at the nearby laptop screen. "You will have to excuse me,

Diego, I have some work I must attend to. A party needs some final details."

"That's fine," Diego shifted in his chair and stood up. "I must go and attend to a few things."

"I am not even going to ask." Jolene said under her breath as if there was a knowledge between the two of them what those 'things' were; Chase remained quiet and continued to drink his coffee. Rubbing a hand over his face, he could feel Diego's eyes on him. Looking up, he watched his finger point at him, shiny rings caught the light and it was clear they were expensive, even though he knew nothing of jewelry.

"You, Chase, what are you doing right now?"

"He's helping me," Jolene commented as she typed furiously into her laptop. "We are *busy* today, Diego."

"It's almost lunchtime," Diego gestured toward a nearby clock and Jolene immediately stopped typing and twisted her face in the same expression from earlier; the expression Chase had never seen on her face before that morning. "Once in a while, Jolene, you need to let your employees out for some fresh air and sunshine."

She raised her eyebrow. "He gets plenty of fresh air and sunshine, Diego. We need to work."

"I will just take him for a short time. I promise I will return him after lunch."

She didn't say anything and Chase oddly felt like a child fought over by two parents. It was ironic considering his recent circumstance with Audrey and for a brief second, he wondered if this would be how his kids would feel if he were to return; pulled in two directions and not wanting to upset either party. Oddly, an unexpected lightness flowed through him. He glanced up at Diego then Jolene, unsure of what the to do.

"Go with him," Jolene appeared irritated as she started typing again. "And Diego? I'm watching the clock!"

"I know, I know, you worry too much."

"Me pregunto porque."

"I promise," Diego called out as he rushed toward the door and Chase reluctantly rose from his chair and did the same.

"Jolene, I-

"Go!" She waved her hand in the air. "Do not worry."

Unfortunately, he did.

Stiffly walking toward the door, coffee still in hand, he followed Diego out and discovered a whole other man waiting for him on the other side. Where he had been intimidating and antagonizing with his sister, Diego now appeared light, practically skipping out of the building, he pulled on a pair of Ray-bans and pointed toward the mountains.

"I cannot get over the mountains!" he sounded like an excited child, an unexpected smile lit up his face and Chase merely nodded. "There," he pointed to the end of the street. "There's a restaurant. Let's go."

It was more a sport's bar. The kind that only hired female servers, all of which were beautiful, resembling models more than the person delivering food to your table. He assumed that's why Diego chose this particular place and sure enough, they weren't there very long, that he was flirting with the girls; complimenting their beauty, asking one if the super high heels were hard to walk on every day as if he was concerned over her possible discomfort. The waitress shrugged and insisted she was 'fine' but Chase somehow doubted that to be true.

After taking their order - pasta for Diego and a chicken for him - the girl rushed away to get their drinks.

"Only water, Chase? Why not join me in a beer? A glass of wine?" Diego appeared quite comfortable on his side of the booth, sliding toward the center, closer to Chase, where he appeared to have a better look at everyone else in the restaurant. He seemed curious, intrigued by his surroundings but swiftly returned his attention to Chase. "No drink?"

"I don't really drink."

Diego's lips formed a grin, a mischievous glint in his eye but he didn't respond, instead turning his attention to their surroundings. "You know Chase, something I never get used to here in America is how people dress for dinner. I know I'm in Canada, but to me, it's the same, you know? To me, you dress nicely for dinner, not sloppy in your yoga pants and jeans. You know?"

Chase shrugged. "I guess…"

"Maybe it's me," He made a face and stared, in a really obvious way, at a young, heavy-set woman wearing black yoga pants and a loose top that barely covered her stomach. She saw him and nervously looked away. "Your country is very different in many ways."

"Is that good or bad?" Chase was curious.

"Sometimes good, sometimes bad," he replied and sat back, his expression turned serious.

The waitress returned with their drinks. A glass of red wine was placed in front of Diego and water with a sliver of lemon for Chase.

"Chase, you should have a drink, this meal, it's on me, order whatever you want," Diego gestured toward the liquor menu, while the waitress waited, her full attention on Chase.

"I, ah…"

"He will have a beer? Wine? What is it you would like? Same as me?" Chase started to nod, unsure of what to say. "The same as me," Diego picked up his own glass and took a drink.

"Be right back," The waitress nodded and rushed away.

"Relax and enjoy yourself," Diego sat sideways in the booth, facing Chase, his arm on the back of the seat, he appeared relaxed, as if they were old friends. "Celebrate the small moments in life."

Chase didn't know what to say.

"So, Jolene, she seems to really like you," Diego began to talk almost right away as he took another drink of wine. "She says nothing but good things about you and believe me, my sister does not say all good things about many people. That's a huge compliment."

"That's good." Chase found himself starting to lighten up.

"She's a picky one," Diego glanced up at the waitress returning with Chases' wine. Both of them thanked her and without missing a beat, Diego continued. "But that is good. I feel better knowing she has someone she can count on."

"I like working for Jolene."

"She's a good girl at times, not a saint by any means but she's efficient as a business lady." Diego's dark eyes stared at Chase and barely blinked. "Her English is improving but it's not there yet. Of course, she won't listen to me and get help with it."

"Get help?"

"Yes, when I moved to the America, I had some help from a coach who helped me with my English and accent. That is why you barely hear it now," he nodded. "Unfortunately, with the US, they like the Columbia look, a bit of accent but they want everyone's English to be perfect." He grinned and his eyebrows shot up as he reached for the glass of wine again. "I believe it's called the melting pot and well, I guess I melted."

Chase smiled and thought for a moment. "Was it hard to move to the US from Columbia?"

"No, I wanted to work for myself and I saw an opportunity there that I would not find in Columbia." He replied. "I was a young man looking for an adventure."

"Did you find it?"

"I found many." He spoke suggestively. "And you, Chase? Have you found many adventures?"

"A few too many," he let out a laugh. "A few I could've done without."

"Nonsense," Diego shook his head. "It's not what you do in life that worries us on our death bed but what we haven't."

"I suppose.

"I've done a lot of things, Chase." He spoke honestly, almost seductively. "A lot."

Chase felt some jealousy by his cavalier attitude and wondered if he would've been the same if he hadn't married so young, not had kids. Would he roam the world, getting into all kind of exciting adventures; adventures that somehow no longer seemed possible, even though he wasn't with his family.

Perhaps it was the wine but Chase began to relax. Diego seemed like a pretty normal guy, not as intimidating as he had appeared earlier, as he spoke honestly about his childhood in Columbia, his life as a 'thug' on the streets, to distinguished business man. Their lunch stretched beyond two hours, with more wine, more talk and it was finally a text from that Jolene that alerted him.

"Oh shit, I gotta get back," he pointed toward his phone and Diego, slightly drunk at this point shrugged.

"The world will not come to an end Jolene," he spoke in the direction of Chase's phone. "But we should get back, shouldn't we? We'll go back, she can reprimand me for not returning you to her sooner and that will be that."

That will be that.

Except, it wasn't.

He didn't see it coming.

CHAPTER FORTY-NINE

Jolene was not surprisingly, irritated by Diego's extended lunch break and didn't hide her frustration upon their return. Shooting off a bunch of words in Spanish, Chase meekly moved out of the line of fire even though deep down, he felt as though he was probably the one she should've been yelling at; after all, it was *him* that was late. It was his responsibility to keep an eye on the clock and leave at the appropriate time.

Not that Diego seemed to as much as flinch when Jolene yelled at him but instead stood with both hands in his pockets, an impish grin on his face, showing no resistance. If she had known he giggled over how late they were, almost the entire way back to the office, she would've been furious. Chase wasn't about to tell her.

Jolene's tone went from anger to almost pleading in tone, as if she were begging him to take her seriously in her simple request. Chase couldn't blame her because they really did have a lot of things to take care of that afternoon, therefore his time away was pressure on her to take on more tasks. He hoped she wasn't angry with him too. Chase didn't want to be the next person in the line of fire; even though, she was already calming before their eyes.

"You must listen," she suddenly switched to English and sitting back down on her chair, while Diego silently nodded.

"You *are* right," Diego graciously replied and took a step closer to her desk. "But in my defense, I was getting to know our employee and I lost track of time."

Chase noted that she shot him a suspicious glance. Leaning on her hand, she listened to Diego negotiate.

"I was actually thinking that if you get your work caught up," he started as Chase grabbed his laptop from Jolene's desk, assuming Diego would try to calm the waters by asking Jolene to dinner. "Maybe Chase could help me with something tomorrow."

"No! Diego, do you not understand how far behind we are," Jolene shot back with her original fury. "We do not have time while you take him off…God knows where, just to play. We have work to do here."

"Ok ok!" He replied, defensively putting his hands in the air as if to surrender. He stepped back and nodded. "I understand, but what about that *dama* that works for you, can she not do work too?"

"Not as well as Chase, no."

Relief flowed through him after hearing these words, as Chase quietly made his way to the chair and sat down with his laptop, opening it up to continue his work, pretending that he wasn't the subject of this conversation.

"Ok, ok, that's fine," Diego shot a look in his direction and stepped back some more "I shall leave you to do your work and I will check in tomorrow, ok?"

"Ok, yes," Jolene curtly replied, moving her own laptop closer as Diego shot Chase a crooked smile and headed toward the door. "Adios…for now."

It was after he was long gone that Jolene suddenly broke the silence.

"He is so infuriating. Now I cannot work!" Jolene complained and moved away from the computer. "I need to go for a walk."

Chase nodded. "Ok, I can-

"No, you come with," she gestured toward the door. "We stay late if we must, but right now, I need a break. The sun is shining. Let's go out."

They didn't end up walking further than the coffee shop. It was mid-afternoon by then and few were there. In fact, their usual barista was finished and met them on the way out, exchanged good-byes before exiting, shoving earbuds in her ears and walking to a nearby bus stop.

"She is a nice girl," Jolene gestured toward the young Spanish woman as she approached a stopped bus. "You should talk to her more."

Not sure of what to say, he merely shrugged.

"She's not crazy like your women," Jolene made a face as they approached an awkward redheaded boy standing at the counter. "Kelsey, Maggie, your ex-wife; they all *loco*, you know? Latino women, we say it as it is and we yell when we want to yell. We don't play the privileged princess on a tower like your white girls."

Chase smirked and nodded. She did have an interesting point.

Ordering both their coffees, Jolene gestured to her favorite seat near the window. It was after they sat down that she brought up the topic of her brother. Chase was hoping she wouldn't.

"So that was an awfully long lunch today," she commented after opening her coffee and inspecting it as if she had no trust for the new barista. Taking a sip, she made a face and jumped up to grab an extra sugar packet from a nearby table and returned. Stirring the sugar into her coffee, she didn't miss a beat. "Did he take you somewhere *nice?*"

"The place over there," Chase gestured toward the nearby sport's bar and felt some relief for the simple question but he had a feeling they were about to get harder.

"Did he try to recruit you to work with him in California? Is that it?" she looked him directly in the eye, as she leaned in.

"It did come up," Chase replied, relieved that their conversation went in this particular direction. It might be a way of explaining any strange energy that had been in the room before Diego left. "I can't see me going to the states, though."

"He will offer you a lot of money," Jolene commented and he wondered if this was a test. Unsure of what to say, Chase decided to say nothing.

"I do understand if you want to go," she continued. "You need the money and you can do good there."

Chase still didn't reply.

"Well, say something," Jolene whimpered. "You make me nervous when you don't talk."

"I don't plan to go," Chase replied. "I didn't even consider it."

"But maybe it is good for you."

"I don't know."

"Well, it's something to consider, no?" Jolene commented. "I would not like to see you go but I would understand, you know?"

"I know," Chase felt like his stomach was churning. He had so many words, so many thoughts and anxieties bubbling up in him and yet, it was almost as if his tongue wouldn't move. He couldn't talk about it. When he was younger, he felt like he was always talking; mostly to Maggie about whatever troubled him, whatever was on his mind, but time had made him silent.

"I would never stand in your way."

"I know."

"Go home tonight and think."

He nodded and looked down at his cup.

"Do you not like my brother?" her voice suddenly held a vulnerable tone that he hadn't expected. He looked up and he noted that her eyes carried the same intensity as earlier. "I know some do not like…"

"No, no, Diego's cool," Chase felt an alarm going off in his brain. She was sniffing a little too close to something he didn't really want to talk about but deep down, he already knew Jolene had figured it out. She always did. She was too smart not to know.

"Did he make a pass at you?"

Chase felt his eyes expand in size, his mouth opened but no words came out, his heart suddenly pounding in his ears. "Ahh…I…"

"He make a pass at you," Jolene nodded as if Chase had admitted something, when in fact, he continued to have a puzzled look on his face. "He likes boys."

Chase couldn't speak.

"He always likes boys," she spoke nonchalantly. "He flirts with girls. In high school, he had a girlfriend for years but he likes boys," She hesitated and took a drink of her coffee and glanced at a stunned Chase. "He would like you. I can tell how he was looking at you. He like you a lot."

"I.."

"I know, Chase, you do not have to hide it from me," Jolene took a deep breath and shook her head. "My brother, he is what you call, gay? What a weird word. I thought 'gay' meant happy, you know, but you English have so many meanings for words."

Chase still struggled to talk. He nodded instead.

"So what happened?" Jolene asked as she relaxed in her seat as if the elephant had left the room. "Did he ask you on a date? Did he kiss you? Did he propose?" she let out a laugh. "He does that sometimes, being the romantic, but he, he will never marry, but in the moment, sometimes, he proposes."

"No, he didn't propose," Chase finally found his voice. "He-

"Kiss you?" Jolene finished, raising a single eyebrow. "He likes being impulsive."

"Yes," Chase agreed, feeling slightly embarrassed. "He kissed me."

"I know, I knew the minute he saw you that he would try," Jolene shook her head and her face was full of worry. "Please, do no sue us for sexual harassment. My brother, he would never do this if it was an employee in the California location."

"It's, you know, I wouldn't do that," Chase stumbled with his words. He was still stunned by the kiss; he hadn't seen it coming, had no idea that Diego was gay and was surprised by the gentleness of his lips and in the moment, he was stunned and yet, intrigued. Was he gay? No, that definitely couldn't be it. Could it?

"Good, because I swear, it will not happen again," she was insistent. "I will talk to him-

"No, no," Chase put his hand up in the air. "I don't want you to talk to him. I don't want him to know that I told you. I just, I feel weird-

"I will not say," Jolene agreed. "But don't be embarrassed or feel weird, Chase. It is just my brother. He does these things you know?" She appeared to struggle with words. "I do not know how to explain. He likes the boys and I accept, but at the same time, he likes to try to convince men who like women that they should like men too, you know? I don't get."

Chase shrugged and silently recalled Diego's final comment to him, just as they were returning to Jolene's office. "I will give you the best blow job of your life."

It was a little awkward. It would've been awkward regardless of who said it to him. It just wasn't one of those casual comments someone made, as you held the door open for someone on the way back to work, after an extended lunch.

Then again, it had been a while, so he assumed that's why it made him feel a little aroused? Intrigued?

Oh my God! Am I gay?

The last thing he wanted was for Jolene to have any indication that these thoughts were going through his head. He didn't want her to know that Diego had every intention of reaching out to Chase again, probably to check back to see if his proposition was something that had an appeal.

"I guess, it's a challenge?" Chase suggested, unsure of what else to say. He was taking big gulps of his coffee, awkward with the conversation and hoping it would end.

"I suppose," Jolene replied, pouting her lips, she played with a strand of hair. "I suppose that makes a lot of sense."

She dropped the topic. Unfortunately, it didn't escape Chase, instead following him around the rest of the day, until he was home alone that night. He briefly considered looking up some gay porn to see if it excited him but immediately knowing that it wouldn't. He dropped the idea of being gay. Wouldn't that be a huge clue if he were? He finally decided he was just flattered by the attention; how intrigued Diego appeared to be with him, his inclination to encourage more alcohol in Chases' glass and perhaps, he recognized a vulnerability in him, after asking about his recent dating life. Maybe it was that final fact that alerted Diego's senses the most.

It was kind of a repeated theme in his life. The women in his life often seemed to see him as a challenge for some reason or another and when he rejected them or showed any inclination to say no, their advances increased rather than faded away. In a way, Diego reminded him of Kelsey and her pursuit to get him in bed. Then again, she was successful in the end.

It was a power thing with Kelsey. Once she had him, she was done. She never tried again. Perhaps Diego was the same. It was a challenge. He clearly liked a challenge and feeling powerful was the essence of his life. Money, looks, charisma, these were advantages that a man like him had and in seemed as if he used them to his advantage. Maybe there was something to learn here, Chase decided. Maybe confidence was the biggest key of all. Then again, maybe faking it was a reasonable substitute as well.

Then again, he *was* a guy, so he probably would know how to give Chase the best blow job of his life. That fact hadn't gone unnoticed.

Feeling slightly aroused, he decided to turn on some porn; with women. Girl on girl. After a few brief moments, he quickly realized that his fears of being gay were unjust.

Diego returned the next day. This time, he arrived when Jolene was out and while Chase finished up on some of his work he didn't have time for the day before, after his extended lunch.

Much to his surprise, Diego wasn't flirting but approached him in a completely different manner.

"You should be behind that desk," he pointed toward Jolene's chair. "Not leaning over a laptop on a pathetic, cheap Walmart chair. I get you the best chair, your own desk, whatever you need."

"What?"

"Come work for me, I get you whatever you need."

"But I-

"I won't flirt with you or offer you blow jobs, I promise," he let out a giggle and sat behind Jolene's desk. "Ok, that's not true but I do want you as my assistant. I've been thinking of expanding our office in Canada. That's why I'm here. Jolene doesn't know yet. Consider it kind of a back door offer, no pun intended." He let out a little laugh and Chase felt his face warm up. "I offer you more than this. Right now, you're Jolene's errand boy and that's fine, that's a start but in my family, we believe that you either are moving up or you're dying. Chase, you don't want to be dying at this job."

Gesturing around the dingy, little office, his attention returned to Chase, "I did some investigating this week and I think there are better places to go. I like Vancouver, near the water. I like Montreal, the culture. I like Toronto, but this city," he made a face. "I don't like it. Too many cowboys. It's all about oil. Not my thing."

"You don't like oil?" Chase had never heard that statement before, especially with all the jobs in that area; although, not as many now.

"No, oil, fossil fuels, they're dying, you know?" Diego made a face and laughed. "They're like the VCR of energy. Sure, you can still plug a tape in and they still work but eventually you won't be able to find a VCR anywhere and even if you do, the tapes will snap. It's the same with oil. It pollutes, it's bad. People are killing for it. People are dying for it. No one ever died from a girl on girl party."

With that, he let out a little grin.

Chase laughed and nodded. "Not usually."

"The point is that I'm not appreciative of this state..er, province…" He smirked and scratched his chin. He was clearly freshly shaved, his hair styled in a popular cut for men and the smell of cologne was vague but noticeable.

"I must take my sister to dinner tonight and talk to her. I think we might have to work out a few things. I want to expand. Men parties maybe, I think we're making a killing here and it's time to look at other options. What do you think, Chase?"

"I think the male parties would be more popular," Chase spoke honestly. "I think there's nothing wrong with heterosexual parties too, same idea. Exclusivity."

"See Chase, this is why I like you," Diego said, his eyes watching him carefully. "I think you and I may have a bright future together."

CHAPTER FIFTY

We often drift a long way from where we started. To do anything else, would not be to live. It's those who stay stagnant for years, always the same job, same house, same town, same city, same boring routine and life, that never truly live. Locked in fear of the unknown, they go to great lengths to avoid breaking away from what made them feel safe and comfortable. His dad was that kind of person and he died having never taken any chances, never wanting to vacation in exotic countries, never wanting to question his beliefs but rather stay stagnant.

Chase was scared every day. He chose to ignore it. The voices of doubt slowly faded and the fears of impending doom became softer as time moved forward. A new confidence formed, assuring him that he had been through many things in his young life and he would be through much more but his strength would always help him find the way through. Something somewhere was looking after him. He wasn't sure what or how but he knew it was there.

Jolene and Diego would have their talk about the future. It would be communicated to him that they would be moving their office to a more reasonable location. Diego was thinking Toronto saying it was central and although Jolene originally turned her nose up at the idea, having had an unpleasant experience while working there, she eventually saw his point; it was more central and since the majority of their business was in eastern Canada in the latter months, it would make more sense to cut travel time and expenses.

Nothing was written in stone yet. Diego insisted that he had some other meetings coming up and might find a more reasonable location.

He had suggested that Vancouver would be a more pleasant city to live in but Jolene quickly disputed the idea, saying that the rent would be too high and it would increase travel time for the majority of their events, scattered throughout the country. Chase said nothing. They were the bosses and whatever they decided would be the answer. He would follow them. He would adjust. Everything would be ok.

Diego's vision was to expand their business to general party planning, with 'private' parties, which is how he classified what they were currently doing, as a part of their business as opposed to the entire thing. He insisted that they had to move forward.

"You got to spring ahead, strike the iron when it's hot, isn't that right, Chase?" Diego attempted to pull him back into the conversation. Before he had a chance to answer, he continued. "I want our main office here in Canada. Jolene, you will run things, Chase will be my assistant and we'll hire some more staff to do the daily odds and ends. We will get a second website for our more conservative parties but we must be known for our discreteness. That's key. People with money like things to be quiet."

"We need more people," he continued and one glance at Jolene told Chase that she was nervous. A visionary, her brother was not one to figure out small details and would hate to do so, he was the man who came up with the ideas, then allowed someone else figure out the rest. Chase suspected that Jolene would carry most of the weight.

"It's going to be a bright, exciting future for us, right Chase?" Diego's eyebrows shot up as he paced across the floor, almost as if he thought better when in motion, rather than sitting in a chair. A smile spread across his face, a spark glimmered in his eyes and Chase was somewhat jealous of his enthusiasm and confidence. Why couldn't he see his own life in such a way; boundless with no end of possibilities?

Perhaps because he had his own dreams cut off so abruptly in his youth after a series of events that closed off a lot of possibilities. Where he once saw marriage and kids as a trap that had taken his life away, he now knew that it was merely an excuse; after all, he was free of his marriage, now well into divorce proceedings and his children appeared to all but have forgotten him, but now he was stuck in a different sort of rut. It was just harder to identify this time around.

Maybe it was him that was the problem.

As if thinking of his family somehow made a mysterious connection over the miles, he was surprised to discover that Leland wanted to talk to him on Skype that night. Feeling slightly unsettled about his day at work and all the changes that were coming forward, some he didn't even fully understand yet, Chase welcomed the simplicity of a conversation with his child. All three of his children on FaceTime, one by one, each child disappeared. Easily distracted, none of them would stick in front of the computer long, while Leland gave a detailed description of a snake he found in the backyard and his confusion about how he couldn't have it as a pet.

Eventually, he ran off too, Albert suggesting taking them upstairs to get ready for bed, the house was suddenly quiet as Audrey took over the computer.

"They're very energetic, aren't they?" she asked with a small grin on her face, she looked happier than he had ever seen her. There was a calmness, an ease of conversation that they never had while married, it was almost as if she shed the old version of herself and now was a lighter, happier woman; something he had never could've foreseen years earlier.

"It looks like they never stop," Chase replied, feeling a smile settle on his lips. "I'm glad they're so happy, though."

"They are. We all are, Chase."

"Now that I'm gone," he made the joke, but deep down, knew it was true.

"It's not that," she corrected him. "We weren't a good fit. We never were and I tried to make it something it couldn't be."

"But I think the kids are happier with Albert than me," Chase spoke bluntly, exposing the small sorrow that he hated to admit. "I think I was a horrible father."

"You weren't a horrible father," Audrey corrected him. "It was a horrible situation. Kids are kids. They are adaptable. They just want love and attention and really, it wouldn't matter if it was Albert or if I was someone else or you again, it isn't like that with them. Kids aren't complicated like adults."

"I can't help feel like…" He drifted off, not knowing how to finish the sentence. "Like something I did or didn't do will fuck them up, you know?"

"Chase we all feel that way," Audrey let out a laugh. "All parents feel that way, regardless of what they do or don't do. I hear it every day at work."

He knew that Audrey continued to study and where she once worked for the minister at her church, she now had a position with the government. It was limited in hours but she was determined to do social work full-time. She'd certainly have her work cut out for her in Hennessey and surrounding towns; fortunately, her strong personality would be ideal for this position.

"No one is a perfect parent," Audrey reminded him and shrugged. "It's a tough job and at least you're there for your kids if they need anything or want to talk. Do you know how many fathers who live outside of the family home, aren't? Think about that Chase."

He nodded.

"So, how are you? How are things in the big city of Calgary? I'm thinking about taking the boys there sometime to see you," she spoke excitedly. "It would be fun."

A spark of hope filled Chase. "That would be amazing, Audrey. I hope it's soon, my boss is talking about moving our offices to Ontario. If that's the case, I guess I'm going too. I'm not sure what to do."

"If you like your job, then I say go," Audrey replied as she rolled her hair up into a bun and clipped it. "I would if I were you."

"I don't know, I-

"Chase, you gotta go," Audrey let out a small laugh. "You even said yourself, Calgary never had any major appeal to you. They'll probably pay for moving expenses and who knows, maybe there will be a promotion of some kind. Why are they moving?"

"Ontario is more central. Diego is also talking about Vancouver, just cause…I don't know, it's prettier or something." He let out a laugh. "I just kind of step away and go with the flow."

"Who's Diego?"

"Jolene's brother. He runs the company. It actually started in the states and Jolene takes care of the Canadian side of things." Chase explained.

"Ah oh, you're twitching, what's wrong with him?" Audrey let out a laugh. "You always twitch when you're anxious."

"I do?" Chase was surprised.

"Yeah, your right eye, I can't explain it and you probably didn't know, but you do," she replied, finally leaving her hair alone. "Trust me, body language is one of the things I'm studying. You make an interesting case study sometimes."

Chase laughed. "I bet."

"So what's the deal. Is Diego shady or something?"

"Nah, he's cool." Chase bit his lip. "Hey Audrey, did you ever wonder if I was gay?"

Her eyes widened and she laughed; heartily, at that. "What? Did Maggie take you to a gay bar or something?"

"No," Chase shook his head, shyly replying, "It's this Diego guy, the boss? He kissed me?"

"Wow! Unbelievable!"

"Yeah, so I thought maybe there was something about me, maybe-

"You're not gay," Audrey quickly reassured him. "Curious, you might be but not gay."

"But I have such terrible relationships with women, maybe that's why?"

"No, you're having a difficult time discovering the real you. Your mother beat that out of you a long time ago and you're slowly getting it back," she spoke honestly. "I'm sure that this Diego wishes you were, though."

"I never thought of it that way before," Chase admitted.

"It's true like I say, you make for a great case study in many things," Audrey's eyes scanned down as if analyzing the keyboard. "You're a work in progress. We all are but you started from a more difficult place."

Chase didn't reply but shared a smile with her.

"So, I have some gossip for you," Audrey quickly changed the subject. "Kelsey's back home. I guess she made some movies?" she rose her eyebrows when she said 'movies' a satirical grin on her face. "Her mom approached me about getting her into counseling which is probably a good idea, that girl is her own worst enemy."

"I agree."

"And your ex, that Lucy girl? Her boyfriend, I think was arrested and so was that Brad guy you used to work for at the bar. Did you know this shit was going down there? Be honest with me?"

"I knew about the movies," Chase replied. "I didn't know about the underage ones, though. I quit when I thought he was trying to solicit Kelsey and well, I kind of threatened him." He was apprehensive to add the last part, fearing she would repeat the story. "Between you and I, that is. I didn't think anything else happened. I certainly didn't know Kelsey went back after I left town."

"Yeah and tried to blame you because you wouldn't pay attention to her," Audrey finished his sentence. "I always thought something was going on with the two of you."

"No, she wanted there to be but I wouldn't let it," Chase felt like a weight was falling off his shoulders. The more he revealed to Audrey, the more they talked about things he had suppressed over time, the more a heaviness inside of him seemed to slide away. "I liked her though and kind of felt sorry for her."

"Lost puppies," Audrey grinned. "Cute till you get them home."

Chase smiled and nodded.

"I'm proud of you, Chase," her words shocked him and he felt any defenses fall to the ground but he remained silent. "I know we've had our differences but you really are a good person. You have a conscience and that says a lot. That's one of the things I discovered about you while doing these case studies. You made mistakes, we all have, but I pushed your buttons a lot and I did it on purpose."

"But you stuck around," she continued solemnly. "You took care of your kids. You protected your friends. When I asked you to stay away from the kids for a while so they could adjust to things here, you did it. I know it wasn't easy for you but you did what was right. Although your moral compass isn't always turned all the way on," she hesitated with a grin on her face, a moment of tranquility connected them and

Chase felt stunned by her remark. "You were a good guy and I never acknowledged that and I think it's time I did."

"Thank you," his voice was barely a whisper. "I never…I never thought you felt that way."

"I did. I do," she replied, her face full of calmness and neither said anything more, but he could see the tears in her eyes as she abruptly ended their conversation and turned off the camera.

He was left staring at a blank screen. Tears falling down his face, each carrying a little bit of the self-hatred that he carried around for far too long. Chase had assumed he ruined every life he touched. Wasn't that really why he was alone? Hadn't he feared of doing the same thing to someone else? Hadn't he felt that he hadn't done enough for his ex-wife, his kids, Maggie, Kelsey, his family? That he had never been *enough* for anyone? That if he had only been a little bit more, that maybe it would've made a difference?

Taking a deep breath, he was shaking and weak as he rose from the chair. It was as if he were a child, reborn into a new world with a brand new set of eyes. He crossed the floor with no destination in mind, no truth in his heart, just a lot of unknown floating on the surface. It was then that he realized that we are all animals; led by our desires, ready to fight in the light of fear and yet with a soul that leads us on a path of wherever we must go. It would never lead us astray.

His hand shook as it reached for a vibrating phone that sat on the counter. He picked it up and a smile crept on his face. It was a message from Diego.

Chase, my friend. Our story is not over. It has just begun. Buckle your seatbelt. You're in for one hell of a ride.

Love the book? Write a review and check out
more on www.mimaonfire.com

Printed in the United States
By Bookmasters